I0661702

# ISABEL HOPE

By Christine Coltman

*For my great Uncle Ronald, who always wanted me to write, and for my Mum who always believed in me.*

# VOLUME ONE

*'Beautiful Evelyn Hope is dead*
*Sit and watch by her side an hour.*
*That is her book-shelf, this her bed;*
*She plucked that piece of geranium flower,*
*Beginning to die too, in the glass.*
*Little has been yet changed, I think -*
*The shutters are shut, no light may pass*
*Save two long rays thro' the hinge's chink.'*

*Evelyn Hope* (lines 1-8), Robert Browning

# I

## THE STORY BEGUN BY THE EDITOR

I said once that she could not die. She has died. My beautiful Isabel is dead.

This is her story. The story of a woman - the most remarkable woman whom I have ever known - whom I loved from the first moment I saw her. It does not matter who I am, though my part in the tale will become apparent. I will simply give voice to the events which befell her, aided by her own words through extracts from her diary entries, in which her voice still rings as clear as day.

For the lady is dead, and her earthly story is ended. But for you, reader, it is just beginning.

# II

*'Perhaps she had scarcely heard my name -*
*It was not her time to love: beside,*
*Her life had many a hope and aim'*

Evelyn Hope (lines 10-12), Robert Browning

## ISABEL'S NARRATIVE
*(Extract from Isabel's Diary)*

*2nd June 1866*

School is over! I can scarce believe it! As the carriage thundered down the tree-lined avenue away from Alverdine School, I felt my heart pounding with excitement, my body urging the horses on as my eyes drank in the bright and exhilarating scenes which rushed past me at a thrilling speed.

I am overjoyed to be leaving; I feel a new chapter of my life opening out in front of me - as long and exciting as the road along which we now race. I am on my way to my Aunt Helen's house, with whom I will stay during the next few months until I come into my inheritance. I hope dear Cathy has arrived before me; it will be so wonderful to see her again - to hear of all her news and tell her mine. If it were not for the joy of seeing her I would wish that this carriage would never stop, taking me on and on and on...But first I will see Cathy, and then I will choose my course.

The paper bounces beneath me as I write and my words are wild and untidy, but I want to capture this moment - this moment that is here and now, and never again. I feel older and yet newer than ever before. What does my future hold? Anything I desire.

## THE STORY CONTINUED BY THE EDITOR

The sun was blazing down overhead as the coach came to a halt outside Harringdon Court. The driver leapt down from his seat to unfasten the door, and out of the darkness of the carriage a small, white, satin-shoed foot emerged, followed by an ivory hand which grasped the proffered hand of the driver to aid her descent, and then purposefully pulled herself into view. It was a young woman, and she was beautiful.

INSERTED ENTRY

*(Titled 'A Memory')*

$2^{nd}$ *June 1866*

It may have simply been the effect of the bright sun beaming down upon her golden head, but it seemed that there was a soft glow radiating from her as she appeared. Her face was arresting, utterly captivating; it was a face that having seen once, you could never forget. The vision of her on that day is always before me - part reality, part hazy illusion created under the influence of time. But I do know that the world stood still at that moment, halting its presence before the glorious creature that presented herself to it so boldly. What kingdom could this maiden not capture, what prince his heart not enslave?

I use romantic terms, I admit that is her influence. I did not know then what lay ahead of me. But I did know that my future was sealed. She held the seal in her beautiful hand, still dripping soft red wax into the balmy air. If only I could have taken her then, taken her away from all that was to come...

But she did not know me yet, and I did not know her. I simply loved her, my swelling heart filling with joy and incredible sadness. For I knew, even then, that I could never deserve her.

## THE STORY CONTINUED BY THE EDITOR

She was slim and stood straight as a poplar, with beautifully arranged golden curls, quite unruffled by the journey, and was exquisitely dressed in a white chiffon gown that shimmered in the sunlight. Her skin glowed softly, endowed with the beauty that only youth, that merciless heartbreaker, can bestow. Her shaped eyebrows arched high over a pair of alert, sparkling violet eyes as she surveyed her surroundings, taking in every detail with an air of habitual authority.

Harringdon Court was an impressive Tudor house on the outskirts of Ashton, surrounded by many large and well-kept gardens. It had long been the country residence of the aristocratic Harringdon family who lived in the area and was therefore treated with some reverence by the local village folk, many of whom tended the grounds and served in the house. It was a good-sized house, although the west wing had been out of use for many years, its current occupant, Lady Harringdon, finding that three wings sufficed for herself and her daughter Catherine. It was here that Isabel Audley had arrived on this glorious June morning and now stood on its wide gravel forecourt, surveying her surroundings with her head held high, and with an air of self-possession not usually found in girls of seventeen.

Just then, voices were heard from the front door and a burly middle-aged man, dressed in the smart attire of a police constable came out, followed by a tall and handsome older woman. Lady Harringdon had a striking face that had once been considered beautiful, and a fine head of dark gleaming hair that was pinned into a high bun at the back of her head. Her piercing eyes were now slightly hooded with age, but had lost none of their intensity. She walked with great poise and was dressed in a lavish and elaborate grey gown that swept out around her as she strode forwards down the steps.

'So please do let me know if there is anything else I can do to help, Constable,' she said to the man beside her in a deep and gracious voice. Then she noticed the young woman in the driveway.

'Oh Isabel, you are here at last.'

Sweeping out onto the drive, Lady Harringdon embraced her niece.

'Let me see you, my dear,' she said, stepping back to appraise the young woman.

Isabel raised her elegant chin high to meet her aunt's gaze.

'My, you and Catherine have grown quite beyond belief this year,' said the older woman. She tilted her niece's head to the side to view her profile. 'And your similarity to your mother grows quite striking.'

Isabel flushed with pleasure.

'How was your journey?' asked her aunt.

'It was most enjoyable,' answered Isabel; and then, with a sudden flash of eagerness, she asked, 'Has Cathy arrived yet?'

'Yes, she arrived not long ago,' replied Lady Harringdon.    'I believe -'

She was cut off mid-sentence by the sound of a loud cry behind them.

'Isabel!'

Isabel's face was suddenly animated with joy as she saw another girl rushing down from the house, her skirts gathered up in haste as she hurried towards them down the wide steps.

'Cathy!' Isabel cried out, and running to her cousin, embraced her tightly. The girls were of the same age, and obviously related, although Catherine was smaller and plumper, with rosy features and dark red curls, her open face beaming with happiness

'I have been so looking forward to seeing you!' exclaimed Isabel, letting her go, her face glowing with pleasure.

'And I you,' said Catherine. 'It has been such a long time since I saw you last!'

'Six months,' said Isabel quickly. 'Far too long.'

'I am sure that you will both have a lot to discuss,' said Lady Harringdon, interposing, 'but we must first allow Isabel to settle in, she has had a long journey.'

She motioned to the driver who was still standing by the cab awaiting his orders.

'Take those cases into the house and leave them in the main hallway. And constables,' she motioned to the two uniformed men: the gentleman who had come out with her, and a second who had been waiting at the front of the house, 'thank you for coming today, and I look forward to hearing from you Constable Hardy.'

The second man who was younger, clean-shaven and also smartly dressed, replied,

'Yes Lady Harringdon, we will be in touch shortly.'

The men turned to leave and Lady Harringdon swept back round to the girls with a gracious smile.

'And now Isabel, let me show you your new room. We have given you one of the best in the house.'

Arm-in-arm with her cousin, Isabel followed her aunt into Harringdon Court, her first station in this fresh new chapter of her life, the destination of which she knew not.


ISABEL'S NARRATIVE
*(Extract from Isabel's Diary)*

*HARRINGDON COURT, 2nd June 1866*


Well I am fully settled in my beautiful new room. Now that I am no longer classed as a child (though I ceased to be one of those a long time ago!) I have been given a much larger room than before, with gorgeous coral patterned walls, cream furniture and broad bay windows that look out across the countryside to the forests that edge the village of Cranwell, and further to the east, the larger town of Ashton. It has always been my favourite room here at Harringdon and I am thrilled to have it to myself. I have unpacked my belongings and my new dresses have been delivered to my room. Cathy, of course, wanted to see each one and we quickly decided that the green taffeta is the nicest by far. It is so good to see her again!

However, before we could catch up properly I was called to Aunt Helen's study (a gloomy and rather imposing room at the back of the house), as she wanted to speak with me about my future plans. She gave a rather long speech about my coming of age and the responsibilities that will soon fall upon my shoulders (a fortune of my own, autonomy and opportunities - those weighty impediments...) and said that I am to stay at Harringdon until she meets with my trustees in April when I turn eighteen, and then I shall decide where I am to live, with their advice. It is just too exciting. I cannot wait to own my own home and finally have real freedom. Obviously Aunt Helen insisted that I will need a companion, probably a drab, unprepossessing older lady, as most companions are – but apart from that the whole plan sounds simply delightful and I agreed in full. We concluded the meeting on good terms and she gave me my monthly allowance in a small purse, so that I may buy any new items that I require.

What I did not tell Aunt Helen was that once these initial basic arrangements have been made, I have other, bigger plans. These I shall keep to myself for the time being and I think they may solve the problem of the unwanted imposed companion as I strongly suspect she will not want to accompany me when she hears of my intentions - which is all the better! Perhaps Cathy could accompany me instead, until the time comes when her future is decided.

Just now, Cathy is asleep beside me. Of course we are not sharing a room, but after Aunt Helen went to bed, she crept along to my room and we chatted for hours in the dark, as we always do. I have missed her so – for I did not see her over the Easter holidays this year due to the measles outbreak at school – but despite almost six months passing, she has not changed in the least. She is still the same dimpled, kind, wonderful Cathy that she always was.

However, it seems that she is not as elated as I to have finished school. Mind you, she has always disliked change and the uncertainty that it brings. I will miss Alverdine School though, with its creaky old staircases, engaging lessons and my group of friends. I have made Claire, Margaret and Jane promise to write to me - and Lucinda, although I know that she will not.

Anyway, I shall continue looking to the future and tomorrow is Sunday and we will attend the local church. I do hope that the vicar is a plainspoken and sensible man. Our chaplain at Alverdine paid rather too much attention to his florid language and disparagement of Eve's sinful descendants than to the meaning of his sermons (I think he disliked having a congregation that was mainly female!).

The sun is setting before me now, the sky radiant with late evening hues of red and orange. I feel as though it is showing me all the possibilities the world has to offer, painted with a masterful hand. I am ready for my future - ready to become a woman and leave behind me the shell of my girlhood. It is a beautiful shell, but I am outgrowing it now and I want to be free, unhindered by any limits or boundaries. I want to see the world and enjoy all it has to offer. I want to shine.

Goodnight.

# III

## THE STORY CONTINUED BY THE EDITOR

*HARRINGDON COURT, 3rd June 1866*

Sunday morning dawned bright and early and Isabel woke to find the curtains drawn and Cathy still asleep beside her. Slipping out of bed softly, so as not to wake her cousin, she went over to the dressing table where she cleansed her face with a bowl of cool lavender water that Catherine's maid had left out for her. Next, she styled her hair quickly and deftly in front of the mirror. She twisted in front of the glass to view her work and then smiled with evident satisfaction, before turning her attention to the important task of selecting her outfit. Since her childhood, Isabel had always preferred to dress herself - a task made possible by her tiny waist as no corset was required. For this, Isabel had always been extremely grateful.

Cathy's maid had already pressed and hung all her dresses in the large wardrobe the night before and Isabel ran her fingers through the textures and fabrics, trying to decide which to wear that morning. She had always taken great pride in her appearance, yet self-awareness of this characteristic had made her question whether she had a tendency for vanity. Guilt would sometimes point its finger as she turned before the mirror in her fine garments, but her pleasure in a well-groomed appearance generally overruled such qualms.

As she walked to church that morning with her aunt and cousin, and their household staff, Isabel knew that she had chosen well. Her princess-line lemon dress and bolero jacket suited her slender figure well and her gold hair, neatly pinned up at the back of her head, complemented the outfit perfectly.

'I simply do not know how you do it,' Cathy said as she struggled to fasten her own bolero as they walked. She had slept over-late as always and her red curls were escaping from their bun. Her eyes flicked down towards Isabel's slender waist that was a constant source of envy. 'I wish I was able to dress like you,' she said, slightly morosely.

'You dress quite beautifully Cathy, and you can carry off many colours that I cannot,' replied Isabel, pausing to help her cousin fasten the clasp. Cathy's bolero was mauve and did not match well with her blue tulle dress. Isabel made a note to make sure Cathy did not wear them together again.

The local church was only a ten-minute walk from Harringdon

Court, straight down a pleasant country lane. It was a beautiful day and Isabel enjoyed feeling the warmth of the sun on her arms and neck. As they walked, her aunt told her of the changes that had taken place at Harringdon since she had last visited: their butler had left for another position and had been replaced by a competent younger man, a storm had uprooted an old tree in the lower gardens in January, destroying one of the greenhouses, and Tom the gardener had become the father of twins last month. The mention of Tom, whom Isabel had noticed tending the lawn when she arrived the day before, roused a question that she had been meaning to ask.

'Why were there two police constables here when I arrived, aunt?'

Her aunt pursed her lips, while Cathy looked rather excited.

'I am afraid we had a break-in,' replied Lady Harringdon, rather sternly.

Isabel gasped.

'What happened?' she asked breathlessly.

Her aunt looked unwilling to talk about it, but after a glance at both eager faces, continued with some reserve.

'William, our manservant, came back late on Friday night, after his evening off, and noticed someone climbing in through the downstairs window. By the time he arrived at the house, he could not find the man inside and asked Mary to alert me. The local constable was sent for, and a full search of the house was conducted.'

'Was anything taken?' asked Isabel.

'My pearl and sapphire brooch,' replied her aunt.

'Goodness!'

Isabel knew the brooch - a large deep-blue stone set in a wide border of gold, with three iridescent pearls hanging from it. She knew it must be worth a small fortune. Her aunt continued,

'Our constable went after the villain, who had fled to Little Wharton, and together with their local constable, tried to track him down - but to no avail. They visited yesterday to inform me of their progress and ask a few more questions of the staff.'

'Do they know who he was?' Isabel asked.

'No. A passing ruffian, perhaps.'

Isabel looked thoughtful.

'Did he take the brooch from your jewellery case?'

'Yes, he did,' her aunt replied.

'I wonder why he only took that brooch,' Isabel asked, curiosity in her voice.

'Excuse me?' said her aunt, her eyebrows rising.

'I mean, if he had all the contents of the box available to him, then why not take a few more items, especially when he already dared so much.'

Her aunt looked displeased by this train of thought.

'I do not know Isabel, but let us be glad that he did not.'

'Of course aunt. It just does not make sense.'

'I do not expect any of us to understand the mind of the criminal,' her aunt said dismissively, 'and I am glad we do not. Cathy!' She turned to her daughter. 'Do not slouch.'

Isabel sensed that the conversation was over, and wishing to avoid the presence of her aunt in a disagreeable mood, began to drift behind the party. Lady Harringdon had now turned her attention fully upon the unfortunate Cathy, rebuking her in muted tones for her untidy hairstyle and the lack of a Bible, which Cathy had left on the hall table in a moment of forgetfulness. Isabel suddenly realised that she had also forgotten to bring her own Bible, and decided to hold back even further until her aunt had dropped the topic. She paused to pick some flowers from an overhanging bush to gain some time. Another party from the village turned into the path from an adjoining lane and Isabel wished them a good morning, as they did her.

'Come along Isabel,' her aunt called out impatiently from the front of their group.

'Go on aunt, I will be with you in a moment,' Isabel called back over the heads of the villagers, now deliberately idling. Her aunt turned to see where she was and Isabel feigned the motions of stopping to remove a stone from her shoe.

By the time the group had turned the next bend, a welcome silence had descended. Isabel was not afraid of getting lost; she knew the way and rather welcomed the tranquillity of her solitariness. Alone for the first time in months, she walked leisurely, swinging her parasol as she went, watching the butterflies as they fluttered around the pollen-laden flowers. They looked like pieces of silk caught in the wind. A striking green and black one caught Isabel's eye and she followed it down the lane until it came to rest on a yellow rose. Perched on a dewy leaf, its feathery wings elegantly folded, it reminded Isabel of a beautiful still-life painting, the delicate pattern on its wings painted by a skilful artist. She felt as though it was watching her, so like a pair of eyes was the design. Putting down her parasol, Isabel stooped down to try and catch it in her hands, when suddenly a large dark shadow fell over the flower from behind her and the butterfly changed from art into life, becoming a blur of colour as it fluttered off the golden flower.

'You know, that rose would look splendid in your hair,' a voice said in a rough, Northern accent.

Catching her breath, Isabel looked round to find a young man standing behind her. Politeness demanded that she should have avoided eye contact with such a stranger, but Isabel was young and curious, and she looked at him openly and frankly, though by no means with a friendly expression. He returned her gaze with an equally frank stare, seemingly unfazed by the blinding look of disapproval she was giving him.

'You gave me quite a shock, sir,' she said, rising almost to his height.

'Forgive me, I thought you had heard me come up behind you,' he replied pleasantly.

'In which case I would have addressed you or turned round,' she said disdainfully.

'Would you like me to cut that rose for you?' he asked, quite unchastened.

Isabel bridled ever so slightly.

'I feel I am adorned quite enough for a church service.'

'Ah, excellent,' he said, smiling. 'That is where I am headed too. May I walk with you?'

Isabel was taken aback: her haughty reserve did not normally have so little effect on strangers. She pursed her lips.

'I do not normally allow complete strangers to accompany me,' she said, reaching for her parasol with a haughty air, but the gentleman was nearer and picking it up, handed it back with a smile.

'In that case, my name is Mr Sam Hardy,' he said amicably.

She appraised him coldly, not allowing his easy manners to disarm her. He was quite young, no more than twenty-eight at most, and had a smiling, tanned face with keen hazel eyes and closely cropped light-brown hair. He was dressed simply but smartly in a brown suit. Ignoring his arm, she began to walk.

'You may walk beside me,' she replied.

The service was long, and the church warm, the morning sun pouring through the stained-glass windows and setting them ablaze with colour. The vicar was a recently appointed curate, young and earnest; a good speaker and a clear one. Having seen Isabel into the Harringdon family pew at the beginning of the service, the young gentleman had then taken a pew at the back of the church. Through the rows of the congregation he could see the young woman now, so striking and fresh among the crowds of familiar faces. She was listening intently to the vicar's sermon on the opening chapter of Romans. From time to time she would frown, or give a slight nod with her head.

Once the service was over the congregation filed out of the church, each stopping to speak briefly with the minister at the church door. Having waited for the front rows to depart first, Mr Hardy watched as Isabel's party took their leave. First the Harringdon girl, plump and smiling, next her severe-looking mother, austere and haughtily gracious, and then - Isabel. He watched as she spoke with the vicar, animated and eager: she seemed to be asking him questions, unaware that she was holding up the line of people waiting to get out. However, her aunt appeared at her side and taking her arm, drew her away. Isabel looked a little flushed and displeased, as did Lady Harringdon.

Making his way outside, Mr Hardy approached the Harringdon party. Isabel and her aunt stood a little apart while Cathy was conversing with another young woman whom he recognised as the mayor's daughter. He walked up to Isabel.

'I hope you enjoyed the sermon, Miss Audley,' he said brightly.

Isabel looked up, surprised.

'I did, sir,' she replied after a moment.

'If you are planning on walking back to Harringdon by yourself, may I offer my services?'

He was greeted with a slightly less disapproving stare than he had received earlier that morning.

'Mr Hardy, I -'

' - Do not think that would be appropriate, do you *Constable*?' Lady Harringdon had turned swiftly towards him, her expression cold and piercing. 'And, as we are a large party, I do not think your services are necessary, today - or any day.'

'I beg your pardon, Lady Harringdon,' replied Mr Hardy calmly. 'I merely wished to continue my earlier conversation with your niece.'

Lady Harringdon's expression was severe as she turned to Isabel.

'Mr Hardy was kind enough to walk me to church this morning, aunt,' said Isabel quickly.

Lady Harringdon's eyebrows raised themselves even higher as she replied coldly,

'Well, I shall have to make sure that you do not lag behind again, Isabel, in order that you do not waste any more of Constable Hardy's time. Good-day, sir.'

And with that, they departed. The young man looked after them and then left in the other direction that led towards Cranwell, swiping at the stray stems of grass that hung over into the lane, an odd half-smile playing on his lips.

## ISABEL'S NARRATIVE
*(Extract from Isabel's Diary)*

### HARRINGDON COURT, 3<sup>rd</sup> June 1866

I suppose he was pleasant enough. It was perhaps the first time that I have ever spoken to a young man on my own. His conversation was engaging, not that we had the chance to cover many topics.

But he also was impertinent and presumptive. Any chivalrous man would surely not approach a woman who was on her own. His approach startled me beyond belief! Nor did he heed my very obvious reproach. Indeed, I would even put him out of my thoughts altogether if it had not been for Aunt Helen's cold treatment of him. I do not wish her to choose my acquaintances for me - I will speak with whomsoever I wish, and walk with anyone I choose. I had not realised he was one of the police constables who was here when I arrived yesterday. It was only when Aunt Helen addressed him (so disparagingly!) as 'Constable' that I made the connection. Of course, I had only laid eyes on him for a few seconds yesterday, so I can be forgiven that oversight.

She also humiliated me this morning in front of the vicar. I had so many questions to ask him about his sermon, which was insightful, but she interposed rather rudely and drew me away, saying that it was not my place to ask such questions of a clergyman. I replied that the church should be a place of learning, and that if we cannot ask the vicar our questions, then whom can we ask? She replied that women have no need to understand all the mysteries of the Word of God as long as we obey its commands. I consider that nonsense: how can you obey something you do not understand?

### POLICE REPORT
By Constable Barnes of Little Wharton

### 4<sup>th</sup> June 1866

Full examination of household staff concluded. It is assumed that the intruder entered through the front gates of the grounds, as several members of the household staff were returning from their evening off through the back gates at this time. As a result, Thomas Greggs the gardener witnessed the intruder entering the house via the pantry window that had been left ajar by the cook (a Mrs Bett) for the house cat. When asked for a description of the man, Greggs replied it was too dark, but he did see 'a flash of red in the moonlight'. This could have been a scarf, or perhaps the colour of his hair (he may have been Scotch). The intruder must have then made his way upstairs to Lady Harringdon's dressing room and spotted the open jewellery case on her dressing table. Lady Harringdon maintains that only a gold and sapphire brooch was taken. It was of considerable value. After further questioning it arose that this case was normally kept locked, but she had been amiss in her security on the evening in question. Her maid, a Miss Susan Figg, said says this was out of character, but her mistress has seemed more forgetful than usual lately.

The intruder was witnessed leaving the Harringdon Court grounds by a villager and then witnessed again entering Little Wharton by the landlord of the White Hart. Both claimed they could not see his face but that the figure was definitely a man, of slight build and moving quickly, taking care to remain in shadow. Constable Hardy, who had been alerted and was tracking the thief, then came to me for additional aid. However, the trail ended on the outskirts of Little Wharton. There were no trackable footprints, nor any outgoing carriages that night. With no further leads the following morning, we returned to Harringdon Court to carry out questioning.

Constables in the local areas have been made aware of the theft and given a description of the man, but it is likely that he is now many counties away. Lady Harringdon has been informed that the chances of capturing the thief are slim and has been advised to keep all doors and windows locked after nightfall. No further action is required on our part.

Signed, Constable Guy Barnes.

# IV

*(Extract from Isabel's Diary)*

*HARRINGDON COURT, 4<sup>th</sup> June 1866*

A glorious, glorious day! At the first sight of the bright sunbeams creeping under the heavy curtains in my room, I was up and slipping on my dressing gown to run into Cathy's room and wake her, so that not a moment of the day would be lost. It is the first day that we have had all to ourselves and we mean to spend every second together. We have both dressed in our lightest white muslin dresses and have our straw hats to hand. I have packed a bag with a throw and some towels and Cathy is bringing her light blue parasol. We will be gone for the entire day, not returning until we have soaked up every last glorious ray of sunshine on the beach – I must go now!

## THE STORY CONTINUED BY THE EDITOR

The excitement of the morning was such that even the dust in the air seemed to sparkle in the early sun-rays as Isabel waited in the large warm kitchen for Mrs Bett to finish packing their picnic basket. Mrs Bett was a rosy-cheeked, grey-haired lady who had worked at Harringdon Court for over forty years. Her signature aroma of fresh scones filled the air as she opened the oven door to check on her baking. Isabel's foot tapped against the stone-flagged floor, impatient to set off while Mrs Bett continued to plod around the kitchen, preparing the food slowly and steadily, unaware of Isabel's eagerness to be gone.

Staring out of the window, Isabel could just catch the faint blue sparkle of the sea, far off in the distance. The sight of it made her heart leap. The cook glanced at her as she placed a freshly baked loaf of bread in the wicker basket. She had known Isabel for many years now. The first time Isabel had come to Harringdon Court, she had been a glowing, pink-cheeked girl of ten, with golden curls down to her waist. Mrs Bett had expected the young heiress to be a quiet child, saddened by the early death of her parents - but instead, she had been full of joy and energy, tearing around the house with Cathy, her cousin who she had heard of all her life. Upon finally meeting, the girls had instantly become inseparable.

The cook had enjoyed treating the girls in her kitchen over the years, giving them warm buns from her oven, candied fruits at Christmas, and occasionally, sugar cubes from the pantry. Isabel was always happy to sit on one of the high wooden stools at the gnarled old table, and chat for hours to Mrs Bett; Cathy hanging around the door, half-enjoying the warm atmosphere and continual treats, half-scared that her mother would come down and find them. If caught, Lady Harringdon was most displeased with them, and ordered the girls not to spend their time with the servants. A haughty woman she was - haughty and cold. Mrs Bett was pleased that Cathy had had such a girl as Isabel burst into her life. She was a fun, imaginative child, unspoilt and full of laughter - just what Cathy needed after years of being alone in the large house with only her mother for company, her elderly father having died when she was just four years old.

It was now almost eight years since Isabel had first burst through her kitchen door, her hair tumbling all over the place, cheeks aglow as she attempted to evade Cathy in a particularly competitive game of hide and seek.

'I am Isabel Audley and I am very pleased to meet you - can I hide in your cupboard?' she had asked, breathless, but full of confidence.

Since then, she had visited every year, spending almost every school holiday at Harringdon Court. Mrs Bett had heard whispers that she had no-where else to go now that Greenwood House had been boarded up, but Isabel did not seem to mind and the cook always liked having her around the house. She had enjoyed watching her grow up from a pretty, animated child, into this confident, lively young woman.

'You are looking so well, Miss Audley, if I may say so', she said, suddenly struck by the young woman's radiance as she stood by the sun-drenched window. 'You are growing into a very beautiful young lady.'

Isabel flushed with pleasure.

'Thank you Mrs Bett,' she said warmly. 'You are very kind.'

The older lady smiled at her, crinkles forming in the corners of her eyes, and then the cook's face grew serious as she contemplated the young woman before her; this girl who had had so much sadness in her life, and yet treated everyone with such kindness and had brought such joy to the sombre household. The cook knew the course Lady Harringdon would want Isabel's life to lead and she suddenly felt sad for the girl - and fiercely protective. Mrs Bett knew she had a tendency to speak out of turn, but she could not help herself and spoke up with feeling:

'Your beauty is a gift my dear – be sure you do not waste it. You find a man worthy of loving you and do not you settle for anything less than you deserve. You only get one chance at love, you know.'

Isabel looked surprised, but touched.

'Thank you, Mrs Bett. I will,' she said, with great sincerity.

The advice was so unexpected and earnest it filled her with a sudden rush of emotion. They stood a table apart, the orphaned girl and the old woman. The cook took a deep breath, ready to say more, but footsteps were heard coming down the overhead stairs and she turned away to open the oven.

'Now', she said, beginning to bustle around again, 'would you like to take some of my freshly baked scones with you?'

'As if you need to ask!' said Cathy gaily, who had appeared in the doorway. 'Pack as many as the basket will hold please, Mrs Bett!'

'I hope you are going to carry the basket then, Cathy,' said Isabel, composing herself. The basket was already bulging, crammed with apples, chicken legs, the great loaf of bread, a wedge of cheese and two water bottles. 'It's a good two mile walk to the beach!'

Cathy's face fell. 'But I am quite weighed down already, Isabel,' she said, holding out the parasol and towels.

Isabel picked up the basket with a resigned smile.

'Well I am sure you will eat half of this food on the way there.'

Cathy opened her mouth in protest and then catching sight of the four warm scones that Mrs Bett had just placed inside the basket, promptly shut it again.

'Thank you Mrs Bett,' said Isabel. 'This should keep us going for a good few hours!'

'Enjoy yourselves, my dears,' said Mrs Bett, glancing out the window. 'You could not have asked for a nicer day than today to spend outdoors.'

'Indeed not,' Isabel replied, arranging her hat on her head and tying the blue ribbon underneath her chin in a pretty bow. Cathy did the same and, lifting their provisions for the day, the girls wished Mrs Bett a very good morning and headed out the back door into the sunshine.

'You know, I do not think I have ever felt happier,' Isabel said to her cousin, viewing the fresh green countryside ahead of them, a sparkling blue line visible on the horizon where the ocean met the clear morning sky. Cathy smiled back at her, her cheeks dimpling in pleasure.

'Nor I. Come on, let's run!'

And she broke into a gay run across the grass, her white skirts billowing out behind her. Isabel called out, laughing,

'Cathy - wait! You forget I am the one carrying the basket!'

It took the girls less than half an hour to get to the beach. They walked along wide lanes, over two small bridges and then finally through several large green fields as they headed towards the sea, the countryside spreading out before them like a beautiful patchwork quilt, a hint of vivid blue always visible in the distance. The air shimmered with a wonderful balmy heat, so dense that they could almost see it glistening and rippling around them. Isabel felt that if she let herself fall slowly backwards it would simply carry her away, towards the sea.

When they reached the fields, Isabel slipped her shoes off, enjoying the feel of the fresh grass, cool and soft against her bare ankles. The sun was already hot overhead, kissing every bare piece of skin it could find, bringing up soft freckles on the girls' arms and cheeks. Isabel knew Aunt Helen would not be pleased – she had firmly warned the girls to make sure they kept their skin covered against the sun's rays, for fear that they would turn red and freckled like the working girls in the village. Isabel did not care: she stretched out her arms in the warmth and brushed a flock of dandelions as she passed. Reluctantly they released their little travellers to roam the great expanse of blue sky above them.

As they neared the beach, heading down some narrow rabbit tracks, suddenly the ground fell away before them and they found themselves standing upon high sand dunes, looking down over the breathtakingly blue sea. It sparkled and danced underneath the azure sky, little white waves spurting across its glistening surface. The girls smiled mischievously at one another and took the sandy hills at a run, laughing and screaming as their feet slipped and slid down the incline, creating avalanches of sand around them. Isabel had a harder job to stay upright as she tried to keep the basket held high, away from the sand, but both of them reached the bottom in one piece, coming off the slope at a run.

'You know, I do not think we will ever be too old to enjoy that,' said Isabel happily.

The girls wandered along the beach, and then chose a spot close to a cluster of rocks surrounded by soft sand. Isabel placed the basket on one of the flat rocks and together they rolled the blanket out across the sand and placed stones at each corner to hold it down, although there was not yet a breath of wind. Apart from a large flock of gulls, the girls were the only visitors that day and the beach rolled out before them like an uninhabited golden meadow, met by the sparkling blue waves of the gentle sea.

'Oh Cathy, this is glorious!' exclaimed Isabel, stretching out on her front upon the blanket and wriggling her toes in the warm sand. 'I have looked forward to this all year!'

Cathy did not answer; Isabel twisted round and found her cousin already tucking into the scones Mrs Bett had made.

'Cathy!' she exclaimed.

'Sorry – I was hungry!' said Cathy apologetically from between a mouthful of scone. 'That walk was longer than I remembered.'

'Well just make sure you leave some for me!' said Isabel, laughing. She stood up and surveyed the view before her. 'Come on, let us dip our toes in those delicious waves.'

Isabel grabbed her cousin by her hand and together they ran down the golden beach and into the shallow waves that were lapping at the shore.

'Oh, it is so lovely and cool!' said Isabel, feeling the refreshing water rush past her warm feet and up to her ankles. Pulling up her skirts, she waded farther in, her feet sinking into the soft wet sand below.

A sudden spray of water splashed against her back and she shrieked as she turned to find Cathy sending another splash towards her. Dashing through the water, Isabel returned the favour and soon the two young ladies were indulging in a spirited water fight, their shrieks ringing out across the beach and their beautifully arranged hair hanging wet and scattered across their happy faces as they danced in and out of the waves.

When they were both fully soaked, they graciously gave up the fight and sprinting out of the water, they ran up the beach where they threw themselves onto the warm blanket and lay breathless under the hot sun.

'Shall we eat now?' asked Cathy a few moments later, rolling onto her front to look at Isabel.

'Only if you wipe that sand from off your face – I am not eating food with you when you look like that!' replied Isabel, wiping the sand from around Cathy's mouth with a gentle swipe of her finger. Cathy sat up and removed the offending sand particles with a napkin from the basket.

'Is that better?' she asked.

'Much,' said Isabel, setting up the parasol and beginning to lay out the delicious spread that Mrs Bett had prepared for them.

'I love Cook,' said Cathy warmly, as she lifted out the chicken and the freshly baked loaf of bread.

'She is marvellous,' replied Isabel appreciatively, setting out the sliced ham and red apples.

'Is it good to be back, Issie?' asked Cathy, glancing across at her cousin with a smile.

'Wonderful,' replied Isabel, returning the smile wholeheartedly.

The two girls made surprisingly short work of the food, and finished their meal with a scone each. Isabel stared out at the sea as they ate, so blue and sparkling and endless – wonderfully peaceful, and yet somehow, exhilarating.

'You know, I could live here Cathy,' said Isabel as she finished the last of her scone. 'I would build a house on the hill just there, high enough to see the sea from, and wake up every morning to that dazzling view…Yes, I do declare that when I come into my inheritance that is exactly what I shall do! And once I have tired of it and the dreary winter months have set in, I shall set sail for abroad.'

'Abroad!' exclaimed Cathy in surprise.

'Indeed! France, Spain, Italy – and further still – India, the Americas - '

Cathy gasped, but Isabel continued.

'- I am going to travel – just as I have always wanted to - and you could come too, Cathy!'

Cathy's surprise turned to trepidation in an instant.

'Oh… I do not think I would like it very much. Is it not very dangerous abroad?'

'No more dangerous than London, and you have been there.'

'But is it not very dirty?'

Isabel laughed.

'Again, no more so than London. But think of all the sights we would see – mountains, great cities, wild animals, native peoples, uninhabited islands, oh Cathy, it would be wonderful – and so much fun!'

Cathy looked uneasy.

'Oh Isabel, you know I am not as fond of adventures as you are. I am sure you would enjoy all of that very much, but I, well, I think I should want to come home rather quickly, and you would get very tired of me holding you up.'

Isabel surveyed her cousin for a moment, half-wishing that she had not mentioned her plans. Perhaps it was too soon, too sudden.

'Cathy, dear,' she said suddenly. 'Come sit under the parasol with me – your arms are getting burnt in this hot sun.'

'Oh goodness, yes they are. I had not even noticed.'

Cathy moved over to where her cousin sat and stretched out underneath the shade of the parasol. Before long, she was fast asleep, snoring softly. Isabel kissed her lightly on the cheek and then rose.

Isabel stood, knee-high in the calm sea, the occasional wave rising higher than most and brushing the hem of the white skirts that she held up above the water. She took no notice: her eyes were fixed far out across the horizon. There sailed a magnificent ship heading east, its hull boldly painted in gold, green and blue with a lion figurehead pushing forward through the waves. Its sails were billowed, catching every breath of wind, and the sun glinted on the golden oars that glided back and forth, carrying the vessel onwards. Aboard were a noble crew – hardy, chivalrous, and hungry for adventure. Before them lay vast unexplored lands, full of promise and opportunity.

'Isabel?'

The boat faded back into her imagination, and Isabel turned to find that her cousin had woken up and was standing upon the shore.

'I must have fallen asleep for ages!' exclaimed Cathy, as Isabel strode back through the water towards her.

'I think it was all that food,' remarked Isabel, smiling.

'It must be nearly five o'clock,' said Cathy.

'Mother will be wondering where we have got to.'

'There's no need to worry,' said Isabel. 'She knows where we are. But you are right, we should think about heading back.'

As they walked up the beach, she glanced back over her shoulder towards the blue horizon.

'One day soon I will set sail,' she said to herself. 'There are no limits anymore.'

# V

Lady Harringdon was less than impressed when the girls arrived back well after six o'clock, both red and rosy, with sand and traces of seaweed in their unkempt hair. She deemed them both unsuitable for dinner as her friend Lady Farley was dining with her that night, and sent the girls to eat dinner in their rooms, followed by hot baths. This suited them very well. Lady Farley was (in their eyes) quite elderly and her conversation most unengaging.

After she had washed the last grains of sand from her hair and between her toes, Isabel towelled herself down, put on her long white nightdress and seated herself in front of her dressing table mirror. Her hair hung long around her shoulders, curling upwards slightly at its golden ends; it was almost completely dry now and smelt of the lavender soap she had used to wash it. She lifted the large silver-plated brush that lay before her and began to draw it from the top of her crown to the very ends of each lock in a rhythmic fashion, her lips softly mouthing the mounting number of strokes as she brushed each gleaming strand. The candle next to her glowed brightly, picking out the glints of gold in her hair. The flame flickered slightly from a movement behind her and Isabel turned to see Cathy staring at her from the doorway, also dressed in her white nightdress.

'You can come in, you know,' Isabel said with a smile, turning back and resuming her brush strokes.

'I know,' said Cathy, not moving. 'I was just watching you. You look so lovely, sitting there.'

Isabel paused, and half-turned on the stool to look at her cousin.

'What?'

'You do Isabel. You look beautiful.'

Isabel turned back to look at her reflection. The candlelight danced across her features. She paused for a moment, trying to see what Cathy could see, but all she saw was herself, sitting in her nightdress, completely unadorned. She gave her cousin a quizzical glance and carried on with her brushing.

'...Eighty, eighty-one...'

'You still count to one hundred,' said Cathy, with a smile as she pulled herself up on to the bed, tucking her feet underneath her, 'just as your mother taught you.' Cathy sighed. 'I always get bored after twenty.'

'A hundred-fold keeps it gold,' Isabel recited.

'Well that must be why mine is red,' said Cathy in a tone of mock-resignation.

'And very beautiful it is too...ninety-nine, one hundred. There!'

Isabel placed the brush down, blew out the candle on the dressing table and climbed up onto the bed beside Cathy.

The candles had all been extinguished, but the room was not dark. Isabel had asked the maid, Bessie, not to close the curtains as it was a clear night and the stars were shining brightly. Isabel liked to see them, and she especially liked to see the moon. Sometimes she believed that she loved the moonlight more than the sunlight, so magical was its presence, its beams so dreamlike in the darkness. The large four-poster bed faced the window and they could see the bright half-moon and the stars sparkling in the vast heavens before them. Isabel nestled down under the duvet. It was her favourite time with Cathy, alone in the almost dark. It was the time when they could speak their secrets, whatever was going on in their hearts, the words that they did not want to speak in the daylight. It was their time.

She remembered last summer, when they had laid in Cathy's bed and talked excitedly about heroes and romance. Isabel had been reading Malory's *La Morte D'Arthur* and told Cathy that one day she wanted a chivalrous knight of her own to sweep her off her feet. He would be tall and handsome, with curling dark hair and a fearless nature that thirsted for adventure. Cathy, who (after being given the novel by Isabel) had just finished reading *Pride and Prejudice* by Jane Austen, admitted that she had been dreaming of the courteous Mr Bingley (Mr Darcy being too harsh of tongue for her). She said she would like to meet her Mr Bingley at an extravagant ball and after a lengthy courtship of love letters, he would propose to her during a country walk and then they would settle down in a big house by the sea and have lots of children together.

'It sounds delightful, Cathy,' said Isabel happily. 'And I shall be godmother to your first girl and teach her how to be naughty and unladylike.'

'You could never be unladylike,' said Cathy, laughing. 'But you shall be godmother, and come stay all the time.'

And so they would make their plans well into the night until at last, happy and exhausted, they would fall asleep.

Isabel remembered all this with a smile and searched her mind for a new topic of conversation. The answer came to her quite suddenly, though she had almost forgotten the conversation amidst the fun of the day.

'Do you know what Mrs Bett said to me this morning,' she said, her voice sounding loud in the silence.

'No.' She heard Cathy turn towards her. 'What did she say?'

'She said that...' Isabel tried to recall the cook's words. 'She said that I was to find a worthy man...a man worthy of loving me, and not to settle for anything less that I deserve, because a person only gets one chance at love.'

'How strange!' said Cathy. 'Were you talking to her about marriage?'

'No, her words were quite unexpected. But she spoke so fervently, I was quite moved.'

'I wonder what caused her to say such a thing,' said Cathy, wonderingly.

'She is right, though,' said Isabel. 'We have spoken often about marriage and husbands, but when the time comes, we must be very wise in the men that we choose, and be sure that they are truly suited to us. Marriage is not a mistake that can be unmade.'

There was silence for a few moments and they stared out at the deep black sky. Isabel wondered at how distant the tiny stars were, wondered at the God who had created them. Suddenly she felt very small, yet the thought did not scare her.

'Do you think the perfect man is really out there for each of us, Cathy?' she asked suddenly.

'I...do not know, Isabel. I hope he is for you.'

In the darkness, Isabel heard the change in tone of her voice.

'Cathy - what do you mean?'

She heard Cathy move uncomfortably on the bed and Isabel reached out for her hand.

'Cathy?'

Cathy squeezed her cousin's hand tightly and then her words came out, all in a tumble.

'Oh Isabel! I am to be married – soon. It is all arranged.'

For a moment, Isabel was grateful of the darkness as it covered the shock on her face. She tried to compose herself.

'When do you marry?'

'October.'

'So soon! Who is he?'

'He is from Berkshire. His name is Sir Charles Leicester.'

Isabel swallowed.

'And what is he like?'

'I...I do not know. I have not met him yet.'

'Not met him!' Isabel could not help herself. 'Oh Cathy – but how do you know if you are suited?'

'He is wealthy, Isabel. Mother says we are a very good match and that he will make me very happy.'

Isabel tried to stem the rising tide of resentment and sorrow within her, but she could not.

'Oh Cathy, all your hopes and dreams - all our plans!'

Cathy was silent, searching for the words she needed to express herself.

'Isabel,' she said after a moment, 'I am different from you. I was never destined for an exciting life. I am not even sure I would have liked one - I have only ever wanted to hear about yours. That is enough for me.' She turned and gave Isabel a small smile. 'Honestly, Isabel.'

Isabel did not know what to say, the sadness in her was so great. Cathy squeezed her hand again.

'I am sorry I did not tell you sooner, Issie. Mother forbade me, but I knew I would tell you anyway. I just wanted us to have one last day together with everything as it was...before it all...changed.'

The day rose again before Isabel's eyes – the sea, the sand, the laughter...Cathy asleep under the parasol...Their last day together as girls.

'You have always been destined for great things, Isabel,' said Cathy in a firm voice. 'I have always known that. And you must promise to write and tell me every one of your adventures.'

Tears were now running freely down Isabel's cheeks.

'But I want you beside me, Cathy.'

'You do not need me. I would only slow you down - and you run so fast! Unless you are carrying the lunch basket.'

She laughed then and Isabel half-laughed too, through her tears. Then she clutched her cousin's hands close.

'It is very soon, Cathy.'

'Yes, it is. And you must promise to stay here until the wedding. I shall need you.'

'I will be here, Cathy. I will be right beside you.'

Cathy smiled at her and Isabel managed to smile back.

'Let us get some sleep now, Isabel. Thank you for not being angry with me.'

'I could never be angry with you Cathy... Good night.'

'Good night Isabel.'

They lay awake in the darkness together for a long time. Neither knew when the other fell asleep.

# VI

*(Extract from Isabel's Diary)*

*HARRINGDON COURT, 5ᵗʰ June 1866*

Morning has dawned. Cathy must have crept out of my room during the night.

Various plans suggested themselves to me as I lay awake in the darkness last night. I almost woke Cathy up to suggest that we run away together, but such a thought would only frighten her. The thing is, I do believe that she is quite resigned to this marriage. I remind myself that she has a family name and reputation to uphold; others will be affected by her actions. I am glad I do not have such barriers.

I had always felt quite sorry for Aunt Helen. She has never seemed to know how to love, nor how to show any affection towards her daughter. But now all I feel towards her is anger. Cathy has always tried so hard to win her approval – the least Aunt Helen could have done is let her choose her own husband, in her own time. I do not believe that she would have been short of admirers. But no, Aunt Helen thinks of nothing but money and titles, and so Cathy is to be married to a man she knows nothing of, for duty. It is folly.

## THE STORY CONTINUED BY THE EDITOR

When Isabel went down to breakfast that day, her aunt and Cathy were already seated. Cathy had dark circles under her eyes. Isabel wondered if she had slept at all.

'I understand Cathy has told you her exciting news,' her aunt said as she motioned to the servant to serve Isabel.

Cathy lowered her eyes. She hated secrets and could not bear any form of guilt and Isabel was not surprised that she had confessed to her mother that she had told her cousin of the arrangement. Isabel lifted her napkin and unfolded it on her lap.

'She has told me that she is to be married to a man she has not met,' she replied coolly.

'It is an excellent match,' said Lady Harringdon, ignoring her niece's tone. 'I can only hope we can find such an eligible young man for you, Isabel.'

Isabel lifted her knife and fork and replied with mock pleasantness,

'With the greatest of respect, I shall choose my own husband, thank you aunt.'

Cathy looked uncomfortable and kept her eyes down. She could not bear disagreements.

'I doubt that at your young age, Isabel, you will be able to identify such a suitable husband,' said her aunt evenly, stirring her tea.

'Then I shall wait until I am older. I believe seventeen is far too young to be married,' replied Isabel dexterously.

'Seventeen is the ideal age to take a husband,' said her aunt swiftly, setting down the spoon. 'It is the right time to secure your future and take up a woman's responsibilities.'

'It is too early to be locked in a cage of someone else's choosing,' Isabel said defiantly.

She knew Cathy was uncomfortable and that her words would sting, but she was too riled by her aunt and was determined to make her voice heard. She would make it known now that she would not be condemned to the same fate as her cousin.

'So you would scorn the advice of your elders and build your own cage?' said her aunt, coldly. 'You assume you know better than those who have gone before you.'

'I will do as my parents did and marry for love alone,' said Isabel hotly.

'Then you choose a life of exile and wretchedness,' replied her aunt bluntly.

'No - I will choose a life of happiness and freedom!'

Isabel stood up, anger coursing through her. She would not hear her parents abused. Cathy looked up at her, her face pale and upset.

'I am no longer hungry. Please excuse me,' Isabel said sharply, and turning on her heel she left the room.


### ISABEL'S NARRATIVE
*(Extract from Isabel's Diary)*

*HARRINGDON COURT, 5th June 1866*

How dare she speak so of my parents! The only exile imposed upon them was by those too small-minded to accept their love, of which Aunt Helen was one.

I am beginning to understand why my parents were glad to be left alone and live their life away from those who could not see past their shuttered view of the world. I find myself wondering again why Aunt Helen brought me back into her life, for it was several years after my parents died that she wrote to me, not on the eve, or even the year of their death. At the time I thought it was the passing of her husband that had softened her heart and made her yearn to mend broken ties. Now I think it was so that she would have one more life to control.

Well, she may try, but I will not be made subject to her will.


## THE STORY CONTINUED BY THE EDITOR

It was several hours later that Isabel calmed herself enough to go downstairs again. She had heard the front door close and expected that her aunt had gone out on her morning visits. She hoped to find Cathy and speak with her, for she suspected that her cousin might be quite upset. However, upon descending the stairs she found her aunt in the hallway, handing an envelope to the footman.

'Where is Cathy?' enquired Isabel evenly.

'She has gone on a visit,' her aunt replied, not looking at her.

Isabel was surprised. There were few people in the surrounding area that Cathy would visit alone.

'How long will she be gone?'

'A week.'

'A week! Who has she gone to see?'

'She has gone to stay with her fiancé's family in Berkshire.'

Isabel was stunned.

'I did not know of this.'

'You did not know of it, but you are the cause of it.' Her aunt turned to face her, her expression taut and cold. 'I will not have you upsetting my daughter and questioning her course of action. I have sent Cathy away to spend some time with her future husband, and away from your influence. You may be as headstrong as your mother, Isabel Audley – and as reckless as your father – but I will not have you destroy my daughter's chances at a settled and respectable life.'

She turned and left Isabel standing upon the stairs. After a moment's furious reflection, Isabel decided that it would be best to leave the house, lest she say something inexcusable in her anger, and so she put on her bonnet and closed the door behind her, her heart beating fast.

She decided to head for Ashton and was part way down the lane when she realised how displeased her aunt would be that she was out on her own. The thought pleased her greatly.

'Miss Audley!'

Isabel turned sharply, her skirts swinging out. Coming up behind her was Mr Hardy, dressed in his constable's uniform, the silver trimming on his hat glinting in the morning sun. Embracing her rebellious mood, she allowed him to fall easily into step with her.

'Good morning, Mr Hardy,' she replied pleasantly. 'And where are you coming from?'

'I am just returning from a visit to the cottages up the road. They have lost five chickens this week.'

'How shocking. Was it poachers?'

He smiled.

'Alas not. It was a particularly hungry fox.'

Her face quivered as she tried to conceal a smile.

'I suppose there are not a great number of elaborate crimes for you to solve in Harringdon, Mr Hardy,' she remarked.

'It is certainly not like London, but then again, not every town can boast of having a disappearing jewel thief.'

'Ah yes, my aunt's stolen brooch. Have there been any leads since Saturday?'

'None, I am afraid.'

'Well I am sure she will not miss it too much, she has much more interesting affairs to meddle in.'

Mr Hardy glanced at Isabel's irritated expression, a faint twinkle in his eyes.

'Have you perchance had a disagreement with your aunt this morning, Miss Audley?'

'And what on earth would give you that idea?'

'I am simply using my skills of deduction.'

'I do not think it takes much deduction to know that my aunt can be altogether disagreeable,' Isabel said with resentment.

'Would that explain why you are out walking on your own again?' he observed.

Isabel pursed her lips.

'I do not feel the need to be constantly chaperoned,' she said, tartly. 'I am not a child.'

'No. But it is unusual to see a young woman like yourself walking on her own around these lanes.'

'Perhaps I am trying to aid the cause of progression.'

'Then you should stop bumping into me,' said Mr Hardy, a smile playing on his lips. 'I make you look far too traditional.'

'Walking out with a man is only traditional if you are engaged,' Isabel replied quickly.

'Then you can be satisfied that you are continuing to break with tradition.'

There was silence for a few moments. Mr Hardy was smiling. Isabel felt slightly breathless.

'And are you enjoying your time here in the country?' he asked, after a few moments more.

'What makes you think I am a city girl?'

He turned his head and observed her outfit for a moment. She was smartly dressed in a pale blue morning dress, with an elaborate chemisette and wide pagoda sleeves

'No country girl dresses like you – not even your cousin.'

'Perhaps no girl dresses like me,' she replied, unsure if he was complimenting her or mocking her.

'Perhaps not. You have your own style which suits you very well.'

He smiled again. Isabel realised that he was not mocking her but showing polite interest.

'I am not from the city,' she said, in a friendlier tone, 'but I was a pupil at Alverdine Ladies School. I finished a few days ago. And yes, I am enjoying my time here, for as long as it lasts.'

He glanced at her and asked,

'Are you not staying for long?'

'I will stay until April - I come into my inheritance then, and I have great plans to travel.'

'And do you have any particular country in mind?' he asked, sounding curious.

Isabel glanced sideways at him, once more unsure if he was mocking her or being sincere. He showed no sign of surprise at her plans, which probably meant that he did not believe her.

'Perhaps India – or America,' she replied tentatively, but as she continued her reserve was overwhelmed by enthusiasm. 'Beautiful places that I can explore, with mountains and rivers, hot skies and new people with their own histories and legends. I want to see new cultures, learn their stories, travel on new forms of transport, taste new food and see all this world has to offer.'

Her speech was warm and energetic – he could feel her passion in every word.

'No wonder you want to travel – this country could never contain you, Miss Audley!' he said with admiration in his voice. 'I think once you have boarded that first ship, there will be no stopping you.'

She felt quite buoyant.

'No stopping me whatsoever, Mr Hardy.'

They turned into a narrower lane, past some tumbledown cottages. The ground was not so good underfoot here and Isabel's skirts were beginning to trail in the dust.

'You will need to buy an entire new wardrobe for your travels,' he said, noticing this.

'Of course,' she said, lifting them up from the ground. 'I will purchase much more practical clothing.'

'And who will travel with you through these wild and wonderful countries?'

'Whomsoever I require. If I need a guide, I shall hire a guide. I will not be tied to one person.'

'You are going to truly embrace your freedom.'

'I am young and independent –'

'– And modern,' he added.

'Thank you,' she acknowledged the words as a compliment with a nod of her head. 'I know that the idea of going anywhere on my own will be viewed by many as improper, but I will not be bound by conventions. Men can ride about this country and do and see what they please, while women must sit and *wait* for things to happen to them. We see so little of life, as a whole. I will not be one of those women.'

'Well I admire your courage Miss Audley. And your hope. I like to see people planning for their future, whatever their age or sex. God gave us life to live, and make the most of. I am glad that you will do that.'

There was no hint of criticism in his words – indeed he spoke in a tone of praise. She stared across at him as they walked and he returned her gaze, levelly and fully. He was perhaps the most unusual man she had ever met, she remarked silently to herself.

They walked in silence once more. Isabel attempted to compose her racing thoughts and as she did so, her manners slowly began to catch up with her. He had asked so many questions about her, she should really return his polite attention. She glanced across at his dark blue uniform, with the bright metal buttons shining in the sunlight and stiff buckled collar pressing in against his neck. She reflected inwardly that he must be very warm.

'So, Mr Hardy, are you the only police constable in Cranwell?' she asked, after a moment.

'Actually, I am officially the constable for Ashton as villages do not warrant a constable, but as I live in Cranwell, I look after the surrounding areas as well.'

'That is quite a large area to be accountable for. Do you not need a second constable?'

'Apart from London and the other large cities, most towns only have one constable, and even that is only a recent occurrence.'

'And how did you come to take this position?'

Her questions were coming more easily now.

'I fell into it actually. Someone kindly put me forward and I was given the job.'

'I suppose only the most trustworthy and respectable men can be given such a responsibility.'

'That is a most flattering way of looking at it,' he replied.

'And do you have family here?'

'No, my family live in Manchester.'

'And do you have any children?'

'No – I am not married. My family are my mother and three sisters. My father left when I was young.'

'I lost my parents when I was young,' said Isabel.

Mr Hardy glanced at her, slight concern in his eyes.

'I hope you will not mind me saying, but I have heard of your family history. The story of your parents is well-known amongst the village-folk, but I did not want to trouble you by asking any more about it.'

Isabel was a little taken aback. Of course, she knew that many local people must be aware of the tragedy as her mother had been Lady Harringdon's sister, and the disaster had hit national news. Most people that she met used the death of her parents as a talking point, almost to the point of bad taste, but Mr Hardy clearly did not wish to speak of it. She supposed he was being kind.

The butterflies were out again, attracted by the clover that grew amongst the hedgerows. They were approaching the spot where they had encountered each other the previous Sunday, where an adjoining lane met with the one that they were now walking along.

'Well, here at the crossroads I must leave you, Miss Audley,' he said to her graciously. 'My travels take me down the opposite road from you towards the mayor's office. It has been most enjoyable meeting you again.'

Isabel was surprised. She had presumed he was also going into town and felt slightly disappointed that he would not be going all the way with her.

'Thank you for your company,' she replied courteously. 'And your understanding.'

He smiled and tipped his hat to her.

# ISABEL'S NARRATIVE
*(Extract from Isabel's Diary)*

*HARRINGDON COURT, 5th June 1866*

I did not mean to add the last part. The words seemed to tumble out. He smiled at me though, as if he understood what I meant. It was a kind smile.

After he left me I continued into town and visited the dressmakers to look at some new hats that had come in from London, and then bought some writing paper at the Post Office. The walk back to Harringdon was warm and as I walked, I mused over our conversation. The words we had shared seemed to be still floating along the lanes where we had spoken them and snatches of the conversation rang softly in my ears as I walked along. He had not treated me like a child. He had not even treated me like a woman. I appreciated that.

# VII

The days at Harringdon Court dragged without Cathy. Isabel kept out of her aunt's way as much as possible as they had still not resolved their disagreement. Fortunately Lady Harringdon often dined out at the homes of her friends Lady Marley and Viscountess De Bere who both lived short distances away, so Isabel regularly had the house to herself in the evening. During the day however, her aunt was very much present and Isabel found retreat and solitude in the one room she loved above all, no matter what house she was residing in: the library.

Sitting back contentedly, Isabel sighed and allowed herself to slip deeply into the red velveteen armchair by the window, its soft cushions enfolding her. Despite its welcoming chairs and good views of the gardens, the library at Harringdon Court had hardly been used since its master died. Lady Harringdon had no great fondness for reading (Isabel was strongly of the opinion that this was why her aunt had such a severe and unimaginative view of the world) and while Isabel had pressed several 'excellent' books into the hands of her cousin over the years, Cathy did not visit the library unless Isabel insisted upon it.

Isabel's current text of choice was Dickens's *Dombey and Son* and she was nearing the end. Despite its hefty page-count, few of its leaves were left unread. She pinched them between her forefinger and thumb; those silent pages which held the final, mesmerising conclusion. A noise from the hall caused her to look up, but it was the sound of her aunt leaving the house. She heard the footman close the door and then waited until the house was silent so that she could savour every word.

Mrs Tabitha Black, her old housekeeper, had once remarked that Isabel did not read books: she devoured them. Not believing that Isabel, at the age of ten, had in fact read her way through the *Waverley* novels, Mrs Tabitha had questioned her upon their content and characters, and had been quite taken aback when Isabel had answered every question in full. Now, as she read, Isabel's eyes drank in the words greedily as she sped through page after page, the scenes coming to life before her eyes as Carker's life was crushed from his body, Walter returned home and Dombey at last enfolded his daughter in his arms.

Finally the concluding lines swam before her eyes:

*"Dear grandpapa, why do you cry when you kiss me?'*
*He only answers, 'Little Florence! Little Florence!' and smooths*

*away the curls that shade her earnest eyes.'*
(*Dombey and Son*, Chapter 62, Charles Dickens)

Isabel could not stem them: the tears that had threatened for the last ten pages overspilled and splashed down onto the fresh paper. She may have been a fast reader, but she was also a deep reader. They were not just characters to her, these people she read about – they were friends, family. She felt every emotion they felt. She had ran with little Em'ly along that jetty, flinched as the strikers hurled their stones towards Margaret and Mr Thornton, sobbed when Maggie and Tom drowned in one another's arms, and was filled with joy when Wentworth revealed the hearts of men to be more constant than Anne had ever imagined. The faces of those dear companions who never failed her came to greet her in her dreams each night, and her imagination by day. She would let them take her hand and lead her into their worlds of words and wonder.

For Isabel had an imagination that never slept. Indeed, she spent much of her time wishing for the adventure, romance and even terror of the novels in her own life. She wanted to laugh, to fear, to grieve, to love – to experience life in all its fullness. Although some would have said that her life had in fact been filled with drama from an early age, she could scarcely remember any of it. Those events were hidden by the shrouds of time, deep within her memory. Sometimes she wondered if this was why she felt such emotion now, because somehow she could understand, because she had gone through it before. But that time was hazy and indistinct. Any romantic memories of distraught weeping and gliding through the house like a ghost at midnight, lost in grief for her parents, were forgotten to her. But then, she conceded, she had been very young.

What she did remember, however, were the books.

Books had filled Isabel's life from a very young age. Her mother and father's library at Greenwood was breathtaking. As a four-year-old, staring up at the mahogany shelves that stretched from the floor, to the very top of the tall ceiling, filled with every colour, shape and size of book you could imagine; from new copies bound in shiny leather, to old originals crumbling at the spine: they filled her with a sense of wonder unlike any other.

It was the reason why James and Marianne Audley had bought the house. Having gathered a huge and varied collection of books throughout their individual lives, they wanted to display their combined treasures in a room worthy of such a collection. Each book was inscribed with their signature, and the year they had got the book. As a young girl, Isabel loved to run her fingers along the coloured spines, then pull a book at random from the shelf and guess which parent it had belonged to, finally opening the cover to reveal the answer. If her mother and father had been there, they would have smiled at their little girl, sitting on the wooden floor, surrounded by their open books, learning about her parents from those faded pages.

It was not surprising therefore that Isabel loved to read – and read widely. With no parents to guide or restrain her, no book was out of bounds and she consumed Austen, Spenser, Coleridge and Tennyson in equal measure. If she did not understand the text, she simply put it down and picked up another, whiling away the hours, surrounded by an ever-growing pile of books, until a servant came to call her down for her dinner, or up to bed.

Her favourite of all the books in that wonderful library was a very small, very faded soft red leather-bound copy of Blake's *Songs of Innocence and Experience* that her father had given to her on her third birthday. I will let her describe this memory to you, for her words touched me when I read them.


## ISABEL'S NARRATIVE
### *(Extract from Isabel's Diary)*

My father had bought me the edition when I was very small; too young to read or understand the poems when he read them to me in his deep, warm tones as I sat upon his knee in the library. But he loved them, and I loved them because he did. I remember poring over the intricately coloured illustrations that were all the more beautiful because the prints used to make them had been hand painted. The colours were so vivid, the images so alive. Each picture seemed to swirl and move before my eyes: a glorious mythical world contained between the pillars that bordered each page. My favourite pages were those of *Innocence*. The colours were brighter, the images more appealing to my childish imagination. And as I grew, though without my father there to read them to me any more, I learned the words of the poems that he had gifted to me by heart. I knew, even then, that their words were profound, their meanings fierce. I felt that Blake was speaking to me. And through the poems, I understood a little more about my father, and that he had loved me very much.

I have very few memories of my early years. I grew up not knowing what it was to have a mother. But sometimes, just sometimes, when my heart hurt for no reason and there was no one to tell, I missed her. I felt that I knew my father better. When I picked up that little book I was with him again, his strong arm around me, his voice reading out the words I did not yet understand. When I felt like this, I would rub my cheek softly with the palm of my hand, and somehow that helped. I wonder now, if that is what my parents used to do when I would not sleep. It comforted me and made me feel that I was not alone.

### THE STORY CONTINUED BY THE EDITOR

And so, perhaps it was inevitable that when her parents were taken from her, books became Isabel's life. As Mrs Tabitha said of the orphaned girl in her care, she was a child born of books, ghosts and dreams. And once again as Isabel sat in her aunt's library, she was grateful of their company as she waited anxiously for her cousin to return.

# VIII

It was almost a week until Cathy returned to Harringdon. Isabel heard the carriage pulling up the drive late one Friday afternoon and jumped from her seat in the library, cast down her volume, and rushed to the front door.

'Cathy!' she cried out with joy when she saw her cousin coming up the steps, rustling in one of her best crinoline gowns. 'How was your visit?' she asked, her eyes searching her cousin's face for any changes.

Cathy opened her mouth to reply and then shut it as her mother appeared at Isabel's shoulder.

'Hello Isabel, hello Mother,' said Cathy, embracing one after another, her face calm and betraying no emotion. 'I had a very good trip, thank you, and am only a little tired from the journey.'

'Did you meet him?' asked Isabel quickly. 'Did you meet Sir Leicester?'

'Catherine,' Lady Harringdon interposed. 'Come and rest in my study. You have had a long drive and I do not want you overtired. Come, my dear.'

She took Cathy by the arm and very firmly led her down the hallway. Cathy cast Isabel a quick backwards glance of apology, but allowed herself to be steered away. Frustrated, Isabel turned on her heel and went out to the gardens. She knew her aunt would not let her see Cathy for several hours, not until she herself had learned every detail of the trip.

It was an overcast day, but still warm, and Isabel wandered round to the back of the house where Harry, the elderly handywright was attaching bolts to the back garden gates. She perched upon the three-legged stool that he always carried around with him and chatted to him to pass the time. He had been asked to carry out the work as a result of the recent burglary. Isabel, always curious, was interested in the device he was using to attach the bolt to the door – a metal tool called a screwdriver. Harry explained that this twisted the metal nails called 'screws' into the wood and that they held much better than nails.

'So if tha' crook comes back 'ere again, e'll 'ave a nasty shock,' Harry told her with a toothless grin.

Isabel thought it kinder not to remind him that the thief had entered through the much more conspicuous front gates and assured him that the bolt looked very secure.

It was almost time for dinner when Isabel returned to the house. She quickly changed into her evening gown and entered the dining room where Cathy and Lady Harringdon were already seated. The conversation over dinner was stilted and sparse. Isabel was glad when the last plates were cleared away and she could bid goodnight to her aunt. She and Cathy went to their separate rooms to get ready for bed, but it was not long before Isabel was creeping barefoot along the first floor corridor to her cousin's room.

Silently, she opened the door and went in. There were several candles still burning and she could see her cousin sitting upon the chaise longue in the corner.

'What a foul dinner,' Isabel remarked with a whisper, closing the door behind her, and then giving Cathy a warm hug. 'I am so glad to have you back.'

'It is good to see you,' said Cathy with a smile. 'I wondered often how you and mother were getting along while I was away. Is she still very angry with you?'

'I barely saw her while you were away, but I expect so,' Isabel replied dismissively.

'She has been in a terrible mood recently, ever since the burglary. I do not think it is your fault.'

'It does not bother me if it is – but enough of that, how was your trip? Did you meet him?'

'No,' said Cathy, her face falling slightly. 'Sir Leicester was not there. He was staying with friends in London and because I arrived so unexpectedly, he could not get back. I am to meet him in two week's time instead. However, I did meet his mother and sister who were very pleasant and kind to me.'

'Is his sister older or younger?'

'Younger. She is fifteen and called Lydia, full of fun and conversation.'

'And his mother?'

'She is a very attractive older woman, well-dressed and very affable.'

Isabel nodded, drawing a picture of them in her mind.

'Do they not find it strange that you are promised to be married without even having met?' Isabel asked, trying to imagine the introductions that must have been made when Cathy arrived.

'I do not think so. They said that Sir Leicester is happy with his family's decision and is ready to take a wife. They welcomed me warmly.'

'I am glad. How does your mother know the family?'

'My father and his father were great friends apparently.' Cathy smiled. 'It is good to know that papa would have been happy about the marriage.'

Isabel kept silent. Cathy glanced at her and then added,

'There was a portrait of Sir Leicester above the staircase. He looks... very handsome.'

Isabel groaned inwardly. It would not do to have Cathy falling in love with a portrait. According to her experience, a painter's eye was often clouded by the wealth of the commissioner.

'Well, let us reserve judgement until you have met him in person, Cathy. In the meantime, I am very glad you are home. I have missed you.'

'And I you.'

Life at Harringdon Court almost resumed its happy course now that Cathy was home, but the knowledge that her cousin was to leave again soon for another visit to Berkshire hung over Isabel like a dark cloud. Isabel resented that their summer of freedom, the time when they should have been celebrating the start of their new lives now that school was over, had been so suddenly clouded by the news of Cathy's engagement. Cathy sensed that her cousin was downcast and as a result was continually suggesting things for them to do, to make the most of their time together.

'Shall we go into town today, Isabel? Mrs Donachie, the dressmaker, has just had some new fabrics delivered. Perhaps they would suit us and we could order some new dresses?'

Isabel knew that Lady Harringdon must have given Cathy permission for this, but agreed warmly, and soon they were both heading down the lanes towards the town centre of Ashton. Lady Harringdon would have preferred them to take the carriage, but the carriage had broken a wheel and was being mended, so the girls, not wanting to wait until Monday for their visit, decided to go on foot. It was a busy Saturday afternoon and by the time they had reached the outskirts of Ashton, the roads were already busy with horses and carriages.

As a result, having reached the town centre, they were struggling to cross the main road to the dressmaker's shop - so many horses were rushing past.

'I have never seen Ashton so busy!' exclaimed Cathy, turning her face away from a large cloud of dust raised by a particularly speedy hansom that had just rattled past.

Isabel gripped her cousin's hand; the next hansom was only just turning the corner and she spotted their window.

'Now, Cathy - run!'

Together they stepped into the road, but a speedy phaeton drawn by two young horses came rushing towards them from an unconsidered side street. Cathy shrieked and leapt back onto the pavement, pulling Isabel with her.

'Are you having trouble, Miss Audley?' called a familiar voice.

Isabel turned to see Mr Hardy striding towards them, dressed in his uniform. Cathy looked rather alarmed at his address and a light flush rose on Isabel's cheeks. She smiled, despite herself.

'Hello Mr Hardy,' she said, trying to keep her voice normal. 'Yes, we are struggling to cross. The carriages simply will not stop coming.'

'Let me solve that problem for you,' he said, stepping from the pavement into the middle of the road amidst the pandemonium. Isabel gasped as he disappeared amidst the clouds of dust, the carriages continuing to hurtle along from all directions. A moment later they heard several short sharp whistle blasts and the smoke cleared to reveal Mr Hardy standing in the middle of the road, his arms outstretched, horses and carriages frozen around him, a silver whistle between his lips. He removed this and called out,

'Now ladies, if you would like to cross.'

Cathy at first seemed reluctant, but Isabel took her arm and together they made their way along the path he had cleared through the suspended chaos. Horses and drivers alike eyed them with curiosity and mild annoyance as they passed. Once safely on the other side, Mr Hardy gave another blast of his whistle and the commotion resumed.

'Thank you very much, Constable,' said Isabel. They were now standing directly outside the dress shop where he joined them.

'You are now where you needed to be I presume?' he asked with a smile.

'Precisely,' replied Isabel – and remembering her manners, added, 'Mr Hardy, may I introduce my cousin Catherine Harringdon.'

'A pleasure,' he replied, with a slight bow.

'Thank you for your assistance, sir,' Cathy replied, with some nervousness.

She was clearly eager to end the conversation. Isabel knew what was on her mind. If her mother found out she had been speaking to men whilst out on her own, such trips would instantly cease.

At that moment a crowd of grubby looking boys ran towards them, a three-legged dog following at their heels.

'How're you doin' peeler?' one of them called out, a cheeky look on his face.

Mr Hardy gave him a friendly cuff round the ear.

'You stay away from the baker's shop today, Jack,' he shouted as they ran off down the street. He turned to Isabel and Cathy once more. 'Well ladies, I must be off. I hope you have a very pleasant day and if you need any assistance on the way home, I will be happy to help.'

'Thank you Constable Hardy,' Isabel replied, and the two girls made their way into the shop.

'Why did they call him peeler?' asked Cathy, in a low voice.

'It is because of Sir Robert Peel – he created the police force, and it has become a sort of nickname for them,' explained Isabel, watching through the shop window as Mr Hardy walked smartly down the street, greeting people as he went. She noted the tangible air of authority and warmth about him that Sir Peel surely would have approved of. Cathy followed her cousin's gaze.

'Isabel, Mother said you were not to speak to him again,' she said reproachfully.

'Oh Cathy,' she replied, irritated. 'He was simply doing his job.'

'I do not think he stops the entire street for every woman who needs to cross.'

Isabel felt the heat rising in her cheeks again.

'And he spoke so familiarly to you,' continued Cathy, suspicion in her voice. 'Isabel, have you met him since that Sunday?'

Isabel could not hide her annoyance.

'I did accidentally meet him whilst out walking one morning. But our conversation was civil, and....' - she could not say brief - 'perfectly acceptable.'

'But Isabel, he is a police constable - a villager!'

'And I doubt we shall ever see him again,' Isabel replied shortly, trying to control her rising temper. 'Now please let us drop this subject, Cathy, it is disagreeable to me. Where are the new fabrics you spoke of?'

An hour later they left the shop. Cathy had ordered several yards of lilac silk for a new evening gown. Isabel had ordered a plain bloomer dress that she had found a pattern for, having read that they were very sensible for travelling. This had caused some outrage on behalf of the shopkeeper, 'bloomers' being deemed unsuitable for the female sex. Isabel had therefore enquired whether she would like to change her views on the subject or lose a paying customer, and Mrs Donachie had quietly accepted the money. This altercation had upset Cathy and further vexed Isabel.

Little was said during the walk back and Isabel, in her annoyance, was walking quickly, her long legs striding much faster than Cathy could keep up with. Her lips were pursed and her brows drawn as she marched ahead, lost in thought.

'Isabel, slow down!' exclaimed her cousin, puffing with exertion behind her.

Isabel paused and looked round.

'I am sorry Cathy, I did not realise I was walking so fast.'

Feeling a little ashamed, Isabel altered her pace and fell in step with her cousin. After a few moments, she took Cathy's arm, and slowly conversation between them returned.

## ISABEL'S NARRATIVE
*(Extract from Isabel's Diary)*

*HARRINGDON COURT, 17<sup>th</sup> June 1866*

Matters between Cathy and myself are now quite resolved. I believe it is simply the suddenness of her news that has caused the strain, for we never usually argue. We stayed up late talking and as a result she overslept this morning. I wish she had not, for something very strange happened at breakfast.

As usual there were several letters for Aunt Helen when the butler delivered them on the silver platter. One envelope of thick parchment with a heavy wax seal caught my eye. She opened it first, and when she did, her face went white and she became so still, it seemed for a moment as though she was carved from stone. I do not think she had even read it much of the letter when this change came over her - she could not have had time to take in more than the first line - but so affecting was the news that she reacted instantly. When I asked her what was wrong, she jumped at the sound of my voice, as though she had forgotten I was there. I repeated my question and she glanced back to the letter and then looked me directly in the eyes. It was the first time in many days that she had done so, but the moment she met my gaze, she dropped it, as though the very sight of me burned her. I must admit, it shocked and disturbed me. I asked again if she was quite well and she seemed not to hear me, turning her eyes back to the content of the letter to read it in full. Cathy was still not yet at the table, and at that moment I wished she were beside me, for I felt quite unsettled.

Aunt Helen continued to appear pale and agitated all day. When the doorbell rang this afternoon, she rose from her chair with such haste I thought she was going to break into a run. Never would she normally rise from her seat for a visitor, preferring to wait for the butler to announce them, but today she went to the door herself (despite it being an unwanted caller). When she returned to the room I felt her gaze on me again. There was a dark, almost haunted look in her eyes, as though she was looking at me, and yet not at me. A shiver ran up my spine.

Cathy was not present during either of these incidents. I mentioned them to her, but while she agreed that her mother has been out of temper, she is not as concerned as I. I am worried about my aunt - for while her behaviour is never overly warm towards me, her coldness and sharpness during this visit has been out of character. Again, I wonder why she asked me back into her life after so many years of silence. I wonder if she has any love for me at all.

## ISABEL'S NARRATIVE
*(Extract from Isabel's Diary)*

### HARRINGDON COURT, 19<sup>th</sup> June 1866

Aunt Helen announced today that we are to have a guest to stay. The news gladdened me. Perhaps the presence of an 'old friend', as she described him, will cheer and gladden her spirit.

He is to arrive in four days' time.

# IX

## THE STORY CONTINUED BY THE EDITOR

The change in Lady Harringdon's behaviour became more noticeable as the days passed. Isabel wondered if indeed she was fit to have guests. She seemed distracted and much agitated, her usually impeccable dress becoming quite disorderly. She spent most of her time in her study, writing letters, and also made a great many trips into town. Again and again Isabel tried to guess at what was troubling her; again and again her mind returned to the arrival of the letter that had troubled her so.

Cathy, who was also concerned by this point, even dared broach the subject with her mother, but Lady Harringdon denied that anything was wrong and quickly turned the conversation to her daughter's forthcoming wedding. She was determined that Cathy should meet her future husband as soon as possible, and from the way she spoke, Isabel was certain that the wedding would not take place in October, as planned, but as soon as her aunt could possibly arrange it.

She was pondering all of this as she sat before the long windows in her bedroom after breakfast, staring out over the grounds. It was an overcast day, the first in a long time, and looking up at the dark clouds, Isabel wondered if the parched gardens would finally get a fresh drink that was not from Tom's rusty watering can. Cathy was downstairs with her mother and silence reigned upon the first floor. Hearing an unexpected creak behind her, she turned around. The window seat was set around the bay windows at the far end of her room, and from where she sat, the long curtains obscured her view. She drew the curtains softly aside to see what had made the noise and had to stifle a cry. In the centre of her room stood a creature – nay, it was a man – of hideous appearance.

She felt as though she was watching a character from one of her books come to life – never had she seen such a man, and to find him in her room made his presence seem even more unreal. Against the plush colours and soft fabrics he stood, his torn black cloak reaching to the floor. He had a lean, sunken face, deeply pitted with smallpox scars, and his red hair hung dull and lank in long thin strands around his shoulders. His skin was curiously colourless, and he appeared to have no eyelashes or eyebrows, giving him a queer, unnerving expression. But what unsettled Isabel more than anything were his eyes - she had never seen such eyes! One was bilious green, like that of a cat, piercing and luminescent. The other was as black as night: empty, searching. His head was cocked to one side, like a curious bird, and his grotesque gaze was fixed upon something in her mirror. She followed his gaze to the glass into which he stared, unblinking, and realised what he was looking at: herself.

In the mirror Isabel met his eyes, both repellent and mesmerising. She swallowed hard and tried to maintain control of herself.

'Who are you, and what are you doing here?' she said, as firmly as she could.

The man's head cocked to the other side at a strange angle, his gaze still unblinking.

'You are Isabel Audley.'

Ice seemed to be creeping through her veins.

'Who I am is no concern of yours,' she replied in the most imperious tone she could muster. 'Who are you and what are you doing in my room?'

He held her fixed in his parti-coloured gaze.

'I am Rester Gaunt, servant of Sir Branden. And I have come to stay.'

Thoughts whirled, confused, in Isabel's head – her aunt's guest was not supposed to arrive until tomorrow. But regardless whether or not this was true, it did not explain this man's presence.

'That is no concern of mine. I ask again - why are you in my room?' she said firmly.

He stared at her with a strange smile on his face, his expression sour and mocking.

'I took a wrong turn,' he replied.

Isabel suddenly realised that she was still staring at the man's reflection, his cast counterpart. Unnerved, she turned to face the man that stood in the centre of her room. He imitated her movement.

'Then please leave,' she said, trying to sound as commanding as possible.

'As you wish,' he replied, with a strange half-bow, the crooked smile still upon his lips. 'Forgive me.'

He turned and left the room, his ragged black cloak sweeping the floor, leaving an unsettled feeling of foreboding behind him. Letting the curtain drop back into place, Isabel found that she was shaking.

Pouring herself a small glass of water with a trembling hand, Isabel sat down on her bed and took a few moments to compose herself, sipping the water at intervals as she tried to calm her racing mind. When she felt calm enough, she rose and went downstairs. At the foot of the stairs stood her aunt and an unfamiliar gentleman. Lady

Harringdon turned. She was impeccably dressed in black silks, her hair swept high at the back of her head. She gestured in front of her, her hand glinting with her finest jewellery, and said,

'Isabel, I want you to meet Sir Aubrey Branden.'

The gentleman who stood before her was tall and slim. His hair was black with streaks of silver, carefully brushed round at the temples. He had thick black eyebrows that arched over a pair of grey eyes. They reminded Isabel of pieces of polished granite. He was also immaculately dressed; gold cufflinks glittered at his wrists and he held a polished cane. Isabel stepped forward and took his hand.

'Sir Branden', she said, giving a slight curtsy.

He raised her small hand to his lips and said in a rich, velvety voice, 'Enchanted.'

His eyes sought hers and held them for a moment. She tried to gauge him from them, but they were shielded and cold, revealing little, while his lips twisted into a seemingly warm smile. Sir Branden turned and beckoned to another figure standing in shadow by the doorway. The man came forward and with a shudder Isabel recognised him as the man who had stood her room only moments before.

'This is my manservant, Gaunt,' said Sir Branden.

The servant turned his unnatural gaze upon Isabel and she looked down, feeling disturbed and uncomfortable. Her aunt acknowledged the man and turned back to her guest.

'I hope you will want for nothing while you are here at Harringdon, Sir Branden,' she said smoothly.

He smiled with gently-curving lips and replied,

'I am sure it will be a most satisfying stay.'

He glanced at Isabel once again and she stared back, granite and violet colliding in unnatural union.


ISABEL'S NARRATIVE
*(Extract from Isabel's Diary)*

*HARRINGDON COURT, 22nd June 1866*

I felt quite queer when Sir Branden looked at me. I felt like he was seeing more than I wanted him to – as though he was looking deep inside me and I had been laid bare before him. In that moment, I wanted to gather up my image and hide it where he could not look. Despite his smiles and gracious manner, he made me feel uneasy.

Why on earth has Aunt Helen invited these people into her house?

Strange as it may seem, she seemed no more comfortable with their presence than I did, and yet she claims that Sir Branden is an old friend?

Dinner was a strained affair. Aunt Helen made polite conversation, but she seemed ill at ease and I could see her hands twisting at the napkin in her lap. Sir Branden had no shortage of conversation however and while he was polite and spoke to all three of us in turn, saying nothing to cause offence, I do not like him. I cannot put my finger on why. Everything about him is smooth – his voice, his clothes, his wooden cane. I believe that if anyone got too close to him, they would slip and fall upon his polished surface.

And the episode with his manservant truly left me shaken. When I close my eyes, I can still see his before me: large, pulsating and hideous.


## THE STORY CONTINUED BY THE EDITOR

Isabel and Catherine ate breakfast earlier than usual the following morning. After a brief discussion the night before, they came to the same conclusion: they did not like the new guests and wished to spend as little time with them as possible. Lady Harringdon entered the dining room just as they finished eating.

'Good morning,' they said together.

She looked up, as if noticing them for the first time.

'Good morning,' she replied distractedly.

There was the sound of footsteps coming down the stairs.

'Shall we go for our walk now, Cathy, while the weather holds?' Isabel asked in a bright, clear voice, anxious to get away.

Cathy quickly assented. They rose and went into the hallway. There stood Gaunt – looking as foul and unkempt as he had the day before. Cathy had to cross his path in order to get her bonnet; he made no effort to get out of her way, and she scurried past him like a frightened mouse. Isabel walked past, eyeing him with disdain. Sir Branden appeared from the drawing room.

'Do not upset the women, Gaunt,' he said in his rich voice.

Isabel disliked being referred to as a separate species.

'Fortunately we are not of a fainting disposition,' she replied coolly. 'Good day, Sir Branden.'

Isabel took Cathy's arm and together they left the house. Gaunt stared after them from the doorway with his mismatched eyes.

'What a horrid servant!' Cathy exclaimed as they hurried down the gravel pathway.

'Your mother has very strange taste in friends,' Isabel agreed. 'I hope he does not stay for long. He frightens me a little – and his manservant positively terrifies me!' She suppressed a shudder. 'What he was doing in your room yesterday, I simply cannot imagine.'

'He spoke to me in such a strange manner – almost as though he was mocking me.'

'How impertinent!' exclaimed Cathy.

'Yes, but I do not understand why,' said Isabel, wonderingly.

'Mother told me that Sir Branden made a lot of money in the cotton business and that he is very rich. You would think he could afford a more suitable servant. He is practically dressed in rags!'

'How does she know Sir Branden?'

'I am not sure…I believe it was from before she was married.'

'Perhaps my mother also knew him, then. Although I doubt that she would have liked such a man.'

'Yes, I often forget that our mothers were sisters… Do you think our mothers were great friends, like we are?' asked Cathy, with a smile.

Isabel pondered the thought. She had heard the servants at Greenwood say that she was very like her mother in character, but Cathy could not have been more different from Lady Harringdon. Yet, perhaps Aunt Helen had been different when she was a girl.

'I hope that they were,' she replied at last.

'Yes,' said Cathy with a smile. 'They must have been even closer than we are - for we are only cousins.'

'I think I should have liked a sister,' Isabel said softly, after a pause.

Cathy squeezed her arm.

'Well, at least you have me!'

'Yes, you who are leaving me soon to get married!' exclaimed Isabel. It was said in jest, but she could not hide the hurt in her voice.

'Isabel, I – ' Cathy sounded pained.

Isabel hurried to cover up her blunder.

'I only mean, that I shall miss you terribly and you must have me to visit – very often.'

A smile flooded Cathy's face.

'Of course I shall! And you never know Isabel, you may well marry soon, and then we shall be wives together. It will be a whole new adventure.'

'Ah, but only if I have not disgraced myself and been banished from your presence,' said Isabel, a naughty twinkle in her eye.

'Whatever do you mean?'

'Well, I might have run away to elope, like your French governess.

Then I shall never be allowed in your grand home!'

Cathy looked shocked at the suggestion. The incident was scarcely mentioned in the Harringdon household, least of all by Cathy and her mother.

'Isabel! How scandalous!'

'Well – it is practically what my parents did! Not that I would ever have to elope,' Isabel continued with energy. 'I shall marry who I choose and no one will stop me.'

Cathy looked on, half-admiring, half-shocked.

'Your parents were very brave,' she admitted, after a moment.

Isabel smiled proudly.

'I wish I had parents like yours,' continued Cathy in a slightly awe-struck tone. 'I have always admired your mother's daring. To give up everything for love... how brave.'

'Neither of them settled for second best, or allowed anyone to order their lives for them,' said Isabel with pleasure, but then she noticed Cathy's eyes clouding over and added, 'But you will be happy, Cathy. I am sure of it.'

Cathy looked away, clearly upset.

'Tell me what is wrong, Cathy?'

Cathy stopped walking and raised her eyes to meet Isabel's. The branches of the great oaks lining the path along which they walked were swaying gently in the wind, casting shifting shadows upon her concerned face.

'I am to meet him in two day's time. Mother came to my room last night to tell me.'

Isabel did not need to ask to whom Cathy was referring. Trying to be positive for her cousin's sake, she replied:

'But that is good news, is it not? I thought you were looking forward to meeting him?'

'But what if he does not like me, Isabel?'

'Not like you? My wonderful Cathy – with your beautiful face, pretty curls and, most importantly, wonderfully kind nature – he will love you! And if he does not, he is a fool and does not deserve you.'

'But I am not beautiful Isabel. If I try very hard, sometimes I look pretty. But he must be expecting so much more. I feel sure I shall disappoint.'

'His mother and sisters liked you very much,' said Isabel reassuringly.

'They are women.'

'But why should he judge you any differently?'

'Because he is a man. Because he is to be my husband.'

Isabel could feel the waves of panic coursing though her cousin. She knew what she wanted to say to her, what she wanted to do. She had been fighting the words for so long, ever since Cathy had told her that she was to be married. Suddenly Isabel realised that it might well be her last chance to say the words. She breathed deeply.

'Do you want to marry this man, Cathy?' she said slowly.

'I…well, it is hard to say before I have met him.'

'Because it seems to me that you are to be married to him, regardless of what he is like. Is that what you want? To be deprived of any say in the most important decision of your life?'

'I do not have a choice, Isabel.'

'You *do* have a choice, Cathy! You always have a choice.'

She took her cousin's hands in hers.

'Cathy, you know that I have access to money, and I will come into my inheritance next year, which will be substantial. That money was left to me by two people who believed that marrying for love was more important than anything else. I cannot stand by and watch you marry someone you do not love – do not even know - with no control over your future. I will not see you entrap yourself in a life that will be nothing but duty and submission. Run away with me Cathy. Run away with me tonight and we shall start our own life, where you will be free, not forced and prodded into a course of action that you do not want to take.' The words flowed out like water, her heart pounding with passion. 'We can go back to the house, pack a bag and leave for London. Tomorrow we will go to my father's bank and withdraw money. We will board a ship together under assumed names and be out of the country before your mother can discover where we have gone. It will just be the two of us. We can do whatever we want, go wherever we want. You would not be trapped any longer.' Isabel's voice was pleading; her eyes flamed with an inward fire.

Cathy's face was flushed and her eyes wide, entranced by Isabel's passionate words and imploring expression. She squeezed her cousin's hands tightly. The wind rose and the branches of the tall oak trees creaked overhead, complaining at being woken from their slumbers. A flutter of small birds took flight from their nest at the sudden movement. Cathy raised her eyes and watched them soar up above the trees. Isabel thought suddenly that she would assent and a bright and glorious future rose up before her.

Just then the clatter of horses' hooves was heard behind them and the girls had to break apart and move quickly aside as a carriage approached. Inside the carriage was Lady Harringdon. She was dressed in black, her lips taut. With a shrewd, hard look she acknowledged her daughter and drove on. All too quickly, real life came flooding back into place for Cathy, and the moment was lost. Isabel surveyed her cousin silently, watching the flush die down in her cheeks and her eyes cast themselves downwards again.

'Oh Isabel. That sounds wonderful – and terrifying. But I cannot,' said Cathy softly.

Isabel's expression was full of sadness.

'But Cathy - dearest Cathy, must all your dreaming come to an end simply because your mother commands it? We are young - the whole world is just opening out before us, and should you choose marry this man, your whole future will be decided at seventeen and there will be no going back.'

Isabel realised her cousin was shaking. She took Cathy by the arm and led her to an upturned log that lay by the side of the road. Together they sat down, side by side.

'This is a good match, Isabel,' said Cathy, her voice trembling. 'Sir Charles Leicester is wealthy, and from a good family.'

'He is rich, yes. But he is one rich man among many. Do you really believe that there will be no other offers, that this is the only man who will ever want to marry you – and without even seeing you? I am vain enough to want a man to wish to marry me because he likes what he sees. And there is so much to like about you.'

'But that is not how it works, Isabel,' said Catherine softly. 'I know that your parents defied convention and it worked out well for them, but this world turns on money and titles. In the end, we can only hope that we are chosen by a good man, and that he will treat us well.'

'It is not wrong to expect affection before marriage, Cathy,' Isabel replied gently. 'I may speak out of turn, but to marry without love - I would rather not marry at all.'

There was a moment's silence.

'I am not like you, Isabel,' Cathy said quietly. 'You talk of running off and having adventures and seeing the world, but I could never do that. You speak of independence and equal marriages and of men who will do things your way, but I cannot see so far ahead. It feels like a different world to me.' She laughed softly, and with the movement a little shiny tear tumbled from her lashes. 'But then I always knew that you would lead a different life from most girls. Such a life is too big for me, I do not have the head for it.'

Her face set with resolve, heartbreaking and unswerving.

'I will marry Sir Charles Leicester,' she said resolutely. I will be a good wife, I will work hard to make him happy and give him lots of children. I will be content.'

'Content,' replied Isabel.

'Content.'

## ISABEL'S NARRATIVE
*(Extract from Isabel's Diary)*

*HARRINGDON COURT, 23rd June 1866*

I wore a smile to mask my sorrow as we walked. I wore it all day and all evening when I was with her, but now it is gone.

I would have fought – I would have taken her by the hand and led her into the London coach there and then, but I could see the resignation in her eyes. I think, if I had looked hard enough, I would have seen it there all along. There was no hope. Our futures were already written and they lay far apart. The realisation brings tears to my eyes.

# X

## THE STORY CONTINUED BY THE EDITOR

The day of Cathy's departure dawned far sooner than either girl would have wished. It had been agreed that Cathy would be staying in Berkshire for a month, which was deemed time enough for the proposal to take place and for the newly engaged couple to make the necessary arrangements for the wedding, which was now to take place in early September. All of this was duly agreed through correspondence between Lady Harringdon and Lady Leicester.

Isabel helped Cathy choose her dresses and pack her cases. The maid had come in to help, but Isabel had sent her away. She wanted to make the most of the precious few hours they had left together.

'You do not mind staying here with Sir Branden and that odious servant of his?' Cathy asked again. She had spoken to her mother several times about Isabel coming with her to Berkshire, at least for part of the duration of her stay, but Lady Harringdon had refused absolutely. Isabel was not surprised.

'Not at all,' Isabel replied, keen to assuage any fears Cathy may have about her. 'You know that they do not frighten me in the least, and that I will not allow your mother to condemn me to spend much time with them.'

Cathy folded up the last of her nightdresses. Her hands looked very small and pink against the white cotton.

'You must write to me, all the time,' Cathy said suddenly. 'I do not know what I will do if I do not hear from you.'

'You know I will!' exclaimed Isabel. 'What are the two things I love more than anything?'

'Reading – and…' Cathy hesitated.

'You!' replied Isabel, hugging her cousin around the waist. ' And we will be back together very soon. At least your mother cannot forbid me from attending the wedding, so the next time you go to Berkshire, I am most definitely going with you.'

Everything was packed. Isabel rang the bell to summon the manservant to take the cases downstairs.

'It is time,' said Cathy, looking round her room one last time.

'The next time I see you, you will be an engaged woman,' said Isabel, trying to keep her voice bright and cheerful. 'I hope the ring will be very pretty.'

She smiled at her cousin and Cathy smiled back and then said, with some concern,

'I just hope I do not lose it – you know how clumsy I am with jewellery.'

It seemed very strange to be speaking of an engagement before it had happened with such certainty. It felt cold, somehow, lacking all the surprise and jubilation that usually occurred on such an occasion. But Isabel was determined to make much of it, for Cathy's sake. She suspected that Cathy knew she was feigning, but it did not matter – Cathy needed support this morning, and there was no one else to give it to her.

'Catherine! The carriage is ready.' Lady Harringdon's voice echoed from downstairs.

With a deep breath, Cathy turned to leave the room. Isabel followed her out of the door and down the stairs. Lady Harringdon stood by the doorway with Sir Branden, who was dressed immaculately as ever, polished cane in hand.

'I hope your stay will be most profitable,' he said smoothly to Cathy, taking her hand and raising it to his lips. She dropped her gaze, made uncomfortable by his gesture and his piercing stare. Lady Harringdon appraised her daughter coolly. Cathy was wearing her newest gown, of lilac silk, with her hair carefully pinned up by Isabel and pretty amethyst earrings dangling from her ears.

'You look very smart, Catherine,' her mother said at last. 'Be sure and make this effort every day during your stay.'

She embraced her daughter briefly, and then, with a hand in the small of Cathy's back, motioned her down the steps towards the carriage. Isabel followed after Cathy, frustrated by her aunt's lack of affection towards her daughter.

At the foot of the stone steps, Cathy turned to her cousin, her face pale but her eyes bright. With a full heart, Isabel held her close and bade her farewell with a kiss. Aware that her aunt was watching impatiently, she made to let Cathy go, but Cathy held her tight for a few moments longer. Then, without glancing backwards, Cathy lifted her small bag and walked across the gravel driveway towards the carriage. Isabel fought an intense desire to stop her, to hold her back. She felt full of sadness, as though she was not bidding farewell to Cathy for a few weeks, but for the final time.

## ISABEL'S NARRATIVE
### *(Extract from Isabel's Diary)*

### HARRINGDON COURT, 25<sup>th</sup> June 1866

When Cathy reached the carriage, she paused. She looked back at me then, a strange look in her eyes. To this day, I cannot describe it – whether it was sadness, or fear, or simply that she was looking at me as if she would never see me again. It seemed as though she was memorising each little detail of my face. But she looked at me intently for a long time, the morning breeze stirring her curls, so red and beautiful. Then, she was gone.

It was that look that prompted my visit to Aunt Helen's study that afternoon. I have never been afraid of speaking my mind when I thought I could make a difference. I knew that in this case, the chances were slim, but there was a chance, nevertheless. We had dressed Cathy up like a doll and sent her off to an unknown end. I had to make one last stand.

## THE STORY CONTINUED BY THE EDITOR

Isabel knocked on the oak-panelled door of her aunt's study, with a short sharp rap.

'Enter,' a voice called from within.

Isabel entered the dimly lit room, directing her steps towards her aunt's dark silhouette seated in front of the window at the far end of the long study. Lady Harringdon was sorting through a pile of letters, and looked up when Isabel entered.

'Isabel? What do you want?'

Lady Harringdon's tone was harsh. Her manner towards Isabel had become even colder since Sir Branden arrived. They had had no major disputes, yet still Isabel felt as though her aunt was deliberately distancing herself from her.

'I wonder if I can have a few moments of your time, Aunt Helen,' she said, determined to persist.

'Very well.'

Isabel took a few steps forward. Her aunt's face was cast in shadow. Isabel took a deep breath.

'Aunt Helen, I am not convinced that Cathy is really happy about this marriage. Is it necessary that she must marry Sir Leicester, when she is still so young?'

There was silence. The sun came out from behind a cloud, casting a shaft of light upon her aunt's countenance. It was stony.

'I do not believe that this is any of your business, Isabel. We have discussed this before. Catherine is not a child. Many girls marry at her age.'

'You did not,' replied Isabel, undaunted.

'Indeed', said Lady Harringdon, her voice brittle, 'and yet I would have been grateful to be married at Catherine's age. It is a great honour: she will be well provided for, and her children will have a good future. What more could any girl wish for?'

'Choice – and free will?' replied Isabel, frustrated.

Her aunt laid aside the paperwork she had been ordering, folded her hands and focused her cold gaze upon the girl who stood before her.

'Let me tell you something Isabel Audley. You may have been born into an enviable inheritance, living a life of few rules, with parents who believed they could do exactly as they pleased - but the world does not operate on those principles.' She looked Isabel up and down. 'What do you know of life? You are young, foolish, with a head stuffed full of romantic notions – notions which your parents did nothing to dispel, I might add. You are going to have to learn that life is made of hard choices not fanciful dreams. I know what it is like to live in the real world. Therefore, in my house, I will decide what is most advantageous for those living under my roof - without question. Do you understand me?'

Isabel stared at her aunt for a moment. A thin blue vein was pulsing in Lady Harringdon's forehead and the knuckles of her tightly clasped hands had turned white.

'No, aunt,' replied Isabel. 'I do not understand you. And I am glad that my future does not rest with you.'

Her aunt made no reply, only stared at her niece with eyes of ice, and the sun again passed behind a cloud, shrouding her in darkness. Isabel turned and left the room

## ISABEL'S NARRATIVE
*(Extract from Isabel's Diary)*

*HARRINGDON COURT, 25ᵗʰ June 1866*

I understood more fully than ever before why my mother made the decision she did. She had stood before the same precipice as my aunt had, the same precipice before which Cathy now stood. My mother had chosen to jump rather than fall – one glorious jump that must have required a vast deal of courage. That courage now flowed through my veins, pounding with every beat of my heart. I know one thing: I will fight for what I want, whatever that may be.

## LETTER FROM ISABEL TO CATHY

*HARRINGDON COURT, 26ᵗʰ June 1866*

*My dearest Cathy,*

*I know I said I would wait a few days before I wrote, but I am afraid my patience is somewhat lacking, as always.*

*How are you enjoying Berkshire and Lancombe Place? I hope Sir Leicester's mother and sister made you feel quite at home when you arrived. I also hope you did not have to wait too long until you met the man who has occupied our thoughts so often, Sir Leicester himself. You must write soon and tell me all about him – with a full description both of his looks and his character. I am quite impatient to hear about him. Tell me also what you have been doing, and the conversations you have had. Then I shall be able to imagine myself with you, and will not feel so cut off here at Harringdon.*

*I have been quite petulant since you left. Due to a rainy spell, I have taken to spending my days in the library (no surprise there, I hear you say!) Having completed the works of Dickens (Pickwick Papers was simply charming!), I have turned to a rather different author, whose works I have been keen to read for some time – a Mrs Anne Radcliffe. I have heard people say her books are quite shocking, but they must not be too scandalous as she is married. Were she Miss Anne Radcliffe, I suspect they would not have been published at all! If I write, I suspect I shall have to lie about my marital status, or write under a pseudonym as the Brontes did...Anyway, I digress.*

*I have decided to begin with The Mysteries of Udolpho and Cathy -*

*it is quite chilling! But I need something very distracting to fill my time now you are gone. The pages take me through dark castles and reveal dark secrets... I fear I may not be able to sleep at night without you down the hall! I crept to your room last night as I had a dream that you and I were back at the beach and I woke missing you. It is strange being here without you, Cathy. Write to me soon.*

*Yours always,*
*Isabel*

## EXTRACT FROM CATHERINE'S LETTER TO ISABEL

*LANCOMBE PLACE, 28th June 1866*

*Dear Isabel,*

*Thank you so much for your letter, it was very good to hear from you so quickly. I hope you are not too lonely on your own and that mother is treating you well. I also hope that you are not having to spend too much time with Sir Branden and his frightful servant.*

*My first few days at Lancombe have been very busy. Lady Leicester has been most kind and made me feel very welcome, as has Margaret. Charles Leicester did not arrive until late evening upon the day of my arrival. When I first saw him, I was surprised that he looked so little like his portrait, but I shall do as I promised and describe him as fully I can (although you know I do not have a way with words like you do, Isabel).*

*He has a pleasant face, with brown hair that curls a little round his ears. His ears are a little large, but he has blue eyes, which I like. He is quite tall – taller than me – and not fat at all. Does that give you a clear enough picture?*

*He sat next to me at dinner and we spoke together for most of the meal. He knows a lot about architecture and so he talked mostly about buildings that he liked. I know very little about that subject, so I tried my best to sound interested and asked lots of questions. He seemed pleased enough with me and I went to bed feeling relieved.*

*The next day, it was beautiful weather and so we all drove out to a nearby hillside for a picnic with neighbours of the Leicester's, the Granston and Helliver families. I did not see much of Charles that day as there were so many people about and he was always busy speaking with them.*

*But yesterday – oh, now I must try to remember everything, as I know you will want to hear all the details - after we had eaten breakfast we sat in the long sitting room at the front of the house. I was sitting in the window seat, a distance away from the rest of the family. Sir Leicester came over and asked if he could sit with me. I was so nervous, I could barely reply, but he sat down next to me and began to speak of how desirous our parents were of this match, and that now he had met me, he was very pleased with their choice. Then – it was just like in your novels, Isabel – then, he went down on one knee in front of everyone and asked for me for my hand. It was very romantic. I gasped out my assent and then he drew out a beautiful sapphire ring. As soon as it was on my finger, his family were all around us, giving us their warm congratulations. I was very happy, but I wish you could have been there Isabel. You should have been there...*


## THE STORY CONTINUED BY THE EDITOR

Isabel put the letter down on the table beside her. It was done. Cathy was engaged to be married.

Restless and unhappy, she stood up from the library armchair in which she sat. Dark clouds hung forebodingly in the sky outside, but she decided to walk out regardless. An umbrella stood by the door, next to where her coat hung, but obtusely, she left it where it was and set off through the gardens, towards the path that led to the fields.

'It was very romantic'.

The words hung in Isabel's mind like lead. Romantic was not how she would have described, this staged engagement in which her cousin had no say. Her words may have sounded cheerful, but there was an uncertainty, a sense of holding back in Cathy's letter that Isabel was all too aware of.

Unhappy with her train of thought, Isabel slipped the bonds of reality for her imagination, and all too soon, although her feet strode through wet grass and crops, her mind was far away...

Standing on the heaving deck, Isabel watched as her defender fought off the villains that were attacking her, with a gleaming sword. Rain was pouring down as he drew her to him, and together they jumped off the sinking ship into the boat waiting below.

'Marry me,' he said, desire flashing in his dark eyes.

'I will,' she replied, breathlessly, and together they sailed off into the storm.

It was very romantic.

# XI

The atmosphere in the drawing room was rigid, the silence so thick that Isabel wondered if it would indeed be possible to stand up, or if the pressure of it would hold her in her place. Not that she was allowed to stand, or leave. Her aunt had instructed her that it was her duty to spend at least two hours each morning with their guests. On this particular morning, the minutes were crawling by so slowly it was as though someone had laid iron weights upon their backs.

She knew it was partly in punishment for yesterday's events. And for that she blamed Gaunt. That sly, obsequious creature, standing behind his master's chair like some overgrown hound. She had realised that very little escaped his notice. Especially when it involved herself.

It was sheer boredom that had driven Isabel into town. Boredom coupled with a desire to avoid the other inhabitants of the house. She had waited until the post arrived, on the off chance that Cathy had written again (mayhap to tell her she had broken off the engagement?) – but alas she had no such luck, and so she set off along the familiar lanes and roads towards Ashton.

When she arrived in the bustling town centre she found that she did not know what to do with herself, and so entered Gentry's tearoom, an overpriced establishment owned by the titular Mrs Gentry herself (an assumed name if ever there was one, thought Isabel dryly). The place was busy so she took a small table for one by the window and ordered a cream tea, the only option available. When it arrived she reminded herself once again that she did not like tea and made a mental note that when she had her own home, it would not be served, no matter how unfashionable she was thought.

Her cup clinked softly against the gaudily patterned china plate as she set it down, adding to the symphony of tinkles and clatters as the many couples around her lifted and sat down their cups. She glanced at the people seated near her. The tables were placed so close together that she could hear snatches of several conversations, all going on at once. One rather buxom woman was speaking of her new lady's maid and how she suspected that she tried on her dresses when she was out; another older woman was discussing possible suitors for her daughter; a gentleman behind her was explaining how the stock market was very much in his favour at the moment; while a young man to her right spoke portentously of his new gun dogs and how well they would do for him in the upcoming season. She looked at their faces as they spoke: most were talking for the sake of talking, some were brimming with the latest gossip, while others were simply boasting. Talking and talking about nothing at all as they always did and would always do. She sighed quietly in her corner, struck by the pointlessness of it all.

She wondered what Cathy was doing at this very moment and if she thought of her at all. A girl who had her back to her had red ringlets that reminded her of Cathy, and her heart ached a little. Another girl sitting opposite her had long blonde hair like her friend Jane from school. Jane would be back in Nottingham now, far, far away. The school days they had shared together seemed so long ago – from a different life. She felt as though she had grown up so much already although not even a month had passed since she left.

Outside a boy ran past, driving his hoop along in front of him. He had dirt smeared on this face and his hair stuck out under his oversized cap. Further along the road, costermongers were selling their wares, and Isabel noticed a pretty girl in a tattered dress flirting with a young man in the corner. He leaned in to steal a kiss from her as a pedlar cart rolled past, obscuring them from view, the driver calling out his wares in a loud voice.

A deep voice coming from the buxom lady to her left spoke out suddenly,

'I do wish Mrs Gentry would move the location of her tearoom, I simply must have a word with her. It is  much too close to those undesirables. They set up closer and closer every day. Soon we will be walking out into their filthy stalls.'

Isabel continued to watch the stall owners and their customers until suddenly a familiar face appeared in the milling crowds. Constable Hardy was making his way along the street, stopping to chat with a few of the mongers and purchasing an apple from a fruit seller. He seemed to know someone every few yards, often pausing for some lively conversation. He was greeted with smiles from the men and curtsies from the women. Suddenly Isabel found herself on her feet.

Putting a few coins down on her table, she made her way out of the tearoom, accidentally knocking the disapproving lady's hat askew in her hurry.

'Well I never!' she heard her exclaim, but Isabel did not stop to apologise.

The constable was directly across the street from her now.

'Constable Hardy,' she called out loudly.

He turned at the sound of her voice just as a breeze picked up without warning and nearly stole her hat from her, but Isabel caught it just in time, laughing as she swept her tousled hair into place. The sight brought a huge smile to his face and he called out to her, crossing the road swiftly as he did so,

'Miss Audley, how good to see you again. Are you in need of some roadside assistance?'

'No, I – well, I saw you from the tearoom window and wanted to… wish you a good morning,' she said, a little lamely.

He gazed at her for a moment, his hazel eyes warm and earnest.

'That was very kind of you, I am glad that you did so. Are you in town for any particular reason?'

'No, I …well, I simply came because I had nothing else to do.'

'I suspected you might find the country life rather dull,' he said, a twinkle in his eye. 'We shall have to find a better way to entertain you.' He pulled out his pocket watch and checked the time. 'I have a short lunch break in ten minutes. Would you like to join me?'

The proposition was so unexpected and delivered in such an unpresumptuous manner that Isabel found herself replying instantly.

'I would,' she said, sounding surprised at herself.

'Excellent. Well, if you will accompany me to the end of this street, I will ensure nothing is amiss and then we shall have some food together.'

Twenty minutes later they were sitting on a grassy bank, just outside of Ashton. Mr Hardy had procured a basket containing several chicken legs, some pork pies and two bottles of ale. He took off his jacket for Isabel to sit upon and she made herself comfortable, removing her hat and laying it down beside him, tidying some strands of hair that had come loose.

'I am afraid it is not a very lady-like lunch', he said, when she was settled, 'but I suppose you shall have to get used to all different sorts of meals with you begin your travels.'

'Indeed', said Isabel, lifting a chicken leg and trying to ensure that the grease from it did not spread all over her hands as she ate. It was delicious: suddenly her appetite, which had seemed non-existent in Mrs Gentry's tea room, returned in full force.

'So, how are you enjoying staying with your aunt?' he asked her as they ate.

Isabel paused before answering, measuring her response.

'I have always loved my visits to Harringdon Court – mostly because I get to spend time with Catherine, my cousin. But she is away for a month now and I am growing bored and restless. My aunt….' she paused, unsure whether to continue. 'I find my aunt's views very restrictive.' She frowned, and a tiny crease appeared between her eyebrows. 'And I do not think much of her choice of guests.'

'She has visitors staying?' he asked.

'Yes, a gentleman called Sir Branden.'

'And does he has any servants with him?'

'A foul man called Gaunt,' she replied with distaste.

Mr Hardy seemed lost in thought for a moment.

'What is wrong?' Isabel asked him.

'No matter.'

She waited, in case he wished to ask anything else on the subject, but he did not.

A horse and cart passed and the driver touched his cap to Sam as he went by. Sam returned the gesture.

'That was my neighbour,' said Sam, after he had passed.

'Do you enjoy life in Cranwell?' Isabel asked, taking a sip from her bottle of ale. It was the first time she had tried the beverage and it had a sharp taste.

'I do indeed,' he said with a smile. 'It is a very friendly village and I enjoy being based in the countryside, rather than in a city.'

'But do you not find it rather dull spending all your time in such a small village?' said Isabel. She heard the apparent condescension in her voice just a moment too late, and berated herself inwardly. 'I mean, after living in Manchester for so many years.'

'No, it is not dull at all,' he replied, taking no offence. 'There is always something going on in Cranwell, always someone to talk to or visit. I enjoy village life – the warmth of the people, the bustle of the marketplace. I enjoy fishing by the river on my days off with the local men, or taking my dog for long walks along the beach, and sitting in the pub at night by the roaring fire while Old Nick tells his old stories to his usual audience. It does not have much drama and splendour, I will admit, but it is enough for me.'

Isabel was intrigued by his enthusiasm.

'And what sort of events take place down in the village?' she asked. 'I have heard our cook speaking of concerts that take place from time to time? I know she enjoys them very much.'

'Ah yes, I know your cook – Joyce is a charming lady, and quite the dancer! Whenever we have a barn dance, she is always the first on the floor.'

Isabel had a sudden strange image of Mrs Bett dancing wildly around a hay-filled barn in her white apron, a far cry from her usual tidy appearance in the downstairs kitchen.

'However,' he continued, 'she was probably speaking of the local band that plays monthly at the Bumblebee Inn. They are really very talented musicians and always give us a wonderful night. Although the Bumblebee is quite small, there are never many left in their seats by the end of their set – everyone is up and dancing, the young couples making the most of the opportunity to be together and Susie the barmaid serving out drinks by the barrel and catching the eye of every man in the house.'

'It sounds like quite a party!' Isabel exclaimed.

His eyes twinkled. 'Probably not of the sort that you are accustomed to, but yes – it is indeed quite a party.'

'And do you – dance?'

'Of course! I am usually one of the first up – I grew up with a mother and three sisters so I am well-used to leading the way where dancing is involved.'

'They must miss you now that you live so far from home,' said Isabel, thinking of them living alone back in Manchester.

'It is hard, but I still see them whenever I have a holiday. Christmas is a particularly jolly time when I go home.'

'I imagine that you do not get very regular holidays?'

'Constable Barnes, who is the Constable of Little Wharton, kindly covers my area during the holiday periods. He has no family of his own and is happy to allow me to return home to see mine.'

'That is very kind of him. He must be a good friend'

'Constable Barnes is possibly the gruffest man I have ever met, but he also has the stoutest heart. He runs a tight ship over at Little Wharton. Have you ever visited there?'

'No, I have not,' she replied. 'Although my aunt has friends in the town.'

'Despite its name, it is actually quite a large town and Barnes is the Chief Constable there, with two younger men underneath him – Fred Gelding and Will Whitburn.'

'Are they friends of yours as well?'

'We get along well and I see them often enough. Fred is a good-hearted fellow with the widest gap in his front teeth that you have ever seen and hair so blonde it looks almost white. Will is harder to spot because he is normally hidden behind a cloud of tobacco smoke. He's slightly older than Fred, but only became a police constable recently. Barnes is training them up quickly though.'

'And where did you train', asked Isabel.

'In London, also under Barnes. He is one of the most experienced constables on the job, and very well respected. It is my aim to follow in his footsteps.'

'How did you find yourself in this line of work?' asked Isabel, intrigued by his passion for the job. 'Was your father also a police constable?'

'I actually started work in a cotton factory in Manchester. It was not work I enjoyed, but the factory owner was a good man and gave me the opportunity to train as his assistant as I had good reading and writing skills. Quickly, he progressed me to manager of another smaller factory that he was starting up on the outskirts of London. It was there I learned of the growing police force and with my benefactor's blessing, moved into this new line of work.'

Isabel noticed he had ignored the reference to his father, but listened with great interest as he continued,

'Barnes trained me quickly, and there is no better place to learn than in London where the crime rate is higher than in any other city. But I grew weary of the dirt and smoke and when they offered me the position in Ashton, I was quick to take it. As I mentioned before, it is only recently that police constables have held these jobs in their own right in smaller towns such as Ashton. Previously men were police constables in addition to their main job, an 'aside', as it were. But it has become clear that there is a growing need for each town to have an appointed constable to maintain peace and order. Barnes was offered a sergeant's position in London, but was concerned about the growing corruption within the London force and instead followed me to this part of the country soon after, choosing to remain as a constable.' Mr Hardy paused and looked up with some surprise. 'In fact, speaking of the man himself – here he is!'

A middle-aged man, tall and broad shouldered, with thick grey hair was walking towards them. He had what Isabel would call a fierce face, partly concealed by a bushy greying moustache.

'Constable Barnes, we were just speaking of you,' said Mr Hardy, jumping up and holding out a hand.

The man surveyed them both sternly.

'And what were you saying,' he replied in a gruff voice.

'I was speaking of our many adventures in London.'

'Humph, yes, terrible place.'

His eyes fell upon Isabel, sitting on the grassy bank.

'And who are you, girl,' he said, no hint of politeness in his tone.

'Forgive my manners - may I present Miss Isabel Audley,' said Mr Hardy, smiling.

'Miss Audley, huh? Niece of Lady Harringdon?'

Isabel nodded a small assent.

'And what are you doing sitting on the roadside with my police constable?' he asked in a demanding tone

Words failed Isabel as she met his piercing gaze.

'We were sharing some lunch,' said Mr Hardy, taking his seat on the grass again. 'Would you care to join us?'

'No time. I am on my way into town.' He stared at Isabel again, who now felt distinctly uncomfortable.

'You seen Fred?' he barked at Mr Hardy.

'I am afraid not. Is he not on duty today?'

'No, Will is. Darned nuisance the pair of them. Wish I could look after the town on my own, it's scarcely bigger than yours. Well, better be off. See you Monday.'

'Yes indeed,' replied Mr Hardy.

Constable Barnes called back at Isabel,

'And mind you don't lead him astray – I know what you rich girls are like.'

Mr Hardy flushed, clearly embarrassed and Isabel cast her eyes down, suddenly wondering if she had been unwise in accepting the offer of lunch.

There was a pause and then Mr Hardy said,

'I am sorry, Miss Audley, I should have realised that it was inappropriate to ask you out here. I tend not to think about proprieties - and I should.'

'Do not apologise for your friendliness, Constable Hardy', Isabel said, standing up and brushing her skirt down. She could not bear for him to feel ashamed; there had been no dishonour in his conduct. 'I know you meant no disrespect to me, only courtesy - and I was glad of your company.'

A rustle in the hedges across the lane made them both look over.

'Who's there?' called Mr Hardy sharply.

There was no answer, but very slowly, the hedge parted and Gaunt stepped through, his clothes as dishevelled as ever, his hair hanging limply around his sallow face.

'You!' exclaimed Isabel in disgust. 'Were you spying on me?'

'Why Miss Audley, what a surprise to see you here!' the servant replied in mock surprise. 'Spying? No, not at all - I was simply taking a walk and happened to hear your voice. And who is this friend of yours?' he asked, gesturing towards Mr Hardy with a sneering smile.

'As you can clearly see from his uniform, he is the town constable,' replied Isabel quickly, her heart sinking at the expression on his face.

'And does your dear aunt know where you are?' asked Gaunt, false concern in his eyes.

'I do not require her permission for my every movement, Gaunt. Be gone!' Isabel's tone was sharp, but she felt sick to her stomach.

Gaunt gave her a deep bow, and then walked off casually down the lane. Mr Hardy glanced at Isabel's pale face.

'Will that man cause trouble for you?' he asked quietly.

'As much as he possibly can,' Isabel replied with certainty.

'I am sorry. We should never have come here. I am a fool.'

'You are no fool, but I must leave now and return home quickly.' She rose determinedly. 'I fear what tales Gaunt may tell otherwise. Thank you for providing such a delicious lunch.'

'If there is anything I can do to help, you will let me know?' Mr Hardy said, concern in his eyes.

'I think, while I am at Harringdon, it will be best if I see you only in passing,' replied Isabel. 'Perhaps once I have left and am making my own way in the world, we can meet up again and share more conversation.'

'When you leave Harringdon, it will be for a place many miles away,' said Mr Hardy, smiling, but there was no merriment in his expression this time. 'You have wider eyes than any woman I have ever met, Miss Audley – you see no barriers and only opportunities. I wish you well in your travels, and in everything that you do. I am sure you will be magnificent. It has been my pleasure to meet you.'

'And I you,' Isabel replied sincerely.

He tipped his hat to her, and picking up the lunch basket, walked back up in the lane in the direction of Ashton.

Alone once more, Isabel suddenly felt worse than when Gaunt had appeared. She wanted to run after Mr Hardy and apologise, but she could sense Gaunt drawing ever nearer to Harringdon, and, disappointed with herself though she was, she turned on her heel and ran all the way back.

Gaunt must have done the same – either that or he could fly - for by the time she entered the drawing room, she found Gaunt standing before her aunt and Sir Branden. He turned and gave her an unpleasant smile. Before Isabel could open her mouth, her aunt greeted her in an imperious tone:

'Isabel Audley. Gaunt has been telling us the most incredible tales about your whereabouts this afternoon. I trust you have a good explanation?'

'Other than the one that you will not believe - that I had an innocent lunch with a friend – no, I do not have an explanation,' replied Isabel stoutly, though rather out of breath.

Lady Harringdon's eyebrows raised.

'Do you realise what this could do to your reputation, Isabel?'

'I have a vague idea, yes. But fortunately I am not your responsibility,' she said tenaciously.

Her aunt's mouth was a hard line. Sir Branden spoke up then, his voice as smooth as glass:

'Miss Audley, what your aunt means is - '

'I know what my aunt means, Sir Branden,' said Isabel quickly. 'That part was perfectly clear, thank you. Now please excuse me, I must go and change for dinner.'

## ISABEL'S NARRATIVE
*(Extract from Isabel's Diary)*

*HARRINGDON COURT, 29<sup>th</sup> June 1866*

Well, I have had my freedom well and truly curtailed after today's events. Branden began the conversation at dinner with a speech about how they see too little of me and would enjoy my company on a more frequent basis, which I take to mean that I will be spending a lot more of my time here with them, whether I wish it or not. Aunt Helen made it quite clear that I would certainly not be allowed to leave the house without a companion from now on.

I did not mean to let my temper get the better of me when I spoke to them after I returned home, but I could not stop myself. I suppose I should have apologised and explained the situation, but I saw in their eyes that they would not listen. A great rebelliousness rose up within me when I saw their disapproving faces, and having run home like a coward, I felt that I must redeem myself.

For I am not ashamed to admit that I enjoyed spending time with Mr Hardy today. He is different from anyone I have ever met. He speaks with such easy confidence and is interesting and good company. Something about him makes me smile. He makes me feel as though we are equals, sharing real conversation and that pleases me.

And I suppose that after today, I shall never see him again.

# XII

## THE STORY CONTINUED BY THE EDITOR

Life at Harringdon had lost all its charm for Isabel now. With no Cathy and no freedom, the days dragged into one long lonely and frustrating stay.

However, now that she was condemned to spend her days indoors, she had much more time to observe the relationship between her aunt and Sir Branden; and the more she saw of it, the more it confused her.

It was clear that Sir Branden had a strange power over Lady Harringdon. Having witnessed the stilted friendships and reserved conversation her aunt usually shared with acquaintances, Isabel was surprised at his cordiality with her. Yet Lady Harringdon, despite her gracious manner, never seemed particularly comfortable around him. Her attitude towards him seemed more one of forced tolerance than easy affection.

Being not uneducated in such matters, Isabel pondered the possibility that Sir Branden had come to stay with the intention of seeking her aunt's hand in marriage: Harringdon was a large estate to run and a joint income would surely be beneficial to her aunt, even if there was a lack of affection. But Branden's attitude to Lady Harringdon was not that of a lover, yet neither was it one of a friend. It was a mystery that Isabel spent a lot of time contemplating during the long dinners and evenings she had to endure.

The mystery deepened one afternoon when she was passing her aunt's study. Isabel had lain late in bed that day, complaining of a slight headache, but as the weather cleared outside, she had dressed and gone downstairs, heading towards the kitchen to enquire of a light breakfast.

Walking past the study, she heard voices. But it was not the tone, nor the topic of conversation that made her pause – it was the name that was used.

'Helen,' she heard Sir Branden say. 'My dear friend, I am so pleased that you can help me in this matter.'

Isabel had never heard anyone call her aunt by her first name alone before. She had also not realised her aunt and Sir Branden were so close, to use such familiar terms of address. And yet, somehow, his tone was not truly friendly - a cold undercurrent seemed to run through it.

'I am willing to do what is necessary, Branden,' she heard her aunt reply stiffly.

Against her better judgement, Isabel paused by the slightly open

74

door, wondering what they were speaking of.

'And if I asked the question of purity?'

'I can assure you, there is no lamb more innocent.'

A sudden creak made Isabel look round. Standing only a few inches from her was Gaunt, his black and green eyes staring directly into hers. Isabel opened her mouth to rebuke him in her fright, but realised that would alert her aunt to the fact that she had been listening outside the door. Gaunt smiled at her, a slow, mocking smile, revealing yellow and uneven teeth. Heart pumping, Isabel turned swiftly on her heel.

## ISABEL'S NARRATIVE
### *(Extract from Isabel's Diary)*

*HARRINGDON COURT, 8<sup>th</sup> July 1866*

How does that man move so quietly? He is more silent than a cat! I am forever looking over my shoulder to see if he behind me.

I still do not know what Aunt Helen and Sir Branden were speaking of. Again, I find myself pondering their relationship... Such feigned friendship and cold glances.

How I wish to leave this place.

## THE STORY CONTINUED BY THE EDITOR

The one thing that brought Isabel willingly to the breakfast table each morning was the prospect of hearing from Cathy. Each morning, she looked up expectantly when the butler appeared at the breakfast table with his silver platter. Each morning, she was disappointed. As the days progressed, her heart sank still further. Why had Cathy not written to her? She had promised to keep in touch and it had been well over a week since her first letter. Isabel had written not once, but three times since then, anxious for news, but there had been no response.

A number of theories had passed through Isabel's head as to Cathy's silence. Had something bad happened? Was she upset with Isabel for some reason? Or was she simply having such a wonderful time that she had had neither the time, nor the inclination to write. Isabel did not know which was worse.

'Have you heard from Catherine this week, Aunt Helen?' Isabel asked as they sat in the morning room with Sir Branden a few days later.

Her aunt glanced up at her from the morning paper.

'I have not. I expect she is far too busy to be writing letters at the moment.'

Isabel looked back down at her book, disappointed.

'You must be looking forward greatly to your cousin's wedding, Isabel,' said Branden from his high-backed chair in the corner of the room. Isabel shot him a disapproving look from under her lashes. She disliked the recent assumed familiarity, and the way he tried to continually draw her into conversation.

'I am sure it will be a most enjoyable day,' she replied evenly.

'Yes indeed, marriage is a most agreeable state, is it not?'

Isabel, thinking of Cathy's description of the staged proposal, did not reply. Branden noticed her pause.

'You would not agree? Are your views of marriage unfavourable?'

'You care to know a woman's opinion on such a subject?' she asked, a hint of mockery in her voice.

'I occasionally stoop to such a level,' he replied with grave serenity.

Isabel straightened her shoulders and set her book down.

'Then I shall reply that I think marriage is a very desirable state, as long as the woman has control over the

choice of her spouse, and is not limited either by her wealth, or lack of it.'

'You wish for equal rights in marriage?' he asked lightly.

'I do indeed. I will not be a mere decorative addition to a man's superior lifestyle.'

'You speak very boldly,' Sir Branden remarked.

'I have got into the habit of expressing myself and will not break it,' replied Isabel.

'Perhaps someone will have to break it for you.'

'I would like to witness the attempt,' said Isabel, a challenge in her eyes.

Her aunt raised a frosted eyebrow and lowered her newspaper slightly.

'Isabel, please mind your manners.'

Aware of Sir Branden's gaze still upon her, Isabel returned his stare with a supercilious glance that it seemed not worth her effort to give, and then turned her eyes away without speaking. Her aunt addressed Sir Branden in a conciliatory tone:

'Please excuse my niece, Sir Branden. She has not seen much of life, and will soon be much less naïve and more respectful of her superiors.'

Isabel surveyed the older couple before her, taking in her aunt's cold expression, her handsome but severe face, those thin lips which never smiled: here sat the woman had abandoned her sister and had let her own child leave her without so much as a kiss; the widow who had forgotten how to love, who was as withered inside as the dried flowers in the vase beside her. And then there was Sir Branden, a bachelor with no one around him except an unpleasant servant; a man who feigned real friendship where there was none; the guest whom no one wanted. She saw before her a barren wilderness of human emotion, lacking in kindness and any form of hope. She could not allow herself to become such a person. She would not. She spoke out, her voice echoing in the silent room:

'If my 'naivety', as you call it allows me an outlook of joy and hope, rather than one of submission and duty then I would not trade it for anything.'

Her aunt opened her mouth in rebuke at this sudden retort, but Sir Branden held up his hand to stop her. He surveyed Isabel for a moment, his grey gaze heavy.

'My dear girl,' said Sir Branden. 'You are young, and naturally desiring great things for your life. But let me give you some advice. If you wish to survive and succeed, you will need to learn that obedience and sense are of much higher value than your adolescent fantasies. You see, Isabel, there are some young women who start out in life thinking that the journey is theirs and theirs alone, but it is not. There are rules and frameworks already in place that you will need to fit into - and if you do not, then you will be sadly broken until you fit the mould. Those who do not learn to adapt are thrown by the wayside. I would not wish to find you there in a few years' time, crumpled and broken, because you held to your 'ideals'.'

Giving her a long and conciliatory smile, he returned to his paper.


ISABEL'S NARRATIVE
*(Extract from Isabel's Diary)*

*HARRINGDON COURT, 11<sup>th</sup> July 1866*

And so the charming guest revealed his true colours. He seemed to transform before my very eyes as he spoke, his poisonous words dripping from his lips like honey. I have tried to wash them from my mind but they have left behind a sticky residue, unpleasant and difficult to remove.

The rest of the day passed in tense silence. During dinner Sir

Branden decided to break the silence by talking at length of his great house at Enderton. The topic seemed to make Aunt Helen uncomfortable but he continued nonetheless, moving on to speak of when he used to live near Bristol. The only point of interest in the conversation was when he mentioned a particular party that he and my aunt had attended when they were much younger. It sounds as though they have known each other for a great many years. For a moment I was going to ask if he had known my mother also, but then held to my vow that I would bandy no more words with the pair of them this day.

I gave myself a fright when I returned to my room after dinner. My mother had been much occupying my thoughts during the evening and as I began dressing for bed, out of the corner of her eye I suddenly thought I saw her standing by my window. I started, and so did the woman staring at me. Recollecting myself, I realised that the maid had neglected to draw my curtains that evening, and the woman staring back at me was in fact myself. It was a black, starless night outside and my room had been reflected back to me against the glass in stark reality.

I stood there and marvelled at my mistake. Was it really myself, that figure that I saw before me? Surely not. She was so elegant, so mature…almost a woman. I had not thought of myself as a woman before.

I moved closer and the impression seemed to dissipate. It was just a reflection, glimpsed in a dark glass. And she was crying: a sudden fall of raindrops outside ran down her glass cheeks, through her long hair and down her gown. The beauty I had seen before me was quite marred now, melting away before my eyes until I blew out the candle and all was dark.


### THE STORY CONTINUED BY THE EDITOR

The rain continued the following day and Isabel, still stinging from the previous day's conversation, decided to retreat to the library rather than joining her aunt and Sir Branden in the morning room, as she was expected to do. However, any hopes of solitude proved to be foolishly optimistic and it was not long before she was disturbed. Within ten minutes, she heard the door creak open and glanced up to see Sir Branden entering the library, with Gaunt following noiselessly. Isabel bristled but made no comment.

'May I join you, Isabel?' Sir Branden asked.

'As my aunt's guest, you need not ask my permission to enter,'

Isabel replied in restrained tones.

'A mere courtesy,' he replied, and settled himself in an armchair by the unlit fire. Gaunt stood behind him like some oversized watchdog. Isabel turned her face towards the window, away from their gaze.

Branden's voice broke the silence once again:

'And what are you reading, Isabel?'

'I am reading *The Italian*,' she replied in pinched tones.

'Ah yes, by Mrs Anne Radcliffe. Does your aunt approve of such novels?'

'My aunt does not dictate my reading, Sir,' Isabel said irritably.

'No matter', he smiled, revealing rows of white teeth. 'Your choice of book is most interesting. I shall leave you to its fantasies.'

Isabel watched him rise with superb indignation. Finding her hands quivering, she put the book down. Only then was she aware that the room was not yet empty. She looked up to see Gaunt now standing just behind her chair, his unnerving eyes fixed on her trembling hands. She looked at him, her disdain tainted with fear.

'What do you want?'

'You have very delicate hands; such narrow fingers,' he said softly.

Isabel drew her hands into her chest.

'Leave me alone,' she said sharply and then added in an undertone, 'You bother me.'

Gaunt cocked his head to one side, smiled at her queerly, and followed his master out of the room.


## ISABEL'S NARRATIVE
*(Extract from Isabel's Diary)*

### HARRINGDON COURT, 13<sup>th</sup> July 1866

The situation is intolerable. I shall go to Aunt Helen tomorrow and suggest my departing Harringdon for London as soon as is convenient. I will take a companion if she insists, but I cannot stay here. Some small sacrifices may have to be made, but anything is better than my current situation. I suspect she might welcome the suggestion and allow me to leave soon. She has not spoken a word to me since Wednesday's dispute. I see no pleasant conclusion to this disagreeable state of affairs except to leave her and Sir Branden to continue their strange relationship here at Harringdon without my presence.

I must admit that Cathy's lack of correspondence has hurt me. I can see no excusable reason for her silence and feel I must come to accept the hard fact that she is happy in her new situation and thinks little of me now. I suppose I should be glad that it is so, and let her go; but it is a great wrench. It simply serves to further stiffen my resolve to leave here, where even the memories are beginning to become painful.


## THE STORY CONTINUED BY THE EDITOR

'Aunt Helen? May I enter?'

Isabel stood in the open doorway of her aunt's study, where Lady Harringdon sat at her desk, writing. She looked up to find her niece awaiting her response.

'You may.'

Isabel entered and stood before the desk, her hands clasped behind her, her back very straight. Her dress was yellow lustring and seemed to gleam in the morning light, casting a delicate glow across her features.

'How can I help you, Isabel?' her aunt asked, her dark eyes narrowed.

Her tone was pleasant, but there was a tautness about her lips, a glitter in her eyes, that proclaimed her ill at ease with Isabel's presence. Isabel's expression was grave, her words rehearsed but earnest:

'Aunt Helen, I feel that my presence here at Harringdon is no longer desired nor required. I seek your permission to take up lodgings in London along with a companion of your choosing. I feel this would be most beneficial for everyone involved.'

Her aunt went very pale. Isabel wondered if she had turned white with anger, but her voice sounded more anxious than angry when she spoke:

'Why would you suggest such a thing, Isabel? You know we agreed that you would stay here until you came of age. Such talk of leaving is both inappropriate and insulting.'

Isabel looked surprised. This was not the reaction she had expected.

'I meant no insult, Aunt Helen. But with Cathy gone and your guest now staying long-term, I feel both out of place and in the way.'

'You are not in the way, Isabel. Your place is here until you come of age. I will hear no more of this matter.'

She picked up her pen and drew another sheet of paper towards her, indicating that the discussion was at an end. But Isabel was not finished. She realised she would have to make her position quite clear.

'Forgive me, but you are not my guardian, aunt. You may have recently begun dealing with my trustees, with regards to my inheritance, but you have no power over me. You never came forward to declare yourself for me when my parents died. I am held to you by no more than a family bond, not a legal one.'

Her aunt looked up, outraged.

'I have taken you in, cared for you in my own home many times, Isabel. Why do you speak so unjustly to me?'

Isabel found the question that she had pondered for so many years rising to her lips.

'Why did you take me in Aunt Helen, after so many years of exile? What changed in your heart?'

For a moment Isabel thought she glimpsed a flicker of emotion in her aunt's eyes, but then her expression hardened.

'Nothing changed, Isabel. Catherine needed a playmate and none of my friends had children. You were cheaper than hiring a live-in companion.'

She stared at Isabel, convincing in her heartlessness, but something did not ring true.

'I do not believe you,' Isabel replied softly.

Lady Harringdon's mask faltered. Then, through the open window they heard something rustle amongst the bushes. Isabel caught sight of a flash of red amongst the leaves and wondered if it was an early robin. Her aunt looked back round, her jaw set firmly.

'Believe what you will, Isabel. You always do, just like your mother. You are young, but you will learn your place and your duty.'

'I have a duty to no one. I have no parents to delight or disgrace, and no arranged suitor to impress - '

'You have a duty to your family name and to the name of womanhood. You shall not live as you please, Isabel.'

'My parents would want me to make my own choices.'

A sudden flash of anger gleamed in her aunt's eyes.

'Your life is not your own to live, Isabel, and they are not the example you should be following.'

Isabel sensed the bait, but left it untouched. Losing her temper at this point would do her no favours.

'Since we disagree so completely on this point, aunt, I see no point in continuing this conversation.'

Her aunt stood up, her fury giving her added height as her tall frame blocked the light from the window behind her. There was an edge of desperation in her voice that Isabel did not quite understand.

'Isabel Audley. You will stay at Harringdon until you come of age. You will be a respectful niece and better company to my guest. You will obey my commands or regret it severely.' There was a note of weariness in her voice now. 'I speak thus for your own good. There will be no further discussion of this matter. Go and entertain Sir Branden at lunch, I will join you shortly. Now leave me.'

Isabel turned on her heel and left the room, then left the house, and finally left the grounds.

The sun was shining high in the sky and somehow the beach seemed even more beautiful that it had done when Isabel had last visited with Cathy. Perhaps it was simply the effect of her troubled mind luxuriating in its release. She lay on her front upon the warm sand, and stared down the beach into the sea, alone at last with her thoughts.

The soft sand around her seemed to glitter in the sunlight, as though flecked with gold; then becoming steadily darker as it rolled down towards the sea which came running up to meet it, casting shells in its wake. The low, soft waves were singing their afternoon lullaby, seagulls hovering overhead. The sun had brought up a gentle flush on Isabel's cheeks and a light breeze ruffled her curls. She sunk her toes deep into the sand behind her, luxuriating in its caress. Here, at least, she was wanted.

Above the murmuring sea was the motionless blue sky. Clouds like great palaces held forth in the vast expanse, their towering white battlements and pearly soft towers reaching high into the heavens, so high that no bird could ever reach them.

From the height of their peaks, Isabel's imagination swooped downwards, captivated by the turquoise gleam of the sea beneath. Thoughts of great caverns in the forsaken depths rose up before her. Secret lands beneath where no person had ever been, far removed from all that troubled her, where the heart of the sea revealed itself, pouring out its secrets...

'A penny for your thoughts, Miss Audley.'

Glancing up and stifling a gasp, Isabel saw Mr Hardy standing beside her. He was wearing a light shirt, unbuttoned at the neck, with short sleeves that revealed muscled brown arms. His casual trousers were held up by a pair of brown braces. Apart from when they first met and he was dressed in his Sunday best, it was the first time she had ever seen him without his uniform.

'Mr Hardy. Have you been here long?'

Sunlight, that great reader of faces, revealed the answer.

'You were many miles away, Miss Audley. I am afraid I was quite fascinated by you,' he said seriously.

She turned a little pink, but did not look displeased. Just then a lively black and white collie came bounding towards them.

'Killie! Heel,' called Mr Hardy. The dog immediately sat down by his side, its tongue hanging out and its tail creating small waves of sand at either side as it wagged enthusiastically.

'This is my dog Killie,' he said, stroking her head. 'We always come here on my afternoon off for a good long walk. She loves being by the sea.'

'Well Killie and I have a lot in common,' said Isabel sitting up and reaching out to stroke the dog's soft coat. The dog's tail began to wag even more vigorously at the attention.

'You have a friend, Killie,' said Mr Hardy, smiling.

'I have a great fondness for dogs,' said Isabel. 'But I have never had the pleasure of owning one.'

'Killie is my most constant companion. Except when I am on duty. Then she guards the cottage very fiercely, do not you, my lovely?'

The collie stared adoringly up at her master.

'Well, I shall not trouble you any longer, Miss Audley. It was good to see you, as always. Enjoy your time on this glorious beach.'

Isabel felt a strange sensation steal over her. She did not want him to go. She did not want to be alone. She did not ever want to have to return to that house, to her aunt and Sir Branden. She wanted someone to talk to, someone to understand. Someone who would not try and shape her future, but who was simply interested in what she thought and appreciated what she said.

'Please stay,' she said suddenly.

He looked at her, surprised, and saw the appeal in her eyes. Instead of the self-possessed young woman he had met many times before, he now saw a girl before him – lonely and perhaps afraid.

'I will gladly join you,' he replied, 'but I do not want to cause more trouble for you, nor do I want to disturb your solitude.'

'I have decided I care little for my reputation, and I am weary of solitude,' Isabel said. 'I would be grateful if you would join me for a short while.'

Mr Hardy sat down beside her in the warm sun and together they stared out at the blue sea. To her embarrassment, she realised that tears were tumbling from her cheeks. She turned her face so that he would not see.

'Are you very unhappy?' he asked, his eyes still fixed on the horizon.

She bit her lip, trying to control herself. He gave her a moment and then asked another question,

'Did you get into much trouble for being seen with me the other day?'

'As much as I expected. But that is not why I am upset.'

'Why then?'

'I feel... trapped. I feel as though I do not have a way out of my situation – not a simple one, at least. I am angry with myself for allowing others to control me. I feel that I am not behaving as my parents would have wanted. I am not being brave enough.'

Mr Hardy gazed at her for a moment and breathed deeply.

'Miss Audley. I was rude the other day in not asking you about your parents. I did not want to seem intrusive, but if you wish to speak of it, if you ever wish to speak of it, I am more than happy to listen.'

Isabel was surprised, but pleased.

'That is kind of you, Mr Hardy. I have been thinking often of my parents recently, but I seldom speak of them. That is probably because whenever I mention my mother and father to other people, I can almost feel the vultures hovering overhead, ready to pick apart the bones, preparing to pounce upon whatever secrets I may know. The truth is, I remember very little about them, or the time when they died.'

'Nothing at all?' he asked, surprised.

'I have little scraps of memory, here and there, but I suspect that most of them are formed from what other people told me.'

'But, forgive me, you were not so very young when they died?'

'I was four. Old enough, I suppose.'

'You have had to grow up very much on your own,' he remarked.

Isabel smiled in recollection.

'My housekeeper, Mrs Tabitha, said I was old before my time.'

He could hear the warmth in her voice when she spoke the housekeeper's name.

'Will you tell me about your childhood?' he asked.

'I am afraid it was not terribly exciting. In fact, the years seem to have all flowed into one endless day that lives on in my mind. I do not know how much of it is true.'

'Then tell me about you – what were you like as a child?'

Isabel stared at the horizon, the sea reflected in her violet eyes, her expression thoughtful.

'I was…I was very wild…and yet very quiet,' she said reflectively. 'I lived inside my mind, very much on the outskirts of life. I was never more alive than when everyone had gone to bed, and I was never happier than when I was alone. I believed I could do anything. I wanted to walk between the worlds.'

# XIII

*Editor's note: Isabel did indeed tell the story of her childhood story at this point, but for the sake of brevity I have taken the liberty of summarising her recollections which I hope will provide a smoother and more consistent read. I have also inserted some additional extracts that may be of interest.*

At the age of five, Isabel Audley had an imagination as far-reaching as the stars. She loved to weave her fancies from nothing but the air around her and the pictures in her head. Her father once told her that stories happen in the space between the teller and the audience. It was her greatest dream to find that space – the space between the worlds.

It was just as well that her imagination was her most constant companion for she often had no other, except for the servants of Greenwood House. After the death of James and Marianne Audley, no one had come forward to claim the orphaned girl of the banished couple, and the lawyers, satisfied that she was not being neglected, decided to leave her in the care of the butler, Mr Ronald Arthur, and the capable housekeeper, Mrs Tabitha Black, until she came of age. It was a mark of how shunned the Audleys had become that even these men of legal standing would not deign to treat the child with the proper care due to her. The servants knew that having Isabel kept at home meant that Greenwood would stay open. If the little one left, then they would all have to leave: this was a certainty. The boards would go up and all would be dark. So they let things carry on as before, always keeping Isabel's well-being the priority, and trying to give the child as normal a childhood as possible.

The lady of the house at just five years old, Isabel had free reign of Greenwood. She ran wild in the gardens, wandered the wood-panelled corridors, explored the servant's quarters; she got up to watch the sunrise and stayed hidden in a corner of the library until midnight. No book, tree, creaky stair or stream was unknown to her as she lived out her days within the beautiful confines of her home.

'The patient child', Mr Arthur named her silently one day, as he watched her standing on the front steps. She was staring out over the gardens - her gardens - waiting for life to find her, wondering what lay ahead.

Sometimes Isabel dreamed of the shadowy parents who should have been there to watch her grow, but when she woke and turned to look at them, they would fade away. They were always there, in the corner of her eye, but never present. It was this sense of absence that instilled in her a conflicted sense of wanting to please, yet having no one there to please.

She lived in her own little world of long summers and dark winters. Thoughts and impressions lay deeply on her heart. She had no one to tell her what to do, no one to offer or impose their views of the world. She had a library of books that did not know to whom they spoke, an army of servants who never strayed beyond their diligent and kindly duties, and an absence at either side of her that did not yet make sense. Every year on her birthday, there would be a small pile of presents waiting in the drawing room for her. She would open them on her own and then when she returned later, the papers would have been removed and the toys placed in her bedroom. The servants never overstepped their mark and behaved exactly as they would have done had her parents been in the house.

Isabel was not unhappy for she knew no better. She imagined other little girls who lived in similar large houses on their own and wished they lived nearer so that they might be friends. In her books she read of other children who had mothers and fathers, but like the imaginary worlds in which they lived, equally as imaginary seemed the parents who cared for them.

The few people who visited Greenwood (mostly friends and family of the other servants) would look at her with sad faces when she appeared and Isabel would work hard to make them smile with her dances and jokes.

'Why are they so sad?' she would ask Mr Arthur.

He did not tell her that their sorrow was for her.

'They should smile,' she would say, looking up at him. 'I am smiling.'

'Yes you are,' he would reply, pinching her rosy cheeks gently, making her laugh.

The housekeeper would look at him sadly then, remembering how Isabel's father once used to do the same.

Mr Ronald Arthur was a tall man in his fifties, with thinning hair, a warm smile and kind green eyes. He had been at Greenwood for thirty years, longer than anyone else, and had been very fond of his master and mistress. Mrs Tabitha Black had arrived at Greenwood with Mrs Audley, whom she had served for most of her life, staying loyal to her amidst the clouds of scandal. She was a little younger that Mr Arthur, also tall, and wore horn-rimmed spectacles, her dark hair pinned back tightly at the back of her head. She had a long fringe that somehow was never cut straight, but whether she had not noticed and no one ever told her, or she simply liked it that way, the staff at Greenwood ever knew. Young Isabel certainly loved her all the more for it and used to imagine that Mrs Tabitha (as she called her, preferring to use the servant's more familiar first names) sat on a stool with one leg longer than the other when she cut her fringe, resulting in the crooked style. When asked by the conversational chimney sweep that came once a month, to pick her favourite between the housekeeper and the butler Isabel was hard-pressed and decided that she loved them both the same – very much.

It was these two members of staff who worked hardest to keep Isabel's life as normal as possible, continuing the routines that her parents had begun, but always keeping the necessary formalities that were required of their station. One of Isabel's favourite times of the day was late evening, just before bed. It was then that she would perch on her dressing room stool and Mrs Tabitha would knock, then enter and open the top left hand drawer in the dresser, in which lay her mother's enamelled hairbrush. Then Isabel would shake out her long blonde curls and Mrs Tabitha would brush and brush and brush until all one hundred strokes were complete and Isabel's hair gleamed in the candlelight. The motion of the gentle pulling would always make Isabel sleepy and sent her off to bed with pleasant memories of her mother brushing her hair and then stroking her forehead until she fell asleep. Of course, Mrs Tabitha did not stroke her forehead, but she would wish Isabel a good night and close the door quietly behind her as Isabel slipped off into sweet dreams.

Another important element of her young life was the local church. The staff of Greenwood House attended the local village church every Sunday and Isabel had accompanied them for as long as she could remember. She enjoyed going and led the house party each Sunday morning, with Mr Ronald and Mrs Tabitha by her side, her head held high in its little bonnet, the ribbons flapping underneath her chin. One of her most treasured possessions was the small green leather-bound Bible that her mother had left behind her. The pages were as thin as tissue paper and finished with gold trim, and a green satin ribbon ran down the centre. She would read this Bible every morning and every night, delighting in the Old Testament stories and marvelling at the New Testament ones. Many of the words were beyond her knowledge, but Mr Ronald was always on hand to help her understand any particularly mystifying phrases. She carried this special book with her each week to church and opened it proudly during the sermons, following the passages fervently as the vicar took them through the word.

She remembered sitting in church when she was seven years old, listening ardently to the vicar, whose rolling tones captivated her every Sunday. This particular Sunday, he was preaching on the Second Coming:

'Jesus is coming soon', he said in his rich bass voice. 'You must be ready, for He will take with him those who believe.'

The excitement that filled the young girl was inexpressible. She had always longed to meet the Saviour who she learned about every Sunday, and gazed upon in the vibrant stained glass windows of the church. In Jesus, she saw the father that she never had, and somehow sensed that He would fill that longing she had deep inside her to be loved by someone that she truly belonged to.

That night, she made sure she was ready. She had her brown leather suitcase in one hand and her jacket in her other, just in case it would be cold on the journey. Her heart was full of yearning, her fresh and untried faith strong within her breast as she padded softly down the staircase to the main hall. Finally, she would get to see the stars, and find out what heaven was like. She opened the front door of the house very quietly, filled with excitement as she sat down upon her suitcase on front steps.

There is nothing to match the certainty of a child. Isabel sat, waiting, firm in the knowledge that he would come. He would come for her and he would take her away to heaven, she told herself with anticipation.

In the morning, when the gardener started work, he found Isabel curled up asleep on the cold steps, her head on the little suitcase. He carried her inside and laid her gently on her bed. She sighed, very deeply, and carried on sleeping. No one asked her what she had been doing. She was the lady of the house.

By the time Isabel was nine years old, she was beginning to bruise herself against the edges of her pretty pen. Life flowed through her in abundance, and often it felt like she had too much of it, so desperate was she for new experiences and places to explore. She spent more and more time on her own at Greenwood, making new discoveries in the grounds, learning her limits. She never felt more alive than at night when the house was quiet and truly her own. It was then that she loved to go to the library and read, or walk the length of the great dining room table in her bare feet, or climb up to the window in the top bedroom on the fourth floor and stare out at the stars.

When she felt very wild, she would slip out of bed when all the servants were asleep, creep down the stairs, unlock the big front door and enter the great unknown. Greenwood's gardens, so familiar during the day, seemed terrifying and magical at night: the trees became dark towering strangers, the air cold and full of adventure. Isabel would run, and dance, and twirl and laugh, completely alone, revelling in the wonder of it all.

One particular night stood out in her memory. It was a late September evening and an autumn breeze swirled around her, the clear sky vast and never-ending, stretching right up to heaven itself. If Isabel could fly, she would have flown, she thought - she would have flown right up past the stars to that shining city. But for now, she was here, a small and earthly child, held firmly to the ground by gravity. So she ran instead, revelling in the headiness of her race. Faster and faster her little feet went, light and able as they traversed mounds and hillocks and streams, gathering momentum with every step. On and on she leapt and bounded - until at last she stopped.

She had reached the end of the grounds, and the land fell away below her, creating a ridge upon which she stood; her hands grasping the wooden fence that marked the boundary, her breath coming quickly, creating faint white puffs in the night air. Before her, in all its brilliant glory, hung the moon. It was the night of its fullest appearance, which was perhaps why the blood pounded more furiously in her veins. It looked bigger than she had ever seen it: glorious and majestic, standing before her and shining its great face upon hers, vast silver upon rosy skin. It reflected itself in her eyes, upon her hair, in her heart, bathing her in its mystical light. She wanted to reach out and touch its glowing surface. But however close it looked, she could not reach it. So she sat down in the grass, her arms resting on the bottom rung of the fence, her head resting on her arms.

She spoke to the moon then, telling it about her day and the lessons she had learned and the stories she had written. She asked it about the sky, and what lay behind it, and how she wanted to go there, to go farther than anyone else, because she was special. That was the one thing she remembered her parents saying to her,

'Isabel, you are special.'

She could not recall which of her parents had said this to her, but she remembered the words, the tone of the warm voice whispering them in her ear, and the feeling it gave her.

'And you are special too,' she told the moon. 'Because you are always there.'

By the age of ten, it was clear that Isabel Audley was going to grow into a beauty. Her face was as fresh and vibrant as the first morning of spring, every emotion sparkling across it like ripples on a pond.

'She will break many hearts, that girl,' Mr Ronald used to say to Mrs Tabitha when they thought Isabel was not listening.

She was a confident girl, for she had never had any reason to fear anyone, and so carried with her the happy impression that no one would ever give her cause to do so. She had a strong spirit and having made her own decisions her whole life, she had every intention of continuing in this manner. Her extensive reading had filled her head with strong-willed heroines who became her constant role models. Exacerbated by the fact that she had been the head of the house for most of her childhood, her lack of a father had imbued her with a sense that everything stopped with her. She had lived like a child on an island, believing that everything was forever, that her tiny world reflected the vast world that was out there. She was strong, untried, but eager for her future.

The next stage of her life began rather sooner than she had expected. Mrs Tabitha and Mr Ronald (I will continue to call them by the same names that Isabel did) had thus far managed Isabel's schooling between them, teaching her to read, write, count, draw, and all other aspects of her education. The child had always been a fast learner and it was with heavy hearts one morning that they realised she now knew all they could teach her.

By happy coincidence, however, Mr Ronald's brother, a Mr William Arthur, had just opened up a school in Alverdine and after consultation, was happy to take Isabel on as a pupil. Alverdine was a girl's school with a progressive outlook. It accepted girls from the ages of ten to seventeen and taught them subjects that would normally only be taught in boy's preparatory schools. Piano lessons, singing and needlework were very much sideline subjects, with mathematics, languages and history at the fore.

'The aim is not social display,' the headmaster would tell visitors sternly. 'At Alverdine, creativity is valued, not condemned.'

Mr Arthur had received much scorn for taking on a girls' school, but he had been fixed in his course and his aim was to produce female students who were fully equipped for the changing world that lay ahead of them.

It was with a few tears that Isabel left Greenwood House for her first term at Alverdine. However (to her slight chagrin), she soon forgot to be sad when she arrived at the school. It was a beautiful manor house, much grander than Greenwood, and surrounded by beautiful gardens. However, these soon faded into the background when the teacher at the door directed her into the great hall. A sea of new faces, sounds and conversations engulfed her as she stood, suitcase in hand, cheeks glowing with the sheer exhilaration of it all. Around her stood more than a hundred girls, of all shapes, sizes and ages, with different coloured hair, different voices and all manner of expressions on their faces. For Isabel who had never met another child outside of the chimney sweep who visited occasionally at Greenwood, the experience was staggering. Yet, while some children may have clutched their suitcase close and closed their mouths, Isabel was filled with excitement and immediately attached herself to the nearest group and within moments they were laughing and chattering together, marvelling at their surroundings and discussing what lay ahead.

Alverdine was exactly the type of new life that Isabel had been craving during her long quiet years at Greenwood. It was a world of engaging lessons, new friends, midnight feasts, weekend excursions and all manner of fresh discoveries. Isabel absorbed these new experiences like a sheet of white silk over spilled ink. Every detail, every word was taken in and recorded in her eager brain.

The teachers were kind and always full of knowledge and stories. There was not a lesson that Isabel did not enjoy, her bright young mind racing along as each new subject caught her imagination. Sections from her early report paint a clear picture of her attitude to her studies:

'Isabel is a well-conducted pupil in every respect. Politely spoken and extremely intelligent, she brings a unique creativity to all her lessons and learns with a quiet gusto,' wrote her Classics teacher.

'She has a certain spark about her,' her English teacher wrote. 'Give her open, bright mind an idea and she will run with it, further than anyone else, until she comes to an obstacle – and then she will leap.'

Isabel loved to write and her creative stories were always full of wonder and adventure – perhaps too much so, for some readers:

'This piece of writing is really quite shocking for a young lady,' remarked one parent who was reading through a display of the girls' work at an end of term event.

Isabel's tales were full of pirates and knights and daring escapades, of far-off lands and perilous exploits. Her mind never stopped, for it never hit those brick walls so carefully constructed by the parents of the other girls.

Yet this did not prevent Isabel from making friends. Her warm, open and enthusiastic nature drew a number of girls to her and they quickly formed a tight-knit group. She loved them all, and revelled in the newfound company, finding herself the natural leader of the group. To her surprise, however, she found herself still wanting something more. Her companions were full of fun and she had many wonderful times with them, but she sensed that they were different from her. They had families and homes to return to, and Isabel did not; their futures were fixed and Isabel's was unsecured. She did not know what lay ahead of her and often spoke of her future, wondering what it would hold. The other girls did not understand, they gave her curious looks and smiled at her, never joining in her flights of fancy. Their imaginations never could lift off from the ground in the same way that Isabel's could. It was then Isabel realised that this was a temporary period, that these girls may not be her friends for life, but were simply momentary companions during this pleasant period. And so she began to long for someone who would understand her fully; who would stand by her side and never leave her.

This longing for a kindred spirit, a protector, occupied most of Isabel's nights while the other girls lay asleep in their beds. Isabel never fell asleep easily, and after many years of her own company, she enjoyed having that time to herself, to unlock her bursting imagination, which was mostly kept in check throughout school hours. This created figure often took the form of a knight – fearless and devoted. He was tall and strong, and though she could not see his face, she knew it was a kind one. She was too young to imagine any kind of romance between them - he was simply her hero and he made her feel safe, guarding her until she finally fell asleep, her soft breathing joining that of the other girls as they slumbered together in the quiet upstairs dormitory.

However, it also was during her time at Alverdine that Isabel realised that not everyone was as pleasant as at Greenwood, and that people had a capacity for meanness and selfish acts. She witnessed no real unkindness during her school years, but gathered a general understanding that human nature was more flawed than she had believed it to be. Despite the many times that she had heard this mentioned during church sermons, she had had no real experience of it until now.

This was made particularly evident to her at the end of each term, when parents were allowed on the premises. She did not notice it at first, but as the years progressed, she realised that she was the object of much speculation, with many adult eyes upon her. She knew that the story of her parent's death had been widespread, but found it strange and uncomfortable that people she had never met in her life had heard of her, their hungry eyes feasting on the girl whose parents had eloped amidst so much scandal, the little girl who had grown up alone. She caught snatches of the gossip that was whispered when she entered and witnessed some expressions of dislike. However, far from making her feel small, such behaviour only served to make her feel proud of her mother and father. It instilled in her a sure sense of self, for she knew that she was made from a different mould and was determined to stand apart from these small-minded people – a determination that only grew with time.

The headmaster's comment in her final report gives evidence of this:

'Strong-minded and surprisingly independent, Isabel is a preternaturally self-possessed girl. Her overwhelming trait is her great kindness. This, along with her unshakable self-assurance will give her a firm foundation in the world she longs to enter.'

It was with a feeling of surprise that Isabel realised that her seven years of school were over. The time had passed so quickly that she had barely noticed the terms flying by. She had enjoyed her time at Alverdine, but the reigning emotion was one of excitement as she looked forward to her future.

As we reach the point where this narrative began, many pages ago, I feel the need to backtrack slightly to cover details missed during the account of her school years. As you will remember Mrs Bett saying, Isabel first visited Harringdon at the age of ten. The reason for this was an unexpected letter from Lady Harringdon that arrived at Greenwood in December 1858, enquiring whether Isabel might like to come to Harringdon for the Christmas holidays. Mrs Tabitha, much surprised, wrote to Isabel at Alverdine and asked if she would like to meet her aunt and her cousin for the first time. Isabel wrote back excitedly that she would indeed like to visit, and so began the first of her many trips to Harringdon.

As you already know, Cathy quickly became Isabel's dearest friend. She connected with her immediately, and Cathy, with her warm and loving nature, welcomed Isabel into her heart as no one had ever done before. They were two fatherless daughters who, with little maternal love to share, found solace and great joy in one another. Isabel astounded Cathy's mind with her talk and Cathy warmed Isabel's with her love.

It was the recounting of this friendship, compounded by the fact that Harringdon was many miles closer to Alverdine than Greenwood, which caused Mrs Tabitha, with a heavy heart, to write to Lady Harringdon and ask if she was willing to have Isabel to stay for every holiday until she came of age. All the servants conceded that it was better for Isabel to stay with family, than continually return to a lonely house where she had no companions her age. Lady Harringdon agreed by turn of post and so Mrs Tabitha wrote to Isabel to tell her of the arrangements. In her letter she told Isabel that Greenwood would be kept for her, but that the servants would have to move on for the time being. The reality of the situation, of course, was that the house was boarded up, the servants forced to find new positions. The key to Greenwood was left with the family lawyers until Isabel came of age and could make her own decision about Greenwood's future.

At the age of eleven, however, Isabel did not fully grasp all of this. She was sad that she would not see Mrs Tabitha and Mr Ronald every holiday, but the pleasure of having Cathy for company outshone this sacrifice. It was only when Mr Arthur wrote to her, many months later, telling her of his new position with another family that she felt slightly strange, as though she had somehow missed a step without noticing. She looked around the new bedroom at Harringdon in which she sat, and at the enamelled brush that lay on her dressing table where she brushed her own hair every night. She felt a sense of something falling away, but then Cathy entered the room and smiled at her and Isabel smiled back, and it was forgotten.

# XIV

'...I spent every holiday at Harringdon from then on, and hence you find me here, sitting on the beach, almost a woman grown, with a story behind her that you are probably now feeling was not worth the telling,' finished Isabel with a smile.

'On the contrary, I found it fascinating. I feel I understand you better for the telling,' Mr Hardy replied amicably.

The sun was high overhead now and he was stretched out on the sand, leaning back on his hands. Then he sat up and dug his hand deep into his trouser pocket.

'Would you like an apple?' he asked, sliding out two very shiny apples. 'I grew them myself – well, that is to say, they grow on the tree in the garden of my cottage.

'Yes please,' Isabel said, taking one. The taste was sharp and refreshing on her tongue as she bit into it with a crunch. She finished hers before him and glanced over at him as he ate. The sun had brought out hints of gold in his cropped brown hair.

'You wear your hair very short,' she remarked.

Mr Hardy ran a hand through it and laughed.

'It because, alas, I was blessed with curls as a child. They were my mother's delight – I had very blonde hair as a boy, and she loved to brush my curls until they shone and then parade me around the town. By the age of twelve however, I was not so fond of them and one night, without her permission, I took a pair of scissors and cut them all off. My hair lost its lustre then and looked more brown than blonde. My mother never forgave me and I stopped being mercilessly teased at school. All in all, I thought it a fair compromise.'

'So you were a rather rebellious child?' said Isabel mischievously.

'I suppose so,' he said, hanging is head in mock shame.

'And if I said that it is only fair that you now tell me the story of your childhood in return for my account, what would you say?'

'I would acquiesce that it is due to you, but apologise in advance for its lack of interesting features, of which yours had so many.'

'I disagree,' Isabel said with a smile.

'Then I shall begin.'

95

'I grew up in the heart of Manchester, along with my mother, father and three younger sisters. It was a busy, bustling city where there was always something going on. We rented two rooms of a large dwelling that we shared with several other families and there were always plenty of boys around who were willing to play games with me in the street outside. I attended the local school and, unlike many, I enjoyed my studies and did well in my class.

'Unfortunately, when I was thirteen, my father left us, walking out one day and never returning. To this day, I do not know why he left and having never seen him since, have not had the chance to ask why. What was clear however was that I had a mother and three sisters who needed fed and clothed, and as school did not help to pay the rent on our rooms, I had no choice but to leave and take up a job in a local cotton factory.

'The work was hard, the hours long and I was very angry for many months. I realised that my future was to be one of menial work and provision, very different from what I had envisaged for myself. One morning, in my selfishness, I decided to run away - so I left the city and set out into the countryside intending to find a better life for myself in another town where I would not have four dependents, nor have to enter the unbearable factory ever again. I said to myself that if my father did it, why should I not also - and this I repeated to myself again and again as the day drew on and the city landscape gave way to one of woods and rivers.

'I tried to appease my conscience by imagining that the workhouse, to which my sisters and mothers would surely be sent to, would be a kind and warm place that they would be happy in.

'I will come back for them once I have made my fortune,' I said to myself. 'Then all will be well.'

'I had always attended church, as you had done, but the words and songs had held no real meaning for me. Yet now, in my folly, I cursed God, holding Him accountable for the situation I now found myself in.

'It is not fair', I said aloud, trying to shift the guilt I felt on to another. 'This is your fault, why have you done this?'

'Dusk was descending by then and I found myself in the middle of a thick forest. The trees were so tall I could not see the tops of them; evening light was falling in shafts through the branches. The smell of damp pine filled my nostrils and above me a buzzard circled, looking for prey. The only sound was that of a stream nearby. I was alone – more alone than I had ever been, and yet aware of a presence that was closer to me than any person could be. I suddenly felt as though God had formed a wall around me: I could not go back; I could not go forwards. All my shame and guilt came crashing over me as I realised what I was doing – abandoning those who now looked to me for provision and protection. I fell to my knees amongst the soft pine needles and asked for his forgiveness, ashamed of all that I was, and offering up my life to him completely. I knew he asked for no more and no less.

'It was very dark when I got home. I said nothing of where I had been, and knowing that I often worked late at the factory, my sisters thought nothing of it. But my mother, picking up my boots to clean them, seemed to notice something. From the bottom of my boot, crushed in with the mud, she had pulled off a bruised buttercup. I froze, wondering what she would say as she must have known that I had left the city that day: no wildflowers grew in the centre of Manchester.

'A yellow flower,' she said, her soft eyes meeting my tear-filled ones. 'Yellow is the colour of hope.'

'And you know the rest of the story,' finished Mr Hardy. 'It turned out that working in that factory was the best possible place I could have been, for the owner gave me the opportunities I needed, and had it not been for him, I would not hold the position I do today. In conclusion, I suppose the moral of the story is that God's plans always work out, if we will just be patient.'

Isabel's throat was dry with emotion.

'Thank you for sharing your story with me,' she said fervently.

'You are very welcome,' he said, stroking Killie, who had grown tired of racing along through the waves and had settled down beside them.

'I suppose we know each other quite well now,' Isabel said seriously.

Mr Hardy looked at her shrewdly, his strong brown eyebrows slightly furrowed.

'Yes indeed,' he replied, 'and yet I feel there is a rather large topic that we have not covered?'

'What is that?' she asked.

He paused, staring at her seriously, and then continued:

'Believe me when I say that I ask this not out of my own curiosity, or to satisfy any need for gossip - but the death of your parents has affected every aspect of your life, and yet you say you can remember nothing about it?'

'I was very young,' Isabel replied.

'Yes, but I can remember feeding the pigeons in our street with crusts of mouldy bread when I was two,' he replied, with energy. 'Not a particularly picturesque scene, I admit, but I was always told that the most important events in our life are engraved in our memories – and yet at the age of four, you cannot remember a single detail?'

Isabel frowned at the sand, as if trying to draw the memories from the depths of the shore.

'I remember…fragments,' she said hesitantly.

'What do you remember?' Mr Hardy asked

She frowned again. It had been so long since she thought back to that time. Or had she ever thought back properly to it at all? Slowly scenes and faces began to swim to the surface of her mind.

'Let me tell you about my parents,' she said at last. 'Perhaps that will help me remember.'

*Editor's note: Once again, let me take this opportunity to add to Isabel's words with additional details from other sources that may be of interest.*

Marianne Laidenhead was a society beauty who grew up amidst wealth and luxury in the fashionable town of Bath. Her fiery auburn hair was envied in every social circle, and women tried in vain to emulate her style and charming mannerisms. Since her first season, she had been on the guest list of every ball and fashionable social occasion both in Bath and London, and her active interest in charity work had only served to garner her great respect.

At the age of nineteen, she was formally engaged to a rich aristocrat of her parent's choosing. Slightly older than her, he was well liked within their social circles and greatly enamoured of his bride-to-be. He bought a house for them on the coast and the date for the wedding was set for the following summer, to which everyone was looking forward with great excitement, for it would be the society event of the year.

A month before the wedding was to take place, Marianne was introduced to a young man named James Audley at a dance. A dashing young man of twenty, his forward-looking views and fresh, unconventional manner connected strongly with her, and after just a few more meetings, they ran away together one night, returning to Bath a week later as man and wife. With his handsome looks and her fierce beauty, they made a striking couple, but found themselves entirely on their own.

James Audley had money that helped cover over most of the disgrace, but Marianne's jilted fiancé had been popular and James Audley was a stranger. Most acquaintances shunned the newlyweds, unwilling to associate themselves with such scandal and keen to follow the example of Marianne's influential parents who had swiftly disowned her upon hearing of the elopement. Commenting that James had stood out to her because of the narrow-minded, inward-looking crowd that she had been brought up among, Marianne claimed that she was glad to leave them behind. The young couple left the area and moved north to Greenwood House. With no friends, nor any visiting family, they very much lived within their own world.

James Audley had always been a lively character with an appetite for fun and novelty. When he met Marianne Laidenhead, he told friends that he had fallen for her instantly and was going to devote himself entirely to her. The absolute sincerity of his love once they were married surprised some who thought he would tire of her, but as he wrote to one friend:

'You could not tire of Marianne.'

Marianne also blossomed under his love. Freed from the structures and regulations of society life, she was finally able to live her life the way she had wanted. She enjoyed taking control of the renovations needed at Greenwood, making the house into a home, and when she gave birth to a beautiful golden-haired little girl, their happiness was complete. Isabel embodied everything that they stood for and had achieved together.

'You are called Isabel because it means 'God's promise',' Marianne told her baby as she rocked her back and forth in her arms. 'A promise of hope.'

The couple were blessed with the marvellous Mr Ronald Arthur and Mrs Tabitha Black who not only helped to run their household staff with expertise, but were also happy to look after Isabel at regular intervals when James and Marianne went on holiday. Sadly, Marianne's parents passed away a few years after they married, never meeting their granddaughter, but at the funeral Marianne made amends with her godfather, Lord Wainston. He had recently purchased a property in the popular French Riviera, and they gratefully accepted his invitation to stay in his house for a couple of weeks in the summer of 1853, while he was away.

On the second last day of their visit they decided to take a trip in Lord Wainston's yacht that he had made available for their pleasure. It was a warm day and the sea was calm. James had been an excellent sailor in his youth and guided them quickly out of the harbour towards quieter waters where they spent several hours enjoying the tranquillity of the ocean.

The storm broke suddenly and without warning. The staff at the house immediately put out an alert, but until the waters calmed, there was nothing they could do for the young couple. The waves were now higher than the large houses that lined the shore, and lightning cracked the black sky as the rain cascaded down.

The bodies washed up shortly after the wreck of the boat. Marianne had been tied to piece of the cracked hull, most likely in an attempt to keep her afloat after a blow to her head had left her unable to swim. She reached the shore first, carried by the timber that was meant to save her life. James followed a few moments later. The tide cast them together on the sand, where they were found by the butler who was leading the search. Their hands brushed gently together as they floated in the shallow water.

The little girl sat under the tall oak tree in the front garden. The sun was shining overhead and she was dressed in a white muslin dress, her golden curls tumbling around her face as she concentrated hard on her daisy chain. Mary, the laundry maid, often made daisy chains for Isabel and had shown her how to make the slits in the green stems and thread the next flower through, but Isabel's fingers were so small, and the stems kept splitting. A pile of broken flowers lay to her right, but she kept going. She was determined to make a full chain by the end of the day - for her parents were returning that evening and she wanted to place the triumphant chain around her mother's neck to welcome her home.

She could see Mrs Tabitha coming down the path from the house and Isabel wondered what she was doing. Mr Arthur was in charge of her today as Monday was laundry day and Mrs Tabitha was always kept busy making sure that the laundry maids got every last mark out of the sheets and clothes (particularly Isabel's clothes, which were often mud-spotted and dirty from her 'adventures').

Mrs Tabitha came towards her and then sat down in the long grass beside her. Isabel was surprised and put down her chain. Mrs Tabitha took her small pink hand in her own.

'Isabel.'

'Yes, Mrs Tabitha?'

Her small, bright face was upturned towards the housekeeper's.

'I have come out here to talk to you about your mother and father.'

'Yes, they are coming home tonight,' said Isabel, her face alight with excitement.

Mrs Tabitha's eyes were very bright and she swallowed hard.

'I am afraid that they are not, Isabel. They are not coming home.'

'Why not?' asked Isabel, confused.

Mrs Tabitha took a deep breath, struggling to fight back her tears.

'They have gone to the best place you can possibly imagine, Isabel. They have gone to the place they have been longing to go to their whole lives.'

Isabel thought about this for a moment and then, whilst confused by Mrs Tabitha's sadness, decided that this was a good thing. She was happy that they had gone to such a wonderful place.

'When will they come home?' she asked the housekeeper.

Mrs Tabitha blinked. She saw the expectation in Isabel's eyes and could not bring herself to say the word.

'They will be gone for a long time,' she said finally.

'Will I see them again?'

'Yes. You will, Isabel.'

That was all Isabel needed to know to feel reassured.

'Thank you, Mrs Tabitha,' she said, turning her attention back to her daisy chain.

The housekeeper watched the little girl for a moment and then, unable to hide her tears any longer, turned and went back up to the house. Isabel was used to her mother and father being away for long periods of time and then returning with beautiful gifts and wonderful stories. She wondered what they would bring her this time. She had joined five daisies together without breaking any stems and smiled at her achievement. Suddenly, though, she was filled with apprehension. What if the daisies did not last until her mother got home? She decided that she would have to ask Mary to put it in water for her, to try and stop them fading.

The next day the clouds had turned dark and the house was filled with sadness. Isabel was greatly distressed as she went down to breakfast, for no one laughed or pinched her cheek, and her always-cheery cook could barely smile at her – indeed, many of the servants turned away to avoid her gaze.

After she had eaten, Mrs Tabitha dressed her in black and then they all got carriages to the local church.

'But it is not Sunday,' Isabel said several times and the carriage rattled along.

'We must say goodbye to your parents,' said Mr Ronald gravely, his thin face drawn with grief.

When they stepped out of the carriage it was raining and Isabel was very wet and cold, despite Mr Ronald holding the umbrella over her. The vicar was there and spoke words she did not understand as they stood on the damp grass.

'Why must I say goodbye to you, Mother?' she asked silently as two black boxes were lowered into the wet earth, where a large hole had been dug.

Mrs Tabitha had said that she would see her mother and father again, so why was the minister speaking so solemnly of farewells and endings and sadness?

The service finally ended and they all returned to Greenwood. Isabel hoped that the strange day was over now – all she wanted was for everyone to be happy again, but they looked sad, so sad. When she looked round, even Mrs Tabitha was crying. Completely discomposed, she ran out of the room and up the two flights of stairs to the library. The last time she had been in here, her father had taken her on his knee and read to her long passages from his favourite books. She had not understood the all words, but loved to listen to his warm voice. She had never been in the room on her own before, and felt very small as she entered in her crushed damp black dress. The smell of the books and the silence of the room comforted her.

'Where are you father?' she asked aloud. 'Why are they so sad?'

She climbed up into her father's rocking chair and tried to initiate the smoothing rocking motion that he created when she was in the chair with him, but her legs could not reach the floor.

'Why are they making me say goodbye to you mother?' she asked again, giving up trying to rock herself and hugging a cushion to her small body. 'Please come back soon.'

But somehow, even as she spoke the words, she knew that they would not.

Days turned into weeks and weeks into months and Isabel's parents did not come back. Mr Ronald and Mrs Tabitha were honest with her and tried to explain the situation but Isabel could not seem to grasp what they were saying. Strange men appeared at the door wanting to speak to the servants and Mr Ronald chased them away with angry words.

'Heartless men,' he said to Mrs Tabitha after the third group of reporters had tried to gain entry.

Then the serious men came, with their black briefcases. They went into the study with Mr Ronald and Mrs Tabitha and Isabel, listening at the door, caught fragments of the conversation.

'She is nobody's child,' she heard them say to Mr Ronald.

Isabel wondered of whom they were speaking.

It was after their visit that things changed at Greenwood. The servants started to smile again, for her sake, and life began to return to normal for Isabel. Slowly, her parents began to fade from her mind, becoming distant memories from another time when the sun shone more brightly and she was not always alone.

Isabel paused, her eyes bright, her memory far away. There was only one more part of her story to tell.

'Over the following years I came to terms with the fact that my parents were not returning, but it was not until the day I left for Alverdine that I found out exactly how they died. Mrs Tabitha was busy packing my clothes and sent me to her room to find the key for the suitcase. When I entered, the top drawer of her dresser was open and inside were a number of newspaper clippings. I realise now that day happened to be the anniversary of my parent's death and that my mother would have been much on her mind. I would not have looked at her private things, but the headline of one article caught my eye: '*Doomed Audleys Drown at Sea*'. I lifted it out and read the copy underneath. It told the story of my parent's boat trip, of the storm that sunk the boat, and my father's last attempts to save my mother. The story that I had never known, never fully been told, and never asked to hear.

'I stood there, waiting for the emotion to hit me as it always did when I read a story in a book, of characters who had come to a tragic fate. I should feel much worse now, for these were my parents, I told myself; yet the tears did not come. The terrible words were before me, in undeniable black and white, but somehow they did not upset me. Instead, I felt strangely empty, as though I was reading about someone very distant from me. I could not connect with these people, could not imagine how they had felt. All I could imagine were my beautiful parents, reading to me, sitting with me on their laps, running in the garden with me at Greenwood. These wet, drowning, terrified people I read about were strangers to me. I suppose, in some ways, they still are.'

Isabel stopped to wipe the falling tears from her cheeks.

'It is good that you can only picture them as they were to you,' said

Mr Hardy. 'It is what they would have wanted.'

Isabel's tears continued to fall, making dark sunken marks in the soft sand below.

'I am sorry if this has upset you,' said Mr Hardy, looking concerned.

'No,' replied Isabel said, trying to control herself. 'It has been good to remember. I did not realise how much of it I did remember – it has all been locked away for so long. Indeed, that morning when Mrs Tabitha came to me under the tree, I find I can still remember every detail. It is as though your question has turned a key in my mind. Thank you.'

'I am afraid I feel more worthy of blame than thanks,' he said, handing her a handkerchief to wipe her tears. 'You seem quite upset.'

'I am not crying for me,' she said, smiling at last through her tears. 'I am crying for the girl who did not understand.' She gazed out at the calm sea with her violet eyes. 'And at last, I think, she feels some peace.'

It was that time in the late afternoon when you feel most lazy. Everything was calm and peaceful and it seemed as though the day would go on forever. Then Isabel felt a slight nip in the air and realised with surprise that the afternoon had gone and evening was already on its way. They had been talking for longer than she thought. She gathered her shawl around her shoulders. The sun was beginning to cast long shadows from even the smallest objects on the beach and the tide had retreated farther than she had ever seen it.

'It is getting late,' she said reluctantly.

'Indeed it is,' replied Mr Hardy.

Neither of them moved. Isabel glanced at him.

'You have been very kind to me, Mr Hardy, sitting and listening to me for such a time.'

'Not at all, it has been my pleasure. And you have done your share of listening also.'

Killie stretched and then stood up beside them, her tail wagging as though keen to start walking again.

'I suppose I should return,' Isabel admitted with a reluctant sigh.

'Shall I walk you back?' he asked.

'I would like that,' she replied.

They walked back together through the fields and lanes, and all too quickly Isabel realised that they were at the gate at the bottom of the sweet-smelling herb gardens that led up to Harringdon Court. She wondered where the time had gone - so quickly had the afternoon passed - but her heart felt lighter than it had done for many weeks.

However, as she glanced towards the path that led towards Harringdon, her buoyant mood began to disappear.

'I had better leave you here,' Isabel said softly. 'This path cannot be seen from the windows of the house and my aunt's remonstrance should be lessened if she thinks I have been out alone.'

'Did she not know where you were?' Mr Hardy asked.

'I am afraid I left without her permission. She does not want me to leave the house on my own.'

He looked surprised,

'Are you a guest or a prisoner here?' he asked, sounding a little shocked.

'I am not quite sure,' Isabel replied honestly.

Mr Hardy took her hand and clasped it in both of his. His hands were rough and warm.

'Remember that I am only down the road if you need me.'

'Will I see you again?' she asked, with some concern in her eyes.

'I think that will be your decision.' His brown eyes stared straight into hers, clear and steady. 'You have made your own decisions almost all your life Isabel, from a far younger age than I ever did. I trust that nothing will stop you from doing that now.'

He let go of her hand and stepped back lightly. She was thinking hard.

Her actions over the past few weeks had not been consistent with those of the girl of whom she had just spoken on the beach. That girl had an unswerving spirit, the daughter of two people who had followed their own course, against all opposition. Why should she now return to a place where she was a prisoner, with her friendships and very thoughts dictated for her?

A rustle in the bushes made her look up. Was it a bird? She realised that there had been too many rustles, too many spying eyes for her liking since Sir Branden and his servant arrived. She wondered how often she had been truly alone since that day. A shiver ran down her spine and she glanced around uneasily. She needed to leave this place.

She stepped close to Mr Hardy.

'Where will you be this evening?' she asked quietly.

'I will be at the Bumblebee,' he said, his voice low and uncertain.

'Can I meet you there?'

His eyes met hers, full of questions, but she did not see them. Her mind was a whirl of plans, hopes and fears, all racing back and forth. But one thing was clear to her now.

'I am leaving Harringdon. This will be my last night. But I would like to see you before I leave. You have been a very good friend to me. You have reminded me of who I am.'

There was a strange expression in his eyes – a mix of pride and sadness.

'I think you have made the right decision, Isabel,' he said softly. 'Although I am very sorry that you will be leaving. We shall have to make tonight a night to remember.' He paused, thinking quickly, and then said, 'I will meet you here, at nine o'clock, and then we will go to The Bumblebee together.'

Isabel could hear footsteps coming along the path that ran down the far side of the house.

'I have to go,' she said quickly, her heart pounding. 'I will see you here in a few hours.'

She opened the gate and stepped through. Mr Hardy smiled and tipped his hat to her.

'Until then, Isabel Audley.'

She smiled back at him.

'Until then.'

# XV

The house was quiet and still when she entered. Only the hall lamps were lit, the rest of the rooms were in darkness. She knew it was the servant's evening off but wondered where her aunt and Sir Branden were; she had expected to find them in the drawing room. She breathed a sigh of relief at the unexpected reprieve - perhaps the furious rebuke she had expected from her aunt would not take place tonight.

Isabel went softly up the stairs, for while her aunt and Sir Branden were obviously out, she did not assume that meant that Gaunt had gone with them. She kept her eyes and ears alert as she went to her room but saw no sign of him. Perhaps she would indeed have the peace and solitude she required to make her final preparations.

She dragged out the small suitcase she had brought with her to Harringdon and quickly began to load it with a few items of clothing. Two dresses, a pair of boots, her cloak, a nightdress and some undergarments. She moved with speed, hardly daring to think about what she was doing, lest she change her mind. She placed on top her precious personal belongings – her Bible, her diary, and the copy of *Songs of Innocence and Experience* that her father had given her. She also took the small purse of money, which contained her monthly allowance.

Then she sat down at the small desk in the corner of her room and pulled out her diary. Time was short but she wanted to record this moment – the moment when she finally took control of her life.

### ISABEL'S NARRATIVE
*(Extract from Isabel's Diary)*

*HARRINGDON COURT, 14th July 1866*

Wonderful, wonderful recklessness.

My plan of action is both perfectly simple and perfectly foolhardy.

Tonight I will go the The Bumblebee with Mr Hardy. He has been my one and only friend here at Harringdon since Cathy left and it seems most fitting that I should spend my last night with him. I will then get the midnight carriage to London from Ashton (I know Mr Hardy will help me in this when I ask him), and tomorrow visit my trustees to sort out matters for myself and inform them that my aunt will no longer be controlling my finances.

I will also write to Cathy and explain everything. I will of course attend her wedding and brave my aunt's outrage there. I suspect, to my benefit, that Aunt Helen will not dare make a scene in front of Cathy's new family on such an important day.

I commit to paper that I readily admit the imprudence of this course. All I know is that in this moment of decision I am my own person – my actions, my decision are now wholly mine, and this is how I want my life to be. I feel like laughing at my audacity and wild thoughts are running through me.

Let me now flick ahead in this diary, one month, two months, three months. In the margin I write:

*'Where am I now?'*

I wonder what my entry will be.

I have a nervous flutter in my stomach and a feeling of suspense. Everything will change tonight.


## THE STORY CONTINUED BY THE EDITOR

Isabel then placed a fresh sheet of paper in front of her. Her heart pounded as she dipped the pen in the inkwell and began to stroke onto the page the words that marked the end of her time at Harringdon.

*Dear Aunt Helen,*

*It is with regret that I write to tell you that I will be leaving Harringdon tonight. I am a woman grown now and must begin to make my own decisions. As discussed, I feel most strongly that I should no longer stay here now that Cathy is gone.*

*I want to thank you for inviting me to stay for the first time, all those years ago. I suspect that I shall never know what made you decide to invite me into your life, but believe me when I say that I am grateful. For having the chance to meet and come to love my cousin Cathy has been one of the most wonderful experiences of my life.*

*I know we shall meet again at the wedding and that you will probably be very angry with me. However, I hope that you can forgive me and wish me well, as I do you, for we are family.*

*Yours truly,*
*Isabel.*

She slipped the page into a white envelope and addressed it to her aunt. Then she took off her day dress and changed into a plain white muslin gown. She chose her simplest throw and tied it around her shoulders, glancing at herself in the looking glass. At least now she would not look so out of place amongst Mr Hardy's friends at The Bumblebee, she thought to herself.

Armed with her suitcase and the letter she took one last look around the room where she and Cathy had spent so many happy times. She knew she would not be allowed back, and took a moment to paint the room clearly in her mind so that she would not forget it. Then, she turned and closed the door behind her.

She went downstairs to her aunt's study and quietly opened the door. Again, no lamps were lit but the light from the hall lamp just outside filled the room with a soft glow. She went over to the desk, the floorboards creaking underneath her, and placed the letter on the desk. She was turning to leave when she noticed something amiss. The small polished wooden chest that had sat upon her aunt's desk for as long as Isabel could remember was turned at a strange angle (her aunt's desk was always in perfect order) and its lid was ajar. This chest was always kept locked – her aunt kept the key in her pocket at all times and Isabel knew that no servant was allowed to touch it.

Fearing another burglary, Isabel took a closer look and noticed that the key was in the lock. She thought this very strange – had her aunt simply forgotten to lock it? Or had she been disturbed in the process? Hesitantly, Isabel opened the lid fully and glanced at the contents to see if they would give her a clue to the mystery.

Inside the chest lay a pile of letters. Isabel recognised the handwriting at once - she knew those sprawling letters better than she knew her own hand – it was Cathy's writing, and the top letter was addressed to '*Isabel Audley*.' She lifted it off and looked at the letter underneath. '*To Isabel Audley*', it read. She went through each one in the pile, '*Isabel Audley*', '*Isabel Audley*', '*Isabel Audley*'. The writing grew more untidy with each letter – Isabel could almost hear Cathy's concerned voice calling out to her. The dates in the corner of each envelope were closer and closer together as she got further down the pile – indeed, the last three had come only days apart. She realised her hands were trembling with rage – how dare her aunt keep these from her – and, more importantly, why had she done so? Was Cathy in trouble?

There were nine letters in all, the final envelope blotched and ink-stained. It sat at a strange angle in the box, for there was something else underneath it. Isabel lifted the last letter out to see what lay beneath - any thoughts of her aunt's privacy now disregarded in her anger - and suddenly saw her own face reflected in a dark gleaming surface. Her mind reeled and she put out a hand to steady herself. At the bottom of the box lay the stolen sapphire and pearl brooch that had disappeared many weeks ago, its facets shining in the moonlight. Isabel stared at it, her eyes wide with confusion, her mind filled with troubled thoughts.

Suddenly she heard a soft noise behind her and turned to look round. Then, all was darkness.

*'Is it too late then, Evelyn Hope?*
*What, your soul was pure and true,*
*The good stars met in your horoscope,*
*Made you of spirit, fire and dew -*
*And just because I was thrice as old,*
*And our paths in the world diverged so wide,*
*Each was nought to each, must I be told?*
*We were fellow mortals, nought beside?'*

*Evelyn Hope* (lines 17-24), Robert Browning

# VOLUME TWO

*'No, indeed! For God above*
*Is great to grant, as mighty to make,*
*And creates the love to reward the love, -*
*I claim you still, for my own love's sake!*
*Delayed it may be for more lives yet,*
*Though worlds I may traverse, not a few -*
*Much is to learn and much to forget*
*Ere the time be come for taking you.'*

*Evelyn Hope* (lines 25-32), Robert Browning

# XVI

## THE STORY CONTINUED BY THE EDITOR

The chandelier glittered overhead, a thousand tiny facets twinkling in the candlelight, reflecting fragments of the scene beneath. Had you looked down from its height, you would have seen a vast dining room, resplendent in its extravagance, with a great feast laid out upon the lengthy dining table. Tall portraits mounted in gold frames hung along the length of one side of the room, the forbidding stares of their subjects falling upon the long rows of guests seated at either side of the mahogany table. Liveried footmen lined the wall beneath the paintings, statue-like in their stillness, crystal decanters in their white-gloved hands. Along the other side of the room, the black velvet curtains had been drawn across the long casement windows, to shield the guests from the cold emanating from the glass. Outside the sky was dark, the clouds heavy and ominous.

The tall candles that stood in the centre of the table cast a red shade around the room. The subdued lighting caught and brought to life brief movements along the table: the sparkle of wine in a glass, the steel gleam of a knife, the shimmer of light across a woman's jewelled earrings.

There was a great deal of conversation, but somehow, perhaps because of the size of the room, it all seemed very hushed, as though the speakers were talking under their breath. There were, however, two people present who were not speaking - indeed, they appeared to hardly move.

A young man and woman sat opposite each other in the centre of the table. Their beauty lit up the room like watch fires set alight atop a high hill, so breathtaking was their appearance. Yet although they were often glanced at, they spoke to no one, and neither did anyone speak to them. The gentleman's eyes were fixed upon the lady's countenance, while her eyes were downcast and distracted, as though she was at the table in body but not in mind. Her face was passive and sad, eloquent in its melancholy.

It was clear that she was a lady of great fortune. The diamonds that hung magnificently around the beautiful contours of her neck were of such a cut and size that most women, even wealthy women, could only ever dream of owning. Her dress was opulent jade silk that shimmered as she shifted listlessly in her chair. She had not touched her food, nor her drink, and her hands rested idly in her lap. But it was her pride that

113

caught his attention; that proud gleam in her eyes of a spirit bowed, but not broken.

The gentleman watched her with his dark eyes, taking in every detail of her appearance; his handsome face, had she looked upon it, was both captivating and captivated by her mystery.

## ISABEL'S NARRATIVE
### *(Extract from Isabel's Diary)*

*ENDERTON, 9th November 1866*

A dreadful day. I feel cold to my very bones, as I have done for many months – but now the weather seems to have taken up my complaint and become as icy as I feel. I am not sure how much longer I can do this. When the silk dress slipped from my shoulders as I undressed, I let the cold embrace me fully, longing for its cold touch to numb the pain inside me, but no relief came. I can only pray that sleep might come now and take the rest away.

## THE STORY CONTINUED BY THE EDITOR

Blowing the candles out at either side of her bed, Isabel sank down under the covers, waiting to be absorbed in the blackness. She wanted it to swallow her up, that she might never be found again. But tonight the room was not utter darkness. There was a strange light coming from the window - a curious luminescence emitting from the gap where the curtains did not quite reach the floor. She felt a presence outside that seemed to draw her towards it. Shivering, she got up and walked to the window, and slowly drew the curtains apart. Before her lay a brilliant white world that she barely knew.

The garden of her prison had been transformed into a silvery wonderland, surrendering fully to the heavy, slow-falling snow that had come without warning or sound, drifting down in ghostly silence. Silver and opalescent blues had taken the place of brown and dull greys, creating a new world, full of perfect beauty. The clouds of flakes swirled outside her window and she stared into them: worlds within worlds, each snowflake making its own journey into the great unknown. She gazed out at the deep stillness of the gardens below. All the magic and mystery of the night had met there, waiting for her, calling her out.

And so it was that she found herself pulling on her boots, fastening her cloak around her neck as the thick white blanket quickly formed itself upon the perfectly cut grass and bushes outside. Brushing all other thoughts from her mind, she rushed down the stairs and through the house, and before the final tree relinquished its last inch of green, she was outside upon the stone patio, breathing in the deep, fresh air that stung her lungs and made her feel more alive than she had done in many months.

The garden stood still, cloaked in its pearly gown that made even the darkness seem bright. The snow lay thick and unbroken on the ground, calling her on, inviting her to make her mark upon the spotless landscape. She took her first step onto the white grass, her foot sinking deeply, making the very first muffled footprint in this new world. A feeling of otherness stole over her as she walked deeper into the not-quite darkness, her feet making soft crunching sounds in the fresh snow, her long red cloak whispering on the ground behind her.

Over this silent landscape, the snowflakes continued to fall like soft feathers - as though God had ripped open a down pillow and was casting handfuls all around her; down they fell from the heavens, carried on the ever-varying currents of the silent wind. To her left they fell fast and straight, to her right, they spiralled and twirled, sometimes even rising upwards as the wind tossed them in its playful arms.

As Isabel walked further and further away from the house, the light from its windows was snuffed out by the walls of snow all around her. She wished that the snowfall would become even heavier. The flakes were huge now and already her footprints, made just moments ago, were being filled in, even as she walked. She wanted the snow to envelop the whole world, to wipe everything that had existed from its surface and start anew – a fresh, white, magical world.

She was walking past the trees at the end of the garden now. Snow was piling up, inch upon inch, on each branch, from the smallest twig to the largest bough. The great oaks seemed to have doubled in size in their ivory robes and had become grand, majestic white sentinels, guarding her walk. She felt as though she was in some far-off land and all her troubles had happened to a different girl - a sad lonely girl - not her. And if she was lonely now, it was a wonderful, thrilling kind of loneliness. She felt the vastness of the moment, the innumerable possibilities of the night. She felt more alive, more herself, than she had done in months – perhaps even in her whole life. Staring into the wonder of the deep white expanse before her, her girlish fantasy re-awoke in her mind: she had finally found the world between the worlds.

Energy surged through her and she began to run. She felt the clouds sigh above her, releasing yet more of their beauty with quiet regret; she heard the trees sway and murmur as the wind picked up, whispering their secrets to one another; she felt the grass underneath her shiver beneath its white prison; she watched the cold breaths of air before her dancing with the falling flakes, a glorious waltz of nature. She began to understand that the world is not silent at all, but always speaking to those who will listen. In this moment of magic, it unveiled itself before her and spoke, calling her into its majesty. She ran, she danced, she spun. She spoke to the night in its own language and it spoke back to her. The world was alive in her and she was the world.

The snow was falling faster now. Isabel was in the centre of the flakes, spinning inside her very own snow globe, trying to wrap herself in the never-ending sheets of ivory – trying to hide herself, lose herself. The snow around her seemed to glow whiter than in any other part of the gardens, her red cloak billowing out behind her, her ungloved hands held upwards, moving and dancing in time with the glorious music only she could hear. The icy coldness of the night seemed to slow down time itself, as though she was in the narrow centre of an hourglass where the particles flow through so very slowly. The snowflakes landed on her cheeks, her lips, her lashes. As they melted, more fell, each one more beautiful that the next.

And as she moved in time with the snowflakes, she did not realise that she was not alone. Someone stood watching her, taking in the scene. He had stumbled upon it quite by accident, but now he could not move, he could not take his eyes from her. There was mastery in that moment, a rightness to his being there. It was a moment that had forever sat in his future, waiting for him to find it, and now he had. But he did not know this yet. All he could see was her – the perfect, magical girl who danced in the snow – captivatingly young, astonishingly beautiful, so full of life that in that moment it seemed as though life itself could not contain her. He knew that if the world ended that night, this image would stay with him forever. Isabel sought and found herself in the white world around her. The nameless man sought and found himself in the dancing girl in the snow.

## ISABEL'S NARRATIVE
*(Extract from Isabel's Diary)*

*ENDERTON, 10th November 1866*

I awoke feeling alive again. The snow - instead of chilling me - has filled me with fire and given me a desire to live once more. My life is not over, I have much still to see and do; I realise that now.

Tonight is the ball. I will be extraordinary.

# XVII

A gradual hush descended upon the company and slowly their eyes turned towards the top of the curving marble staircase to watch the figure descend. Her dress was vibrantly blue, picking out the azure tints in her sparkling eyes. It was cut in a sweetheart neckline at the front, the full skirt flowing from her bustle in endless lengths of taffeta that rustled as she moved downwards, forming a shimmering cascade. Her hair was a mass of curls, swept up high at the back of her head - though several of them had escaped and strayed mischievously round her shapely neck. A cluster of glittering diamonds hung there, complemented by a pair of dazzling earrings. She was luminous.

The host watched her from the doorway to the ballroom, his face cast in shadow, his expression unreadable. Something was different about Isabel tonight – never before had she assented to present herself in this way, certainly not of her own accord. There was a heightened colour in her cheeks, a deeper red in her lips and a brilliance in her eyes that he had not seen for many months. Even her sense of dress was unusual. Something within her had changed.

Her heart beat painfully against her ribs as she made her way down, each step a steep cliff to her feet; she feared she would stumble at each one. But to the spectators she glided down, her head held high, her expression proud. She felt their eyes upon her – at least a hundred – no, more, many more. Suddenly she felt that the stones of her necklace were cutting tightly into her neck and the bones of her bodice slowing her breathing. She glanced up quickly, raising her gaze above the general company, to the tall paintings that hung around the entrance hall. One of them was of a young woman with fiery red hair. She reminded Isabel of her mother, and somehow it gave her the courage to carry on. She held her chin high as she reached the bottom of the stairs and the host moved forwards to greet her. She was fixed in his piercing gaze, but tonight she did not flinch under its weight.

As she made her way into the incandescent ballroom, the gathered crowd began to file in after her, enticed by this young beauty and the lively sound of the band that was beginning to play. It was a sumptuous affair – so many candles had been lit that the golden ballroom simply glowed, and the casement doors had been opened to a garden, so bedecked with candles that it looked like a fairy grotto.

As usual Isabel did not lack the offer of a partner for the first dance, but today she did not resent the presence of every gentleman who asked for her hand. A young gentleman introduced himself as Mr Roderick, gained her hand and led her to the centre of the floor. He placed one hand on her waist and grasped her in the waltz position, seeming delighted with his prize. A second dance quickly followed, in which she was asked to dance by a Mr Farringdon, and then thirdly by Sir Kent. She danced well, but not like clockwork, as she had done at previous balls during the past few months. Instead, she enjoyed the music and smiled as she moved in time with her partners, moving around the dance floor with feet as light as air, her skirts swinging out with gusto.

However, after the fifth dance, she found herself in need of some refreshment. Excusing herself from the large group of young men who were now vying for her hand, Isabel made her way into the dining room where refreshments were being served.

The dining room seemed very dimly lit after the blaze of the grand ballroom. She was poured a glass of champagne and, warm from the vigour of the dancing, stepped over to the open patio doors to sip her drink. As she lifted the glass to her lips, a figure suddenly stepped out of the shadows to her right. Expecting to see the one person she dreaded above all, she stepped backwards, the champagne spilling over the edge of her glass. But it was not him.

Instead, she found herself face to face with a young man. He was tall, dressed in a smartly cut dress suit and cravat. His thick shock of brown hair fell carelessly over his eyes, which seemed dark and wild in the moonlight, for she could not see the depths of them. He had a well-shaped face and handsome mouth that turned down slightly at the corners, lending his face, when he was not smiling, a melancholy air. Standing a head above all the other men in the room, he had a slim figure, his poise careless but graceful. He smiled at her, deep and warm, and she wondered who he was - this stranger with the haunting face. She could not think that she had seen him before, but then, she conceded, she had been rather distracted, and there were many guests.

'There is hardly anyone here who knows me,' he said to her, matter-of-factly. 'So we cannot be introduced. But I would not want to let that stop me from making your acquaintance.'

Isabel did not quite know how to reply. The gentleman watched her, taking in her striking looks – her fine nose, beautiful violet eyes, soft red lips. Isabel could actually feel his gaze resting upon her, but for the first time in many months, she did not resent being looked at.

'Certainly not,' she replied, as though in a dream. 'I am most pleased to meet you.'

'I take it that the polka is not a particular favourite of yours?' he said, with another confident smile, gesturing towards the ballroom where the guests were now partaking in a particularly lively version of the aforementioned dance.

'One cannot dance every dance,' she replied calmly, coming back to herself, though she found that her heart was racing for no explainable reason. It beat a little faster as she added,

'And I do not believe that I have seen you on the dance floor at all tonight.'

'Ah', he stepped forward, pursuing his advantage. 'I do hope I have not appeared rude. It was simply that I could not find a desirable partner.'

He had a self-assured and easy manner about him that she liked.

'Are the present females so objectionable?' she asked, raising a perfectly shaped eyebrow.

'Oh not at all. It is simply that the female with whom I wished to dance was continually engaged.'

His admiring look was unmistakable. Isabel breathed in tightly and half-consciously raised her hand to her hair which had become loose during the dancing, tucking it back behind her ear.

'Well, perhaps the lady for whom you have been waiting may be available at some point this evening, should you choose to engage her,' she said in as calm a voice as she could muster.

'That would be most agreeable,' he replied, smiling.

'Although,' said Isabel, growing bolder, 'With your previous record, this woman may now have come to the conclusion that you are not a very skilled dancer, hence your unwillingness to take the floor.'

She took a sip of her champagne and continued to look out across the moonlit gardens, half-amazed at her own daring.

'Oh dear,' he pretended to look disheartened, stealing a glance at her profile as he did. 'Well perhaps you would be so kind as to allow me this dance in order for me to prove my skills, Miss -'

'Audley,' she said quickly. 'Isabel Audley.'

She held out her hand and he took it in his.

'Isabel,' he said, his dark eyes holding hers firmly in their grip. 'Your name sounds like silver bells ringing in the wind - but I must not call you that yet.' He smiled warmly at her. 'Miss Audley, would you do me the honour of the next dance?'

The pressure of his hand was tight upon hers and she flushed brightly with pleasure at his request.

'I will dance with you,' she said, attempting to regain her calm reserve, 'If you will tell me your name.'

He looked at her deeply for a moment and then replied,

'Gladly - I am John Treador.'

He bent his slightly tousled head to her hand and kissed it. Then he raised his wide, fascinating eyes to meet hers, adding,

'And I am at your service, Miss Audley.'

Taking her arm, he led her back into the blaze of light and onto the dance floor.

## ISABEL'S NARRATIVE
*(Extract from Isabel's Diary)*

*ENDERTON, 10<sup>th</sup> November 1866*

I could not describe the dance to you. It was like one of those perfect dreams, from which you awake filled with the most wonderful feeling and yet have only a faint recollection of what has passed. All I remember is that he held me close - so close - and I could feel his heart beating against my own. His arms were strong and held me tight, and I wished that he might never let me go. I was utterly intoxicated by him. The sea of faces around us seemed to blur while we danced until all I could see was his face, looking down at me, so wonderful and unlike any I had ever seen before.

## THE STORY CONTINUED BY THE EDITOR

The young couple danced together exclusively until the band announced their final number. Many more couples got to their feet for the last dance of the evening and, noticing the emptying gardens, Mr Treador gestured towards the patio doors. Isabel assented, and gladly took his arm, noting his careless grace and easy charm as he manoeuvred them through the busy throng towards the quieter outdoor area. There were a number of warm furs hanging by the door and Mr Treador lifted one, placing it around Isabel's shoulders. His hands were warm as he fastened it around her neck.

'I hope you do not mind this break,' he said courteously, 'but the dance floor was becoming rather crowded. Are you quite warm enough?'

'Oh yes', Isabel replied, although was thankful for the furs as the air was bitingly cold. She hoped that her nose would not turn too pink.

They were left quite alone as the last few guests made their way past them into the ballroom. Mr Treador turned to her.

'So tell me, Miss Audley - where did you learn to dance like that? You have lighter feet than any woman I have ever danced with – I felt like we were dancing on the clouds.'

Isabel smiled, pleased by the compliment.

'I had dance lessons at school, but have not had much practice since I left.'

'Have you been out of school long?' he asked amiably.

'Yes,' replied Isabel, slightly defensively.

'Forgive me, I mean no insult,' he said quickly. 'It is just that I seemed to be attracting a few unfavourable looks from my distinguished host as we danced. I thought perhaps you were his young ward?'

Isabel thought quickly, anger and uncertainty flowing through her.

'He is not my guardian - and I am not 'young',' she said after a moment.

She looked up at the tall stranger standing before her from under her long lashes, wondering how much to tell him; wondering if she could confide in him. Her cheeks were flushed from the cold and her eyes sparkled in the candlelight.

'Well, that is good news. I...' his voice trailed off as he gazed at her.

He seemed to lose track of what he had been saying and gazed intently at her face. She gazed back, turmoil in her eyes as she tried to weigh up this man who stood before her.

'You are absolutely beautiful,' he said in a captivated voice.

Something seemed to burst within her, like a firework setting off a thousand vibrant colours.

'Isabel, it not time you were in bed?' A deep voice spoke from the darkness, unmistakable in its tone.

The champagne glass slipped from Isabel's hand, falling through the air and shattering into fragments on the stone floor. Her eyes were transfixed in fear on the figure that had approached, and Mr Treador, watching the colour slip from her face, turned to find his host behind him.

'Ah, Sir Branden', he said, slightly taken aback. 'I did not see you there.'

Sir Branden stepped forward out of the shadows, his expression unfathomable.

'Mr Treador, I do hope you are enjoying the evening?' he said, his voice smooth and powerful.

Mr Treador uncertainly nodded his assent as his host moved towards them, his eyes fixed upon Isabel.

'You must forgive me for stealing your partner away,' said Sir

Branden in an apologetic tone. 'It has been a late night for her and my wife does need her sleep.'

The words ripped through the air like an unsharpened knife. Mr Treador flinched as through struck and inhaled sharply.

'Your wife...she never... I did not know she was your wife.'

Sir Branden twisted his mouth into an amiable curve. His eyes had a new, harder gleam.

'Did she not tell you? It must have slipped her mind. Ah well, no matter, you know now.'

He turned to Isabel, whose face was very white.

'My dear, I think that it is time that you went upstairs; it has been a long evening for you. I will be up soon to join you.'

Isabel stepped backwards involuntarily onto the broken glass at her feet, crunching it beneath her satin pumps.

'Now now,' said Sir Branden, said in a silky tone, reaching out a hand to steady her. 'Be careful or you will hurt yourself.'

She froze at his touch, her red lips pursed tight, her hands clenched into tight white fists - and then, without a word to either, she turned and ran back through the garden and into the ballroom, a beautiful streak of vivid blue through the crowd. Both men looked after her.

'She is such a lovely girl but I must discipline her on her manners,' said Sir Branden lightly. There was a beat of silence and then he turned to John and laughed, 'Come, let us return to the ballroom.'

Sir Branden led the way and Mr Treador followed, his face full of perplexity and unease.

## ISABEL'S NARRATIVE
*(Extract from Isabel's Diary)*

*ENDERTON, account written 11th November 1866*

Somehow, I had always managed to keep him out, but this night was different.

I could feel the blood pounding through my hands and legs. I could hear it in my ears and behind my eyes. Tonight, tonight, the door would fail. Tonight, he would get in.

Perhaps I should not have taunted him this morning, or riled him this evening. Perhaps the wine had been more potent, or the frustration more prevalent, but tonight he was using all of his brutal, masculine force. And he was about to enter my room.

I sat in the centre of the bed in my nightgown, my knees drawn up, and my hands clasped around my legs. I did not look at the slowly shattering door, at the lock that was buckling with every blow. Instead I stared in front of me at my white hands. I moved my fingers, and wondered at how my brain knew how to tell them to do that. I wondered if they would still be able to do that after tonight.

As that outer defence gave way, I felt as though all my inner defences were began to break down also and pure fear shot though me. Tonight, what I had managed to prevent for so long, was going to happen. And then suddenly it was as though one of my dreams were coming to life.

I looked up at the first creak. I knew exactly where it was coming from and yet it did not make sense. It truly did look as if the painting of the knight that hung on the wall – that knight, who had been my immovable protector for so long – had come to life before my very eyes. One moment he was oils and paper; the next he was a real-life man stepping out of the frame and into my room.

It took a few moments for my brain to overcome my imagination. I blinked and looked again. There was no frame anymore – and the man was not wearing armour. Instead, the place where the painting had hung was now a black hole in the wall, about four feet high and two feet wide. The painting was still attached to the wall, but was hanging back to front, attached to the wall by some sort of hinge that had swung back to reveal the opening that I could now see.

And the man – he had leapt down from the hole, his hair over his eyes. He straightened up, pushed his hair back roughly and I saw who it was. Mr Treador stood before me, concern and anger on his face.

He must have seen my frightened eyes and flushed cheeks, the faltering words on my lips and my pale hands, but he asked no questions of me, turning his full attention to the situation in front of him. To the right of my buckling door stood an ancient chest of drawers, tall and solid. Mr Treador darted over to this and pushed his weight against it, his arms straining as he heaved it into position in front of the door. It stood, strong and impenetrable even as the lock gave way behind it, allowing the door to open not even a fraction. I heard Sir Branden give two final, desperate blows to the oak and then, cursing with all the powers of hell, he ceased his attempt. We both listened as he turned away, dragging his heavy footsteps into the darkness.

I watched as Mr Treador relaxed his tensed body against the saving piece of furniture and turned round to me. A million questions swirled in my confused my mind; a thousand emotions surged within me. Yet all that came out were two tiny little words:

'Thank you.'

He stood back, and surveyed me - that pathetic creature crouched on the bed in her nightgown.

'You are most welcome,' he replied. He gave the chest of drawers one final shove to ensure that it was wedged securely by the door, and then came nearer to me.

'Miss Audley,' he said, placing his hand upon my arm as I took a deep, shuddering breath. 'Tell me what is going on - how can I help you?'

I am not sure why I began to weep - perhaps it was because he said my name - my own real name; or because this was the first kind human touch I had had in a long time; or because no one had asked how I was for many months - certainly not with real concern in their voice; or because I knew for the first time that someone was protecting me and I did not have to do it all myself – perhaps it was all of the above - but I broke down on my bed, releasing the tension from my body, and sobbed.


## THE STORY CONTINUED BY THE EDITOR

It was good for Isabel to cry, for she had been strong for so very long. Mr Treador held her close, his hands upon her shaking shoulders. He was warm, and his smell unfamiliar, but she felt comforted, and let all her pain, and fear, and anguish flood out unreservedly, feeling safe in the presence of someone who was so clearly on her side.

After the last tear had fallen and been wiped from her cheeks, she sighed deeply.

'Do you feel better,' he asked, the tiniest hint of a smile mingled with his concern.

She gazed up at him and found herself smiling back.

'Yes, much better,' she replied. 'I feel as though a load has been lifted from my back.'

She looked around and her eyes fell upon the dark hole at the far end of her room.

'Is there a passage behind the painting?' she asked, aware of how absurd her question sounded.

'There is indeed,' replied Mr Treador. 'A very ancient passage that connects this room and the one which I am staying in, one floor above. I discovered it by accident when I arrived yesterday and wondered where it led. When I opened the access point again tonight, which is behind some false bookshelves, with the intention of exploring further,

I heard some rather worrying noises that I attributed to an intruder, and followed the roughly hewn stone steps to a small ledge. Pushing aside the hinged door, which is in fact that painting,' he motioned towards the painting of the knight, 'I found myself here and realised that...' his eyes hardened as he glanced back at the blockaded door, '...that brute, was trying to enter. I could see that no lock would hold him, so I had to take the liberty of entering and providing more - physical - assistance.'

Isabel stared at the passage. A sense of calm descended on her heart.

'God must have put it there,' she said softly.

'What?'

'The connecting passage.'

'I do not believe in God,' he said matter-of-factly. 'I was able to get here because you needed me.'

'I needed you very much,' she said quietly.

She sighed deeply and pushed back her covers. She suddenly felt very warm.

'Your cheeks are flushed,' he said, straightening up. 'Come and have some fresh air.'

He reached for her warm dressing gown, and once Isabel had stepped gingerly out of bed, he helped her into it. He led her over to the window and drew back the thick curtains, opening the central pane. A cool breeze flooded the room, fluttering the curtains and her nightgown.

'They say you should not have your windows open at night as you will catch a cold,' he said, watching her, 'but I think it calms you – that cool night breeze. It can wash all your cares away.'

The stars were shining brightly tonight, and the frozen snow glittered in the gardens beneath them. She turned to look at Mr Treador. His face was calm, as though this was the most normal situation in the world. She felt herself wondering at him – at who he was, and why he was so unlike anyone she had ever met. He could sense her looking at him, and he turned. His eyes were also full of questions.

'If you do not wish to tell me, I will never ask you again,' he said softly. 'But if I can, may I ask: why are you here, in this godforsaken place?'

She looked at this - this impossible man, her rescuer, who had burst into her life as suddenly as any knight on horseback - and she decided to trust him. She had nothing else to lose.

# XVIII

*'God hath delivered me to the ungodly, and turned me over into the hands of the wicked. I was at ease, but he hath broken me asunder: he hath also taken me by my neck, and shaken me to pieces, and set me up for his mark.'*

*Job* (Chapter 16, verses 11-12), King James Bible

## ISABEL'S NARRATIVE
### *(Extract from Isabel's Diary)*

*ENDERTON, account written 19<sup>th</sup> July 1866*

She must have heard me screaming her name. She must have heard me clawing at every doorway we passed, kicking and fighting for my life.

She must have heard the man holding me slam his fist into my temple to silence and stop me. She must have seen the drips of blood that fell onto the floor below.

She must have heard.

She did not come.

## THE STORY CONTINUED BY THE EDITOR

If Isabel had been conscious as she was dragged down the front driveway of Harringdon Court, what would she have seen at the upstairs window?

Some say there stood a tall woman, pale, even to her lips, with a face that strove for composure until its proud beauty was as fixed as death.

It was nearly an hour later that Isabel came round. A strange smell filled her nose and when she opened her eyes, she nearly cried out in fear for she could see nothing around her. Slowly she realised that something had been placed over her head, but when she tried to lift her hands to remove it, she found that they were tightly bound behind her back. The floor upon which she had been thrown was moving and bouncing and it did not take her long to realise that she was in a carriage of some form. She could feel the blood pounding in her ears as her bound form was tossed to and fro, her head aching horribly from where she had been hit. The slow dawning realisation that she had been kidnapped was mixed with sheer confusion – who had done this, and why? Her questions were gradually overcome with choking, excruciating fear as she wondered what was to come. She could hear muttered voices above her and tried to listen to what they were saying, although their tones were too low and her head swam with sparks of pain when she tried to concentrate.

They travelled for some time, the rough hessian bag that covered Isabel's head chafing at her skin as the road became more and more uneven, every jolt of the wooden wheels shooting a bolt of pain straight through her. The weather outside sounded terrible and soon rain began to splatter the carriage in heavy drops, while gusts of wind howled through the gaps in the floor. Far-off Isabel could hear the faint rumble of thunder.

When they had journeyed for ten minutes or so up the worst road so far, the carriage drew to a halt and Isabel heard the door being opened from the outside and felt rough hands pulling her up and outside into the wind and the rain. She heard a knife being drawn and fear ripped through her, but it was used not to harm her - instead she felt the cords that bound the hessian bag around her head cut, and the bag pulled away. For a moment, she could not recognise any discernible shapes - a tall winged figure, dark tablets of stone, great iron gates – they all swam around her like a nightmare, but slowly she realised she was in a graveyard and before her stood a church, its spire striking high into the sky like a dagger.

The wind was wailing through the trees around her like a woman in pain, as the men behind her pushed her roughly to indicate that she should start walking. Fear seemed to have her legs in its grip, and she found she could not move so they dragged her forward by her bound arms – one man at either side, and one following behind. Her feet struggled on wet, muddy cobbles, as she tried to begin walking and she tried to pause to stop herself from slipping, but they pulled and pushed her on.

As they approached the church, there was a great clap of thunder and the wind rose up suddenly. Isabel's hair, which was now almost completely undone, was whipped up in a great wave, and wrapped itself round her face so that she could barely see. Rain was streaming down her neck and bare arms. At the shout of the man to her right, the great wooden doors of the church opened slowly before them and Isabel caught sight of two more men inside the church, at either side of the doors. They seemed to leer at her.

At the entrance, the men beside her paused long enough to cut the ropes that bound Isabel's arms. She took advantage of one brief second to sweep the wet hair from her face so she could see what was before her. The storm was raging directly overhead now, and a great flash of lightning shot down, illuminating the ancient stained glass windows and casting an unearthly light on a dreadful scene.

They were in an ancient church, with a long central aisle and high windows. No candles were lit, save a few at the front where two men stood. One was wearing a vicar's collar and robes, though his face was hidden by the hood he wore, while the other man was dressed in an expensive black suit, holding a polished cane. He had a gold pocket watch open in his hand and as he looked up from it, Isabel recognised his face with a thrill of fear. It was Sir Branden.

'Welcome,' he said, with a wide smile.

A feeling of unreality stole over Isabel. This cannot be real, she thought to herself. It looked like some grotesque wedding ceremony. Another flash of lightning above them lit up Isabel's white dress with hideous irony. The panic that had seized her at the moment of her kidnap now mastered her completely as the terrible realisation of what was about to happen hit her with full force. She was frozen in terror for a few moments. The men at either side of her released their grip and motioned her to walk forwards, but then sanity returned and Isabel whipped round towards the doors to seize her chance. Instantly, two of the men had her by the arms. Lashing out frantically with renewed energy, she somehow managed to throw them off, bolting for her freedom. The open doorway was before her - she could see the empty horse and carriage at the end of the path – but then she felt a terrible tug behind her and she cried out in agony. They had her by her hair in an iron grip, and slowly, mercilessly began to haul her down the aisle. Behind her, the doors were slammed shut.

Branden's smile never faltered as he stood waiting at the altar. His grey eyes were fixed upon the terrified girl, who was being relentlessly drawn ever closer in her mud-splattered gown, her dripping hair hanging over her shoulders in a blonde mass, her face as pale as death.

The hooded vicar began to speak before she had even reached the end of the aisle, and Sir Branden assented to his vows quickly and calmly. When Isabel reached them, Sir Branden took her arm in a vice-like grip and the same vows were presented to Isabel. She tried to use her voice to reply in the negative but nothing came out of her pale lips.

Instead, she began to numbly shake her head, but Sir Branden signalled for the vicar to move on quickly and he did, not even glancing at Isabel.

'The rings,' Branden then commanded to someone behind him.

From behind the pulpit came a cloaked figure with a wraith-like face. It was Gaunt. In his hand were two gold rings. Isabel clenched her hands as he approached, but one of the men standing behind forced her wet, shaking hand open and Branden pushed the icy cold band onto her wedding finger.

'A perfect fit,' whispered Gaunt, who had crept round behind her. 'I did say you had such delicate fingers.'

Lightning cracked the sky in two as the faceless vicar pronounced them man and wife.

The ordeal was not yet over for Isabel, but she barely noticed. She must have walked back up the aisle herself, and back down through the graveyard, but she was no more aware of anything than the eroded statues that they passed. Once back inside the carriage, the foul bag was once again thrust over her head. She wondered why; wondered what more there was that they could possibly do to her.

The second journey was much longer than the first. Isabel passed it in a state of half- consciousness, unaware of anything other than her own shock and confusion. However, one change did filter through her senses. She could hear a low rumbling noise to her left, which she at first attributed to returning thunder, but the sound was less threatening, more constant, and somehow, strangely comforting. When a waft of salty air penetrated into her hessian prison, she realised with a jolt that they must be near the sea. The next sensation that greeted her was that of travelling uphill, and on a much smoother road than they had previously been travelling. A moment later, they stopped.

Isabel did not struggle this time when they lifted her out of the carriage, nor when they set her on her feet and led her into what seemed like a house, for there was flooring underneath her feet now, and the echoes of being inside a passageway. She was led roughly down several flights of very narrow stairs – one man in front and one behind her, and then she felt the man in front step away and she was pushed into a space in front of her. The bag was removed from her head and, blinking, she stared around the dimly lit room that she found herself in. It was a very small lavatory, foul and unkempt. On the floor was a small chipped jug of water and several crusts of dry bread. Horror rose up within her like a flood.

She turned, aghast, and found herself face to face with Sir Branden himself.

'What is this,' she demanded, trying to sound braver than she felt. Her voice sounded cracked and quivery, as though she had not used it in years.

'A short period of sequestration,' he said with an air of gravity, yet a faint smile hovered around his lips. 'It will do you good.'

'They will come for me!' Isabel said sharply, trying to inject her voice with confidence that she did not feel certain of.

Sir Branden's mouth curled upwards still further.

'Who will come?' he said simply, and he closed the door.

As she listened to him draw the lock on the other side of the door, Isabel felt as though she could not breathe. Hearing them leave, she tried the door once. It did not open. Pushing all her weight against, she tried to force it, but she may as well have been a mouse for all the difference she made: it moved not an inch. She sank down to her knees. Aunt Helen would come for her, she told herself, refusing to listen to the quiet, terrified corner of her mind that knew her aunt had not heeded to her screams.


## ISABEL'S NARRATIVE
*(Extract from Isabel's Diary)*

*ENDERTON, account written 19$^{th}$ July 1866*


I was alone. So utterly alone. I had never been so aware of myself, and so aware of the lack of anyone around me. I had little comprehension of what the time was – both to begin with, and in the hours that passed. I rubbed my hands together for warmth as the cold air around me made my aching body hurt all the more. Something cold and smooth rubbed back against my fingers. I held out my hand and saw the gold band wound around my finger. It had been forced on so roughly that my knuckle was red and raw. I stared down at the circlet, as the slow, numbing realisation of what had happened in that awful church dawned upon me afresh. Suddenly, the nightmare in which I found myself became filled with much darker implications. The horror of what had befallen me in that church was suddenly far more unbearable to me than my current imprisonment. My future, all my hopes and dreams screamed out in dismay upon seeing the miserable metal hoop upon my finger. I could not be married! Could one even be married without consent? Was that monstrous ceremony legally binding? Would a court of law take up my case – if I was indeed ever able to leave this prison cell? Thoughts and fears and questions tumbled around in my aching head, but the only one I could focus on was the thought that I was no longer my own person, no longer free to give my heart to whom I chose. I wept until weariness overcame me, and I fell asleep in the narrow room, my skull pressed against the cold, damp wall.

## THE STORY CONTINUED BY THE EDITON

A girl. Far from home. With no one to ask where she was.

Who watches over these lost souls? Who keeps them from utter wretchedness? Isabel did not know. She simply slept.

When Isabel awoke her head ached so sickeningly that she nearly retched. Tenderly touching the area where it hurt, she found she had a raised swelling where she had been hit. Her throat was dry and she reached for the clay jug of water beside her, thanking God that she had not knocked it over during her sleep. There was no cup, and the water was very stale but she was grateful for it all the same. However, she was not yet so hungry that she wanted to eat the dry bread crusts that nestled amongst the dirt and dust on the floor.

Feeling more refreshed, Isabel attempted to take stock of her situation. She knew that she must be many leagues from Harringdon, judging by the time she had spent in the carriage - and that she must be by the sea. The sea...she found herself thinking of Cathy and of their summer days at the beach, at Harringdon. Suddenly all those happy memories seemed to be slipping away from her and she felt herself falling into a deep abyss...This cannot be real, she told herself in an attempt to stay the rising darkness. It was a dream. Sir Branden, his men, the kidnap, the church...people did not behave like that in real life...

Trying to marshal her thoughts, Isabel looked around in an attempt to distract herself. The lavatory was old and looked unused. The walls were bare and patches of damp were visible in the plaster. There was one small window, set high up in the wall, but it was beyond her reach, and let in very little light. Feeling very weary, Isabel found her eyes closing and allowed herself to drift off into sleep.

When she awoke, she drank again from the small jug, draining it dry. That was foolish, she thought vaguely. She had no more water now. Head aching, she closed her eyes once more.

Dreams came amongst fitful waking. The hours passed slowly, and yet so fast as she slept and woke, slept and woke. The wall across from her was only two feet away and she stared and stared into the swirling patterns made by the spreading damp – hideous and curling, repeating, unsymmetrical lines of varying shades of brown. Her weary brain puzzled over the swirls, seeing shapes at first in the lines, and then, as the thirsty days passed - faces. At first it was unknown faces, but then they began to take on likenesses. There was Tom the gardener at Harringdon, and there was Mrs Ramsell, her dance teacher...then came the terrible faces, of the hooded vicar, and the men who had dragged her by her hair down that endless aisle. And last of all came Cathy and her aunt. Isabel wept then, and then wished she had drunk her tears, for she was so thirsty. She ate the crusts soon after that.

It was three days before Isabel was released. Sleep had deserted her by then and she heard the footsteps coming down the stairs, and the lock drawn open with a screech.

Rough hands hauled her out into a dark corridor and a foul rag was tied tightly over her eyes. She was pulled along and then up flights of stairs – one, two, three – she lost count. Her feet hung behind her as they dragged her upwards, banging against each step - but she was too exhausted to cry out or even attempt to struggle. She heard a door open and then she was thrown down upon the floor, with relish. However, this time, instead of hard cold stone, she felt something soft against her cheek. She sat up slowly, her head spinning, and tried to make sense of the different sensations impressing themselves upon her.

The first thing she noticed was the change in smell. No longer did the scents of damp and sewage abound – now the air was clean – nay, floral even. Isabel could smell the soft scents of fresh flowers. She closed her hand over the long luxurious fibres beneath it, and slowly realised she was sitting on carpet. She heard the door behind her open again and was aware of someone entering. Hands moved behind her head, untying the rag around her eyes and light flooded her vision. She blinked, and slowly a room came into focus, rich colours fighting to impress themselves upon her eyes.

She was sitting upon the floor of a large bedroom. Heavy pink velvet curtains were drawn across the wide window (she realised later that it was already evening) and a huge four-poster bed stood to the left of her, with floral hangings. Arranged around the room was expensive mahogany furniture, beautifully carved, and an extravagant dresser stood to her right. It was the most luxurious room Isabel had ever been in. A gilt washstand stood beside the dresser, filled with steaming scented water. Pure white towels with a wrapped piece of soap lay beside it. How she longed to wash herself – to feel clean and fresh after so many days of travel and torture. She turned to see who it was who stood behind her when her stomach suddenly lurched and growled. Her nostrils had caught the heady scent of cooked food somewhere nearby. She half-rose in her hunger, trying to identify where it was. Then, there – to the left of her, she saw it. Standing on a gleaming polished table was a silver tray holding a huge plate of roast beef, Yorkshire puddings and vegetables. A crystal decanter of wine stood beside it and her parched throat longed for even just one drop. Her stomach groaned with hunger.

'You are hungry,' a deep voice said.

She turned to find the towering figure of Sir Branden behind her. The other men had left. She stared up at him, fury surging through her, mingled with fear. He did not even seem to notice her expression as he smiled down at her.

'The food is for you,' he said smoothly. 'As is this room, and everything in it.'

Her anger subdued the fear and exhaustion within her and trembling with rage, she rose to her feet, standing with nothing but her self-possession to guard her.

'How *dare* you kidnap me,' she said, her voice shaking, yet she was surprised to hear the defiance in it. Red-hot fury and resentment rose up in her like a wave. 'How *dare* you force me to marry you - you have taken *everything* from me!'

Sir Branden waved her words away as if they were no more than puffs of smoke.

'Nonsense, I have taken nothing from you that was of any value. I have taken neither your life, your wealth, nor your sanity. I have simply relieved you from some foolish romantic notions, and granted in their place a title, a position, a comfortable home and every material thing your heart could desire.'

His voice was sleek, his tone coldly courteous. He glanced at her dishevelled form.

'I want you to know that I did not enjoy forcing you to marry me, Isabel. I would have rather you had naturally come to respect and wish to marry me on your own. But I saw from your rebellious and obtuse nature that that day would take too long to come -'

'- Never!' Isabel broke in, incensed.

'Excuse me?' he asked politely, his eyes glittering.

'That day would never have come,' she said, with furious resentment.

Sir Branden smiled, condescension lining his face, and carried on:

'You see, I was going to wait until after your cousin had married, but you forced my hand, Isabel. The only advantage to your planned escape was that you packed your own case for me.'

He motioned to the end of the bed, where her suitcase lay, small and forlorn-looking against the rich colours of the room. Isabel's heart gave a sudden leap at the sight of it. Inside were all her most precious items – her diary, her mother's bible, the book her father had given her – she had thought she would never see them again. Sir Branden saw her expression and stepped in front of her, blocking her sight of the case.

'As I was saying, force and coercion are not part of my nature, but you made them necessary. Should you behave in the manner expected of my wife from now on, no such measures will again be necessary.'

At his words, Isabel felt her legs begin to give way beneath her, exhaustion and sheer lack of energy sending her sinking back down to the floor.

'Why have you done this?' she said weakly.

Sir Branden paused behind her, and bent down, his lips at the level of her ear.

'Because I like beautiful things,' he said, in a voice that both thrilled and terrified her.

He rose and walked slowly around the magnificent room, past the gold-painted cabinets, the tall, intricately embroidered screen that stood in the corner, the expensive rocking chair, the satin hangings on the four-poster bed. Fresh, foreign flowers stood in a tall crystal vase on the bedside table – orchids, black lilies and frangipani – flowers that Isabel had heard of – read of - but never seen. Sir Branden brushed their petals with his fingers, filling the air with their expensive, intoxicating scents.

'Have you ever looked upon something of great beauty and wished it was your own,' he said, glancing over at Isabel, '– like a butterfly, settled upon a flower? You do not want to let it fly away, for then you will never see it again – so you catch it, and keep it in a glass so you can see it every day.'

Isabel could hear the soft beating of the butterfly's wings against the glass as he spoke, but then she realised it was her own heart, beating fast and furious under her gown. She shivered violently and Sir Branden paused in his circle around the room, turning to look at her.

'Be still,' he said softly.

Isabel tried to control her fear.

'You are my prize, Isabel, but not my prisoner,' he continued. 'I want you to have everything you could possibly desire.' His eyes met hers and led them on as he moved past a large wardrobe, its door ajar. Inside, Isabel could see luxurious fabrics, dresses and furs.

'You will be a showcase for London fashion, the envy of every woman in this country,' he said, smiling.

He then paused at the dresser. Here, it was not only the wood that gleamed. Upon the polished surface lay a vast number of necklaces, rings and earrings in their display boxes. Rubies, emeralds and sapphires of immense size sparkled at her. Hungry though Isabel was, she could not help but stare at them, so dazzling was their beauty.

'Yes, it is all yours,' he said, thoughtfully. 'In every sense. They have been waiting for you.'

Isabel was silent; weak and confused thoughts passed through her mind. Sir Branden turned to her, as if coming out of a reverie.

'This is your home now, Isabel. You are at Mount Enderton, my residence, and I want you to feel most welcome here. And now I will leave you and you can eat, refresh yourself and sleep. All I ask is that you will fulfil your rightful role and stay here, with me.' He stood directly in front of her, his height made all the more intimidating by her forlorn position on the floor. Isabel stared up at him - what choice did she have? ...But she must be strong. She glanced away from him, determined to resist. She looked at the comfortable bed, the hot water and towels and then, finally, at the plate of food. It was her undoing: all at once she felt her strength melt away.

'I will stay,' she said, her throat dry and cracked. It was all she could manage, but it was enough for him.

He left her then, and she ate and washed and slept, trying to think of nothing else but that she was much better off than she had been an hour ago, and pushing from her mind the thought that she had entered into a bargain she would very much regret.

# XIX

The sound of horses' hooves outside penetrated deep into Isabel's slumbers. Drowsily, she wondered if it was Cathy returning home. She turned in her bed. The duvet was soft and warm. She passed a hand over the satin covers and wondered why they were not her usual cotton ones. Had Cathy's maid changed them while she was sleeping? Rich, heady scents filled her nose and she opened her eyes slowly. Her heart sank. The nightmare was still before her – it had not been a dream. And yet, when had a dream looked so beautiful, and smelt so wonderful? Trying to focus herself, she glanced down to see the gold band around her finger. It reminded her of the deadliness, the treachery of this beauty.

The sound of more clattering hooves roused her and she got to her feet, slipping off the high bed. A pair of velvet slippers met her feet with a soft embrace. They fitted perfectly. Isabel pulled on the dressing gown that lay at the end of her bed and padded over to the window to see where she was.

Beautifully kept gardens stretched out as far as the eye could see, with tall oaks visible at the far end. She was on the third floor of the house, its walls of grey stone reaching far above and below her as she craned her neck to see its exterior from the bay window at which she stood. The driveway that she remembered from their arrival must have been at the other side of the house, and it sounded as though there was much activity going on there, as the sound of yet more horses and carriages met her ears.

Seeing no one outside, she turned her attention to the room itself. The first thing that caught her eye was a large painting in a heavy gold frame that hung in the right-hand corner. It was a painting of a medieval knight, his visor down, his sword drawn, ready for action. The colours were rich, the brushwork traditional, steeping the image in elegance and history. He was an Arthurian knight, his visor down to shield his eyes as he prepared to face an unseen danger. Isabel could picture his face underneath – kind, strong and fearless. It made her feel calmer to look upon him. He was the night of her childhood dreams, standing silent and steady amidst the turmoil that she had found herself thrust into.

She heard a soft sound behind her and turned to see that someone had slipped a note underneath her door. It was a small envelope, freshly sealed with red wax bearing the seal of an intricate coat of arms. Opening the envelope, she found a small card inside featuring the same coat of arms. It read, in an elegant scripted hand:

*'Be downstairs at 8 o'clock, dressed for dinner.'*

A chill ran down Isabel's spine. Checking the gold carriage clock that sat upon her bedside table, she saw that it was a quarter past seven. The thought of refusing the command did not even occur to her; she was too afraid of the consequences.

There was a rap on the door. Trembling slightly, Isabel opened it. An old woman in a smart maid's uniform stood at the door. She had watery, yellowish eyes and an ancient sunken face.

'What do you want?' asked Isabel, uncertain.

The maid gestured towards the open wardrobe. Isabel realised she was here to dress her. The thought of the old woman's hands upon her skin made her flinch.

'I will dress myself,' she said in as commanding a tone as she could muster.

The woman said nothing, but continued to stand in the doorway.

'Go away please,' said Isabel, beginning to close the door. 'I do not need your help.'

The woman took a step back and Isabel shut the door. She turned to face her wardrobe and, taking a deep breath, she headed towards it, opening the doors fully and staring at the wild profusion of colours that thrust themselves upon her: rich plum velvets, scarlet red satins, emerald silks and vibrant blue chiffons. She gazed in confusion as the colours assaulted her gaze, obscenely confident in their splendour. She felt terrified even to touch them lest the scarlet should drip from the satin and splash onto her pale skin. The gold clock ticked softly behind her. Half past seven. She must change now. Trembling slightly, she reached for a pale brown gown with gold stitching. It had a high neck and mid-length sleeves. Her hand shook as she lifted it out, sending waves down the expensive fabric.

At eight o'clock, when she opened the door, Sir Branden was waiting. He stood at the end of the corridor with four gentlemen she did not recognise, all expensively dressed and smoking cigars with glasses of champagne in their hands. They were standing around the head of the staircase and Isabel had no choice but to approach them. Her hands clutched at the fabric around her, pulling it a little closer.

She felt Sir Branden's gaze sweep over her as she walked towards them.

'Ah gentlemen, will you excuse me a moment,' he said suavely, breaking away from the group and coming towards her.

The men looked around and Isabel felt four pairs of appraising eyes look her up and down. Sir Branden met her halfway down the corridor, and she stopped, unsure of what to do. He stood before her, blocking her from the gaze of the other men, and laid his hand upon her arm, his black velvet dinner jacket giving him the appearance of a predatory panther. She felt his hand tighten upon her, and turning, he began to lead her back towards her room. She half-tripped on her hem, fear gripping her tighter than his hand. He spoke softly in her ear, his voice as smooth as silk:

'You look quite charming my dear, really, quite charming. But you are not a middle-aged woman. You are a beautiful young hostess, and my guests expect to see you looking your best, as I do. So why not take off the dress you are wearing, which is really more suited to be worn under a riding habit, and put on something a little more appropriate.'

Isabel raised her burning face to his. His expression was inscrutable. Sir Branden's hand was on her door handle now, her back against the door.

'Do you understand me?' he asked, his face inches from hers, his lips curling slightly upwards.

'I do,' she half-whispered, sliding herself through the door that he opened behind her.

'I am glad. I will expect to see you downstairs in half an hour. You are a jewel, my dear, and I expect you to shine.'

She was inside her room and he shut the door upon her, leaving her facing the closed wood panelling. The grain swirled before her eyes and the floor felt unsteady beneath her feet.

It was half past eight. A girl left Isabel's room and made her way to the top of the stairs. Her long hair was swept up into a high knot, the back of her neck bare, her white arms sparkling with gold and gems. The bright scarlet satin of her gown scooped low on her back and lower still at the front, embracing her tightly around her narrow waist. Her exposed shoulders were pale and beautiful against the colour of the fabric, and around her shapely neck hung a sparkling ruby the size of a guinea that gave off a deep glitter. The weightless fabric rippled down her body as she took her first step down the staircase.

Isabel felt bold, shameless; the red of the satin matching the scarlet in her cheeks. She felt as though she was wearing nothing at all, despite the fact that the material pulled tightly against her chest. The dress fitted like a glove – as though it had been made for her. Yet she had never worn anything like it in her life. She could feel blood pounding through her as she turned the curve of the staircase. Below stood a gathered group of men, drinking and smoking, dressed in lavish evening wear. She was descending into the lions, dressed like a woman of the Devil. And there – there in the centre was Sir Branden.

## ISABEL'S NARRATIVE
### *(Extract from Isabel's Diary)*

*ENDERTON, account written 19th July 1866*

Are you judging me?

Are you muttering that I should have made a stand, that I should not have subjected myself to him in this way?

If you are wondering if I was questioning myself – I was. Could I see any other option? No, I could not. I was alone and very much afraid.

Judge me if you will.

At dinner I sat at the head of the table, his hand resting on mine. Men leaned across the table to speak to him, their gazes grazing me from every angle. I spoke not a word, heard not a word, and barely moved, except to eat the food that was put before me (for I was still feeling very hungry). Absently, I took small sips of the wine before me and, almost too late, realised it was heady and strong. Immediately, I put it down and asked for water.

The meal was long, the courses never-ending. Stewed pigeons, grouse, mutton, jelly, Charlotte russe… on and on they came. Yet still I sat, upright and unfeeling. I was like a stone statue, my numbness protecting me from the all that lay without, and within.

Drinks and cigars followed. I had prayed that I might escape from this part of the evening, but his tight grip on my arm banished this hope from my mind. I sat stiffly in a leather armchair in his billiard room, the cold fabric hard and ungiving underneath me, the masculine conversations around me passing in snatches through my consciousness.

I glanced up at wearily at the clock that hung on the wall. The hands, stealing their way round the dial, pointed five to midnight. When the witching hour struck, I saw the men around me rise like figures in a dream world, and passing back into reality, I realised the night was over. With a sudden rush of energy, I rose and sought my captor's permission to leave. With a nod, he granted my request, smoke curling around him from the thick cigar in his hand.

'I will join you shortly,' he said to me.

I hardly heard his words in my rush to escape. In the huge mirror by the door, I saw that my dress flashed like fire as I left the room.

I moved swiftly up the carpeted staircase, when suddenly his parting words hit me like a tree falling. I stopped as though I had been struck. The fear had been there, creeping, slithering in the dark, but I had not understood it. I involuntarily scratched at the red satin that covered me like a second skin. I felt tainted, unclean – but the thought of him... No! I could not even comprehend it.

I began to move again, counting the steps to my door. I heard movement in the hall below and panic gripped me. I hauled up my skirts and began to run, faster and faster, and suddenly I was at my door. I thrust it shut behind me and retreated backwards, slowly, slowly - and then I was at my bed. I felt the satin skirts clinging to my legs and with a movement of disgust I stripped the foul fabric from my body. It lay in a heap at my feet, slowly sinking into hateful folds.

A noise at my door – I looked up in terror, but the person passed. I got into my nightgown and pulled it up high around my neck. I dared not blow the candles out, lest the fears that were pressing in on me danced their way into hideous reality amidst the darkness. So I lay on my back and prayed for dawn. The night could not last forever, I told myself. Morning must come.


### THE STORY CONTINUED BY THE EDITOR

Morning did come, and Isabel awoke, grateful beyond belief that none of her fears had been met. A breakfast was awaiting her upon a small table by her bed. The maid must have entered silently while Isabel had been sleeping. The thought sent a shiver up her spine. A note, in the same sealed envelope awaited her also. It read:

*'I imagine you are tired after your late night. Rest and then join me for lunch at one o'clock.'*

Isabel ate the food gratefully, and as she finished the last few mouthfuls, she suddenly remembered her suitcase. At first she could not find it and she feared that it had been removed to serve as some further torture, but at last she discovered it underneath the bed. She unfastened the buckles and breathed a sigh of relief to see her possessions still inside. Lovingly, she ran her ringers over the three books: her mother's Bible, her copy of *Songs of Innocence and Experience*, and her well-worn diary. It was this third book that she picked up first. She went over to the gleaming desk in the corner of the room and examined the inkwell. It was filled with fresh ink, a gold pen sitting on the side. Instinctively, she sat down, opened her diary, and began to write.

It was three hours later, when the clock had struck midday, that Isabel finally lay the pen down. The inkwell was nearly dry and many, many pages had been filled with her flowing hand. She had made an account of all the days that had passed since she left Harringdon – some of which you have already read. It had been hard – nay, hideous – to recall much of it, but somehow the writing of them had soothed her. Consigning them to paper meant that those times were in the past; they were finished. And although she knew that there was much more to come, for now, at least, she felt calmer.

A noise at the door made her look up. It was the maid from last night. She had an unpleasant smile upon her ancient face. Isabel realised it must be time for her to dress for lunch.

'Do not enter,' she said, standing up.

She was going to take control of this unwanted repeat visitor. Her voice was steady and her tone clear, unlike the previous evening.

'I want you to understand that I will be dressing myself today, and every day. I will be doing my own hair, and washing myself. You may bring me food, drink and hot water, and you will always knock before entering. I may be a prisoner in this house, but you will obey me. Do I make myself clear?'

The woman opened her lips – she had no teeth and a strange hissing noise emitted from her throat. Isabel stared at her in alarm, but the woman then turned and closed the door behind her. Isabel breathed a sigh of relief.

The next thing to do was to place her possessions out of sight. Looking around, Isabel saw drawers, cabinets, closets – but nowhere safe. She stared over at the knight - her knight - as if for help. He made no reply, yet his painted gaze, from behind his visor, was pointed upwards, fixed firmly upon a high shelf above the dresser. Isabel stared up at it. It was set beyond the reach of any man, and looked dusty, as though it had not been touched in years. If she placed her belongings up there, the books at least – the clothes did not matter – they would not be seen from below.

Clambering onto the dresser, Isabel stood up to her full height, marvelling at how tall the ceilings were in the room, and pushed her precious bundle of books onto the shelf with her fingertips, out of sight, but not out of her grasp. Something moved against her hand as she did so. Lifting it down, she realised it was a key. Making sure her books could not be seen, she climbed down again. The key was heavy and looked very old – it was thick with rust. It was too large to fit the wardrobe or any of the drawers in the room. Excitement suddenly filled her. Quietly, she went over to the door and tried the key in the lock. It fitted, and turned noiselessly as the latch clicked into place, giving Isabel the first peace of mind she had felt since arriving at Enderton. Finally, she was gaining some small measure of control.

Isabel came downstairs feeling far calmer than she had done the previous night. Morning had brought with it a sense of perspective, and having had time both to reflect and write, and also having found the key to her room, she felt strong enough to face whatever the rest of the day would hold. However, she did note for the first time, with a chill, the distance between her room and any other guests. She seemed to be alone on the third floor. She tried not to think of the reason for this.

When she reached the main hall, she was motioned towards a dining room at the back of the house by an austere-looking servant. He also spoke not a word to her, despite the several questions she put to him. The room she entered was much smaller than the banquet hall in which they had eaten the night before, but was still large and housed a long dining table at which Sir Branden was already seated. He rose and greeted her with an approving smile. Isabel had made an effort to make sure her day dress was one of the most elaborate available. She had decided to be amenable until she had found out more about her current situation.

'Please sit, my dear,' he said, pulling out the chair next to him. A large Newfoundland dog stood by his side. He growled as Isabel stepped towards them.

'Be quiet, Hadrian,' Sir Branden said in a commanding tone.

The moment she had sat down, the first course was placed in front of her by an unseen footman: vermicelli soup. This was one of Isabel's favourites and, finding herself quite hungry, she began to eat.

'I understand you have refused the help of your lady's maid?' he said impassively, watching her sip hot soup from the silver spoon.

'Only with certain tasks,' replied Isabel steadily. 'I have had many years of dressing myself and will continue to do so.'

Displeasure flickered across his face.

'You are my wife, Isabel, the lady of my house – you are expected to raise yourself above such tasks.'

Despite her revulsion at hearing him call her his wife, Isabel kept her temper under control.

'They are not tasks to me,' she said calmly. 'I enjoy them and I will look more presentable if I do it myself.'

Sir Branden's eyes narrowed, but he cast his eye over her and clearly approved of what he saw. She saw her chance.

'I want to look my best here at Enderton. I know what suits me better than an old maid.'

He nodded then, apparently satisfied that she was making reference to her new life without further protest. He gestured to the footman to pour him some coffee, staring at her profile as she continued to eat. She wished, once more, that she could prevent him from looking at her; his gaze was so intrusive it sent a chill down her spine.

The second course arrived: baked salmon. Isabel was pleased that she liked this dish also, but then she noticed Sir Branden's eyes flick towards her, awaiting her reaction. Too many things had fit perfectly at Enderton so far, she realised. The dresses, the slippers, the food... Suddenly she began to realise the extent of her aunt's treachery. Although not yet full, Isabel pushed the salmon away – she could not eat food tainted with betrayal.

'Are you not hungry?' he asked, his eyes narrowed.

'I am afraid I am not fond of salmon,' she said smoothly. 'In fact, I feel the need for some fresh air - especially as I have not had any for quite some time,' she added pointedly. 'Would I be able to go outside? I would like to see the grounds of your home and explore where I am going to be living.'

This notion seemed to please him.

'Of course,' he replied. 'And you must refer to it as our home now.'

Isabel rose from her seat, glad of the reprieve.

'Your will enjoy your explorations, I am sure,' he said as he began to cut into his salmon. 'The gardens are well looked after by the many gardeners I employ. They tend the plants almost every hour of the day to ensure they always look their best. Indeed, Enderton is the finest house for a hundred miles. Not, of course, that this has anything to do with the fact that there are hardly any other dwellings within a hundred miles,' he added with a smile, as though he had made a pleasant joke.

Isabel smiled sweetly back, well aware that he had just told her in no uncertain terms that there would be eyes on her every step of the way, and that there was little point in attempting to escape, for there was nowhere to go. Whether that was true or not, she was determined to find out for herself.

'Thank you, Sir Branden. I will see you at dinner,' she replied pleasantly.

Mount Enderton was a labyrinthine house, ancient in every sense. Isabel's first impression of the residence, as she surveyed it from the lawn that afternoon, was one of stern grandeur. Its huge walls were built from vast blocks of grey stone, and rose some six storeys high, with Gothicised octagonal towers at either end and castellated parapet along the front. Tall, leadlight windows in a variety of styles punctuated the walls - from extravagant coloured-glass designs on the lower casement windows, to simple pointed panes on the upper floors. The lines of the building were clean and elegant, yet robustness and strength emanated from its immense size. The great front doors stood open to reveal a lofty entrance hall, flanked by marble pillars, and a pair of crossed swords hung above the doorway. The elegance of the house welcomed Isabel; its sternness repelled her, yet she could not fail to be impressed. It was a most beautiful prison.

Behind her ran a broad and handsome avenue, flanked with elms, which ran down from the house to an ivied gatehouse flanked by high stone walls. Through the open doorway of the gatehouse, Isabel could spot the tiniest blue gleam of the sea that lay just beyond, visible as the steeply sloping road dropped away.

Around the house, gardens spread like ripples, each more inviting than the next. Enticingly scented herb gardens lay to the west, while to the north there was a large arboretum several acres in length, populated with a whole host of ancient and magnificent oak, ash and beech trees. A walled garden stood next to this, with rockeries behind, and to the east was a gardenesque style garden. Glasshouses ran along the west side of the house filled with all manner of exotic flowers and seedlings. Elaborate sculptures, statues and sundials were scattered around as Isabel passed from one garden to the next. Finally she reached the stables and coach house at the far side of the house, which were modern and well kept. Wondering at the sheer size of the ample estate, she completed her circle of the house by arriving at the entrance once more. She could see no movement inside, apart from Hadrian padding down the stairs, and she decided that there was no reason why she should not also explore the interior of the house also.

Inside Mount Enderton, all was cleanliness, delicacy, and elegance. No servants were visible as Isabel moved from room to room, unobserved and undisturbed. The ballroom was the loftiest she had ever seen – five chandeliers of varying sizes were suspended in perfect beauty from the high ceiling. Sunlight hit the crystals through the tall arched windows and the glass blazed red and blue, casting sparkles upon the gleaming wood floor. The large dining room she had already been in the night before, but in her discomposure, she had not noticed the elaborately carved wooden ceiling, the huge tapestries on the walls, or the tall chairs with their backs sculpted in intricate Gothic designs. The table was laid for dinner, last night's meal already a ghost, and the linen tableware and napkins were all embroidered with the Branden coat of arms that she recognised from Sir Branden's letters.

The drawing room was sumptuous, laid with thick carpet and filled with armchairs upholstered in red velvet. The morning room next door had a crescent of bay windows that looked out over the arboretum and was filled with comfortable day chairs. The billiard room, which looked less imposing in the daylight, was long and elegant, with dark wood panelling throughout. Next-door was a wide breakfast room with tall French doors and an elegant table in the centre. Isabel glanced into the room in which they had eaten that morning, which was now empty, the tables cleared. She had almost visited every room on the ground floor – all but one.

She knew it must be a small room from its corner position at the back of the house. She pushed the door open with a creak and entered. The pleasant stillness of the glass-filtered sunlight gave Isabel a sense of peace before she had even realised where she was. Half-remembered memories of childhood filled her senses as she closed her eyes and breathed in the cool, secretive scent of the beeswaxed wood. She had found the library.

It was an exquisite oak panelled room, with books stretching from floor to ceiling, many accessible only by the sliding ladder that ran round the glass-covered shelves. A thick burgundy rug ran underfoot, ensuring utter silence, and well-worn leather chairs sat comfortably around the edges of the bookshelves. There was one tall diamond-paned window in the corner, with a wide window seat set into it.

She walked round the shelves, her eyes scanning the books. There was everything from Shakespeare to Diderot. She smiled as she opened one cabinet door and picked out the text she had been reading at

Harringdon – *The Mysteries of Udolpho*. She opened it up at the page she had last read and within a few moments was immersed in the story, her feet tucked up underneath her as she settled down into the window seat. She knew that she should not take pleasure from anything in the house but somehow this felt different from the food and the clothes. This book was here by chance, and if anything, Sir Branden would not be pleased that she was reading such fiction. This was her own private pleasure and she would not deny herself the only comfort available to her in her confinement.

It was not until several hours later, when she heard movement in the hall outside that Isabel rose. She was about to check that the way was clear to return to her room, when a collection of maps in the cabinet by the door caught her eye. She fingered through the titles and then pulled out one titled 'Enderton'. On the front spread she could see the house by the sea, its title marked in black ink. Then, kneeling down upon the floor, she unfolded and unfolded the map, trying to find the next dwelling in the vicinity. It was 40 miles out that she finally found a small village labelled 'Carstone'. Sir Branden had not been lying when he said the estate was isolated.

She was in the south west of the country, at least four hours from Harringdon (although she had guessed that from the journey). She had never been so far south before and knew little of the area, not that she supposed that she would be seeing much of it. Even if she did attempt to escape, where would she go? She could not trust her aunt, and she had no real friends to take her in. She thought of Mr Arthur and Mrs Tabitha, but she had no addresses for them, even if she could escape. The rebellion rising in her chest was quenched by cold, undeniable fact. She was trapped. But she stored an image of the map in her mind, just in case it ever came in useful. Then she folded it up and left the room.

She met no one on her way up the stairs although she could hear people either arriving or returning at the front of the house. There were no carriages this evening and she realised that the men who had dined with them last night must be staying again. There was a half-expected letter awaiting her when she opened the door. She sliced it open using a gilt letter-opener that lay on the side.

*'I hope you are impressed with the house and grounds. I sent the guests out so that you could have freedom to explore in peace. Dinner is at eight o'clock.'*

Isabel realised that this would be her evening routine from now on. Resignedly, she chose a shimmering gold gown from the wardrobe.

# XX

*'He hath hedged me about, that I cannot get out: He hath enclosed my ways with hewn stone.'*

*Lamentations* (Chapter 3, verses 6-9), King James Bible

Life at Mount Enderton was unusual, to say the least. It was like a continual house party, or gentlemen's club. There were never less than twenty visitors – always gentlemen, who were clearly wealthy – and they passed through either on their own, or in groups, after staying for varying lengths of time.

Every morning the house rustled with morning papers, and by night it was filled with clouds of drifting cigar smoke. During the day, the myriad of activities on offer varied from shooting to riding, hunting to fishing, or long hikes along the beautiful coastline that Isabel was never allowed to see. The men seemed to use the house as a kind of retreat, an escape from their everyday lives.

As she had done with her aunt, Isabel puzzled over the men's relationship with Sir Branden. At first she thought they were visitors of leisure, but as she padded back and forth throughout the house as the days passed, she noticed that there were frequent visits made to Sir Branden's study by many of the guests. She picked up that some of the men were involved in the London stock market. It was clear that Sir Branden was very rich and therefore was probably involved in some form of trading. Although, from the number of different areas that these men were involved in, it seemed as though Sir Branden had a finger in every financial pie, if these were indeed business conversations that took place. And yet, for a man who clearly did not like to be alone in his own house, he did not spend much time with any of his guests apart from these brief meetings, and kept to his study when they departed on their regular day trips. The visitors seemed to act as a kind of façade, creating an illusion of sociability around a very private man. But each night, Sir Branden struck an impressive figure at the head of the long table, his collection of guests treating him with an air of respect, bordering on reverence.

It was clear that their Sir Branden was, in every respect, a powerful man, and the men around him, firmly in his grasp. In any other similar environment, surrounded by so many men in such a large house, Isabel might have feared for her safety – or at least her virtue - but despite there always being an admiring eye, she was safe in the knowledge that no one else would ever have dared overstep the mark with her, for fear of the repercussions from their host. Should any of the guests spend too long with her, or say anything untoward, there would be a sudden moment of silence, an uneasy glance around, and then they would slink away, avoiding her for the rest of their stay. Who or what they saw in the shadows, she was never quite sure. However, while the guests were, for the most part, nothing to complain about, there was a subtle oppressiveness at Mount Enderton, a sense of being utterly feminine amongst a very masculine pack, that meant that soon Isabel began to long for the sound of a female voice. She was a revered outcast, admired and very much alone.

It was therefore with some favourable anticipation that Isabel looked forward to the announcement of a ball, to be held at Mount Enderton in two weeks time. Sir Branden held such a ball methodically each quarter, to which all his many acquaintances and their partners were invited.

On the night of the ball, Isabel enjoyed the strange independence of her situation for the first time. She realised that, had the situation been more favourable, her position would have been every girl's dream. Her room seemed even more beautiful, with fresh flowers on every table and every jewel she could possibly want to wear at her disposal. A gorgeous new turquoise-coloured gown had appeared in her room when she returned from the library. It was a strikingly modern design and as she admired herself in the mirror, Isabel was very aware of the noticeable curves that the dress showed off, emphasising aspects of her figure that she had not appreciated before. As she set off from her room, she was relieved to see that Sir Branden was not waiting outside and, exhilarated, descended the stairs, looking forward to female company and conversation, however frivolous.

The house was brightened by the sound of female voices as she came down the staircase, though she did notice a hush when she entered the ballroom, and a sense of turning away. The hired orchestra began to play a lively waltz; a hand was offered and Isabel began to dance, a sense of bright hopefulness rising with in her. However, as the night progressed, while the female guests treated her with the greatest of respect and eyed her with much curiosity, they never once engaged her in conversation, instead taking pains to ensure that there was no opportunity to do so. After several futile attempts, Isabel gave up, feeling frustrated. The only positive aspect of the night was that Sir Branden never danced with her, leaving Isabel free to enjoy the music and energy of the dancing. However, this sense of freedom began to dissipate as she noticed his fixed position in the corner, his eyes always upon her, the guests always keeping his view of her undisturbed. The look of possession in his eyes repulsed her.

The moment the last note of the final dance played, he stepped across the dance floor and claimed her for his own. Age and power mingled with youth and beauty as they walked through the parting crowd to the dining room. He kept her on his arm for the rest of the night, until she was finally allowed to retire at an early hour of the morning. The women stayed that night only, for when Isabel awoke the next morning, they were gone.

## ISABEL'S NARRATIVE
*(Extract from Isabel's Diary)*

*ENDERTON 10<sup>th</sup> August 1866*

Lonely. Beautiful and lonely – that is what this house is. It is big enough to hold a small world within its walls, is filled with a continual stream of guests, and yet I am desolate.

Not even the servants will speak a word to me. They are like ghosts – almost entirely unseen and flitting from one room to another. They chill me too. I have not heard one of them speak a word since I arrived. Not a single word! Having grown up in a house where the servant's voices rang from every room, this unnerves me. But while I admit that Greenwood House was unique, surely most servants converse at some point during the day? The thing is, I do not think they can speak.

The only conversation I have, is to exchange a few words with Sir Branden at breakfast, lunch and dinner. He seems less provocative than he was at Greenwood. I like him no more for it – indeed, I despise him for what he has done to me - but for the moment there is no reason to cause a disagreement, when he is so completely in control. I am beginning to comprehend that this is not a visit, not another school term, but my life now. The enormity of this terrifies me, though I am determined not to accept it indefinitely.

Four Sundays have now come and gone. I asked in my first week if I might attend a local church, even with supervision, but Sir Branden refused quite absolutely. When I persisted, he became angry.

'I will not temporise on this matter with you,' he said, impatience riddling his voice. 'My word is final.'

The thing is, I have not even been reading my Bible as I used to. Each day when I reach for my diary on the shelf, my hand skims the top of it. It was not until yesterday that I realised I was brushing over a layer of dust. I know I should read it, but somehow it seems like an object from a different world; alien and irrelevant, its old comfort too childlike to be of any use to me now. I feel that even the immovable things in my life are slipping away from me.

The memory of being dragged down the aisle still wakes me in the middle of the night. I tell myself, it was only a dream, and the violence has ended. He has what he wants, I hope. A young wife to adorn his palace. Yet when he looks at me, there is no sense of conclusion, of satisfaction. I feel as though he is waiting for something...

My days are filled with wandering. My body wanders through the gardens (which are growing dry from a lack of rain during these hot summer months) and also through the house. When there are fewer guests during the week, the floors are filled with empty rooms. In one sense it reminds me of my early years at Greenwood. But there is no sense of security here. Growing up, no matter how far I had tucked myself away into a room, I was always aware of a loving presence – likely my caring servants – although I thought it my parents at the time. Here, all is cold and unfriendly and I am no more than a shadow.

My mind wanders through the books. There are many that I have not read that I am working my way through. The library is my refuge, the one place where I feel at home. Sir Branden must have realised that I love this place and today there were several new volumes on the table – shiny leather-bound versions of some new women's fiction from London. While I admit they looked interesting, out of spite I ignored them and turned to the old classics. I may have little control over my life in this house, but I do have free will over what I read, which I will exercise.

As an aside, he asked me the other day if I would like some embroidery materials. I replied coolly that I do not sew.

'Then perhaps some easels and paints,' he attempted.

I informed him that neither do I paint.

'Then what do you do?' he said, a hint of exasperation in his voice which he did not trouble to hide.

I turned to face him and replied that I used to do exactly as I pleased. He did not bother me again after that.

After these daily explorations, it is time for dinner. We eat, sometimes with guests and sometimes by ourselves in the smaller dining room. And so the clock tolls on into the evening. I feel it does so out of frustration as I sit in silence, waiting to be allowed to leave. There is no memorable event for it to mark, no interesting conversation for it to time, nothing to do but to tick on, and on, into the endless evening. I am haughty and alone. That is, haughty through choice (my natural protective fallback) and alone through imposition.

Will I be trapped here forever? I think my voice might vanish from lack of use.


## THE STORY CONTINUED BY THE EDITOR

It was the last day of summer, remarked one of the guests as they sat at breakfast. But somehow it felt too hot - almost unnaturally so. By 11 o'clock the skies outside were dark, black clouds hovering ominously overhead, waiting to break.

The house was unusually silent that morning as the guests retired to their rooms, too warm to partake in any activities. Isabel wandered from room to room, listless, alone – like a pale white ghost in an abandoned house. It was so quiet she could hear the soft breathing sounds of the house as she padded around in her soft pumps. Too hot to sit still, she kept moving around from one ground floor room to another, although even when she moved, no breeze was created. She seemed to walk from one wall of heat into the next.

Her hair hung limply on her damp skin, her body's moisture causing her muslin dress to cling unbearably. She opened the drawing room window in the unlikely hope of a puff of air, but the light wind that had stirred the trees at breakfast had died away, leaving behind a dead calm of sultry heat that prevailed inside and out. Everything had slowed down, hanging motionless in time. Everyone was waiting, waiting, the heat rising to an unbearable level. An oppressive sweet smell rose from the geranium bushes outside the window. Her head felt like it was about to burst; a tight pain pounded behind her eyes. She could hear the sound of silence all around her, the sound of nothingness, so loud she could almost touch it. It disturbed her. Surely this could not hold?

Far, far off in the hills, she heard a distant rumbling approach, and the windowpanes rattled gently with the ancient call of the storm. Then – it broke.

The thunder rolled across the countryside like a roaring lion at full speed, racing to devour its prey. The lightning cracked, violent and shattering, splitting the sky in a great chasm of light. And the rain fell like an ocean bursting from the black skies, crashing through the leaves of the tall oaks, cascading down the steep roof of the house and striking the earth with aggressive force.

Isabel stared out at it all. The world bellowed before her; the rain, held back for so long, was venting its anger on the parched landscape.

Dust transformed to drops in an instant, brooks into rivers, the aligning thirsty trees bending down to welcome the much-anticipated deluge.

The blinding strikes of lightning above lit the scene up for a moment – and in that moment the landscape transformed. Suddenly she was no longer looking at Enderton – but a separate world of blistering light and water – a magnificent display of power and surrender. And then it was England again, dark and furious in the face of the overpowering downfall. But the thunder bellowed its dominance and the land was subdued.

The rain fell for hours until every last drop had been hurled and every thunderous echo faded. And Isabel watched from the window, feeling very small, until the world returned to its familiar state.


## ISABEL'S NARRATIVE
### (Extract from Isabel's Diary)

*ENDERTON, 20th August 1866*

I thought that life here had settled into its lonely, luxurious pattern, but a most unwelcome figure reappeared today: Gaunt.

To make matters worse, he was not alone. He was accompanied by the men who had taken me so forcibly from Harringdon and ensured that I stood before Sir Branden at that false altar, despite my struggles. Their faces swam before me, as they have done so often in my dreams these past weeks. They all seem to have been away on a long journey, but Gaunt is now a fixed presence at Sir Branden's side. He greeted me with his usual obsequious smile and welcomed me as 'Lady Branden'. The title sent shivers down my spine, but I knew he was only trying to rouse me. Seeing him again reminded me of that terrible episode in the church that I have tried so hard to forget. He frequently glanced down at my ring during dinner, as though reminding me of my entrapment. I could feel it getting tighter upon my finger – it was only the heat - but I imagined it gripping me ever tighter, burning its mark upon me. I have often considered taking it off, but the thought of Sir Branden – or worse now – Gaunt's hands upon me once more, flesh upon flesh, put that idea to rest.

His presence seems to have re-awoken an unpleasant look in Sir Branden's eye that I have not seen since that terrible night. A shadow seems to have fallen over the house. I sense that this brief period of relatively peaceful imprisonment may be at an end.

*(Entry added later that evening)*

Tonight, the knocking began.

## THE STORY CONTINUED BY THE EDITOR

Let me go back to earlier that evening. Isabel was not wrong when she predicted that things were about to change at Mount Enderton with the arrival of Gaunt and those other unwelcome, familiar faces. The interested male gazes that she had previously been subjected to at Enderton were now replaced by openly hostile, leering expressions. Many of the regular guests left upon the arrival of this band and their ringleader. It was obvious that these men were of a much lower class than the usual standard of guests, and their presence was little appreciated by anyone except Sir Branden.

Dinner that night was long and tedious. The conversation was lewder than Isabel was used to, made bawdy by the group who had arrived that day. Isabel gathered that their names were – Messrs Cugh, Knowles, Lursted, Ratch and Drent – there were no members of the aristocracy amongst this group. The other guests filtered away quietly once dinner had ended while Branden retired with these six men to his study, taking Isabel with him. Gaunt accompanied them, silent, but alert.

The wine flowed more freely than usual after dinner and soon bottles of whiskey and gin were called for which also went down in abundance. While Branden joined in the conversation infrequently, he seemed to enjoy the men's company, though Isabel wondered greatly at his choice of companions. He also seemed to be enjoying the drinks on hand, which surprised her as he normally only took one small glass of wine. She watched him from her chair at the back of the room as he sat there in his great armchair, acting the Lord. She hated him for making her sit in a room with the very men who had treated her so inhumanly only a few weeks before. Now that she saw them in a less frightening situation, she realised that they were little more than commonplace thugs, with little intelligence and even fewer manners. She despised them.

It was not yet gone twelve, and Isabel was not normally allowed to leave until after midnight, but she was tired and irritated by the present company.

'I am going upstairs,' she announced in a loud, clear voice.

The men looked round to find her standing behind them. She looked at them coldly and then met Sir Branden's eyes. He looked a little startled, but displeased. She decided she would take his silence as an assent and ignore the angry warning in his eyes. Turning, she made her way to the door and found Gaunt standing before it.

'Get out of my way,' she said succinctly.

He glanced at Sir Branden and then moved aside. Isabel heard murmurs from the room as she left, which grew to a riot of noise as she made her way up the stairs. When she reached her room, she fetched the key, closed the door and locked it, feeling uneasy.

It was as she blew out the last candle that she heard the noise. A slow tap, tap, soft at first, so soft that she could not be sure at first where the noise was coming from, and then growing steadily stronger, like a steady drum beat. She froze, the wick in front of her still glowing red-hot in the darkness. There was a pause – another heavy knock, and then a hand reached for the handle. It turned - she could almost sense the anticipation – but the locked door would not open. The handle lifted and was then drawn down again, to no avail. She could taste blood on her tongue where she had bitten into her lip. It tasted of repulsion and fear. A few moments later, soft as a shadow, she heard the footsteps retreating.

ISABEL'S NARRATIVE
*(Extract from Isabel's Diary)*

*ENDERTON, 21st August 1866*

At first I could not account for the slow, creeping fear that prickled up my spine when the knocking began – softly, so softly. Then I realised with a rush that I knew full well who stood outside my door, and that I knew what he wanted from me.

I realise now that I had almost been expecting it, ever since his words to me after the first dinner. I told myself then he had said he would join me simply for the sake of appearance. I am aware that some husbands and wives do not have separate rooms (my parents did not). Why that was…well, I had never fully explored that notion, never having had any reason to, but now ... I admit that I know more about it than I thought I did.

I act with confidence during the day, dressed in my fine clothes, wearing my painted smile. But at night, in this unfamiliar house, I feel no more than a child. I sat in the rocking chair after he left and rocked myself back and forth for a long while, trying to find some comfort in the motion. My feet touched the floor this time, but I felt no less alone than I had done that afternoon, so many years ago, when my parents left me.

## THE STORY CONTINUED BY THE EDITOR

It took every ounce of courage Isabel had to dress and go down to breakfast the next morning. When she entered the room, Sir Branden did not greet her. She glanced at him, half-hidden behind his paper, Hadrian at his feet. He was dressed elegantly in his usual black, his silver-streaked hair swept back, as always, in perfect neatness. He turned the pages of the paper in a calm, unhurried way, yet every inch of him posed a quiet and terrible threat. She wanted to recoil. She wanted to turn and to run as far away from him as she could. But he looked up at her, his grey eyes glinting, challenging, and very quickly and quietly she sat down.

Isabel went to the library earlier than usual that day, for it was raining heavily outside and she did not fancy her usual morning walk in the gardens. It was the sort of day that she enjoyed spending reading – when the world outside closed in on itself and her paper worlds opened up. She picked out *The Vampyre* by Henry Colburn, finding the foreign title intriguing. She had not heard of the book before, but it was described as a 'thrilling tale' in the introduction and she looked forward to the distraction. It was indeed a thrilling story, and she read quickly, losing herself in the fantastical adventure. It told the story of Lord Ruthven, an aristocratic fiend of mysterious origins who preyed upon beautiful young women. He was a creature quite unlike any Isabel had read of before and dark undertones ran deliciously through the novel. The story carried her from intriguing beginning to breathless ending in just a few hundred pages and she enjoyed it immensely. By the time she left the library, she felt almost normal once more.

After dinner that night, Isabel was allowed to leave the company earlier than usual, the men obviously wishing to be freed from her censorious presence. She ran quickly up the stairs, climbed onto the dresser and reached for the key, feeling a rush of relief when her fingers grasped the cold steel: it was still there. She climbed down and locked the door, breathing a little more easily.

Her room was dim, lit only by a couple of candles, and having changed into her nightdress, she slid into bed. This was the time that she usually enjoyed most at Enderton: the soothing hush of night when everyone else was downstairs and she had time to herself, safe in the knowledge that her door was firmly locked. However, the solitude that she usually revelled in felt less pleasurable to her tonight. She lit the candle by her bed; the wick caught and the flame steadied, but then began to sway. The darkness seemed alive tonight. Indeed, as the minutes crept by and she sat in silence, she realised that the night felt like a horror to her, the dark room seemed filled with shadowy terrors. Again and again she told herself she was safe. The door was locked: he could not get in.

The fears of the previous night crowded round her in the growing shadows, suddenly becoming much more vivid than they had been in the bright light of day. A slithering noise came from inside the wardrobe, soft and unnatural. A prickle ran down Isabel's spine. Summoning her courage, she got to her feet and approached the wardrobe. She opened the doors to find that her satin dress had slipped from its hanger to the floor. Shaking her head, she hung it up again, and then jumped, promptly dropping it again. There was a rattling noise at the window. Leaving the dress on the floor, she pulled back the curtain slightly and gazed out to find a small bat fluttering by the glass. She knew they nested in the roof above. Berating herself for her foolish fears, she closed the curtains, hung up the dress and got back into bed, her feet cold from the bare floor.

Leaving the candles burning, she tried to close her eyes, hoping that sleep would come quickly - but her mind carried her, against her will, back to the story she had read that afternoon. Those delightful fears that had risen up as she had read, that had been so much fun to tangle with, now began to take terrible, full-bodied form in the darkness. The tale which had seemed so fantastical, almost laughable in the daylight hours, suddenly felt much less distant, much more believable as she lay there, waiting for the knocking to begin. She suddenly wished she had not read even half the pages she had of *The Vampyre*. They had been safe then, contained within their paper borders, but her imagination felt ravaged and exposed now.

She opened her eyes again, afraid of the dreams that might come, but sleep had its grasp upon her brain and began to pull her back towards the abyss. The figures of Sir Branden and Lord Ruthven began to converge in her mind as she tried to fight the oncoming tide of oblivion. A man stood below her window, three floors down.

'I am safe; he cannot get in,' she murmured uncertainly.

But the figure rose up, half flying, half climbing, a black cloak billowing out behind him in the wind. He was outside her window – with a flick of his gloved hands, the panes shattered and he glided inwards and across the room, ready to take her, to consume her as she lay motionless on the bed.

Isabel woke up with a start. She gazed round in panic, but there was no one there. A noise came from under her bed and she curled her legs into herself, sleep still clouding her brain. The noise came again. She could not bear to look into the darkness underneath her bed. Trembling, she picked up the drinking glass that sat on her bedside table. She laid it on its side and with a push, set it rolling across the floor underneath her bed. Meeting no obstacle, it came rolling out the other side. A mouse followed out after it. She breathed a heady sigh of relief, and settling back into her pillows, sleep claimed her once more.

## ISABEL'S NARRATIVE
### (Extracts from Isabel's Diary)

### ENDERTON, 24*th* August 1866

Now that the terrors have entered my mind, I cannot get rid of them. Indeed, they seem to become more real every day, almost as if he knows what dwells inside my head. I had despised him, but now I fear him.

### ENDERTON, 26*th* August 1866

Last night, he entered my room. I was getting ready for dinner and had not locked the door as the maid had been gathering up my clothes for washing and I had forgotten to lock it after she left. He came in so silently I did not see him until his image entered the mirror into which I was looking as I brushed my hair. I did not know what to do, so I remained sitting at my dressing table, the brush in my hand. He came up behind me, so close, and took the silver brush from me, laying it down on the table. I placed my empty hands in my lap, trying to resist the trembling that had come upon me. He began to sink his hands into my hair, his touch light and terrible, sweeping my hair up high upon the top of my head so that my neck was completely exposed.

'Such a beautiful girl,' he murmured, freeing a hand to run a finger along my cheekbone and then along the red curve of my lower lip. I could feel his body pressed into mine.

He stared at my reflection so intently. I remained quite still, praying that he would leave me, curbing the thought that he might not. It seems strange, but he seemed almost not to notice my physical presence, but continued to gaze deep into the glass at my parallel self for what seemed like hours. Finally, with a swift movement he let my hair fall softly down where it hung long over my shoulders.

'I have a gift for you,' he said, addressing me for the first time.

He placed an open box in front of me that contained a pair of dazzling ruby and diamond earrings. They sparkled deeply.

'Wear them,' he said in a deep, resonant tone. 'I will see you shortly.'

Bending down low over me, he kissed my bare shoulder. Then, softly, he walked out of the room and closed the door behind him.

I sat still, continuing to tremble; and then, almost mechanically I lifted the brush from the table and continued to brush my hair, counting out the remaining strokes of my usual hundred. I did not know what else to do.

I hardly noticed anything that evening, except his eyes upon me. I wondered how Lord Ruthven's victims had felt as they fell prey to him. Before too long, I found myself back in my room again. I stood numbly by the locked door, and then began to undress for bed, taking the heavy earrings from my ears. I turned them on the palm of my hand; this way and that, watching the candlelight catch them, feeling the weight of the stone and the cool touch of the yellow gold. Then it came - his step outside the door, his hand leaning on the handle, then feeling it locked, he went on his way. When I heard the retreating footsteps, I began to shake, the rubies glinting as I trembled. He knew the door would be locked; he wanted only to terrorise me. When I looked down at the shaking jewels, I saw Branden's eyes staring out of them. With a cry, I hurled them against the wall where they hit off the skirting board and rolled under the wardrobe.

I saw them in my dreams that night – burning red eyes staring at me from under the wardrobe. I tried to retrieve them this morning to dispose of them properly, but they had rolled too far for me to reach.

## THE STORY CONTINUED BY THE EDITOR

The next few weeks stumbled by in a tangle of panic, fear and confusion. Every night Isabel expected her door to be forced open, but it was not; every morning she expected a rebuke, but none came. She did not understand – she was one young woman with a key, and he was the Lord of the manor, with the whole household at his disposal. Why did he not manage to get past her feeble defences? And yet, while she was glad he had not overcome her, somehow the waiting was worse than the inevitable ending.

The thought of running away presented itself to her once again. Yet, even with the obstacles of distance, transport, and the terrible consequences of getting caught – one impediment loomed larger than all the others.

Gaunt had become the echo to her every footstep since he had returned. Solitude, which had plagued her for so long, was now a stranger to her. While Isabel was sure that Sir Branden had ordered this surveillance, there was no doubt that Gaunt took a savage pleasure in his task. She could not deny, even to herself that she was afraid of him, but his incessant tailing roused anger in her. Finding him in the library – her library - at the very hour in which she would usually seek solace in its pages – her temper broke.

'I wish to use this room alone,' she said angrily, noting that he had taken her favourite position at the window, his slovenly clothes conflicting with the plush green cushions that lined the window seat.

'I do not take orders from you,' he said curtly, not moving.

'Have you forgotten, or did you and your foul companions not make me the Lady of this house?' she said contemptuously.

'As I said, I do not take orders from you.'

He discordant eyes met hers and then he turned and slowly slid out one of the books from the shelves. It was *Lady Audley's Secret,* the very book that Isabel had been reading yesterday. He opened it, letting her bookmark fall to the floor, his loathsome hands fingering the new pages and leaving stains behind. Her eyes clouded in anger.

'Oh, run back to your master, you dog!' she cried, and unable to bear it any longer, she turned on her heel, slamming the door behind her.

Burning with frustration, she turned into the gardens. Autumn was coming, but it was still warm and she needed no coat. Taking advantage of her momentary freedom, she walked further than usual, over acres of manicured lawns, until she met the open fields. Unwilling to attempt an escape for freedom with nothing but the clothes on her back, she lay down upon the short soft grass, still within the boundary of Enderton's gardens. The sun was warm upon her arms as she looked up at the clouds moving across the sky.

Time seemed to pass so slowly as she lay there. A second gone, another second gone. She counted them in her head and watched them pass before her eyes, swept along by the clouds. A minute gone, another minute gone, and nothing changed, except that her memory

161

was fuller – crammed with more emptiness. A question crossed her dull mind - does time pass us, or do we pass through time?

Slowly losing her grip on reality, she began to wonder if it was the clouds that were moving, or was she? She felt suddenly dizzy and clutched at the strands of grass underneath her hands as though they would support her, hold her to the earth. Was she lying flat, looking down - or standing up, with a wall of grass at her back? Was she about to fall into a scudding pit of blue and white? Her stomach lurched and she sat up.

'Truly, I am going mad in this place,' she said to no one.

The sun went out before her very eyes.

'Oh no, not yet,' came a voice as she blinked and stared up in front of her.

A black silhouette burned itself into her vision: it was Gaunt.

'That comes later,' he said with a sly smile. 'For now, your husband commands that you return to the house to dress for dinner. Oh,' he added as she made to move, 'I enjoyed the book.'

Isabel jumped to her feet and ran back, before he could follow her.


ISABEL'S NARRATIVE
*(Extracts from Isabel's Diary)*


*ENDERTON, 16th September 1866*


I think they can read my mind. Every time I even think of running away, Gaunt is there, by my side, leaving me with no-where to turn. He watches me with such a malicious scrutiny, and is almost pestilential in his adherence to me. I can smell the vile odour of his breath even when I go to sleep at night. I wonder if he lies by my door.

For they are of one mind – that man and his dog. Branden hardly has to speak a command and Gaunt has carried it out. And yet I hardly understand his role – for it is more than a manservant, and yet as menial. I know he dresses Branden (how strange that such slovenliness produces such perfect grooming), yet attends all his meetings. He never eats with us, and yet is in the billiard room every night, along with all the other invitees. He even goes on errands to London for his master (not often enough for my liking), though for what business I do not know.

I have never seen a servant so devoted to his master, yet somehow it is not in a healthy way. He seems intensely jealous of anything that holds Branden's affection, even Hadrian. I was called to Branden's study this afternoon (as I have been most days this week), to assist him with some menial letter-writing tasks. He seems to prefer to have me near him during the day now, most likely to allow him to keep an eye on me. Gaunt knocked and then entered, coming over to the desk where we sat (as far apart as I could manage), my attention focused on the addresses and stamps which I was applying liberally.

While Gaunt spoke to Branden in a low voice about some business matter in London (a venture had been successful and he wanted to know the next steps), Hadrian sat down in front of him, whining for attention. Gaunt ignored him impassively, but then the dog began to jump up on him, desperate to be heeded. I could see the irritation in Gaunt's eyes as he waved him away impatiently, but Hadrian continued, pleading for attention with his large brown eyes, until a sudden, savage kick from Gaunt sent the dog limping away.

'Do not kick him, Gaunt!' Branden's voice rose sharply. Gaunt flinched and then bowing slightly, backed away, remaining at the back of the room as another guest entered, holding a briefcase and an armful of papers. Branden waved this man forward and motioned that it was time to for me to leave, at which I rose gladly. As I passed Gaunt, I saw upon his face a look of such fierce hatred that I was startled. I glanced back towards the desk and saw the object of his malice. Hadrian was now being petted by his master as Branden spoke to his new guest, the dog's paws up on his master's knees, his tail wagging joyfully. Defended and adored by his master.

Hadrian's body was found down the well in the stable courtyard the next morning, his throat slit. The gardeners hoisted the slumped body up using the well bucket and Branden had him buried at the bottom of the herb garden. It was the first time I think I have seen genuine emotion upon his face. Gaunt stood behind, his eyes hooded.

I wondered if Branden suspected that Gaunt had done it. I had no proof, but in my mind's eye, I saw him do it. I watched him lure the dog out at night, hatred etched in every line of his miserable face, and then slice the life from it.

They say your imagination can dream up more horrors than real life could ever hold. I am beginning to think that is not true. Not here at Mount Enderton, anyway.


## THE STORY CONTINUED BY THE EDITOR

The incident with Hadrian did not seem to damage the relationship between Sir Branden and Gaunt. At first Isabel wondered if Branden even suspected his manservant, although she intuited that there was little at Enderton that escaped his notice. It was as she watched them together over the next few days that she realised Sir Branden knew exactly what had happened. She could see it in the cold glitter of his eyes as he looked at Gaunt. Yet she also knew that he would not react. He needed Gaunt by his side: his servant was too valuable to him - and so he kept his emotions completely under control. Isabel felt a strange admiration mixed with abhorrence at Branden's detachment. He was always able to keep his focus on the main objective, and would not let anything get in his way - even when it was something he cared about.

Isabel's days were little improved by the frequent visits she was now forced to make to Sir Branden's study in the afternoons, nor by the continued presence of Messrs Cugh, Knowles, Lursted, Ratch and Drent. Continued fear of intrusion each night made her sleep fragmented and her temperament irritable, and on this particular Friday evening, she wanted nothing more than to be left alone. But of course she was in attendance upon them in Sir Branden's drawing room, while the men drank their port and sherry.

She despised these men almost as much as she despised her captor and his servant. The ruffians were hired by Sir Branden for specific jobs, and handsomely paid and rewarded by long visits to Enderton where they were served with all the food, drink and entertainment they could desire.

Mr Knowles had a sniff, a constant sniff. Mr Ratch bit his nails until Isabel thought there could be no more nail left. Mr Lursted had a laugh that would pierce metal. He laughed when someone made a joke, a dry comment, or even a remark about the weather. The noises built up in her head until she could feel them rapping a symphony of antagonism upon her brain and she thought she would scream.

'Excuse me, I must get some fresh air,' she muttered finally, and rose to leave the room.

As she did, she saw Sir Branden motion with his finger to Gaunt, who was standing by the door, to follow her out. Isabel's temper rose further still. She strode down the hallway, and taking advantage of Gaunt's momentary pause to close the door behind him, turned to her right and slipped silently into the ballroom, hoping that Gaunt not seen her turn, thus giving her a few moments of peace. One of the tall windows had been left open to air the room and she went over to enjoy the welcome breeze, which felt calming and cool after the overly warm, smoke-filled drawing room.

The vast ballroom was shrouded in darkness, having not been used for a few weeks, and the wide silence was soothing to her aching head.

She only just caught the sound of the ballroom door creaking open at the far side of the room. Swinging round, she could just make out a figure wrapped in shadow, entering. Phantomlike, he made no noise.

'I am not going to run away, if that is what you are here for,' she called out, knowing full well who was there. 'I merely need some air and I wish to be alone.'

The figure did not move. Her last vestige of patience left her.

'Be gone! I do not want you here!' she said loudly.

With a chill sensation of horror, she heard his mocking voice as clearly as if he were standing beside her, though he stood at the other side of the huge room:

'My *lady.*'

She supposed it must have been the way his voice travelled around the walls to reach her, but she shivered and strained to see if he was still in his original position. The moon had gone behind a cloud and she could no longer see him amongst the dark shadows. The voice spoke again, seeming to come from everywhere and nowhere:

'I must remind you that your will and your wishes do not matter here. Your husband commands me to be always by your side, and so, by your side I will be.'

She could feel breath on her ear – or was it the wind from the open window? Cold spectral fingers ran down her spine. The voice continued:

'He does not trust you and I do not trust you. If you run, I will find you. You will submit to him. Or I will make you.'

Something glinted to her left – was it his hideous eyes? Isabel tried to breathe calmly and stand her ground, but fear gripped her - she could not bear to be in the same dark room with this wraith. The horror that he might appear beside her was too much and she took to her heels and ran – back to the light, to the warmth, to the unbearable noises.

She felt ashamed of herself when she returned to her bedroom that night. There was no knock at her door when the men retired, and in the morning when she sat down to write her diary, she took the time to flick back and read a few of her earlier entries during her time at school, her time at Harringdon. They reminded her of when she was stronger and much less afraid. She knew the issue of Gaunt would not go away. Therefore, she would have to take the matter boldly into her own hands.

'I demand that Gaunt stops following me.'

Isabel had burst into Sir Branden's office. He looked up, surprise crossing his usually inscrutable face.

'It is in your best interests that Gaunt keeps an eye on you,' he replied, quickly regaining his composure.

'It is not in my best interests,' Isabel retorted. 'I have no privacy - none at all. If you insist upon keeping me trapped here against my will, then at least allow me the dignity of being able to cross from one room to another without being followed like a shadow.'

Branden gave a singularly humourless laugh.

'My dear, you are not trapped here. You are my wife. This is your home. And as your husband, my will is your will and it is my will that Gaunt knows where you are at all times.' He paused, and looked at her closely, before adding, 'I could of course ask him to be more discreet in his viewing.'

'No, that is not what I want.' Isabel shuddered at the thought of the already ghost-like figure becoming less visible.

Sir Branden stared at her, false sympathy in his eyes. 'I know the move here must have been hard, Isabel, but your ungratefulness towards the protection I am providing for you through my manservant - as any husband would do for the one he loves - makes me question your loyalties and motives. You would not want to put me in a position where I am forced to make sure that Gaunt watches you even while you sleep?'

Isabel froze, horrified. The thought of those eyes, watching her from the corner of her room was more than she could bear.

'No,' she replied, her throat dry.

'Of course, that would be a last resort,' he added pleasantly. 'I am reluctant to intrude any further upon your personal space.' His eyes darkened as he added, 'But do not force my hand, Isabel. Abide by my rules and I will make sure you are always comfortable. Do you understand me?'

She looked back at him, her frightened eyes signalling assent.

'Is that all?' he asked, his iron gaze locked upon hers.

There was no use in her defiance, she realised too late. There was no sympathy to be found in this man, nor any decency. With her heart thudding in her chest, she nodded and turned to leave.

'And Isabel.'

She stopped, but did not turn round.

'I would like to come to you tonight. Please make sure your door is open. Your displays of defiance are very amusing, but they will end now.'

Isabel walked very slowly and erectly to the door, every nerve in her body tingling; but when she reached the hallway, she ran.

Fear tight in her chest, Isabel headed for the stairs, but Branden's band of friends were coming down towards her. Startled, she turned and headed for the gardens, but then caught sight of Gaunt upon the front steps. Panicked, she swung round and fled towards the smaller staircase at the back of the house. She ran up three flights and then stopped, out of breath upon the landing. She had not been in this part of the house before. A long corridor stretched out before her, rows of doors along each side and a tall window at the end, looking out over the arboretum. A thick mist had descended outside and it enveloped the house in its eerie mantle.

It was colder on this floor and a feeling of damp penetrated her bones. Clearly no fires had been lit here for many months. She entered one of the rooms that must have been an unused guest room; a thin layer of dust lay upon the furniture. She went to the window seat and curled up upon it, looking out at the October landscape. The sky was white, the trees gently rocking in a light wind. Her fingers felt like ice, so she sat upon them to try and warm them. All was silence up here and she was filled with a strange sense of foreboding.

Still shaken from her experience in the ballroom the night before, it seemed that she could hear evil thoughts whispering through the walls, creeping along the floor and taking hold of her. She shivered and got up, trying to shake them off. She drew her shawl around her, thin as it was, but did not want to return to her room for fear of being caught there again. Anger suddenly flared through her, heating her more than the movement. Why should she allow Branden to dictate her steps? She had her key; she would be safe. She set her shoulders and made for the door.

The sound of steps coming up the stairs made her halt, her hand on the door handle. She listened to the soft footsteps stealing along the corridor. It was Gaunt, she was sure of it. Stepping back quietly, she caused one of the floorboards to creak and instantly the footsteps halted on the other side of the door. She froze, hardly daring to breathe. All thoughts of defiance melted at the thought of being caught by Gaunt in this area of the house. There was no one around, no one to call to if – she did not even know the end to that sentence. But then – she heard another noise – perhaps he had passed?

Slowly, very slowly she knelt down by the door and put her eye to the keyhole. She breathed a sigh of relief - there was no one there, the hall was empty. Then -

A black, searching pupil slid instantly into place, staring into her eye, only an inch away. A shrill, terrified cry cast itself from her lips and she fell backwards onto the wooden floor. Thrusting her feet out, she pushed her legs against the door to stop the creature from entering. One second passed – two – three. There was no movement from the other side of the door, no desperate forceful pushing. Her chest heaving, she crawled towards the door, but could not bear to look through the tiny hole once more. There was a sick taste in her mouth as she leant against the crack of the door, listening for a sound – a slither – that would give away his presence. But there was nothing. He had left. Putting her head between her knees, she sank down, utterly exhausted.

I suppose it will be no surprise to you that despite Sir Branden's warning, Isabel still locked her door that night.

She had curled herself up in her bed, like a chick in a nest, blankets and pillows around her, as she had been wont to do as a child. She had her diary open beside her and was flicking through the pages, reading of happier days at Harringdon when she ran free with Cathy and danced in the waves. Cathy would be married now, she realised with sorrow.

She recalled conversations with a young man with blue eyes, who would have helped her, had he known what was coming, and she thought back over all her hopes and plans that seemed so distant now. Wearily, she turned to write her entry for this day. It was a fresh page, but in the top right hand corner was a small note, written in a rushed hand:

*'Where am I now?'*

The words hit her like a blow. The girl who had written that line, full of such excitement, had expected to be far away by now – living her dreams, becoming the woman she wanted to be. From outside Isabel's door the knocking began. Isabel ran her finger across the ink-stained words, as though trying to transport herself back to that time. How different the reality is, she thought desolately. Tears began to fall from her eyes as she sat, pale and miserable. Why had this happened to her?

The knocking continued. She could not bear it. Going to the window, she drew open the curtains. She knew the ground was a long way down but instead of staring into the darkness below, her gaze was instantly captured by the moon.

The clouds were scudding by, hurried and frantic, on their way to destinations even they knew not, borne along by the unseen wind. A circle of light bore through these rushing travellers; the shining face of the faithful one. It was unmoving, steady and serene – and to Isabel, unspeakably comforting. It gazed at the buffeting puffs of cloud from a position so far removed that she could not even comprehend it.

'Look at the things of earth', the moon said to her. 'So frantic and uncontrolled. Look at me. Nothing can move me, I belong to a higher plain, and I will always be here.'

She gazed in wonder at its beauty, feeling the tension release and wash away from her. She felt somehow comforted by its otherworldliness.

'You do not change,' she said softly. 'You are always there.'

And so the moon looked down at her, a solitary companion for a solitary girl, both seeing the world from a lonely perspective.

Isabel had defied Sir Branden's warning. She refused to move her knight from his position in the face of adversity and he made his next move with equal ferocity.

### ISABEL'S NARRATIVE
*(Extract from Isabel's Diary)*

*ENDERTON, 3ʳᵈ October 1866*

It was clear from the instant I entered my room what had happened. I suppose I had almost expected it. My drawers were thrown open, clothes strewn over the floor. My bed was stripped back, the curtains in disarray and the rug was pulled up at one end. There was no need to climb up upon the dresser and slide my hand around the empty shelf. The key was, of course, gone.

Gazing around at the chaos, the ransacked room reminded me of my dreams. They had looked so beautiful in the beginning, but were now ruined and destroyed.

The room, however, I could put back together. I managed to keep myself surprisingly calm as I lifted, tidied and finally sat down on the bed. It was then I realised my small pile of books hidden on the shelf were also gone. Surely he had not taken those also? He had not.

On my pillow they lay, bound up with a red ribbon – his signature envelope on top. I opened it with distaste. It read:

*'Forgive my intrusion. I have found what I was looking for. You do not need it.'*

Anger billowed up inside me. I thought back to a warm day and a meaningless conversation with a handywright. I got up and went to the outbuildings.

## THE STORY CONTINUED BY THE EDITOR

It did not take Isabel long to find what she was looking for. She took several of them, along with the same tool she had seen Harry use, and a handful of the screws. A wicker basket lay by the doorway, left lying by one of the maids. Isabel lifted it, put her precious bundle inside and then spent a few moments gathering a large bunch of flowers that she placed on top, creating a pretty flower basket.

At the front door she met Sir Branden.

'Where have you been, Isabel?' he asked, eyes surveying her curiously.

'I have been gathering some flowers for my room,' she replied with dignity.

'Are the varieties I provide not enough?' he asked politely.

'These remind me of Harringdon,' she said, glancing down at the poppies and lavender. 'Cathy and I used to pick them in summer.'

He looked uncomfortable at the mention of Harringdon and motioned her to go on. She walked past, smiling broadly.

That night, nothing, not even a raging bull, could have got through her door. Her handle turned once, twice, but Isabel did not fear. Perhaps Sir Branden was embarrassed to have been outwitted once again, perhaps he was too angry to mention it, but Isabel was granted another few weeks of undisturbed sleep.

She held her head a little higher from then on.

# XXI

It had been a warm autumn and the trees had clung on to their leaves past their usual time. But after several nights of light frost and several days of strong winds, at last they gave up their fight. From green to red, and red to gold, the leaves turned their final hues and then finally bade their branches farewell. Isabel watched them from her window – marvelling at the colours, enjoying their dance as the falling leaves moved with the wind, which tossed them back and forth, left and right, but always downwards from the heights of their crowning glory. They fell slowly from grace, down to their final resting place in the damp grass and soil where already they began to decay, the burnt gold turning to muddy brown and their unique forms disintegrating, never more to reign resplendent.

And yet, what a beautiful way to die, Isabel thought as she looked at the blaze of colours as the leaves lived out their final days in defiance. To leave in such glory, dying whilst burning out bright.

As the days passed, the trees grew barer and barer, until one morning when she awoke, they were stripped completely, their glorious mantles destroyed. And yet still their great forms stood, defiant and proud, their branches naked for all to see. She felt an ache of pity for them.

'You will not be this way for long,' she said to them silently. 'Soon spring will come, and all will be restored.'

She went out that day. Gaunt was in Sir Branden's office attending a meeting so she was guaranteed a few hours of freedom. She drew her cloak around her; it was needed now the season had turned. All was cold and quiet as she sat down on the bench at the edge of the arboretum, the herb garden to her back, its soft scents calming and fragrant.

She was always drawn to the dim, mysterious charm of the trees. As a child, she used to imagine that birds could travel between worlds, and that the seeds and twigs they brought back were from distant, magical woods. It was why the trees appeared in so many forms and bore such different fruit, she would tell Mrs Tabitha.

It was late afternoon and the light was low. She watched the moving branches cast shadows upon the steady trunks. Shadows – those silent whispers of all that exists, given life by the light, but never a presence of their own. Just like her, thought Isabel as she sat there.

Once again, she felt time slipping past her. She reached out, her hand pale in the cold air – she could almost feel it running across the tips of her fingers, cold and vacuous. An invisible stream of eternity that she could not halt. She used to live every second to the full. Now, she was trapped in a continuous pattern of nothingness. She felt the waste of it all so acutely.

'Is this what my life will be like now?' she asked out loud.

A silent answer to her silent question resounded in her ears. She was truly alone.

But not quite – a flock of birds settled in the empty branches above her and began their friendly chatter. Isabel remembered how she used to make up dialogue in her head for the little creatures – the young sparrows returning to their parents and telling them about their day upon the horse chestnut tree, the blackbirds were old friends reminiscing at the top of a tall oak, and the sparrows were two young lovers hopping on the grass by her feet. They made her feel less lonely, and when a robin landed at the end of her bench, it even raised a smile from her.

The cool and sombre shade of the evening stole upon Isabel without her noticing. It reminded her of when she was at school and she would spend her free hour before bedtime upon the quiet lawns at the back of the house. She would dream then, of her magical place between the worlds.

'Sometimes you can see it,' she would tell her friends, when she rejoined them later – 'at dusk, when the darkness steals upon you without you realising, or when you walk along a beach on your own, or very early in the morning, before anyone else is awake – you get just a glimpse of what it is like. That very still, very quiet place where everything is just that little bit more beautiful than in our world.'

'Please let me get there now,' Isabel prayed. 'Please let me escape.'

She opened her eyes, the skies were darkening and evening was drawing near. It was time to return to the house. She got to her feet when suddenly all around her, rain started to fall. Looking up, huge heavy drops hit her forehead and exploded into tiny droplets that scattered across her nose and mouth. The grass around her began to move, as if hundreds of tiny creatures were scurrying away beneath the blades. It took her a moment to realise that it was simply the weight of the drops moving the blades with their force. Quickly, silently, she was completely soaked. She thought of running to escape the sudden deluge, but there was little point. So she stood there, water running and dripping down every inch of her body, the ground beneath her feet suddenly moist and soft. She did not yet feel cold, and did not care about her gown, and therefore there was nothing identifiably unpleasant about her situation. Hardly able to see two feet in front of her through the walls of water that surrounded her, she took a moment to enjoy the strange solitude of her situation. Had a stranger walked up to her and into her odd, wet world, she would have talked as comfortably to them as to an old friend. The usual rules of conduct did not apply here.

After one minute, ten minutes, an hour – she could not be sure – the rain stopped. She looked at the gardens around her that had suddenly reappeared. They seemed very solid, very normal. She could see the house not far away. She sighed, and headed in.

Gaunt continued to skulk in the dark corners of the house. He skulked in the darker corners of Isabel's mind. She had learned to sense his presence. She felt a chill creep over her whenever he was near. And on this particular October afternoon, as she stood in the hall, she felt his menacing presence approaching. She froze and tucked herself into a stone alcove by the stairs. A shadow fell across her face. Across from her, on a pedestal, stood a creamy marble bust of a woman, with curls of stone hair falling gently over her carved features, her arms wrapped around herself to hide her nudity. It was the only statue Isabel had seen in the house and she was curiously fond of it. At this moment, it reminded her of herself, frozen in time. Quietly, Gaunt passed, unaware of her, his long strands of hair clinging to the shoulders of his worn brown leather coat.

A strange impulse gripped her. For the first time in many months, Gaunt had not seen her – had she finally eluded him? He seemed completely unaware of her and continued down the hallway. A strange emotion thrilled through her body - now he was the watched and she was the watcher. Insane as she knew it was, she began to follow him. Down the stairs he went, and then down another flight to the basement. Still she followed, fear in her throat, excitement in her heart.

He entered a room at the far end of the basement corridor. She noted the door and then stepped quietly into a cupboard, leaving the door very slightly ajar. She realised she was on the same floor where she had been kept captive all those months ago. The thought should have filled her with horror, but somehow it did not. Ten minutes later, she heard Gaunt emerge from the room and close the door, but he did not lock it. She let him pass and then, once she was sure he was upstairs, she crept along and entered the room.

It was like entering a dark pit, foul smelling and seemingly endless. There was no window and it took several minutes for her eyes to become accustomed to the gloom. A musty smell filled her nose and caught in her throat. What had seemed like dark towers in the semi-darkness emerged as great mounds of papers and letters as her eyes adjusted and the shapes around her became more distinct. Some piles stood upon tables, some were heaped on the floor. Boxes and roughly hung shelves lined the walls, with ledgers, folders and notebooks crammed into every available space, newspapers strewn around the floor. There was an air of curiously organised chaos about the place.

A worn sofa was tucked into the far corner of the room, the shape of a man impressed into its cushions. This was Gaunt's room, she realised. She had never thought of him sleeping before – in her mind he was the eternal stalker, always awake, always watching, his miscoloured eyes continually alert and never closed.

There was one desk at the far end of the room. It was slightly more orderly than the disarray around it, but only slightly. Isabel made her way carefully over to it, trying not to disturb the pages beneath her feet. A folder lay open on the desk, its inserted paper files marked with dates and names. She read through the file names – partly, out of interest, partly out spite and a desire to finally rebel against her torturer, no matter how small the act was. One caught her eye as she flicked through. It was titled: 'Helen Harringdon'.

Isabel grasped it in surprise and drew it out of its folder. Inside were two certificates, and a signed paper of some kind. She looked at the certificates first. The first was a birth certificate, faded and stained, and torn at the edges. It was dated the 1st May 1848 and Helen Laidenhead was listed as the mother. The first thing Isabel noticed was the sex of the child – it was male. At first she wondered if they had got Cathy's sex wrong – but then she realised that it was her aunt's maiden name that had written above, while the father's box had been left blank. Also, this was over a year before Cathy had even been born. There was no name given for the child.

Isabel turned over to read the second certificate. It was a certificate of death for an unnamed boy, who died on the 4th May 1848. No parents were listed. He had been buried at Watergate cemetery in London. Beside this entry, written in a cramped hand, was the following account:

*'Seen at grave 4th May 1852, 6th June 1853 and 4th May 1866. Only witness, a Ms Rachel Frain, ladies maid to her Ladyship during confinement in France.'*

The final piece of paper was a roughly scrawled statement:

*'I, Rachel Frain, attest to this being the burial place of the only male child of Lady Helen Laidenhead. I delivered the child in Lyons and was there when he died of whooping cough, a few days later.'*

Underneath, in the same cramped hand that had written on the previous certificate, was the note:

*'Price paid for information - £5. Current occupation of Ms Frain – prostitute.'*

Isabel felt dizzy. The words seemed to swim before her eyes. Her aunt had had a baby boy before she had Cathy - before she was even married? And he had died, so quickly, so young... She looked back at the empty box on the birth certificate for the child, the box that should have held his little name within its black lines, the name of the cousin she had never met. She felt a strange feeling in her stomach, like when you step out into a bitter cold wind in winter and it catches you quite by surprise.

Her mind was a rush of questions, but one rose up more strongly than the others: who, then, was the child's father? She looked through the papers, but there was no record of this information. Isabel knew enough to understand that a child born out of wedlock was a shameful offence, both for the mother and the child. She suddenly felt a wave of pity for her aunt: to have lost her first born child, to have kept such a secret for such a long time, grieving only in private – it must have been unbearable. Isabel glanced back at the dates that her aunt had been seen at the graveside. She had visited on the anniversary of the boy's death this year, only a few months before Isabel had arrived at Harringdon. She recalled her aunt's tight lips and hard eyes. Isabel wondered if she had wept as she knelt at the pauper's grave, her face shrouded with a veil to shield her from preying eyes.

But prying eyes had seen her. And from the notes in the file, it looked as though they had been watching her for some time. Isabel closed the file with a heavy hand. It was then she noticed a stamp on the front. The stamp read *'Paid in Full'*, and a date was scrawled underneath: *'14th July 1866'*. It was the date Sir Branden had kidnapped her.

Suddenly everything made sense. With a sudden rush, Isabel realised why she was here, why her aunt had given her up. It was so clear, as though someone had lit a lamp in her mind. She had been traded for Branden's silence. He had used this evidence that she now held in her hand, written to her aunt, confronted her with it in person, hung it over Harringdon House like a boulder waiting to crash, and then taken his payment. Herself.

Isabel glanced around the room, this place where papers and letters, containing such revelations lay in huge piles. Names and acts and dates caught her eye – the secrets of the world, ready to be bandied and utilised for foul purposes. Ledgers of debts and crimes, that could fetch any price most desired. She felt sick. Secrets lived and breathed in this place – they were physical, tradable entities. She finally understood her master's relationship with his servant. Gaunt was the spy and Sir Branden was the debt collector.

## ISABEL'S NARRATIVE
### *(Extract from Isabel's Diary)*

*ENDERTON, 15th October 1866*

My mind is very full as I wrestle with this revelation. Again and again I ask myself, do I blame Aunt Helen? Somehow, I cannot find it in myself to do so. Had Branden been allowed to go public with his secret, Cathy's life would have been destroyed, her marriage prospects ruined by the worst kind of scandal. I realise now why Aunt Helen had been so desperate for the marriage to take place quickly, why she was so desperate for me not to dissuade Cathy to take this step. It was in case Sir Branden had reneged on his deal. One Cathy was married, she was safe – she had a future, no matter what happened afterwards.

Aunt Helen had not had a choice. She had to save her daughter. Yet, she must have known what sort of a man she was giving me to. She must have heard my screams...

No, I must push those thoughts from my mind. I am glad that Cathy is safe, at least and married now...but I cannot think of that. I am married now also, I remind myself. I do not blame my aunt, but I do not know that I can forgive.

Isabel walked into the drawing room that afternoon with none of her usual fear. It seemed to be slipping from her, as though a heavy cloak was falling from her shoulders. Sir Branden looked up, surprised at her voluntary entrance into the occupied room.

'Do you mind if I take a seat?' she asked, sweetly.

'Of course not,' he replied, 'I am glad to see you.'

She noticed a wavering in his gaze, an uncomfortable twitch in his shoulders. She wondered at the cause of it. He could not know what she had discovered – and even if he did, surely it would make no difference to him? She knew how he made his money; she knew that his 'speculations' were in secrets, and not in shares - but it did not help her in her current situation. No – his behaviour was that of awkwardness. It struck her for the first time that they were very seldom – nay, never – alone together, unless he willed it. This was the first time she had entered his presence without being forced, and therefore he had no control over the situation. They were suddenly man and woman, not master and wife. And he was uncomfortable.

She looked at him as he feigned continuing to read his newspaper, though his eyes were not moving. What was he thinking of? Was it of last night, when he came to her door again, this time armed with a key (thinking perhaps that the reason he had not got in previously was that she had found another), only to be thwarted once more?

'Let me in Isabel,' he had hissed.

She had ignored his voice, as he now attempted to ignore her.

He was ashamed, she realised with a jump. He was uncomfortable in her presence for he knew he was in the wrong. This was a surprise to her. It gave her fire.

'I stumbled across a strange room today,' she said in a clear, ringing voice, and Sir Branden looked up. 'It was an odd place, full of papers and letters. I believe it was Gaunt's room.'

'You should not have entered there,' said Sir Branden, a little startled.

'But you said that this was my home now,' she replied with provoking self-possession. 'You said I could wander as I pleased.'

A flicker of annoyance passed over his face

'Yet you should not enter other people's rooms.'

'Gaunt is a servant – surely I have every right to do so,' she said defiantly.

Sir Branden frowned heavily.

'Gaunt is my servant.'

'And what sets him apart from everyone else? I have been meaning to ask – what is his role in this household beside secret-sourcer and my jail keeper?'

Branden looked taken aback at her impetuosity; a crack appeared in his composure. However, it did not take him long to recover himself. He stared at her a while, as though weighing her up. Isabel straightened her back and looked at him squarely, to ensure she was not found wanting. Then he leaned towards her, bending his dark gaze full upon her. To her credit, she did not flinch.

'I took Rester Gaunt into my household when he was just a boy,' he said, pleasantly, though there was an undertone of darkness to his voice. 'I found him on the streets in London, alone and half-starved, abandoned by his parents at an early age. They told him he was from the Devil and cast him out, unnerved by his strange personality and unusual eyes. Yet it was something in his eyes – those fascinating eyes – that caught my attention, so I took him in and trained him up as my manservant. You see, I can be kind when I want to be, Isabel.'

She gave a half-smile, neither assenting to, nor negating this claim. Sir Branden continued,

'He was extremely grateful to me, eager to do whatever I desired, and quickly I found he had other skills besides serving. I began to use him for ever greater and more important tasks, and he always delivered admirable results. He is has always anxious to do my every will and this has served him well. He now has money at his disposal, a comfortable lifestyle and anything he desires. I am a loyal master, and reward him for his duties, although all he wants is to be by my side. Therefore I trust him implicitly and involve him in all my affairs.'

Isabel felt disgusted.

'And so you use him to do your dirty work,' she said coldly. 'What an honour that is. You are right, you are kind indeed.'

Sir Branden smiled at her.

'Yes, I am kind. I am kind because I could make his life hell. I am his Master and he is my servant. I could make him dread each sunrise and nightfall, for he has nothing else but me. But I do not. Therefore, I am kind. Kindness is what you can achieve with your power. Be sure I do not have to turn the coin upon you, Isabel.'

She smiled pleasantly back at him.

'I would like to read that paper when you are finished with it, if you do not mind.'


ISABEL'S NARRATIVE
*(Extract from Isabel's Diary)*

*ENDERTON, 16<sup>th</sup> October 1866*

Make no mistake, I feel nothing but abhorrence for him, but he is a very lonely man. I wonder if he saw something of himself in Gaunt, that day when he stared at the starving child on the street. No wonder Gaunt worships him – he is his whole life, and I doubt if anyone else holds Branden in such high regard.

It certainly explains why Branden will only hire servants who are mute (I have worked my way to the bottom of that mystery during my time here). Otherwise, he could not guarantee the protection of all his many secrets.

I am still not clear whether his guests are invited here to have secrets or payment extracted. I suspect he mainly invites people who are 'useful' to him, in order to gain information. Otherwise, so many of them would not make repeat visits. His little spy will pick up every scrap of information released while they are here, and use it to Branden's advantage.

One thing is clear: Enderton is a dangerous web and Branden is the spider in the centre, controlling every thread.

*ENDERTON, 20<sup>th</sup> October 1866*

Each night he has come since I challenged him in the dining room. He must know he cannot get in, but it is a battle of wills now. I can hear him muttering poisonous words behind the door. He is so pleasant, such an accommodating host during the day... what would his guests say if they could see him there – a bitter, furious creature of the night. I believe the drink does not help him think clearly either.

I suppose I should be scared but I refuse to act like some persecuted heroine. I must hold to who I am despite all this and not be cowed. I cannot just retreat into my shell, much as I want to. I will not let him break me.

## THE STORY CONTINUED BY THE EDITOR

'I will come to you tonight,' Sir Branden said softly to her as they sat at the table that night. More guests had arrived in the recent weeks and the table was full.

'I am afraid I am not available,' Isabel replied, casually.

It was the first time in many months he had brought up the topic while in public.

'I am not accustomed to asking,' he replied quietly, ice in his tone. 'I simply command. There is little choice in the matter. I will not stand for your interminable caprices any longer.'

She did not reply.

He did not even wait until she was in bed. Immediately after the last guest had gone up the stairs, she heard his unmistakable measured step approach her door. Fire burned in her veins, as red as the velvet dress she was wearing, as she stood, awaiting his arrival. Rubies glittered around her neck and ears.

Getting into her nightgown had seemed like a sign of defeat – it seemed to make her weaker, more accessible – and she was neither.

His voice came, low and soft, almost like the purr of a cat, his breathing heavy with fury

'I know you can hear me. This is the end of your defiant disregard for my pleasure. I will have what is mine by right – you shall not deny me! I am your husband – *open* this door!'

And she threw the door open, glowing as if the red light of an angry fire had caught her in its blaze.


## ISABEL'S NARRATIVE
### *(Extract from Isabel's Diary)*

### *ENDERTON, 20<sup>th</sup> October 1866*

I confronted him fully with my furious gaze – terrified, shaking and proud. I felt as though I was on fire, so intense was the heat inside me. He stepped back, as though scorched by my rage.

I raised my eyebrows, laying down the gauntlet, daring him to step over the threshold. And he turned and walked back into the darkness. I stepped back and bolted the door.

I had won tonight's battle. There would be many more to come.

### *ENDERTON, 21<sup>st</sup> October 1866*

I still find it so strange that we greet each other with such polite words in the morning, acting our charade by day, mentioning nothing of our battle by night. It is a power struggle played out behind locked doors and vast dinner tables, but I will win.

I realise now that he will not make too much noise when there are guests, hence the quiet knocking, the whispered words. He cannot want anyone to hear that I will not allow him entry. I often wonder why he does not just send the guests all away. But I believe he feels most powerful when he is surrounded. His guests give him confidence.

For I do believe that he is ashamed of his desires, for he only ever comes to my door alone, and in the dark hours of the night when everyone else lies sleeping.

I can use this to my advantage.

I heard Gaunt speaking with Branden today as I entered the dining room for breakfast.

'What can I do, master? How can I help?' he asked in a fawning tone.

'There is nothing to be done. Leave me now,' replied Sir Branden, irritably.

Too late I realised they were speaking of me. Gaunt looked up and actually snarled at me, pure malice in his eyes. I suddenly realised why Gaunt enjoyed making my life a misery - he hated me because I was humiliating his beloved master, and he could not bear it. I could almost physically feel his hatred pulsing through the air towards me.

'Go, Gaunt,' commanded Sir Branden.

Other guests were now entering the room and Gaunt walked past me towards the door, looking vengeful.

I suddenly thought of Hadrian, Sir Branden's unfortunate dog. If Gaunt had hated a helpless animal so much, how much more did he despise me, the ungrateful, unrepentant rebel? I was suddenly assailed with sinister thoughts. I took a deep breath and brought myself sharply to task, but nevermore walked near the well.

# XXII

## THE STORY CONTINUED BY THE EDITOR

We have almost returned to the point whereupon Isabel began her story of how she came to Enderton, but there is one major event to recount before I return you to Isabel, and the man who had come to her aid.

Isabel was reading a book by the window in the library. Outside one of the many gardeners was sweeping away the last of the fallen leaves to prevent the grass from dying underneath. Glancing upwards, she saw birds soaring overhead, like small black pen strokes that had taken life and leapt from the page of her book, sweeping into the clear expanse above.

Noises were suddenly audible from the billiard room next door. She recognised the first speaker at once. He was one of the more recent guests, a man named Richard King. She knew his voice, for he was one of the first people she had met who had an Irish accent. An old friend of Branden's, Isabel had felt more favourably to him than the usual guests as he had been kind to her the previous night at dinner, asking her about the books she had read and which authors she liked. He was one of the few guests who bothered to engage her in conversation at all during mealtimes, most preferring to leave her sitting in silence. He was in his fifties, with greying black hair, and he had a genial face and pleasantly lilting voice.

His voice sounded angrier now, ringing out into the hallway and through the open door of the library.

'She's just a girl, Branden! She may look like her mother, but she is just a girl – and you are an old man. You cannot wreak your revenge on her like some melodramatic villain!' He paused, and then began to speak in more measured tones: 'We both know that you are involved in some disputable business – it is a hard world; I do not judge you for it. But this goes far beyond your usual actions. This is wrong in every sense of the word, and I will have nothing more to do with you if you persist in this.'

There was silence. Isabel held her breath, wondering what was coming next. Then Sir Branden spoke, his voice much lower, so that she had to strain to make out his words. 'I would not make such foolish comments if I were you, Richard. You know full well your business cannot survive without my assistance. You will withdraw your threat and your intrusion into my private affairs.'

His voice grew louder as he spoke, and Isabel realised he was walking towards the door. With his last words, he closed it and Isabel could not make out the other man's reply. She did not find out what decision Mr King made, but by the next morning, he was gone.

## ISABEL'S NARRATIVE
### (Extract from Isabel's Diary)

ENDERTON, 24th October 1866

His revenge? I do not understand. Have I harmed him in some way? What cause have I given for him to hate me so? I had not even laid eyes upon him before he arrived at Harringdon.

## THE STORY CONTINUED BY THE EDITOR

Isabel was summoned to Sir Branden's study the next morning by the usual sealed note, delivered on her silver breakfast platter. When she arrived, there was no one there, but another note awaited her on his desk.

*'Called away. I will be back in half an hour. Please begin your tasks.'*

She had decided that he used these notes to distance himself and create a sense of mystery and power. However, Isabel thought dryly to herself, it was also a necessity when one only hired mute servants. Her tasks were laid out before her – several piles of letters waiting to be addressed and stamped. She groaned inwardly.

Defiantly sitting down in his chair instead of her usual stool, she looked around the room from his position of power. It reminded her of her aunt's study, but with more masculine excesses of expensive green leather and polished black walnut panelling. Glancing down, something silver caught her eye. The desk drawer to her right lay slightly open, the key half-turned in the lock. Sir Branden had obviously been called away in a hurry as she had never seen any keys left lying around before (although her propensity to use such items against him may have been

183

the cause of this). Urged on by the perverse rebellious spirit that had recently been sparked in her, she pulled the drawer open. To her immense surprise she found herself looking at a photograph. Isabel had not seen many of these modern versions of portraiture, but they fascinated her. What was even more fascinating was that the photograph was of herself, standing beside Sir Branden.

She blinked, trying to remember when such an occasion had taken place. But wait – he looked so much younger, with a shock of dark hair and a thick moustache. His suit was cut very differently as well – and she had certainly never worn a dress of that fashion; it looked like a style from several decades ago. The reality was hard to perceive, but gradually she realised that while the man in the photograph was indeed Sir Branden, the woman was her mother.

Her hair was slightly darker than Isabel's, her forehead a little higher, her face more beautiful. Now that Isabel looked more closely, she clearly recognised the face that for so long had inhabited her dreams. She had never seen a photograph of her mother before, and was struck by her beauty, fascinated by her image. For several moments she stared at her, so young and full of life, until her focus was drawn back to the man in the picture. Why on earth would her mother have had her picture taken with Sir Branden? Isabel looked at the picture more closely, taking in each detail. The more she looked at it, the more it puzzled her. A man and woman would not have their picture taken so intimately if they were simply acquaintances. A tiny sparkle of light was emitting from her mother's left hand. Upon her finger, minute though it was in the photograph, Isabel could see a diamond ring, but it was not the one her father had given her. A cold realisation slowly dawned upon her.

Sir Branden was the gentleman to whom her mother had been engaged. Sir Branden was the man her mother had left to elope with Isabel's father.

The enormity of the revelation staggered her. She felt as though the room around her was spinning slightly and put out a hand to steady herself against the desk. She had thought that Sir Branden had been a man who had entered her life only a few months ago, and yet now she realised he had always been there – he had been a part of her life before she was even born. She looked at Sir Branden's face, so young and beaming with joy at the beautiful woman on his arm. For the first time since she had met him, Isabel felt a very small pang of pity for him. So he was the spurned lover, humiliated and abandoned in the night.

And now he was taking his revenge.

## ISABEL'S NARRATIVE
*(Extract from Isabel's Diary)*

ENDERTON, 25th October 1866

She has left me the legacy of her love, and the curse of her betrayal.

I cannot judge her for what she did. She left a man she did not love for one she did – she left a life of loneliness and misery for one of happiness and fulfilment.

But had she not done so, I would not be here now, at Enderton. It seems that selfishness, no matter how worthy, does not go unpunished. I wonder for the first time how she felt about leaving her fiancé. I wonder if she felt guilty.

Oh mother, if only you had known the final outcome of your actions.


## THE STORY CONTINUED BY THE EDITOR

So now you know the reason why Isabel found herself in the situation she was in. Both secrets were now known to her – the cause and the means of her kidnap. But let me go back to the beginning to fill in a few details that were not immediately obvious to Isabel, but that became apparent over time.

*(In order to gain a full understanding of what had occurred, I have felt it necessary to supplement this account by relating to several conversations overheard by various household persons and diary entries).*

Helen and Marianne Laidenhead were well known throughout the county for being the most beautiful sisters most men had ever laid eyes on. Helen, the eldest, had a darker, more striking beauty than her younger sister, Marianne – and yet while she was much admired, she was generally the less popular of the two. For it was Marianne who would light up a room with her auburn hair and irresistible smile, making men tumble over themselves in an effort to please her, while her older sister would watch from a distance; an amused, yet slightly acerbic smile upon her lips. An often volatile relationship existed between the two young women, particularly when Marianne made a much-admired early engagement to Sir Aubrey Branden.

Sir Branden was an extremely wealthy young man. The only child of the rather eccentric and elderly Lord and Lady Branden, he had initially been a shy and awkward child. However, once freed from his parents' grasp, he blossomed at Eton and emerged as a very respectable and engaging young gentleman. He was therefore welcomed with open arms into the Laidenhead family circle, who, with two eligible daughters to marry off, were most pleased to have made his acquaintance. Although it was expected that he would choose the elder of the two sisters, it quickly became clear that his preference was for the younger one.

However, Helen soon forgave him for choosing Marianne when she found she had an admirer of her own – a Mr Nicholas Harley. A man of little money, but many acquaintances, he was a regular attendee at the Laidenhead gatherings and he and Helen soon became passionately involved. Of course, any lasting relationship between them was not possible due to his lack of means and station. Yet their meetings became more frequent and took place in ever more risky locations. It was upon one of these meets that Sir Branden entered upon their presence and was instantly made aware of their relationship. Helen made him promise he would not breathe a word of it to anyone, but soon her father became aware of the affair through other persons and the relationship was sharply brought to an end. Nicholas, blaming Helen for not choosing to stay with him, against her father's wishes, left for the Continent as a member of the Navy, with no intention of returning.

Having convinced herself she had done the right thing by obeying her parents, the heartbroken Helen then bitterly watched her sister disengage herself from her fiancé and return from her elopement, married to the handsome, golden-haired James Audley. Helen saw before her the relationship that she could have had, if Nicholas had the fortune that John did, and had she had the courage that her sister did. By the end of that month she realised she was carrying Nicholas' baby.

Thinking quickly, she gained her parent's permission to spend a year in France under the pretence of visiting friends and seeking a suitable husband. She took with her her lady's maid, a shrewd woman called Rachel Frain, and on the 1st May 1848, she gave birth to a sickly baby boy. Together, the three of them took the boat back to England, but before they had landed, the whooping cough had already taken hold of the tiny baby and within a few hours, he was dead.

Helen had him buried in a local cemetery and marked the spot with several smooth pebbles in the shape of a cross. She could not afford to have him buried in a family graveyard, for fear of the consequences, and so he lay in a pauper's grave, amidst many other unnamed children. She wore a black mourning gown during the short ceremony, a black veil fluttering over her face in the wind. She would continue to wear dark colours for the rest of her years.

She came home, pale and exhausted. Lady Laidenhead devoted all her efforts to restoring her daughter to full health, but much of her beauty had faded. When the elderly Lord Harringdon proposed to Helen three months later, she instantly accepted, to the surprise of many around her. Having secured her future, Catherine was born one year later, but Helen did not seem to take particularly to the child, leaving her often in the care of her nurse. Lady Laidenhead remarked that Helen was not born to be a mother. The fact was, Helen never had her whole heart to give to Catherine. She had left the largest part of it in the neglected graveyard, where it lay buried in the cold hard soil, beside her baby boy.

As Catherine grew up, her mother was very strict with her, always seeking to crush her romantic ideals and remind her of her duties. Helen's greatest fear was that her daughter would follow her path and her one aim was to get her married quickly and guarantee her a safe future.

Lord Harringdon died not long after Catherine's ninth birthday. He had been wealthy, largely due to some successful shares in the cotton industry and left his wife and daughter in a comfortable situation. Helen believed she was safe and began to relax, even inviting Isabel to come and stay with them, despite the grudge she still held against her sister. What she did not know was that her secret still lived and breathed and was in the hands of a man who was keeping it warm until it had gained as much value as possible. A man who still blamed her for not alerting him to her sister's intentions many years ago, even though Helen had been as much in the dark as he was.

Sir Branden was a shark in business, well-known for always getting what he wanted, though nobody was quite sure how. He had ploughed himself into his business after Marianne left him, channelling all his rage and grief into profitable ventures and schemes. This detached state had served to make him a very good businessman – he cared nothing for anyone and would sacrifice anything, for he believed he had nothing left of value. He trusted only one person, his manservant, Gaunt.

Together they lived at the house he had bought for his fiancée,

Mount Enderton, which slowly became a shrine to the woman he had loved, full of paintings that reminded him of her, a marble statue that he thought captured her likeness, gardens and flowers that he thought she would have liked...but his collection was far from complete.

It was on the 3$^{rd}$ of June that the late Lord Harringdon's stocks reached their highest value yet. The very next day, Sir Branden sent Gaunt to London to source the original birth certificate for Helen Harringdon's illegitimate son. Learning that the document had been destroyed in a church fire, Gaunt then headed North to Harringdon House as his source, Ms Frain, believed that her mistress had had a copy of the birth certificate that she kept still, despite the risk it would pose to her. It was a reminder to Helen of her son, the only thing she had of him. Breaking in through the pantry window, Gaunt found the document in a locked wooden box in her study.

Panicked by the focused theft, and unable to cover up the event, Helen instead told the police that an item of jewellery had been taken from her room, stowing the very present brooch inside the same wooden chest. She waited in terror for another few days, until the half-expected letter arrived. She knew why he was coming. What she did not know was what he wanted in return.

When Sir Branden arrived and told Helen of his price, she was relieved. Yes, the loss of the shares meant that Harringdon's future was perilous, but Catherine had a good marriage offer on the cards and she could quietly sell up once Catherine was safely married. Sir Branden had arrived a day early, to make sure that Helen did not have time to make any unwelcome preparations, and he had booked rooms in Ashton for one night, planning to take his payment and then leave.

Sir Branden saw Isabel quite by accident. He was leaving Helen's study when he looked up and saw her coming down the stairs. For a moment he truly believed that Marianne Laidenhead was alive and walking once more. He did not take his gaze from her as she walked gracefully down the steps, engrossed in the book she held out before her. She had no sense of his presence and passed by his silent figure into the gardens. It was when the sunlight fell upon her golden hair that he realised she was Audley's daughter. Hatred coupled with desire in his churning heart. He turned and went back into Helen's study to demand his new price.

*Extract from a conversation held between Lady Harringdon and Sir Branden overheard by the gardener at Harringdon House*

'She will not be short of offers, why should I let you take first pick? I am sorry for what she did to you, Branden. I really am. But your time has passed.'

'My dear Helen, you are in no position to deny me anything. I only have to speak a few words to your daughter's fiancé and her only hope of happiness will be gone. I know her dowry is already small and she is unlikely to attract another suitor.'

There was a pause.

'We used to be friends, Branden. Why will you not take the shares and leave – they are ample, surely?'

'Yes, we used to be friends. Indeed, I covered for you with Harley for no reason other than I was your friend. But then you let me down.'

'Do not you think I would have stopped her if I had known?'

'You may be telling the truth. You may not be. You always were good at lying.'

*Extract from Helen Harringdon's Diary*

*HARRINGDON, 22<sup>nd</sup> June 1866*

He knows. He knows everything! I have no choice but to aid him. May God forgive me.

### THE STORY CONTINUED BY THE EDITOR

Isabel was in the library, as she usually was when Sir Branden did not demand her presence in his study. She was reading the final page of *Madam Bovary*, a novel that had only recently come over from France. Obviously Sir Branden did not know its content or he most certainly would not have left it out for her to read. In fact, she suspected he knew very little about the contents of his library, having never seen him in there. Getting up, she went over to the eye-level bookshelf to replace the copy. In the black slit where the book had fitted so snugly, she thought she saw something glint. She looked closer and saw an empty knot in the wood, but there was nothing behind it, only blackness. She replaced the book. From behind it came a voice, muffled and twisted, as gnarled as the wood from which it came.

'How he pined... How he wept for her – that spoilt, wicked little wretch.'

The voice began to move, now coming from her right, still from inside the bookshelves.

'I thought he would die when she left him. But he was strong... he got up and carried on. He became a great man, with my help. Untouchable, he was... Until he saw you.'

She spun around as the voice moved along the walls, wicked and echoing. She knew who it was.

'I thought you were her at first, floating into the room like a precious angel on a cloud, trailing poison. But then I realised you were worse than her. For you were hers...*and his.*'

She turned again, but she could not see him – and yet his voice was so close. The voice of the house, the voice that hated her, that never left her. Was he now inside the very walls?

She waited until the echoes had retreated back into the walls; the nightmare had ended. She walked slowly from the room.


## ISABEL'S NARRATIVE
*(Extract from Isabel's Diary)*


*ENDERTON, 27ᵗʰ October 1866*

I know it was Gaunt's voice, whether by some trick or using secret passages in the walls. He must have known that I found the photograph; he must have always known what I now know. But instead of terrifying me, the discovery about my mother has given me strength. She stood up to Branden once and I will do the same. I am no longer afraid of him - all my dark thoughts have vanished. All I see is a broken and lonely man, trying to make up for what he has lost with a great house and a host of visitors, and now, with a doppelganger of the only woman he ever loved. I imagine that, after my mother left him, to the world he was unconcerned and smiling. Only when he was alone, would he have fallen apart. For I believe he must have truly loved her. Only a very great love could have turned to such a bitter hate.

I wonder if a small conscience inside him chides and scorns him for his cruelty, his presumption, with me. Perhaps this is why he seems to lose his confidence again and again at my door. For if he really wanted to gain entry, I am sure he could do; this is his house after all.

But I do not fear him. I even pity him a little.

How he will hate that.

# THE STORY CONTINUED BY THE EDITOR

It had been over a week since Isabel had found the photograph of her mother. Sir Branden had been away on a trip to London since that day (leaving Gaunt behind to watch her) and had only returned yesterday. A large number of new guests had returned with him and an extravagant dinner had been served to herald his return.

Isabel came down the stairs to dinner that night, every inch the immaculate, demure lady of the house. Whispers passed through the crowd like ripples as she descended. She felt forty pairs of eyes appraise her and pass comment behind expensive wine glasses and cigars. The hatred in her heart was well hidden as she approached her husband, but the expression of pleasure on Sir Branden's face when he met her at the foot of the stairs made her want to choke him. As he addressed her with the necessary pleasantries, Isabel searched his eyes but found no change in them. She suspected that Gaunt had not made mention of her discovery. Strangely, this frustrated her.

Isabel was bored and listless through dinner, finding that she had no appetite. The energy that had risen within her after making the discovery about Sir Branden and her mother seemed to have dissipated with Sir Branden's return. Indeed, she felt more hopeless than ever with the arrival of the new guests. She had been glad to see the five ruffians leave with Sir Branden when he left for London; but to see a new group arrive with him upon his return, despite their better manners and more pleasant countenances, only reminded her of the continuation of the endless pattern of dreary life at Enderton. No matter what discoveries she made about the past, it seemed that nothing could change her future.

After dinner, Sir Branden led her to the billiard room with a few chosen guests. Wearily, Isabel prepared herself for another long evening. Sir Branden passed round the cigars and handed out the billiard cues. The clock ticked, the newspaper pages rustled, the cues clicked against the balls. The minutes seemed to pass by, as though weighed with lead, and boredom began to gnaw at her. After a while, she had the strangest feeling that she had died, that she did not exist. Had she become invisible? Time started to bend and the room seemed to move before her very eyes as she stared into space. She had never heard such loud silence. But this was her life now; this was how things would go on. There was no way out.

The commotion inside her rose to a clamour until she could not bear it – she needed to get out of this place, find a way out of her skin, go somewhere quiet and simple where all was well. She wanted to scream. She wanted to stand up and throw the lamp across the room – to rip the newspapers from their hands, smash the leadlight windows into a thousand pieces and then run, barefoot and bare-armed across the soaking grass. But she sat, her hands still, knees one inch apart, eyes fixed on the floor. She had felt herself approaching invisibility and had now arrived at it. And so she remained until midnight struck.

She shivered as she walked through the hallway. The weather had broken as sharply and suddenly as a twig snapping. As she passed by the tall windows up the stair she did not see the first snowflakes fall.

As you have already read, that night the world became white, Isabel went out into the snow and the wondrous experience that followed filled her with fresh strength and fire. I pick up the narrative the morning after, which was the day of the great ball. Despite her late night, Isabel woke feeling as though she had slept for many days; her body and mind more refreshed than they had been in a long time. She went downstairs, feeling calm, but bold. The house was busy in expectation of the night's event; the snow had not stopped them from travelling many miles to attend the social event of the season.

Yet while the snowfall seemed to have released something within Isabel, it seemed to have steeled a resolve within Sir Branden. He found her standing by the French doors in the breakfast room, looking out over the white gardens. She looked up to find a grim expression on his face.

'I trust you enjoyed your time here while I was away?' he asked, ice lacing his voice.

'Yes, my imprisonment continues to thrill me,' she replied, making no effort to lower her voice despite the milling throng of guests.

She felt his hand tighten upon her arm.

'You are not under your aunt's roof any more Isabel. Heaven knows I have been patient with you, for you are still a child, but I will not tolerate your insolence any longer.'

She shook him off, her eyes ablaze.

'I am not a child – but you are old enough to be my father!'

She watched him flush at the rebuke, which was closer to the truth than he would ever admit. She continued, pursuing her advantage:

'And I believe I have been quite dutiful to you. Believe me, if I decided to be insolent, you would be well aware of it. I consider myself to have behaved remarkably well, considering how you have treated me. Or would you rather I raised my voice louder and tell the people in this room exactly what you have done to me.'

A red flush was creeping up his neck. She watched it spread with triumph.

'You bear my name. You are my wife. You will treat me with respect,' he said warningly.

'You forced your name upon me; you branded me as your wife. Therefore you have no more rights to my respect, or any other part of me, than a mongrel dog does to a piece of choice meat in a butcher's window.'

She watched him swell at her insolence.

'You will be silent, Isabel. I am to be deferred to and obeyed. This I demand as my right!'

Her chin lifted in determination.

'You have no rights over me. That which is taken by force and deceit is not lawful.' Her voice grew louder still, 'Only a coward takes by force that which he cannot gain by consent!'

Sir Branden's mouth hardened into a thin line. He took her by the arm and tried to walk her towards the other end of the room, away from the guests, but she held her ground, shaking him off with repugnance. She thought he was going to raise his voice to her, for the first time, but instead he leaned and spoke quietly in her ear.

'You stand there, with your disdainful eyes on me – I will not have it. '

She looked back at him and saw herself reflected in his eyes, tiny but unafraid. She realised then, that when he looked at her, he saw only her mother: defiant, and unsubmissive, ready to abandon him and scorn him all over again. Isabel smiled. Her mother had not allowed herself to be held back by him, and neither would she.

'I am not afraid of you,' she said plainly. 'And I am tired of this charade.'

She tried to pass him but he blocked her way.

'You should be afraid,' he hissed. 'You are going to learn that there is a price to be paid for your acts of defiance.'

Her eyes narrowed, blue and piercing.

'Do it then,' she said, bitingly. 'Be a man, and do it.'

# XXIII

'And - and then you were here. And he did not get me.'

'No, he did not,' said Mr Treador, reaching out a hand to her. They had stood for a long time while she talked, sometimes looking out over the white gardens, sometimes at each other. His hand was warm and held hers firmly, looking at her fully now. Never had she been gazed at so intently; his eyes were large - wondering, dazzling and full of life. She felt herself drawn into them, deeper and deeper; she did not want to blink, for fear of losing the moment.

Breaking the tension, he glanced over at the door and at the bolts that had held the door firmly shut for so long, now hanging from the shattered wood where the force of the blows had buckled it.

'Well, if there's one thing I have learned about you tonight Isabel Audley, it is that you are certainly resourceful,' he remarked lightly.

A short laugh broke from Isabel's lips. The noise sounded almost foreign to her; she had not laughed in such a long time. She turned back to him, her face serious once more.

'I am sorry I was not clear with you about my situation, Mr Treador. Legally my name is not Isabel Audley. But to me, it still is.'

'As it is to me,' he replied. 'I set no store by forced marriages.'

Warmth filled her heart, and she smiled up at him.

'And you must call me John,' he said amiably. 'For I also set no store by formalities.'

'Very well, John,' she said tentatively.

'And now you must get to bed,' he said brightly. 'I do not think you will have much more trouble tonight, but I will move my bed close to the painting behind which the passage lies. Should I hear any noises I will be back down in an instant, and by your side.'

'I am most grateful to you,' she said fervently.

'It is my duty and my honour. I can do no more for you at this moment Isabel, but from now on, I am your protector.'

'I will sleep soundly, knowing you are so close,' she said, stifling a yawn. She suddenly felt very tired.

'Then I must say goodnight,' he replied.

He raised her hand and kissed it, his dark hair tumbling over his eyes as he did so.

'Sleep well, Isabel.'

'And you – John.'

Isabel was standing by the open French doors in the breakfast room, looking out across the perfectly kept lawns, thinking of all that had happened the night before. Sir Branden had not appeared at breakfast, sending a note of apology to his guests for his absence. It was a beautiful day winter's day outside, the sun had melted the snow and the skies were bright and clear. The doors stood open and Isabel had a heavy shawl around her to protect her from the cold.

She was waiting. Each time she heard someone enter the room, she strained her ears to hear who it was, not wanting to look round for fear of seeming overly interested. When she woke this morning, she had half-convinced herself that the events of the previous night had been a dream, but her damaged door proved otherwise. He had been too perfect, too wonderful - her knight who had come to life. He will not come again, she told herself. She was sure he would have vanished into the night, like all her other hopes and dreams.

'And how are you this morning?' said a soft, low voice to her right.

Isabel jumped and looked from side to side: there was no one there. Stepping through the doorway, she glanced cautiously to her right. John stood there, also staring out across the gardens. Shielded by the wall, he could not be seen by anyone inside. Isabel smiled, pleasure filling her heart, and answered him warmly, keeping her gaze fixed outwards:

'I am very well, thank you.'

'Did you sleep?'

'Better than I have done in a long time.'

'That is good.'

He swung round to face her, only a foot away, yet to all the guests, it looked like she was still standing alone. Isabel could see him smiling at her from the corner of her eye, leaning casually against the outside wall.

'This is most difficult, for I cannot look at you,' she said, smiling at the gardens.

'Yes, but I can look at you, he said cavalierly.

'Why are you standing outside?' she said, amused by his audacity.

'I wanted to speak to you privately, to ask what you are doing today,' he replied, not taking his eyes from her.

'My day will consist of standing, sitting, and possibly even a short walk across the gardens,' Isabel replied in a tone of mock gravity. 'I am sure it will be most memorable.'

'Would you like to join me for a morning ride instead?'

She looked at him incredulously. Surely he must know that was impossible?

'I would very much like to spend more time with you, you see,' he continued, ' – if you were willing to grant me such a request. You have been cooped up here for so long and there is something I would like to show you that I think you might like.'

'You know I am not allowed to leave the house,' she replied, her heart beating quickly.

'What if no one were to know?'

'Gaunt follows my every footstep. I cannot so much as turn a page of my book without him noticing,' she said bitterly

'But – menace as he is - surely he does not enter your room?'

'No. At least, I do not believe so.'

'Then what if you were to say that you have a terrible headache and are going to your room for the day?' he suggested.

'Then he would wait outside the door to make sure I kept my word,' said Isabel darkly.

'And does he know that there is a passage that links your room with mine?' asked John.

Isabel thought for a moment.

'I do not believe so – if he did then I am sure that you would not have been given that room, for it could have been put to better use,' said Isabel, her blood running cold at the thought of Sir Branden appearing through the black space in the wall in the dead of night. 'Then shall we use that as your escape route?' he asked playfully. Isabel felt her heart racing.

'But how would I get out of the house?'

'Well,' said John, 'with your faithful bodyguard waiting for you in the hallway outside, we can use the servant's stairs and leave through the back door to the stables - the house will be quite quiet by that time for the guests will be out riding, or reading in the morning room. I can go on ahead and have the horses ready. Your husband is in bed, claiming illness (though I suspect it is actually a case of too much wine and some measure of humiliation) and you will be back before dinner – no one is to know where you really are!'

Isabel fought a burning desire to look at him.

'You must be mad to think this will work,' she said, hope fighting her disbelief.

'I am a little mad,' he said apologetically. 'But life is for living - especially on such a beautiful day – and not for staying inside like a trapped creature.'

Gaiety and gravity danced across his countenance as he spoke, for she could not help but look round.

'What if we are caught?' said Isabel, already deciding that she was going to attempt it.

A cynical smile creased John's lips.

'Then I will tell your husband that I insisted that I took you out and did not realise that he would mind.'

'He will not believe you,' she said with conviction.

'I do not care. Will you come?'

Isabel could feel his fascinating eyes dwelling on her in anticipation. At that moment, if he had told her to take his hand and run into a blazing fire with him, she would have done.

'Of course,' she replied. 'Give me half an hour.'

It was easy enough for Isabel to feign a headache and have two concerned guests escort her upstairs to her room. She leaned heavily on the arms offered at either side of her, and walked very slowly up the stairs. When they reached her room, one of the gentlemen asked her:

'Are you sure I should not call the doctor?'

'No, I just need to rest and shut my eyes,' she replied - and thinking quickly, added, 'and please request that the maid does not knock my door. The noise would be unbearable and I could not think of eating anything until dinnertime, at least.'

They both agreed and said they hoped that she would recover soon.

Gaunt hovered behind, looking suspicious, but the men seemed so genuinely concerned for her, and her performance so convincing, that when the door closed behind her, Isabel heard him go back downstairs, apparently satisfied that she was indeed ill.

Once inside, Isabel realised that there were two fresh bolts on the door, and the broken wood had been replaced on the inside. She smiled at John's initiative and drew the bolts the door quietly. Silently she changed into her soft leather boots and put on her riding habit. As she moved across the room towards the portrait, she caught sight of herself in the mirror. Her face was aglow, her eyes sparkling. It was the first time she had seen herself look happy in this room. She took a deep breath, swung the portrait open and pulled herself up into the high space.

Getting through the house unseen was beautifully easy. John's room was on the fourth floor – there were so many guests staying that the normally unused rooms had been opened for the season - and bypassing the main staircase, Isabel slipped down the back stairs meeting no one, not even Gaunt. Reaching the bottom, she unlatched the back door that led out by the stables. Stepping through the doorway and glancing to her right, she saw John standing there waiting, a triumphant smile on his face. He took her hand; her heart was thumping.

'Are you ready to run?' he asked, smiling mischievously.

Within minutes they were riding out across the fields. John had saddled the horses and tied them to the far gate, so after running through the gardens, they quickly mounted them and set off at speed. The remaining guests were absorbed in their papers in the morning room at the other side of the house, so they were far removed from sight. Isabel could feel the fresh air rushing past her as she rose and fell in the saddle. It tasted like freedom. She turned to look at the man by her side. He looked as she felt – exuberant, excited, and free. He urged his horse on faster, riding ahead of her.

'Where are we going?' Isabel cried out, with incredulous delight as Enderton became smaller and smaller behind them.

'Follow me!' he called back.

They rode fast away from the house, the fields becoming less organised and more open, until there were no fences at all. They were in the uninhibited countryside, and Isabel realised for the first time what a beautiful area she had been living in. The climbing green hills before her filled her with delight and her heart rejoiced in the brilliant blue sea that sparkled on their left.

It was a surprisingly mild day for November and with her fur-lined cloak, she was quite warm. The coquelicot ribbons on her bonnet danced under her chin as they rode up and up until at last the land flattened out in a plateau. John slowed his horse and Isabel did the same, coming to a halt before a tall stone structure that stood before them. It was an ancient folly, weathered and beaten down through many years of abuse from the wind and salt spray that rose up from the sea below. Parts of it had crumbled away, yet the main tower still stood proudly, a testament to the workmanship that had gone into it. A curving stone staircase ran up the side of it, though most of its passage now lay open to the elements. The low doorway that led to the stairs remained, looking forlorn without its supporting walls. Ancient ivy had crept through the cracks and up the stones, knitting the tower together with a strong green blanket. There was a small circular room at the top, the collapsed ceiling now negating any need for the large window that looked out over the blue sea below. Yet, despite the folly's crumbling state, there was something defiant about the structure, which was hewn from the very rock upon which they now stood. Isabel felt drawn to its ruined majesty.

'Shall we try the view from the top?' said John, reading her pleasure of it.

'Yes please,' said Isabel, dismounting alongside him, and handing him the reigns of her mare.

He tied both horses to a rusting hook on the wall and slowly they climbed the tightly twisting stairs.

John went first, leading her by the hand, while she used the other to gather her skirts above her ankles. She glanced up at him as he climbed, admiring the strength and grace of his figure. Reaching the top, she stepped up into the small room at the top and gasped at the view that spread out around her. She was higher up than she had expected. Behind them was the solemn beauty of the woods, to her left, the tiny speck that was Enderton, and before her, the vast, white-specked expanse of the sea. John stood quite close behind her as she moved slowly round, taking in the view.

'You will make yourself dizzy,' he said laughingly, putting his hands on her shoulders.

Isabel continued to move round until she was face to face with him.

'Why was this place built?' she asked.

'Well, the story goes that the folly was built by the original master of Enderton, many hundreds of years ago,' he began, pointing up at a flock of black birds flying above them. 'He loved to train rooks and had one favourite bird, who was quite tame. He would send this bird out from the top of his folly, and the bird would always return from overseas with something for his master – sometimes a twig from a foreign plant, sometimes a shell from a far off beach. The master was a very private man; he had few friends and never left his home: they say he lived his life through this bird. One day, when he was very old, he sent the bird out from this room, but it did not come back. They found the master here one day, still waiting for his bird, his hand outstretched. He was dead.'

Isabel was gazing at him in rapt attention.

'How terribly sad,' she said, finding tears in her eyes when he had finished.

'You know how to let yourself into a story,' remarked John, his eyes upon hers. 'I watched it come to life in your eyes as I told it.'

'I love stories,' replied Isabel. 'Especially when they are true.'

'Even if they are sad?'

'Even then – life is made up of sad and happy stories.'

'I normally only like the happy ones,' he replied. 'Which is why we shall have to give yours a happy ending.'

A little bird fluttered its soft wings against her heart in joyful anticipation.

'I would be most grateful for that,' she said, trying to contain the hope in her voice. 'Though how you will manage it, I have no idea.'

'There is always a way,' he said thoughtfully. 'It may just take some time.'

Her heart began to beat a little faster.

'You are quite extraordinary,' she said, almost without meaning to.

'Thank you,' he replied, with a mock bow, his hair tumbling over his eyes again. He swept it back with a flourish. 'It is my aim in life to surprise and delight.'

'Well you have succeeded with me.'

'Ah, but we have only known each other a few hours.'

'It is enough,' she thought, thinking that they had traversed months of relationships in just those few hours – last night had changed everything.

'A few hours of me might well be enough for you, by the end of the day,' he said, a strange look in his eyes.

Isabel paused, unsure if he was being serious. The corners of John's mouth twitched, his eyes crinkled and then he burst into the merriest fit of laughter she had ever heard. Unsure of why they were laughing, but glad all the same, she laughed heartily with him – the first time she had done so in many weeks.

'You look like a ship whose sails have suddenly caught the wind,' said John as the laughter receded. 'It is good to see you smile.'

'It is good to smile,' she replied. 'Being away from Enderton makes me feel like myself again.'

'Then let us continue our day with a brisk walk along the top of the cliffs. Perhaps I may be able to take you back with a permanent smile on your face.'

'If I know that you will be staying a while, then I can almost guarantee that,' Isabel replied shyly.

'I will stay for as long as you need me,' he replied gravely. 'But', he added with a quick smile, 'do not smile too much or Sir Branden may notice that something is wrong.'


ISABEL'S NARRATIVE
*(Extract from Isabel's Diary)*


*ENDERTON, 11ᵗʰ November 1866*


He has just left me. We got back completely unseen and he replaced the horses while the stable hands were inside having dinner. I need to dress for dinner soon, but I must write down how I feel. I want to capture this feeling forever, to lock it in my mind ... for I feel it may not last – it seems as fleeting as the morning mist.

The exhilaration of the day, the pure raw emotion of it, crackles through me like fire. Today I felt, for the first time, that I suddenly *existed*. Not that I had not existed before – but I had not existed fully. Every fibre of my being had come alive in his thrilling presence. It was the most intoxicating feeling I have ever experienced, and so utterly unexpected. I do not know how he feels - I barely understand how I feel - nor do I expect anything more than what happened today... but it was wonderful. Real life left me and all was a dream.


## THE STORY CONTINUED BY THE EDITOR

It was difficult for Isabel not to look at John when he entered the breakfast room the next morning. He strolled into the room, his untidy fringe giving him a roguish, boyish look. The other guests glanced up at him when he appeared, his hands thrust deep into the pockets of his jacket: relaxed, assured, and confident.

He sought Isabel's eye straightaway and she smiled back, but immediately she let her mask slip back into place when Sir Branden entered the room. She sat down, settled her skirts, and began to sip her morning coffee. She had put especial effort into her outfit that morning and it seemed to have the desired effect: John barely took his eyes from her. Isabel smiled to herself. The irony was that Sir Branden took pleasure from other men admiring her and as long as Sir Branden saw no more than appreciative glances from John, his admiring attention would only raise him higher in Sir Branden's favour as he was clearly a man who commended his host's taste.

The day continued without event. Isabel looked for any opportunity to speak to John, who continued to occupy her thoughts, but her every move was guarded. She contented herself with wearing her very best emerald-coloured taffeta dress to dinner and then, seeing that John had retired early, asked permission to do the same. Sir Branden, seeming mollified by Isabel's efforts to look and behave as he would have her do, consented.

When Isabel got to her room, she felt her heart sinking a little. She reminded herself that she had expected nothing more after yesterday's events, but already she was feeling a longing to see and speak with John again. She told herself that John's actions and words meant little more than friendship; that his rescue of her was nothing more than a gentleman's duty; that he would have behaved so to any woman - but certain glances and phrases that had aroused such hope in her continued to play in her mind.

Trying to shake her feelings of despondency, she began to remove her glittering jewellery. A voice made her look round.

'Mr Treador, requesting entrance.'

Joy filled Isabel's heart and she rushed over to the painting, swinging it open. John was crouching in the gap, still in his dinner suit, his cravat hanging undone.

'I did not want to knock, for I fear that may have unpleasant connotations for you.'

'This was much more pleasant,' she replied, slightly breathless.

'I have not disturbed you?' he asked, swinging his legs down.

His movements reminded her of a young cat – there was a seductive suppleness to his body.

'Not at all! In fact, I had hoped to speak with you before the day was over.'

'And what did you want to say?' he asked, straightening up to his full height and brushing the dust from his shoulders that had gathered as he squeezed himself down the narrow passageway and stairs.

She found herself at a loss for words – what had she wanted to say to him? Most of it could not be put into words.

'I now cannot remember,' she said falteringly.

'Well I wanted to say how much I enjoyed yesterday,' he said, covering over her embarrassment, 'and that I hope we can have a great many more trips together – not too often, of course, as we must escape detection – but perhaps every few days?'

'I would like that,' replied Isabel, her eyes shining.

'Come, let us sit down,' he said, leading her by the hand over to the neatly upholstered sofa by the window, '– that is, if I can invite you to sit down in your own room.'

'You can,' she replied. 'And it is not my room.'

'Of course. It is a temporary residence,' he acknowledged with a smile.

She liked the way he accepted her situation as a passing phase. Settling himself comfortably, John turned to her.

'So shall we go again tomorrow?'

Isabel tried to disguise her enthusiasm.

'That may be possible – but I cannot feign another headache.'

'No, of course not – but where do you usually spend your mornings?'

'In the library,' she replied.

'Does it have a sash window?'

'It does.'

'Then I shall lift it high enough for you to climb through. I am meant to be shooting with the other men, but I will make my excuses and say that I fancy a ride instead. I think we should leave at different times to avoid suspicion, so I will leave your horse tied in the same place as yesterday... What are you smiling at?'

'You have thought this through very well.'

'What else do you think I do during the endless days here?'

'The other men seem to have plenty to occupy them.'

'The other men would not dare to dream as I do,' he said with a smile.

'You know that there is a lot at stake here,' she said seriously.

'For you more than I. Are you willing to risk so much for a walk with me?'

'What else have I to lose?' Isabel replied, fire in her eyes. 'Branden has taken everything else from me. I will not let him rule every part of my life.'

'Your defiant spirit rises again,' John said approvingly. 'And you will be pleased to know that Sir Branden's servant, who seems to keep a particularly close eye on you, is being sent to London for two weeks on important business.'

Isabel's heart leapt.

'Gaunt will be gone? Then there is practically no risk at all!'

'I am sure your captor will have other eyes upon you, but yes, this does make your life much easier.'

Isabel relaxed back into the sofa.

'So I will see you tomorrow?' John asked, rising up.

She smiled up at him.

'Indeed you shall.'

Isabel arrived at the folly just before ten o'clock the next morning. The plan had worked just as John had said it would. She jumped down from her horse and tied it up next to his, glancing around for him. A voice echoed from within the folly:

'How shocking, to see a young woman out on her own without a companion. One would almost think she had an independent mind!'

Isabel moved round to the folly entrance and she smiled as John appeared, his hair ruffled and windswept from the ride. Assuming the air of a haughty debutante, she replied,

'Independent and yet not without a suitable companion,' she replied promptly. 'For it is quite proper that I should ride out alone, as long as I have a gentleman to accompany me.'

'And would I qualify as such a gentleman?' he asked, stepping down to face her, mischief riddling his features.

'I believe so – as long as you behave in a gentlemanly manner,' she replied, stepping away from him smartly.

'You mean I should not refer to you simply as Isabel?'

'Certainly not,' she replied with a tilt of her chin. 'I am Lady Isabel, to you.'

'And should I not do this?' he said, putting his arm lightly around her waist.

'Indeed not!' she replied, delight spreading across her face. 'That would be most shocking!'

'Or this?' He lifted her hand to his lips and kissed it slowly. She swallowed and looked deeply into his dark brown eyes, which were closer to hers than they had ever been before.

'That – that is most definitely - '

'Acceptable?' he posed with twinkling eyes.

'Quite acceptable,' she replied, a little breathless.

She looked up at him: his face was so animated, so full of expression, and totally focused upon her. She was completely in love with him before she even realised it.


ISABEL'S NARRATIVE
*(Extract from Isabel's Diary)*


*ENDERTON, 14<sup>th</sup> November 1866*

For days now I have not walked, but flown.

How many times have I read of love affairs in novels, how many times have I dreamed of such things happening to me and yet struggled to grasp what it would be like? How many girls at school told me of the various boys they were in love with, of the secret whispered conversations and stolen kisses they shared – and I, enviously, wondered when my time would come, wondered what it would be like to be the other part of someone. And now, it seems, the reality is so near I can almost touch it.

It is so much like a fairytale that I keep expecting to have to turn the page - and then I realise all over again that this is my life and that this is really happening to me. It is like the world has shifted and suddenly everything looks different – wonderful, beautiful. I feel every fibre in me re-awakening. When I look at him, I feel hope.

And yet this feels so different from how I thought it would. For although it feels like a story, it is also so real it hurts. It is so different from any other emotion I have ever felt, so completely unrelatable to any previous experience. I feel intoxicated, wild, fearless. I wonder, is this how my mother felt when she met my father? Is this what it feels like to be in love? It seems much more than such a small word – such a huge, deep, tremendous awakening...

Ever since I was a child have ached for more than ordinary, and now I have found it. He walked into my life – no, burst into it – and now, all I can see is him. My time without him is empty; he makes everything else feel stale. Today I read the same paragraph of *Jane Eyre* three times without even taking in one word. I am so unlike myself. But when he is there, he makes everything come alive.

And yet, does he feel the same way about me? I am so scared, so terrified of revealing myself. What if he is not aware of my feelings? What if he is simply being friendly, just doing his duty, or worse, acting out of pity towards me? What if he already has a woman somewhere, whom he loves. The very thought makes me turn cold, and the sun fade from the sky.

### THE STORY CONTINUED BY THE EDITOR

Isabel may have told herself that she did not expect anything more from John, but she was seventeen, and very human. Soon she could not hide from herself that she was utterly in love with him. And why not, you may ask - he was all her childhood dreams personified, all her romantic imaginings come to life in front of her, in human form.

However, her fears about his motives began to beset her more and more when she was with him, on their secret walks and meetings. John was clearly aware of this as they walked together one afternoon, high up on the cliff path.

'What is troubling you, Isabel?' he asked, concern in his voice.

'Nothing,' she replied lightly, keeping her eyes straight ahead.

'I may not have known you for very long, but I do know that you are not telling me the truth,' he said, with a sideways glance.

Isabel stopped walking, her heart drumming in her chest.

'I just wanted to know why you are spending time with me?' she asked, trying to keep her voice normal.

'Why?' He looked genuinely surprised, the sea wind buffeting his hair about his forehead. 'Is is not obvious?'

'Well,' Isabel continued tentatively, aware of how childlike her words sounded, 'I wondered if it was because you felt sorry for me - that you felt it was your duty to look after me?'

'Isabel, how could you think that?' John said, astonishment in his voice. 'Can you not see how much I care for you?'

Isabel's heart began to beat tenfold faster.

'Of course I can – it is just, it is hard to believe that...you would want someone...like me.'

John looked incredulous.

'What - someone who is beautiful, fascinating, brave, strong and wonderful in every way?'

Isabel was lost for words. John stepped closer to her.

'I am yours, Isabel,' he said in a soft tone. 'Completely.'

Her red lips were slightly open, like rose petals that had landed on a soft pile of snow. Unable to resist, he leaned over and brushed her lips with his own. Tense and surprised at his touch, her lips resisted, but then yielded, soft and warm. The connection thrilled her whole frame and the colour came into her face in a slow, rich blush.

'I do not know how else to enforce my words,' he said tenderly, 'but do you believe me now?'

# XXIV

It was with great unhappiness that Isabel realised Gaunt's return was imminent. She knew it would make it much harder to see John, despite his inventive escapes, for she would be watched every hour of the day. She mentioned this to him as they sat in the garden, as close as they dared – Isabel on a bench on one side of a shrubbery, wrapped in her furs, and John on the other, a great stone statue of a headless Roman Gladiator between them. Both of them kept their heads down, Isabel feigning reading and John drawing idly on a notebook he carried with them. Had they been seen from a distance, you would have thought they did not even realise each other's presence.

'You know that we cannot leave the house, or be seen together, from morning to night, once my shadow returns,' she said darkly, turning a page.

'Yes, I know,' he replied from behind the statue.

Isabel paused, waiting for John to lament this tragedy, but he said nothing more.

'It will be hard not to see you, except when we are in public and unable to speak,' she said, trying to keep a tremor from her voice.

'Why only then?' he asked.

'Because I will be tailed, every hour of the day,' she replied, surprised that he had not realised this.

'Yes – but there are many other hours available to us,' he said in a matter-of-fact tone.

'What do you mean?' she asked, wonderingly.

'Do you not enjoy the midnight hours?' he asked, his words sparking a thrill in her.

'You mean for us to sneak away after everyone has gone to bed?' she said in astonishment.

'Why not?' came John's voice, calm and confident. 'If they take your sunlit hours from you then I shall claim the hours of darkness with you.'

'But where shall we go?'

'To our favourite spot, of course.'

'The folly? That would be almost impossible!' she exclaimed.

'I love that word 'almost',' he said, and she could see the smile on his face without turning round.

Isabel tried to think rationally for a moment.

'It will be so cold up there at night –'

' – Then we shall dress warmly,' he replied. 'I will bring coverings and light a fire.'

Isabel thought of flames dancing, their sparks flying high into the sky -

' - But it may be seen from the house.'

'Not from the other side of the hill. Do not worry Isabel,' he said reassuringly, 'I have thought it through and ascertained our visibility already.'

A warmth was spreading through Isabel that had nothing to do with the morning sunlight streaming down around her. She longed to look round at John but already there were other men out walking in the garden, enjoying the fine morning.

'So you do want to see me still,' she said, unable to hide the joy in her voice.

'Isabel, until I can take you away from here, I want to make the most of every opportunity with you,' he said fervently. 'Give me a few days to make the final arrangements and we will be together, I promise you.'

John was as good as his word. Three days later, at the midnight hour, Isabel was creeping down the back stairs of the silent house, dressed in her very warmest outfit, clutching a fur scarf around her neck. John was awaiting her at the back door, and quickly led her to the stables. Within a matter of moments, they were on horseback, speeding through the night. It was the first night of December, and there was magic in the air.

When they crossed the top of the hill and rode down towards the folly, a glimmer of light caught Isabel's eye. She glanced at John in alarm but he only smiled and motioned her to go on. She rode ahead, the lights growing stronger, and soon she was dismounting and heading round to the other side of the tower to see what was causing the glow.

It was like walking into an enchanted castle. All around the stairs and entrance of the folly burned tall taper candles, their flames dancing in the light night breeze. A crackling fire had been lit near the wall, casting a warm glow around the soft blankets and furs that had been scattered nearby. Two cups of hot chocolate were warming by the flames. Isabel was completely amazed.

'How – when did you do all this?' she asked in astonishment.

John pulled her close.

'Did I forget to tell you? I am brilliant.'

He smiled at her – a wide smile so full of joy that it was almost childlike. It lit his whole face and touched Isabel's heart.

'You see,' she said, touching his cheek with her gloved hand, 'that is what I love about you. With you, nothing is ever done by halves – where I walk, you run; where I hope, you make it happen; and when I smile, you beam, until I think your mouth will split from the grin.'

He grinned still wider then, and kissed her.

'I think this is going to be a most wonderful night,' she said, sitting herself down amongst the furs.

It was one of those black nights where the darkness was so thick you could almost feel its velvety folds against your skin. But it was not cold – more like a warm shroud that lay across your shoulders and moved with you. The stars shone above while the candles flickered below. Isabel leaned her head against John's shoulder and sipped her chocolate as he pointed out the constellations to her. Several of the names she had not heard before.

'Do you know the name of every star?' she asked, curiously.

'Not every one,' he admitted, '- but the ones I do not know, I create new names for.'

'And are you allowed to do that,' she asked, laughingly.

'Well after all, each star was only named by a man - so what gives his created name precedence over mine?' he said with humour.

'I suppose you are right,' she conceded. 'You may continue.'

His eyes sparkled as he pointed up at a very small star to the far right of the folly. It was tiny, but very, very bright, twinkling like a beautiful diamond caught in firelight.

'That one there – that is your star,' he said gently.

'My star?'

'Yes – I have just given it to you.'

'You cannot give away a star!' Isabel exclaimed

'Yes I can,' he said daringly. 'What would you like to call it?'

Isabel stared at it - millions of miles away, yet still dazzling.

'Aurora,' she said softly.

'Perfect,' he breathed in her ear, his arms around her now.

She leant back into the soft warmth of his body, the darkness all around them. For the first time since she could remember in many months, it was night, and she was not afraid.

'Will you take me there, one day?' she asked, remembering her childhood dream of visiting the moon.

John laughed.

'What to the stars? I will try.'

'What do you think is on the other side of them?' she said, more seriously.

'Life,' he replied, thoughtfully.

'What kind of life?'

'I am not sure. Beautiful life. Wonderful, glorious life that makes you feel so happy and yet so sad at the same time.'

She stared up at him. Something deep was stirring in his eyes. She felt it was time to ask a question that had been on her mind since she had first met him.

'You said before that you do not believe in God.'

'I did.'

'Then what do you believe in?'

'I believe in people, and their ability to do good.'

'Then why do so many of us do such wrong?' she asked quietly.

John glanced at her, and saw the dark figure in her eyes.

'You are thinking of Sir Branden?'

The figure split and became many more men, dragging a helpless girl down a stone aisle by her hair.

'Him, yes - and others.'

John's face darkened.

'Curse that man for taking you and condemning you to this life of imprisonment.'

'I am glad that he took me!' Isabel exclaimed.

'Why?' asked John, his eyes troubled.

'Because if he had not, then I would not have met you.'

John dropped her hand as though it had burned him.

'I am not worth that cost, Isabel!'

'I believe you are,' she said in surprise.

'I am not,' he said soberly. 'Believe me.'

'Well who are you then?'

The question rang from her lips before she could stop it. John looked surprised.

'I am the man you see here, I am the man you know.'

'But what was your past, where do you live – who are your family? I hardly know anything about you.'

The light from the fire was dancing upon John's face, creating a different expression every time the flames moved. He seemed to sink inward for a moment, no longer aware of her presence.

'John?' she said, uncertainly.

'Does my past matter?' he replied suddenly, coming back to himself. 'It is who we are right here, right now, that counts. The past is just leaves in the wind.'

'But do you not think that your past makes you who you are?' asked Isabel curiously.

An inscrutable look passed across his face.

'No, I do not,' he replied. 'We are eternally shifting creatures. We can be who we want to be, not defined by what has gone before.' His handsome eyes brooded under his dark brows as he stared darkly into the flames.

Isabel feared she had upset him and looked away, pretending to tend the fire while she gathered her thoughts. She had known John for several weeks now (although it felt much longer), but during that time he had hardly spoken of anything but the present. She could not justify her need to know more about him, it was simply the ancient human urge for answers. Did she need to know his past? Perhaps not. But her past had made her who she was, it was important to her. How strange to find that he held it in such little regard.

John noticed her furrowed brow and crestfallen eyes, and his expression relaxed. He pulled her back again.

'I see that you have a curious mind, my lady. Very well, I relent. I will give you seven questions about my past – no more, no less - will that satisfy you?'

Isabel smiled – she could not help it.

'Very well,' she replied. 'I shall make them good ones.' She pursed her lips and thought for a moment. 'Where did you grow up?' she asked curiously.

He paused, but then answered,

'In the south west.'

Isabel narrowed her eyes.

'That is very vague,' she replied.

'Why do you need to know any more?' he said, with an easy smile

She continued, determined to make her questions more focused.

'Are your parents still alive?' She saw how he battled with himself before he answered her:

'No. They are dead,' he said stiffly.

There was silence, as they both sat lost in very different trains of thought. Isabel was weighing her questions out carefully in her head.

'Have you done much travelling?'

'Yes.'

'What is your vocation?'

'Teacher.'

She brought the next question out with a lightness of touch that masked a deep-rooted fear:

'Married?'

She cast a keen glance at him and he smiled.

'No,' he replied, in a slightly reproachful tone.

She carried on quickly:

'Where is your home?'

John tapped his breast pocket.

'Here. I carry my home with me, and am not based anywhere. I do not like to be tied down.'

'That is not a proper answer!' Isabel said, slightly indignantly

'But it is true.'

She gave him a disapproving look, but relented. He pulled her closer and said,

'Last question – use it wisely.'

She gazed up into his eyes, with their many secrets. They looked so much older than the smooth face they sat in.

'How old are you?' she asked at last.

'What an impertinent question!' he said in mock indignation.

'It's only impertinent if you are a lady!' she replied slyly.

'Well, I am old enough to have the right not to answer your question, young madam.'

'Tell me!' she said playfully. 'It is my final question – and I can be just as stubborn as you are, sir.'

'Well you do not want to waste it on such a boring question. I have no age - I am a mysterious creature who defies all facts and figures,' he said enigmatically. 'Now ask another.'

'You are indeed mysterious,' Isabel mused, considering whether or not to pursue the battle. She could see the resolve behind John's merry eyes and with a sigh, gave up the fight.

'And so, sweet interrogator, what is your final question,' he said, brushing a stray curl from her shoulder.

Isabel thought through his previous answers and found something that puzzled her.

'Tell me?' he said, noticing the question in her eyes.

Isabel spoke slowly, thinking it through: 'You are obviously wealthy, for Sir Branden only invites guests from the upper classes to stay at Enderton, and yet you say you are a teacher, which, forgive me, is a middle-class profession.'

'Ah, but I do not teach out of necessity, but out of a desire to do something I enjoy,' he said shrewdly. 'A school environment allows me both company and solitude, and it is also a vocation I can participate in, in whatever country I choose. I speak several languages, you see,' he added.

Seeing further questions in her eyes, John sighed and continued.

'I could not live the life of a gentleman. Those long idle days filled with meaningless pursuits. I like to be useful, to bring my skills to benefit others. I do not think Sir Branden knew of my profession when I caught his attention. It would have been my rather arbitrary attendance at a well-established club in London and a bribed investigation into my financial affairs that would have gained me my invite.'

'And why did you accept?' Isabel asked, curiously.

'I accepted out of boredom and a faint interest in meeting a man I had heard so much about. I knew within seconds that I would learn no more that I already did, however – never have I met a man so reserved, so skilled at hiding his true self behind a wall of manners and civility. Unfortunately, through you, I have learned far more of his character now that I would have ever wished to know.' He paused and then smiled at her. 'There – I have given you several answers to one question. Now you cannot claim you have been hard done by.'

Isabel smiled and conceded. It was true, she knew more about her protector now. But although she could see partway down the dark corridor, the light only shone so far, and there were many locked doors leading off to which she did not yet have the key. She still wanted more.

'So Sir Branden invited you to his house because he thinks you are an interesting character,' she asked, wondering if he would give anything else away.

'Alas, he was mistaken,' said John with finality, a twinkle in his eye. Then he put his finger irresistibly on her lips.

'Hush,' he said, playfully.

'What is it?' asked Isabel.

She leaned over him so that a ripple of her hair played upon his cheek

'Can you hear it?'

She strained her ears.

'Hear what?' she asked.

'The sea,' said John. 'The sea is playing us its music – listen.'

Now that there was silence, down below she could hear the waves breaking on rocks, and further out, the deep roar of the ocean. It sounded like a call, to which the birds above, buffeted by the wind, answered with their wild cries. She even thought she heard the far off bellow of a sea creature, but that may have been her imagination.

'A requiem for our dreams,' he said, in low, sweet tones.

'It is beautiful,' she said softly.

'All life is beautiful,' said John, his dark eyes fixed upon her. 'But only if it is being observed… Just like you.'

He looked at her, his face beautiful in the flame light.

'And when have you been observing me?' Isabel asked, teasingly, putting back his fringe from his eyes so that she could look into them.

He did not return the smile. Instead he glanced away, as if remembering a half-forgotten dream.

'John?'

He looked back at her, a strange look in his eyes: half apologetic, half-revering.

'I saw you… that night in the garden… when it snowed. When you danced.'

Isabel froze. She felt as though John had tread upon the innermost part of her. She felt a strange pain.

'I did not know anyone was there that night,' she said, confusion in her voice.

John looked at her deeply, his eyes captivating, mesmerizing; and Isabel suddenly realised – of course he had been there. That moment had been meant for him, meant for both of them. It was the moment when she had been more herself than she had ever been. It was why he knew her so well, for she had completely revealed herself in that perfect instant when their worlds collided. The pain gave way to a feeling of wonderment.

John took both her hands, uncertain of her response.

'I came across you quite by accident as I walked through the snow. Isabel, it was the most beautiful sight I have ever seen, and it will remain with me forever. I did not know who you were, nor why you were there, but somehow you gave me hope in a world that I had given up on. Your innocence, and your beauty shone so brightly, it was overwhelming. And now I realise, it was amidst horror, and persecution, which makes it all the more incredible. You opened my eyes, Isabel; you have opened my eyes to a future that I am not afraid of.'

Isabel's heart was beating with an almost formidable delight. She did not know what to say, nor, she realised, did she need to say anything. They were meant to be together, and that was all she needed to know.

And so they sat, in the deepening darkness, luxuriating in the quiet hours that belonged to them alone, while the stars shone on above them. There is a safety in the evening sky, a peace that it brings. Isabel and John wrapped themselves in the velvety darkness that was all around them, allowing their thoughts and dreams to intertwine, their eyes drinking in the beauty of the night.

'Let tomorrow hold what tomorrow will hold. Tonight is ours,' they said silently to one another.

ISABEL'S NARRATIVE
*(Extract from Isabel's Diary)*

*ENDERTON, 7<sup>th</sup> December 1866*

I long to see him. Every moment spent without him is spent counting down the hours until I can see him again – those glorious mealtimes and wonderful, wonderful evenings. For the first time I am making full use of the blood-bought gifts that Branden has given me. I utilise them to their best advantage – jewels, gowns and hair clasps. But not for him – oh, no. It is all for John.

When I am alone, I am constantly thinking about him – wondering where he is, what he is doing during those male hours when I can have no part of him. My nights are spent dreaming of him. My imagination takes us away, far away, to a place where we can be freely together, where he holds me in his arms and tells me that he is mine. He is my air in this place, my very own life force in a world that had seemed so lifeless. Every day he makes my chains feel lighter, and easier to bear.

For the first time I appreciate the many guests that Branden has here at Enderton. Despite my ever-constant shadow, John and I are still able to exchange words, for as long as I speak to other guests on rotation, I believe we can escape detection.

These shared moments are brief periods of luxury. We have not been able to escape for almost a week now and this makes every second precious. To make matters far worse, John has been moved to another room. Due to a slightly decreased number of guests, there was a larger guest room available on the first floor and he was relocated, despite his protestations. There is therefore no way for us to communicate after hours unless we leave the house again.

In these fleeting instances when we meet, amidst a busy crowd, or on the way to a meal, I luxuriate in his presence, wanting every second to last just a little longer. I am acutely aware of every one of his movements, of every inch that he moves closer to me, of every fibre of my body reaching out and longing to be beside him. The small space between us feels like acres, and yet I wonder how no one else in the room can be aware of this crackling intensity between us that prickles all over my body. I feel as though we are emanating light and heat, as bright as the noonday sun. He looks at me and I smile back, giving him my full self in the gaze. Can anyone else see that my heart is full? I feel as though I may burst with joy.

And then, we realise our time is up: Gaunt's eye has fallen upon us, or Branden enters the room - and we part - he moves back into the surging crowd, and I turn to speak to someone else, his presence lingering beside me like a beautiful dream.

'I am afraid people will notice,' I told him as we were pushed together as the guests filed into the ballroom for an orchestra performance earlier this evening.

Branden had gone ahead to exchange words with the lead violinist, who apparently was a performer of some note.

'Why do you think that?' John said softly.

'Because when we are together, you set a fire within me that I fear everyone can see.'

'They are invisible flames,' he replied, 'And only I can see them.'

Unseen, I felt his hand slip into mine for an instant, and then he was gone.

When I took my seat, I found to my pleasure that we could see each other from where we were seated. The audience's chairs curved around the circular stage that had been set up, and just over the right hand shoulder of the lead violinist, I could see John's face. I felt Branden take his seat beside me, a glazed smile upon his curved lips. He reached for my hand, as was his custom, but that aggravation was lessened by keeping my eyes upon John. Branden could take my hand, but John had my heart. He smiled at me as the music began, carelessly handsome, his fringe tumbling over his dark eyes.

The first few pieces I had heard before, but the fourth was a new one to me, opening with a violin solo full of soaring tragedy. The player's fingers simply danced across the strings, making them sing out in wonder. Its beauty captivated me so that it was a few moments before I glanced back to John.

The sadness and pain in his eyes was unimaginable. I looked, for the first time, into a huge, aching void that I had never before perceived within him. Despite being at the other side of the room, I could almost touch the pain emulating from him. It scared me in its intensity and strangeness, and in that moment, he became a stranger to me. I was filled with such inexplicable grief, desperate to go to him, and yet unable to move as he sat there, empty, hollow, breaking; his arms crossed across himself as if to try and hold himself together, stop himself from splitting into a thousand tiny pieces.

After what seemed like an age, the piece ended, the final longing notes drawing to a heart-rending close. Drinks in the dining room were then announced. As if rising from a reverie, John got up and left the room. I excused myself, pleading a thirst, and hurried out.

I found him standing by an open window in the dining room. He was staring into the darkness with sorrow-laden eyes, as the music lingered in the air – those notes that had sounded so beautiful but now seemed to drip with blood, so deep had they pierced his heart.

Despite being on his own, I went to him.

'John?'

He did not answer, his eyes fixed on the blackness outside. I do not think he was even aware of my presence.

'John. What can I do to help you?'

His voice came back, little more than a broken whisper,

'You cannot,' he replied, without turning his head.

*ENDERTON, 8<sup>th</sup> December 1866*

I realised last night that nothing hurts more than watching someone you love, hurt. But what was even worse was being shut out.

He is usually so buoyant, so full of joy and jokes. But now I see that there is a darkness in him, crouching in the shadows like a lion. Most of the time, I cannot see it: we are merry, and caught up in our love – but then suddenly it appears, raising its head and letting out a mournful roar, terrifying and sad – so terribly sad, casting a chill upon my heart. I wish I could set him free, but I think the prison is in his mind, buried far deeper than I could ever go.

I ask myself, what is it to know someone? I know much of him - I knew the moods that sweep through his eyes; I knew the sweet curls that fall across his brow, unnoticed by him; I know that he is happiest in that first early hour of the morning when no one else is up, and that he often feels like a young boy, desperate to escape on whatever adventure has caught his fancy. I know when he is telling the truth, and when he is hiding a secret that he will never tell me. I know that I love him.

I took a morning walk today, as is my habit. Often John and I have contrived a meeting on these strolls, or found a way of exchanging words unobserved. I did not expect him to be there today, but I went anyway, my heart heavy in my chest and my head aching from a troubled night's sleep of worrying for him.

To my very great surprise, he was there, waiting behind one of the great elms that bordered the rockeries. I took a seat on a nearby bench while Gaunt hovered by the greenhouses. From his position, behind the broad trunk, John was quite hidden.

'How are you this morning?' he asked lightly.

Surprised, I answered:

'I am worried about you!'

'Yes, I apologise for last night,' he answered quickly. 'Music has always awakened deep emotions within me.'

'It seemed much more than mere emotion – it seemed to pierce your very soul!' I exclaimed.

'Yes, well he was a very talented violinist, I must admit,' said John, avoidance in his voice.

'You will tell me no more?' I asked, already knowing the answer.

'There is nothing more to tell,' he replied.

I kicked at the grass in front of me, frustrated.

'You are a puzzle within a mystery, wrapped up in a riddle, John Treador, and I shall never fathom you, not if I devoted every hour of every day to the task!' I replied, aggravated and not bothering to hide it.

'Then why waste any more time on it when there are far sweeter things we can do?' he said, his voice floating out from behind the tree. 'Come to me.'

'I cannot, Gaunt is watching me,' I replied in irritated tones.

'If you glance up, you will see he has disappeared indoors, content that you are behaving.'

John's lure was too strong. I got up, and went to him, behind the tree. He kissed me then, long and soft, knowing full well that I would succumb to the distraction – and I did.


## THE STORY CONTINUED BY THE EDITOR

Several days passed without Isabel and John being able to exchange a word. As December progressed, the schedule of activity and events at Enderton became busier than usual, with winter hunts, festive dinners and charades in the evenings. Isabel could find no opportunity to get close to John, for Sir Branden kept her tightly by his side as he presided as head of the festivities.

However, as Isabel sat reading in her room one afternoon, she was startled to hear a soft knock at the door. Her old fears rose up – had the terror begun again? But then she heard John's voice:

'It is me – let me in!'

Casting her book aside and rushing over to the door, she drew the bolts to reveal John standing there, slightly out of breath. He stepped in and closed the door, drawing the bolts back in place.

'What are you doing here?' asked Isabel, delight and concern on her face. 'What if you were seen?'

'I was not seen – the men are going out on a hunt and Gaunt is downstairs in his room – I checked. I had to see you.'

He kissed her, and she forgot her concerns all in a moment.

'It has been many weeks since I was in this room,' remarked John a few moments later. 'And there is my dramatic entrance hole,' he motioned towards the painting of the knight.

'I love that painting,' Isabel said fondly.

John studied it for a moment.

'It is quite forbidding, do you not think? I would not trust him.'

'How would you know? His visor is down, you cannot see his face,' Isabel replied.

'Precisely,' said John, and then he turned back to face her in his syncopated manner. 'Shall we go on an adventure?'

'Where?' She was still not used to his sudden changes of mood.

'To explore.' He swung back the painting to reveal the passageway.

She laughed incredulously at the thought of roaming the house together, and then realised he was being serious. 'Have you no fear?' she asked, staggered.

'No – fear only holds you back. Now come on!'

She looked at him in frank astonishment and then followed his quick athletic stride, wordlessly.

'You make me do such wild things,' she said, when she had climbed up beside him in the portrait hole. He smiled at her, his lips not quite touching hers.

'No - I make you realise you have always wanted to do them,' he said playfully, with a wide and irrepressible grin.

Crawling through the tiny space, up the roughly hewn steps and tumbling out into John's old room, Isabel felt her fear leave her. Her hand was in John's, her cheeks were flushed – all thought of danger was gone.

'Where shall we go?' she asked, smiling at his energy.

'Shall we explore the attic? There will be some interesting items up there, I am sure,' said John, opening the door to the hallway and checking that there was no one around. 'Perhaps we can learn some more of Branden's secrets.'

Together, they made their way down the hall, John making a show of avoiding the creaking floorboards, and jumping from one board to another like a cat. Suddenly there was a real creak from the stairs to their right.

'Quick!' John grabbed her hand, and opening the door of a cupboard on their left, pulled her inside and closed the door.

They were in a dark space, hardly big enough for the two of them.

Silently they waited for the person to pass. Isabel could feel the beat of John's heart against her; it was not thudding as nearly as fast as her own. From the keyhole, Isabel caught a glimpse of white – it was almost certainly a servant outside.

'What are we supposed to do now?' she asked in a whisper, when the danger had passed.

'Whatever happens next,' said John, flashing her a smile.

Reason began to reassert itself in Isabel's mind.

'I suggest we go back to my room and remain in safety,' she said sensibly. 'This venture is not worth the risk.'

'Yes my lady,' he replied decorously, a twinkle in his eye.

As Isabel closed the door of the bedroom, she thought she saw something move behind the keyhole of the door opposite. She looked again, but it was gone. Feeling uneasy, she followed John down the passageway, but said nothing.

# XXV

ISABEL'S NARRATIVE
*(Extract from Isabel's Diary)*

*ENDERTON, 11<sup>th</sup> December 1866*

John has been in my life for a month now. Somehow, all the time before that seems slightly hazy, as though it was all a bad dream. This is my real life now, with him by my side.

I admit that there are things that trouble me about him. In some senses, he is a haunted man. There are ghosts that move behind his eyes – when I glance away I can see them shifting in the depths. Trying to pin down who he is, is harder than trying to chase soap with wet hands. Half-truths run from his lips like water. But this is only when he speaks of his past. When he speaks about us, about me, the ghosts disappear and hope fills his eyes. In those moments I believe every word he says, and not in foolishness. You might call me a child, but I believe he has his reasons for not speaking of his past, and for the time being, I accept this. As I remind myself, my parents could not have known so very much about each other before they got married.

In some ways I almost like the fact that parts of him are a mystery to me. I cannot even figure out how old he is, for he has such youthful energy, but such ancient eyes. Sometimes I would guess he must in his be early twenties, with only a few year between us; other times he seems decades older. There is such depth to him, like the ocean - so full of secrets and memories, hidden so deep down that you are not even aware they exist. He is like all my favourite heroes wrapped up in one. He is Arthur, he is Tilney, he is Valancourt, he is ~~Mr Knightly~~ (no, that was someone else). He is Heathcliff. He is the exhilarating stranger who burst into my life so suddenly, bringing with him such joy.

Yesterday, he said to me, his face warm and full of happiness,

'Now there is a smile on my lips and hope in my heart. It has been such a long time since I felt this way.'

'And what has changed in your life?' I asked him.

'You,' he replied.

I realised then that he needs me as much as I need him. It was a thought that delighted and comforted me.

I love him so much it makes me ache inside. Sometimes I do not know what to do with the feeling – it is so intense and terrible and wonderful. Sometimes I feel sad for I feel sure it cannot last and yet if it does not, I fear I shall die. I am utterly mesmerised by him (I must sound like a fool, but I do not care – if you could look into his eyes, you would be too). When his skin brushes mine, I feel as though a thousand butterflies have just flown past me at a great speed, so gentle but so intense is his touch. All I want is to be noticed by him and have his eyes forever on me, for when he looks at me there is nothing else. To look into his eyes is to see everything you are and everything you want to be.

I asked myself last night, what is love? For me, it is all consuming - empowering, and utterly terrifying. I think it is your strength, and your greatest fear. It makes you realise how much you could hurt, and how much you can give someone just by being yourself. And that is wonderful. It causes me to smile without even realising, and makes me feel as if the sun is shining down on me despite the fact that I am inside, on a winter's day. This is love, I think.

Tomorrow John wants to take me away again. We are going to leave just before sunrise, escaping silently by the usual route. It will only be for a few hours, for we must return before breakfast, but it is a few hours alone together – and they will be more precious than gold.


## THE STORY CONTINUED BY THE EDITOR

Isabel and John sat together upon layers of furs laid across the stone floor of the top tower room in the folly, surrounded by blankets and the warmth of each other. The great open window was before them, and beyond that lay the grey majesty of the sea and the night sky, which stood, dark and unsure, waiting for the first wakings of dawn.

'I can see the whole world from up here,' said Isabel dreamily. She moved deeper into the curve of John's arm. It was not muscular like the arm of that other half-remembered man, but she felt safe.

'I can see my whole world right here,' replied John, looking down at her. 'Everything I am – everything I want to be, is here in my arms.' He sighed suddenly, and pulled Isabel closer into him. She felt his chest rise and fall against hers and she slowed her breathing in time with his.


### ISABEL'S NARRATIVE
*(Extract from Isabel's Diary)*

*ENDERTON, 12<sup>th</sup> December 1866*

'We are one', I thought happily as I watched his eyelids began to droop.

I let him sleep; there was still an hour still before sunrise, and I wanted to look at him - he looked so boyish as he lay there. I gently pushed the hair from over his eyes so I could see him better.

His fascinating eyes – so wide and expressive, fringed by those handsome black lashes, were closed now. When he was awake, they were like a burning fire, so incandescent and ever changing, that it was impossible to take your eyes from them. Sometimes when I looked at him, they burned so intensely, so fiercely, that they seemed to penetrate deep within me, burning away the layers until they reached that spot that was truly myself – unprotected and unfeigned.

But they were also such wide eyes - open, yearning, taking in all of life with such a wonderful enthusiasm. Yet when a shadow passed over them they suddenly became dark and terrible. I feared him a little then, but it was a worshipful fear, so different from the loathing fear that I felt for Branden.

And if I were to describe his personality? He is like...nothing on earth, nothing that I have ever seen at least. He is fierce, yes, and wonderful. Frighteningly wonderful, and kind, and fearless...how to relate him to something you might understand...I shall describe him as if he were a piece of music.

He is the theme. The triumphant, uplifting, joyful theme, containing moments of indescribable happiness, of soaring wonder and touching beauty. A theme that is always pushing on to that glorious crescendo where you are lifted up, up – floating ever higher onto wilder and more wonderful notes. The pizzicato brings to life his wildness, the excitement that I feel when I am with him. There is a certain sadness, yes, far down in the bass notes, but it is overcome by a truly glorious finale. And yet, I do not want it to end...

And if I were the accompanying piece? Well I think it would be light and soft – fairly steady, but with moments of surprise where the tune carries you off somewhere unexpected. I think it would start quietly, telling of the girl in the empty house, and then billowing out into the story of the girl who was loved, who was beginning to discover all that life could hold. Perhaps a female voice, slightly mystical, in the background for the woman that I want to be, that I should be...that I must be, if I am to be his partner. For he needs a very great piece of music to match his own.

I wonder if my tune is too naive, lacking his depth. I despair a little then... But – listen carefully, far off in the background – they seem to be coming together. My piece complements his in a strange way, intertwining and harmonising; filling in the areas where his is sparse, bringing joy to the moments when his music is sad.

Yes, I think we will do well together.


## THE STORY CONTINUED BY THE EDITOR

Isabel was still staring intently at John when he woke, her face set in a concentrated frown.

'What are you doing?' he asked, sitting up with a smile and yawning. 'Are you examining me in my sleep?'

'I am memorising your face,' she replied matter-of-factly.

'Why?'

'In case I ever lose you.'

John took her hands in his. They were a little cold.

'I am not going anywhere,' he said firmly.

'It is just...' Isabel straightened up a little. 'Do you ever feel that this is too perfect to last?'

'What, this morning?'

'No.' Isabel pulled his hand to her heart. 'Us!'

John looked surprised.

'No I do not. I think all our lives have been leading up to this point. And I think that we are meant to be together, for a long time to come.'

Isabel stared back at him, wanting to believe him, but something still nagged at her.

'Isabel, I will love, protect and comfort you for as much time is given to me,' he said, trying to make her believe him. 'I promise you.'

Isabel smiled, tears in her eyes.

'I know John, forgive me. I just find it hard to believe that this is all real, that you are real. You are like the hero of every novel I have ever read,' she paused, '- and yet so unlike them, for you are far better, far kinder - a far more wonderful man. I have never met anyone like you.'

For the first time Isabel had caught him off guard. He did not reply and seemed to shake his head a little. His eyes looked very bright in the fading moonlight. Then he spoke:

'Isabel...to you everything is full of hope, everything is beautiful – you are pure, perfect. You must promise me you will try and stay like that.'

'No I am not,' she replied, slightly overwhelmed. 'I am just a normal, very ordinary person.'

John smiled.

'Ah, but that is the wonderful thing. There are no ordinary people.

Each one is wonderful and amazing and unique. You particularly.' The liquid melody of his voice rose and fell as he spoke, captivating her with his tone.

She gazed up at him.

'Did you know that you make people fall under your spell? With you I am a girl enchanted,' she said softly.

'Well, we are in an enchanted place,' said John, looking around them.

The stars were going out and way out on the horizon was the first glimmer of dawn. A glow overspread Isabel's face, as the dawn crept further up from behind the sea.

'And here begin all the colours of the world,' said John softly.

The light stole a little further, like beautiful fingers of gold and amber weaving through hair of the palest blue. The darkness was fading now, returning to rest while the glorious sun took on the world's protection for another day.

'I had forgotten how much I love the sunrise,' Isabel said in wonder.

She had not sat up to watch the sunrise since she was a girl running wild at Greenwood. She wondered why she had not done it more often – it made her feel so alive, so uplifted by the sheer beauty of the world.

'I am glad you are here, Isabel,' John said in her ear.

She slipped round to face him, her face illuminated by the orange and pink glow.

'Where else would I be?' she said, tenderly.

The sky was glowing with a myriad of colours now, as dawn began in all its splendour – flame, pink, purple and deepest red fanned out and upwards – and then, there it was, the first beginnings of the sun. That globe of life and beauty, rising up out of the sea like a goddess from the deep. Around her, the colours spread so widely that the very sky itself seemed to have grown larger.

For a moment Isabel felt as though she was beginning to remember something: something that was half-forgotten, deep within her. She glanced up at John. The wind had lifted his fringe and his eyes were fixed far out on the horizon. She knew he would not like what she was going to say, but she said it anyway, with conviction:

'God is painting a beautiful masterpiece.'

John looked at her quizzically and then said:

'I have so much respect for you, Isabel.'

'Why do you respect me?' she asked.

'Because you do not hide who you are,' he replied.

Isabel was silent for a moment, but then asked:

'And why do you?'

He gazed ahead of him, his brow creased, and then he spoke, his eyes still fixed on the sunrise,

'Because I am not all I want to be.'

By the time morning had fully dawned, the sky looked brand new – as though it had been freshly washed. Isabel and John knew they must return to the house soon, but still they sat, the sound of the long breakers in their ears.

'I wish time would just stop,' said Isabel. 'I wish we could stay here forever, just as we are, invisible to all. In our own little world.'

'But we wish for better than that,' said John in her ear. 'We must look forward to leaving Enderton, to starting our own life together.'

'I dare not wish for that yet,' said Isabel. 'It is an impossible dream and I have lost all my impossible dreams over the past few months.'

'Ah, but you must dream impossible dreams,' he said softly, 'otherwise you will never get anywhere. And it is not so very impossible. I am going to London next week to make arrangements for our departure.'

Isabel felt as though she could not breathe, so tight was the excitement in her chest.

'Our departure. You are planning it already!'

'Of course, I am. You do not think I am idly sitting about while that brute claims you for his own? It will take some weeks, but it is in progress. Trust me Isabel, soon you will be free of this place.'

Isabel felt all her old dreams beginning to unfurl their wings inside her.

'We will be free – we will be together,' she said, hardly daring to believe it.

'We will be together,' he repeated, smiling back at her.

## ISABEL'S NARRATIVE
*(Extract from Isabel's Diary)*

*ENDERTON, 12th December 1866*

I could not but kiss him.

As we rode back, my hair streamed out behind me – we were riding fast to ensure they were back at the house in time for breakfast - but I was not thinking much of that. Our horses were so close together it that I could have reached out and touched him if I chose. He looks at me and we laugh – with the glorious joy, the terror and the beauty of it all. Nothing could ever be sad, nothing could ever end, could ever be real apart from this. Nothing could ever mar the joy of this perfect moment.

# XXVI

## THE STORY CONTINUED BY THE EDITOR

More and more guests arrived during the Christmas period, and by the 20th of December, all of Enderton's sixty bedrooms were full. For Isabel and John, this was somewhat of a blessing as it was easier to get lost amongst the crowds.

As John had said, he was leaving for London on the 21st of December. On the morning of that day, Isabel was in the library, reading on her favourite the window seat. The door creaked, and she looked up to see John entering. There was no one else in the room and he went over to her. He was dressed in his travelling cloak. Isabel looked up with sadness in her eyes.

'I wanted to say goodbye,' said John, looking at her fondly.

'Thank you,' she said gratefully. 'But I wish you did not have to go.'

She had been dreading this moment for many days now.

'Do you not want me to find you a Christmas present in London?' he asked, a twinkle in his eye.

'Of course…' Isabel replied hesitantly, 'but I would rather have you here.'

John took her hand and sat down beside her.

'Just remember that Sir Branden does not know we are together, so you are in no less danger when I am gone. He has not troubled you for some weeks now, and I will only be away for three days. Can you wait that long?'

'I can,' she said reluctantly.

'Then I will be on my way.'

He kissed her softly on her red lips and then stood up, but before he reached the door, Isabel rose up suddenly as if caught on a breeze – her cheeks and eyes bright.

'Do not forget me!' she called out, her voice a little wild.

John turned, a surprised look on his face 'I will not,' he said, a troubled look on his face. 'I could not.'

The door opened at that point and another gentleman came in, unaware of the scene he was trespassing on. He bade good morning to John, and unable to speak further, John gave Isabel one final glance, and left. Isabel remained standing, wanting to run after him with every fibre of her being. She found her hands were shaking, and she looked down at them. The other gentleman turned to her. He was an older man with blue eyes set in a slightly worn-looking face.

'Lady Branden,' he said kindly, 'have you lost something?'

Isabel left the room, for fear of bursting into tears there and then.

## ISABEL'S NARRATIVE
*(Extract from Isabel's Diary)*

*ENDERTON, 21ˢᵗ December 1866*

I pray that he returns to me soon. All at once the house seems cold and forbidding without him here. I feel lost, like a child in a maze.

Come back quickly, my love.

## THE STORY CONTINUED BY THE EDITOR

It was Christmas Eve. The lights were dimmed and Mount Enderton was decorated from head to toe in glorious Christmas excess. The tree itself was so large it had to go in the ballroom, for it was the only room with a ceiling high enough to accommodate it. It sparkled with a thousand baubles and candied fruits, and the scents that drifted up from the kitchens downstairs smelled of cloves and cinnamon, and every Christmas fragrance you could imagine. But Isabel could enjoy none of it without John.

She was in a small room on the second floor that she sometimes used for writing. It contained only a small desk and a few bookshelves, but was far enough removed from the bustle of the house to afford her some privacy. She was reading, but not really reading, her forehead creased and her foot tapping, glancing up at the slightest noise...waiting for his return.

Suddenly, in the dusk of the study, he was there. The room seemed to become strangely airless as he entered silently. He was wearing a blue suit, his fringe, for once, carefully swept to one side, his face flushed from the cold air outside. Everything stopped for Isabel – all noise, even the evening birdsong outside. All she could see was John. Dropping his bundles on the floor, he strode across the room, the candlelight turning the dust in the air into flecks of gold that swirled as he moved through them towards her, and he caught her to himself.

'I missed you,' he said fervently (how Isabel rejoiced in those words!). 'Let us not part again.'

Isabel woke on Christmas morning to find that winter had kissed the ground all over. Thick with frost, each branch and blade of grass sparkled in the pale morning sunlight as though encrusted with diamonds.

Tonight was the Christmas Masquerade Ball and Isabel had ordered a dress especially for the occasion. It was the first important occasion that she and John had shared together, and she meant to look her very best. The dress was made of amethyst-coloured tulle, with the fullest skirt imaginable, and tiny silk rosebuds scattered over the skirt and around the neckline. She fingered the material thoughtfully and began to plan what jewels would best compliment the outfit.

Lunch was a buffet, as the kitchen staff were busy preparing for the night's feast. Isabel had asked for the food to be brought to her room and after eating, spent the afternoon in nervous anticipation. By five o'clock she decided it was acceptable to begin getting ready, but that took far less time than she had thought and found she had another hour spare before the seven o'clock start.

When the bell in the extravagant mahogany clock on her mantelpiece began to chime, Isabel lifted her silver mask, gathered her skirts and began to make her way downstairs. She could hear the now-familiar thrum of the voices of the female partners, who had arrived to accompany their visiting husbands.

Sir Branden gave a nod of approval as she descended the stairs, her mask held to her face. Unlike all of his guests, he had no mask.

'Shall we enter?' he said smoothly to Isabel.

Only half-listening to him, she allowed herself to be directed towards the ballroom. Her attention was elsewhere – she could not see John, and she had wanted him to see her come down, wanted him to know it was all for him.

The ballroom was dazzling. All around her swept huge dresses in a multitude of colours, each figure moving aside to reveal further crowds of guests, each with a decorated mask held to their faces – some in the shape of cats, others elegant half-masks, like hers, others more elaborate, topped with feathers and jewels. Rich food and wine lined the tables at the end of the room, decadently covered in black velvet. Candelabras glowed brightly from every wall, while the stunning chandeliers lit the scene with abundance.

Showing disinterest in the dancing, Sir Branden led Isabel to a pair of large high backed chairs, and after enquiring if she was comfortable, he went to welcome some more guests. It was then that Isabel saw John.

He entered the room – striking, peerless, wonderful – and

unmasked. His eyes sought Isabel's and in them was the sweetest caress. For a moment she was afraid, so unhidden and fervent was his gaze. But then she realised she was not afraid – and she looked back at him, unfettered and fearless. Had Sir Branden noticed and given the order to have them shot, in that room, at that very moment, she knew she would have died with joy in her heart, her eyes still locked in John's, until the very end.

Isabel rose and strode across the room to him, a fearless expression upon her face. Her skirts made a soft rustling noise as she walked, the guests parting to let their hostess through. The band had begun to play a waltz and John pulled her into his arms and together they began to dance.

'You are perfect,' he murmured in her ear. 'I have never seen you look so beautiful. Your dress wakes the colour in your eyes and makes them shine brighter than I have ever seen them.'

'It is because I am with you,' she replied, her voice aching with tenderness.

She pressed herself tightly against him. Others may see, she did not care. She was nearly free of them. John had told her that it would not be long before they could leave. His plans were nearly in place. She nearly yielded to her intense desire to kiss him in full view of everyone, but then she came to her senses as Sir Branden re-entered the room.

All she wanted was to be alone with John, but delicacy was needed, as always. A thin gentleman dressed in black, with a paper mask tied round his eyes was watching from the walls. He was wearing a top hat but a strand of red hair had escaped from underneath it and one green eye glinted from behind his mask. Isabel knew where the real danger was.

'Gaunt is watching us,' she whispered to John.

'I know,' he replied. The dance was ending and he said softly to her, 'Find a way to lose his trail and meet me upstairs in your room.'

Kissing her hand, he relinquished her as his partner and Isabel was immediately asked to dance by another young gentleman. When that dance ended, she danced a faster number with a different man, swirling through the crowds in her billowing, weightless gown. Then suddenly, halfway through, she stopped her partner and asked for a drink. When he hurried off to fetch one for her, Isabel cast her eye around for Gaunt and seeing that he was not looking in her direction, left the ballroom, gliding upstairs at great speed.

Opening her door, she gasped in delight. John had set out a small table before the fire – and on it was the tiniest Christmas tree, carefully decorated with thin red velvet ribbon and tiny painted acorns for baubles. Around it were set many candles and underneath lay a beautifully wrapped present.

'Happy Christmas,' he whispered as she shut the door behind her.

'Happy Christmas, my love,' she replied, going over to the tree. 'Oh John, it is beautiful!'

'And now you must open your present,' he said, leading her to one of the two chairs he had set out by the table.

Excitedly, Isabel lifted her parcel and opened it, taking care not to tear the delicate gold wrapping paper. Inside was a thick red leather-bound journal with gilt-edged pages and a heart-shaped gold lock.

'It is your new journal,' he said earnestly. 'I want you to begin it once we are together, and write in it all the things that bring you joy. It is our little book of hope – for our future together.'

The happiness inside Isabel grew until she could physically feel the warmth of it within her - so wonderful was the moment. Candlelight danced across John's face as he smiled at her. Then he pulled out two glasses and a small bottle of wine. He poured them a glass each, the garnet liquid gleaming in the light of the flames.

'This is the start of something incredible, is it not?' said Isabel, as he handed her the glass.

'Yes. It is the start of our adventure,' John replied, clinking his glass against hers. 'Happy Christmas, my beautiful snow angel.'

ISABEL'S NARRATIVE
*(Extract from Isabel's Diary)*

*ENDERTON, 25<sup>th</sup> December 1866*

I do not think we said anything more. I settled down beside him, my journal in one hand and my glass in the other, and together we watched the Christmas fireworks explode in glorious colours outside my window.

# XXVII

## ISABEL'S NARRATIVE
### *(Extract from Isabel's Diary)*

ENDERTON, 26<sup>th</sup> December 1866

I woke this morning tangled up in my bed sheets, my curls wilting, my journal still in my hand. Coming to, I thought back over the day before. This is the start of our adventure, John had said.

I wandered to the window – the frost was still thick outside and I could hear the horses neighing in their stables as they awaited their morning feed. How soon will it be before we ride off together, never to return? The thought of our future both thrills and terrifies me. John has told me nothing of his plan, saying it is safer that way, but I long to know the details – both for my peace of mind, and so I can start envisaging what our future will be like: where we will go, where we will stay, how we will manage to escape Branden's undoubted searching... The thought of it all makes me feel a little shaky, I must admit.

If someone had told me only a few months ago that I was about to run off with a man I hardly knew, to who knows where, I would have laughed in their face. I like adventures, I would have said, but that sounds like madness. Now that I think about it, John has given me no definites. He has not even told me that he loves me yet. Does that matter? The happiness of last night begins to disappear like smoke amidst my doubts.

## THE STORY CONTINUED BY THE EDITOR

The white clouds had turned to black and the day was dark and gloomy. Isabel felt the change not only in the weather, but also in John's mood when she met him in the library that day. They had the room to themselves as most guests were busy sleeping off their overindulgences from the night before. Even though it was early afternoon, the servants had lit the candles; so black was the sky outside.

John had an open book in his hands, though from the look in his eyes, he was not reading it: he was somewhere far away.

'I am jealous of your thoughts today,' Isabel said at last. 'I feel as though they are wandering some distant land and not here with me.'

John did not reply. She watched the candlelight create dancing patches of light and shade upon his face. The flame cast his eyes into shadow. His visor was down.

'You do not have to pretend to read, you know,' she said, breaking the silence again. 'No one will be downstairs for hours.'

'It is safer,' John replied, keeping his eyes on the book.

'Did you sleep well?' she asked lightly, after a moment.

'Not particularly,' he said shortly.

'Why was that?'

'I had many dreams.'

'Bad dreams?' she asked.

'Just dreams,' John replied stiffly, his expression suddenly shuttered

'Dreams come when there are many cares,' quoted Isabel, her voice kind.

'They were dreams from long ago, nothing to do with my current cares,' he said bluntly.

'Then I do not know how to help you, for you will tell me nothing of that time!' said Isabel, a little frustrated.

John turned away, his profile to her. His face was as dark as the clouds that hung ominously overhead; as dark as his brooding heart that she felt beating between them.

'What is it that plagues you so, John?' she burst out. 'Please tell me!'

He gave no answer, and Isabel continued, a pleading tone in her voice:

'I know your face, your expressions, better even than I know my own and yet I have no idea who you really are, where you come from, what your life has been like. You talk so much and yet you never *say* anything.'

John slammed his book down.

'What is there to say?' he said, with gathering emotion. 'Why must I pour out my soul to you? My past is over, why do you keep returning to it? It is dead, forgotten... I ask no questions of you – all I know, you have told me freely, so do not concern yourself with my former life. It is our future and our future alone that matters.'

'A future that I know little about!' she burst out.

'You know that I will take you away from here – is that not enough?' he demanded.

'And why are you doing that?' she cried, her voice loud, but she no longer cared.

'Why? You know why!'

'I do not – for you have never told me!'

234

'Told you what?'

The candlelight made it look as though real flames burned in his eyes. The effect was eerie. Slightly frightened, Isabel retreated.

'Nothing. It is no matter.'

The moment of silence lengthened between them. Isabel stared ahead as John picked up his book again. Is it too many words to say, she wondered? Those three small words she longed to hear. Those three words that meant she belonged.

Though she could not see John's face, she felt a great tumult going on within him, as though he were struggling with some silent opponent. She looked away, unsure, disquieted. Then she realised John was looking at her. His face was still dark, but calmer. She stared back at him with mute appeal, trying to frame her simple question in a way that he would understand.

'What is wrong Isabel, tell me,' he said in a softer tone.

'Should I be afraid that you never say it?' she asked.

'Say what?' he replied, imperturbably.

'How you really feel!'

His brown eyes tightened under the shadow of his heavily drawn brows. He said nothing, just as Isabel had expected. Then she smiled; a sad, soft little smile, and turned to look out of the misting window.

'It is not so much that I want to hear it', she said in a very small voice. 'It is just that I need to.'

She glanced at him, and seeing his unmoving expression, stood up, and gathering her shawl, made to leave the room. When she got to the door, she looked back at him where he sat, staring out into nothingness, his eyes full of storms.

'I love you, you see,' she whispered, though she knew he could not hear her.

Isabel spent the day with a vague, knowing restlessness and could not settle, wandering around her room, staring out of the window, reordering items in her jewellery box, lifting a newspaper and then putting it down again. She glanced at the clock. It was almost dinnertime.

She sat at the long dining table, her eyes fixed upon the chair that usually held the only person that she cared about. It was empty tonight, yet no one seemed to know why.

*'No purer essence, than the one that burns,*
*Like an untended watch-fire, on the ridge*
*Of some dark mountain...'*

*If Thou Indeed Derive Thy Light From Heaven* (lines 9-11), William
Wordsworth

ISABEL'S NARRATIVE
*(Extract from Isabel's Diary)*

*ENDERTON, 26th December 1866*

I looked out at the full moon, majestic in its splendour. It was smiling tonight. My heart took reassurance in this good omen. I put on my cloak and boots. As I was about to leave the room, I glanced back at the window once more. The wind was up and the clouds were moving. The moon smiled at me, but as the clouds shifted with the wind, its smile turned to sadness. There was no comfort in that face as I left the room, and the sky was turning black with an approaching storm.

I walked down the cold, dark back stairs, through the stone-paved hallway and, unlocking and unbolting the heavy oak back door, swung it open and swept through. Outside a chill mist hung in the air. My eyes took a moment to adjust to the heavy darkness, but picking out the path that led to the shrubbery, I gathered up my skirts and hurried along it. Just past the shrubbery was the hill that led up to the forest. The grass was cold and damp around my ankles and my breath rose up before me like a cloud, hanging in the thick misty air behind me as I passed on. The cold air was laced with the faintest whiff of the sea.

Where was I going? Well, I was going to find John. Somehow, I knew where he was, although I did not know why.

I had heard him mention the cliff walk. We had not visited it together for it was too close to the house, but it was where he liked to walk when he wanted to get away for an hour or two. He said it made feel calmer when something was troubling him and I could sense that it was where he had gone tonight.

Seeing the tall dark trees rising before me caused a shiver to run down my spine but I took a deep breath and stepped into the deep darkness. The threatening storm was now full-blown and wind and rain howled around me. Barely able to make out the rabbit track that led to the cliff top, I headed due east and sure enough, after about ten minutes of fast walking through the trees, I came out into the open, breathing in the heady sea air that rushed upon me. My heart was beating fast, partly from my swift journey, and partly from fear of what I would find. That fear stabbed at me like a sharp knife as my eyes searched for him along the cliff top. The clouds were clearing and a sliver of the moon was visible through them. The wind was blowing wildly, lifting up my skirts and hair around me as I stood close to the edge of the cliff.

I pushed back my hair from my face, eagerly looking for him to my left and to my right, when I heard a small voice in my mind say,

'He is not here.'

My legs felt suddenly weak and my head dizzy at the thought as I tried earnestly to pick out his black figure against the dark sky. The rocks below seemed to take on wild and magical shapes as I stared at them, as though I was in some kind of nightmare.

A sudden gust swept up the spray from an oncoming wave below, lifting it as high as the cliff - and as the dark sparkle of water caught my eye, I watched it fall before a tall dark silhouette standing erect on a jagged formation – a huge standing rock in the sea, which was joined by the sharp rocks below at the foot of the cliff.

'John!' I called out, unable to hide the joy, nor the fear in my voice, but the figure made no movement, unable to hear me over the deafening crashing of the waves on the rocks below. The sheet lightning lit up the hidden black landscape and I saw him clearly – looking out to sea, lost to all the world.

To reach him, I had to climb down the cliff side and then up the side of the huge rock upon which he stood, like a tall tower amidst the tempest. The waves frothed and foamed white against the dark rocks and the wind drove the rain, stinging, into my face as I climbed. Worn hollows served as footholds and soon I reached the top of the rock and rushed towards him. My patent boots were insecure on the damp stone, but I ran nonetheless, calling out his name. As I got nearer, he turned - that tall dark figure - and his eyes met mine. In them surged something more restless and furious than the dark swelling sea below us - they looked almost black in the darkness, gleaming with some unknown emotion that terrified me and yet drew me to him at the same time.

He held out his hands to me as I climbed up the last few steps to get to the high point on which he stood. I reached up and grasped them -

they were warm, despite the lashing seawater and chill misty air - and strong. He drew me to him, and his hands held me firm. I was trembling slightly - and I knew it was not just from the cold night air. John's face was a raging tempest of emotions: rage, terror, defiance, recklessness, despair. The sky swirled darkly above him.

'What are you doing, John?' I asked, my voice shaking as I tried to raise it above the storm.

'I have come out here to think – why did you follow me?' he demanded.

I did not even think of my answer before I spoke it,

'Because you need me.'

His eyes flashed back dangerously.

'Do I look like I need help?'

'You do not *look* like you need help,' I replied, anguished.

'You *look* like a young Adonis that no one could bring down. But there is something broken in your eyes – like a small child crying out. And it has been crying ever louder these past few days - ' I broke off, for John had pushed roughly past me and was standing on the very tip of the rock, staring down into the sea below.

'John!' I cried out. 'Talk to me!'

He turned, his countenance terrible. His fierce emotion terrified and thrilled me to my very core.

'Answer me one question, Isabel,' he said, almost bitterly.

'Of course - I will answer you anything!' I exclaimed. 'I would never deny you anything.'

His question came blunt and fast - like an axe striking wood:

'Do you love me?'

I breathed deeply, as through struck, and with my outward breath gasped,

'Yes.'

The look that came over his face was almost unbearable. It was one of deep torment, mixed with pain and fury, anxiety and fear, love and loathing. I felt myself sway with terror at his reaction, my heart pounding in my chest.

'John? John - speak to me! What is wrong, I cannot bear it!'

He was ashen-white in the darkness, his pallor heightened by the glow of the bright stars and moon in the sky above that came in and out of sight as the clouds rushed past. A tall wave reared up and soaked the rocks behind us. The water sprayed forwards and I slipped a little, my hands reaching out. He caught them. His grip was vice-like, his face only a few inches away, dripping with seawater. It ran in rivulets down his anguished face that he lifted up to the skies.

'I did not mean - I cannot - you do not know!' he half-muttered, half-wailed into the sweeping gusts of wind that swirled around us.

'John, please - please talk to me - whatever is the matter,' I pleaded, trying to get him to look at me as he gazed upwards.

Whatever he could see in the darkness, whether it was the black waves that rose up around us, or the brilliant stars in the huge expanse above, something brought him back to me and he grabbed my shoulders, bringing me close to him, his face close enough to kiss me. The rain streamed into his eyes, his jaw was set. I breathed in his scent, terrified and exhilarated by his passion. When I stared into his eyes I realised they were swimming with tears. I lifted my hands up and placed them against his chest, feeling his heart beating underneath my palms.

'John - '

He shook his head, and then lifted his eyes to mine. They burned with such an intensity that I could not bear it. With a sudden great groan, he caught me to his heart, and just as suddenly thrust me from him. When he spoke, the great storm bellowed with him in its rage.

'You must *not* love me!' he cried in anguish.

And then he left me.

# XXVIII

## THE STORY CONTINUED BY THE EDITOR

I will let you read the letter in its entirety. It is only fair to him. The paper on which it is written is a little worn now, but still pressed quite flat, having lain in her diary for so long. His hand is wild and fills the page from top to bottom, with deep indentations on certain words as though his voice still speaks from the paper – those words which he could not say to her face.

*My dearest Isabel.*

*Thank you for coming to find me last night. I do not know what to say to you, except 'Forgive me' and that I forgot myself. You see, I have to hold on to myself very hard. Many ghosts haunt me, but with you they are dispelled.*

*I need you, Isabel. You make everything better. You give me hope for the future. I will give you everything I am, everything I have – my whole universe of nothingness – if you will share it with me.*

*I know you want to hear me say those words. And yet I am so terribly afraid. It is hard to explain why. But I will do it for you. I love you, Isabel - so very much – and I will try to be worthy of you. Like a splintered piece of glass trying to shine like the stars above. I will try.*

*John.*

## ISABEL'S NARRATIVE
### *(Extract from Isabel's Diary)*

*ENDERTON, 27<sup>th</sup> December 1866*

I went to his door and knocked. He opened the door with a face that was ashen. When he saw that it was I, he caught me to his heart with a sudden groan. I forgave him freely, that impossible man, through whom strange strong passions sweep so suddenly and unexpectedly with such frightening energy. There is a power in him that almost scares me. If he was not such a good man, I think that he would be a terrible one. Yet, I shrug this aside and cling on to him – my love, my only love.

Men do not realise how quickly we fall.


## THE STORY CONTINUED BY THE EDITOR

Isabel was sitting in the breakfast room. She had arrived late for breakfast and was now the only one left at the table. She looked up to see Sir Branden entering the room. It was strange. For the past few weeks, she had felt little more than apathy towards him, rather than her previous hatred. Now that John was in her life, she felt she could tolerate almost anything.

'Good morning, my dear,' Sir Branden said lightly.

'Good morning,' she replied, smiling coolly at him.

'I feel I must apologise for I have spent so little time with you these past weeks,' he said, taking the seat next to her and motioning for some coffee to be served.

It was true - Isabel had not seen much of Sir Branden for the past month, for which she was immensely grateful. Since the last attempted break-in, she had had no more trouble from him at night – she often wondered if he had embarrassed himself one step too far that evening and decided to retreat with dignity. Also, some new piece of business seemed to have come in which meant that he did not want her in his study during the afternoon, and apart from accompanying him to dinner each night, she barely saw him.

'You do not have to apologise,' she replied genuinely. 'I have been quite entertained.'

'No, no. It is quite unacceptable, and I mean for it to change,' he said, a hint of steel in his voice.

Isabel felt a cold stone dropping into her stomach.

'And as for your entertainments,' he continued dexterously, 'they will also need to change.'

'What do you mean?' she asked, keeping her tone light.

He gripped her arm suddenly and so tightly that she almost cried out.

'Do not take me for a fool, Isabel. You are resourceful, I will give you that. But I am not blind. Two of my horses are always gone, your bed has been reported as being unslept in, you are always nowhere to be found. Did you think I would not notice? These 'episodes' will cease.' He moved closer, leaning in and levelling his stare. 'In fact, they will cease today. I have instructed my groom that no horses are to be let out without my permission, and for anyone seen in the stables to be brought to me. It is not your safety that I am concerned about Isabel.

You are my wife, and you will be kept safe – though perhaps, not quite so comfortable. But woe betide the gentleman who should try and take you from me.'

Isabel stared back, her anger blocking out the pain of her arm.

'I know nothing of which you speak,' she replied. 'If you cannot keep your horses under control, or your wife entertained, then that is not my problem.'

Sir Branden's eyes were so cold they looked like they had turned to ice.

'Be careful, Isabel,' he replied as he let go of her arm.

'How dare he! How dare he touch you!' John growled, pacing her room like a caged beast.

'He has done it before, and he will do it again,' said Isabel wearily. 'But we must be careful.'

The angry print upon her white arm was starting to fade, but every time John looked at it, his temper rose. Isabel drew a shawl over her to cover her arms and stood up.

'Well…at least it is nearly over,' John muttered darkly.

Isabel turned to him. It was time to ask.

'Tell me  - when are we leaving John?'

'In two days' time – New Year's Eve, to be precise,' he answered.

Her heart leapt.

'Oh, that is so close!'

'Branden's reign of tyranny is nearly over,' said John, taking her hands.

It thrilled Isabel to see him jealous for her.

'Where will we go?' she asked eagerly.

'Everywhere. The future is ours to find,' he replied with a smile.

'But where shall we settle?'

'Why should we settle? We could roam this earth all our days. You wanted to see the world, did you not?'

'Yes, I did – I still do,' she agreed.

He pulled her closer.

'Our home is each other, Isabel. Wherever you are – that is where I will be.'

She smiled up at him. Excitement prickled her stomach.

'And what is your plan?'

John's expression changed.

'It will be dangerous, and will require a great deal of courage. You are going to have to trust me, Isabel.'

She squeezed his hands.

'Nothing is too frightening – or too much to go through – when you are by my side.'

He smiled back at her, admiration in his eyes.

'We are going to leave at midnight on the thirty-first. I will need to leave the house after dinner. I have arranged for a carriage to meet me at the front gates – Sir Branden believes I am leaving that night as my stay has come to an end. In actual fact I will be travelling to the nearest town to collect two horses. I will ride back, as fast as I can, and collect you.'

'How will I get to you – the doors will be locked and the stable entrance is being watched?' asked Isabel, tension already building within her.

'In the way that all beautiful heroines leave their towers,' he said with a smile, ' – by climbing down a rope from your bedroom window.'

Isabel laughed and then realised he was being serious.

'I will put a long thick length of rope under your bed before I go,' he continued. 'You just need to tie it to the leg of your bed and drop the other end out the window when I arrive. I will hold it steady and you can climb down to me. No one will be in any of the rooms below – they will be celebrating the coming of the new year in the ballroom, and I will be lifting you down into my arms.'

'And then we will be off?'

'And then we will be off – first to an inn, a few hours away, to get some rest – and then on to Dover. I have not booked places on a ship, for fear of Branden's spies tracing us. We will have to take what we can get, to wherever it is going. Does that scare you?'

'Not in the slightest. You are wonderful, John.'

'You are worth it, Isabel,' he replied steadily.

Isabel reached up and kissed him softly. John smiled, slipped his arm round her waist and turned them both towards the window. Outside, the sun was setting in a glorious purple sky.

'It is a beautiful world out there Isabel, and I want to show you it all,' John said, smiling in his wild and exhilarating way. 'I want to hold your hand, run with you to the highest spot in the land and shout to all the world that you are mine.'

'There is no one I would rather see the world with,' she Isabel contentedly.

She suddenly felt quite sleepy. The worry was over, it was all in hand and John was going to take her away from this place. They were finally going to be together.

'I am going to protect you from now on Isabel,' said John, as though reading her thoughts. 'No one will ever harm you again, I promise you that.'

## ISABEL'S NARRATIVE
*(Extract from Isabel's Diary)*

*ENDERTON, 30<sup>th</sup> December 1866*

We leave tomorrow. A world of hitherto unknown possibilities is opening up before me.

Equally, however, the immensity of what we are doing is dawning upon me. The risk, the danger...some would say it is pure folly.

Yet each time that I look into his eyes with their warm entreaty – those eyes that say, 'Go on, I dare you...' - the fear disappears. There is an excitement in choosing to go with him. There is a thrill in trusting someone completely. I have the strangest sense that he is drawing me towards the edge of a cliff, but that the fall – however brief – will be the most exciting thing of my life. How strange that I barely know him, but I trust him entirely.

The adventures I always dreamed of are about to come true.

## THE STORY CONTINUED BY THE EDITOR

The last day of the year dawned bright and cold. John had come to Isabel's room early that morning, as planned, to discuss the final details of their escape.

John had become aware that he was not the only guest leaving that day. In fact, most of the Christmas visitors were choosing to travel back after dinner rather than stay on for the festivities. The reasons for this were unclear, but it seemed that Sir Branden had invited a new group to spend the evening with him instead.

'It is just as well we had planned to leave tonight, for it seems I may have been forced to leave anyway,' remarked John.

'Who are the group that have arrived?' asked Isabel.

They had come after she retired yesterday evening, but John had remained in the drawing room to see them.

'A brutish bunch,' he remarked. 'There were five of them – two tall dark-haired gentlemen, one rather more stocky blonde-haired man, another with hooded eyes and wide shoulders, and a fifth with a shorn head and very blue eyes.' He did not notice the look on Isabel's face and continued, 'The good news is, they all like a drink and the likelihood is that they will be more focused on the gin than their hostess tomorrow night.'

Isabel had got to her feet and was pacing back and forth.

'What is wrong?' he asked in surprise.

'Those are the men who kidnapped me!' said Isabel, fear and confusion in her voice. 'Why have they come back here, now?'

'Probably for no reason than to see Branden,' John said in a calming voice. 'I am sure it is quite unrelated. They seem to be very close with him and Gaunt.'

'They are thick as thieves,' said Isabel sardonically.

'Then there is nothing to worry about. I would rather contend with five drunk men than fifty sober, when it comes down to it – but I am sure it will not,' he added, to appease the horrified look in Isabel's eyes. 'The only thing I am concerned about is the watchman.'

'The blind man who lives in the gatehouse?' asked Isabel.

'Yes – I have been keeping an eye on him and he sleeps during the day, but never leaves his post at night.'

'I always see his lamp bobbing around at night, but I do not understand the point of a blind watchman,' said Isabel, dismissively.

'Ah, but he has extremely keen hearing,' said John cautiously. 'His ears prick up if even a mouse scurries through those gates – I should know, he nearly caught me spying on him, and I always pride myself on being particularly light on my feet.'

'But surely you can out speed him – you will be on a horse and he is an old man.'

'Have you not noticed his greyhound? Should an intruder pass those gates, he sends that dog speeding up to the house faster than a bolt of lightning to warn his master.'

'Then how will you stop him?'

'I have not decided that yet,' said John thoughtfully.

'Well you had better think quickly!' Isabel exclaimed nervously. 'We leave in less than twenty-four hours!'

'Calm, Isabel. Be calm. These nerves will not help you. Everything will be fine.'

'You sound as if you have done this before,' she said, with a half-laugh.

'Sadly not, though if this goes well, I feel sure we can make a career out of rescuing damsels in distress,' he said jovially.

He opened the bag he had brought with him, and drew out of it a long length of thick rope that Isabel was going to use for her escape.

'Where did you get that from?' she asked, wonderingly.

'From the well – they never use it,' he replied, with a shrug.

Isabel had a sudden flashback of a limp, dead body being drawn up from that same well. For a few weeks she had not seen much of her shadow, and for the first time, this thought struck her with ominous force.

'I am worried about Gaunt,' she said suddenly, as John slid the coil of rope underneath her bed.

'Why? I have hardly seen him recently. He has been shut up in that office with his master.'

'I feel he must know, somehow, what is going on,' she said apprehensively.

'Isabel,' said John cajolingly, 'you have been here for six months now. Gaunt has forgotten about you – he has decided that you are not going to try and escape. You have made his life sincerely uninteresting and he has found another task to occupy his time.'

Isabel looked back at him, unconvinced.

'I see you have packed your suitcase?' said John, nodding to the small leather-bound case.

'Yes. I hope I get to take it on the journey I want to take it on, this time.'

'You will,' said John. 'And now, I must leave you.'

Isabel got to her feet. Her bed was made, her suitcase packed, her escape rope stored. John stood by the door and watched her staring around the room that she was preparing to leave.

'This is it,' he said. 'I will not see you again until you are climbing down that rope.'

She looked up at him.

'Yes, I know.'

He surveyed her closely.

'Are you ready?'

'Yes,' she replied, wrapping her shawl around her. She suddenly felt a little cold.

He moved towards her.

'Are you scared?'

'I - ,' Isabel paused and he reached out his hand and she took it. 'No', she answered truthfully.

John pulled her towards him and said gently in her ear:

'There is no going back now - only look forwards.'

She wrapped her arms around him and over her shoulder the knight watched.

The final hours of the old year were dying in a haze of rain, while the new one began with a rising hope. Surely no new year had been so eagerly anticipated as this one, thought Isabel to herself, as she paced her room nervously. Finally she could see the open door at the end of the long dark tunnel that she had been travelling through for so long.

She had re-packed her suitcase to make sure she had not forgotten anything. Her bible, diary and father's book were all inside, as was a change of clothing: a simple muslin dress that she had ordered from her own small purse. She had taken nothing that did not belong to her – not that she would have wanted anything that reminded her of Enderton.

She could hear the men downstairs. Dinner meal had been a rushed affair, with all the guests eager to leave and begin their journeys home. The new visitors had disgraced themselves with crude jokes and rough language. Isabel sensed that the other men were eager to leave them and their host to their drinking in peace. Sir Branden had seemed in an almost jovial mood that night, but when his eye fell upon Isabel, it was dark.

'No matter,' she said silently to him. 'You look upon me for the last time. In a few hours I will be gone, reclaiming the freedom that you took from me.'

He had been happy to let her retire early, clearly wanting to be alone with his friends. Isabel climbed the long stairs one last time, noticing how quiet the house seemed. All the rooms around hers were empty now. The thought gave her a queer chill.

Once back in her room, she recalled John's advice to get some rest before their long night. She lay down on her soft bed, still fully dressed, to try and heed his advice. She looked around her vast room and thought over the terrible and wonderful scenes that had taken place there. She looked over at her knight and said a silent goodbye.

Isabel closed her eyes, not expecting to sleep, but drowsiness suddenly overcame her. She began to think of John's face, and the pleasant notion that he would soon wake her with a soft cry from outside her half-open window lulled her to sleep, his voice calling her into the land of dreams.

She dreamt of a huge stone girl standing in the sea. Waves were crashing around the statue – violent, terrible waves. They did not reach further than her calves, but as Isabel watched, their ceaseless, never-ending work began to take effect, and gradually she saw the layers of stone beginning to wear away, crumbling into the water. Soon the legs were thin and wasted and slowly she watched as the huge form toppled heavily into the sea with a crash that resounded around the world.

A crash. A real crash. Flesh against wood. Isabel sat bolt upright in bed. No, it could not be happening again. The rain was heavier now, splattering in through her open window as the wind moaned around the house as if it were in pain.

Crash.

Crash.

Isabel rose from her bed, as though still in her dream.

John was riding through the walls of rain, leading the other horse behind him.

'Faster, boy, faster,' he yelled above the wind.

The moon hung low in the sky before him. He read it as a warning.

'Another blow, another one will break it!' a voice cried.

It certainly looked that way. One bolt was hanging off now, shattered by the force that was being applied with such ferocity. Isabel stared futilely at the heavy chest of drawers that had saved her once before and then back at the door with half-seeing eyes. What could she do? It was too heavy for her to move, and they were so nearly through. Then, with a final blow, the door gave way and her rising panic mounted to utter terror.

She watched the handle of the door being savagely twisted and then it opened and they tumbled into the room. Their faces were flushed with wine and heavy metal pokers were in their hands, with which they had been raining blows upon her door. With a mournful cry behind them, the door fell from its hinges. The battle was over.

As the five men advanced towards her, a pungent smell filled the room. She could smell strong alcohol, cigar smoke and sweat. Menace was in their eyes and their blood was up.

'She's mine! Marianne is mine!'

Their leader stumbled into the midst of them. He was more intoxicated than even the other men. High colour blazed in Branden's cheeks and he spoke roughly, threat pouring from every word. Isabel turned her unbelieving gaze to the man who called himself her husband.

'Yes, you look at me, Marianne!' he slurred. 'You have made a fool of me for the last time. I have been a kind, and faithful husband to you – I *waited* for you – and you made a mockery of me. I have given you everything you could ever have wished for - and in return? In return, you have defied me – disobeyed me - and refused me my *rights* as your husband.'

The other men muttered encouragement as he spoke. They moved forwards with him – two of them had their hands on his shoulder, anticipation in their eyes. Isabel moved backwards, moving closer to the window.

'And now, now you think you can run off and leave me. You think you can *leave* me – again? I will have what was promised to me. Tonight this rebellion ends. Tonight I will have my rights!'

Murmurs of approval echoed round the room. Hot blood rose in Isabel's veins.

'So tonight you will become even more the monster I knew you were!' she spat at him in disgust. 'My mother knew you were not worthy, tonight you prove it!'

A livid flush suffused Branden's face and he lunged at Isabel, but she moved too quickly for him, jumping from the bed over to the window - and for a moment she thought his wits had left him, so great was the rage that possessed him as he looked up at her from where he had fallen. She knew then that he was not to be stopped.

'Leave me - do not dare take one more step', she heard her voice say in the strongest tones it could muster.

'And who will protect you now?' he said, getting up and coming in closer with the five men ranged around him, two to his right and three to his left, cruel smiles on their faces.

Branden's face was quite transformed - malice burned in his eyes, and for the first time Isabel experienced true, debilitating fear. She was against the stone window ledge now; she could retreat no further, and her legs seemed to have locked beneath her. Behind her was a three-storey drop and she could not reach the rope underneath her bed. Branden's figure seemed to grow in height and bulk before her very eyes. Once again, the demonic vampirish nightmares began to cloud her mind. The memory of the hands clawing and dragging her into the church, the horrific imprisonment, the bag over her head – all the fears that had been pushed so far back in her mind, flooded forward again. The edges of her vision blurred and all she could see was his figure before her.

'You are mine,' he said with a slowly curving smile.

'Do not lay a finger on her, you dog!'

249

The voice that Isabel had longed to hear suddenly rang out around the room. She opened her eyes – John was standing in the doorway, dripping wet, his eyes blazing with cold fury. Down below she could hear a dog barking wildly. Branden's face turned black and he swore savagely at John, grabbing Isabel by her hair.

'She is mine, James!' he screamed. 'You will not take her from me again!'

Branden seemed quite lost in his delusion, seeing only her mother and father before him. The thought sent a shiver up Isabel's spine. How would this end?

John took in the scene – the drunkenness of the men, the madness in Branden's eyes, and finally, Isabel, gasping in pain. At that sight, Isabel watched John's face suddenly undergo a startling transformation. It was as though he had cast off a mask, revealing something dark and strange underneath – a wild animal unleashed. Without a second's hesitation, John lunged with dexterity at the first man. He moved quickly and without fear, striking an expert blow - and the man fell down like a log. For a moment, the other men stood amazed at the savagery of his attack, but then moved in on him. He lashed out, untempered but controlled – fighting like a man possessed. Soon, the remaining men began to flinch away from him, unnerved by the rage of this strange creature. He turned upon the final two, his teeth set in a kind of snarl.

'Run,' he said to them – and they did.

Only Isabel, John and Branden now remained in the room, but Branden did not recoil.

'You do not scare me, you fool,' he said, clutching Isabel to him.

His fingers dug into her throat, but she did not flinch, only kept her eyes fixed on John. An unearthly light was in his eyes.

'Then you are the fool,' he said.

Branden held Isabel still tighter – she was struggling to breathe now, gasping for air. John's lips tightened as he bared his teeth that gleamed white in the candlelight. Black fire burned in his eyes.

'You will *never* touch her again!' said John with a snarl – and then he struck.

Isabel saw Branden recoil – she saw the look of anguish in his eyes as he fell backwards from the force of the blow. She watched that look die as he fell sharply against the window ledge, and slid down to the ground.

## ISABEL'S NARRATIVE
*(Extract from Isabel's Diary)*

*1ˢᵗ January 1867*

I felt the pressure of John's hand in mine; I heard the sound of our footsteps ringing down the stairs and through the hallway. I saw the wild, wonderful look in his eyes as he lifted me up onto the horse; I heard the cry of the watchman as he swung his lamp towards us, shouting,

'Who goes there?'

And then we were through the gates, riding, riding faster than we had ever done before. We rode and the moon rode with us.

Every nerve inside me was tingling, but I felt no fear – only joy, excitement and sheer exhilaration. We were free. Already, the scene that had taken place just moments before felt like a dream. We rode towards a sign with one arrow pointing towards Carstone, and another pointing back towards Enderton. We had reached the edge of Branden's lands. I slipped the gold ring from my finger and tossed it behind me as we passed the sign. It landed in the mud and I glanced back to see it sink out of sight, its weight dragging it down.

# XXIX

## THE STORY CONTINUED BY THE EDITOR

They arrived in the early hours of the morning at the White Hart Inn. The innkeeper was a friendly man who had waited up for their arrival. He and John seemed to know each other fairly well and he led them up to a room at the very top of the house.

'I have had a busier day than expected, Mr Fenn,' he said to John as he led them up the wooden staircase, holding Isabel's case in one hand and a candle in the other. 'So I hope you and your wife do not mind sharing the same room.'

He smiled genially at Isabel, who glanced at John quickly. John gave her a reassuring look. Isabel presumed he was using an assumed name to escape detection.

'Of course not,' John replied.

The room was a fair size and homely, with a low, sloping ceiling. The bed was large and looked clean and comfortable. The innkeeper placed Isabel's case by the bed and bade them a very good night. John thanked him warmly and closed the door. He looked at Isabel. There was suddenly a strange awkwardness in the air.

They had spent much time together, but this was different. Somehow it seemed more real. The air seemed to crackle; the silence seemed deeper than ever before, more alive. John and Isabel looked at each other, standing a few feet apart. For the first time, they were truly alone, they could do whatever they wished: there was no ending to this moment. The reality of it pressed upon Isabel in all its wonderful and terrifying fullness.

To break the silence, Isabel took off her cloak. There was a hook over by the window and she went over to hang it up, for it was mud-splattered and wet from the ride. She glanced out of the window – the rain had stopped and it was a beautiful night, cold and clear. John came over and stood behind her as she undid her bonnet. Her fingers fumbled with the ties; she felt suddenly self-conscious in his presence.

'Let me help you,' he said softly, deftly untying the ribbons.

He lifted it from her head and placed it on the bed. Outside, the stars shone brightly, reflecting in his eyes as she looked up at him, his gaze steady as he looked far out into the night. Suddenly he looked down at her, his face alight with excitement and sudden resolve. He grabbed her hand and swung her cloak over his arm.

'Come on,' he whispered in her ear. 'Run with me.'

## ISABEL'S NARRATIVE
*(Extract from Isabel's Diary)*

*1st January 1867*

I had felt tired after the journey and all that had happened that night, but at John's words suddenly I felt weightless, vibrating with energy, more alive than I had ever felt in my life. The world had no limits as I ran with him across the midnight fields, over darkly sparkling streams, down a sloping valley; my hand in his, my heart in his, my hair streaming out behind me as we ran through the landscape of the night. The hill that rose up before us flew away beneath our feet as we scaled it effortlessly. Then we stood at the top, our chests heaving. My eyes met his in the darkness and suddenly, in the cold night air, I knew that something wonderful was about to happen.

He took my pale hand and laid it on his chest, on his heart. I looked up and saw that tears were in his eyes.

'Your eyes are sparkling,' I said, cupping the side of his face with my hand. My breath came out in white mists in the night air.

'It's the stars,' he replied. 'The light of the myriad above us.'

I followed his gaze up to the vast expanse.

'Can you see it?' he said, his lips close to my ear.

'What?'

'Your star.'

My eyes searched the black velvet, but the arrangements looked different tonight, less familiar. The radiant, sparkling stone was not set in her usual place.

'No,' I replied softly. 'Not tonight.'

His eyes sought mine again. When he spoke, his throat was dry. I felt suddenly unreal, as though the ground below me was not quite firm.

'You asked me once to take you to the stars,' he said, his voice deep and husky. 'I have not yet figured out how to do that – not yet, anyway.'

He smiled at me then, but my tense stomach did not relax.

'So instead,' he continued, 'I have brought one of them closer to you.'

He lifted his hand to his breast pocket and drew out a small black box. I gazed at it with wondering eyes.

'I caught this for you, so you could have it with you always,' he said, placing the box in my trembling fingers. 'Open it,' he said simply.

I lifted the lid, slowly and inside – oh! – Inside was the star! It

253

shone so brightly underneath its companions above that it took me a few moments to see that it was fastened to a ring, a thin band of gold encircling the brilliant stone. I stared into its depths – it drew me into its glistening facets like an ocean.

'Oh John, I –' I paused; he was no longer standing before me, and then I looked down and realised he was kneeling before me, his face white, his eyes steady. Then he began the speech that would stay with me for the rest of my life:

'Isabel. You said once that you did not know me. But you know me better than anyone ever has. You hold my heart in your hands, Isabel, because I love you. I cannot do anything but love you: it is the simplest, most powerful emotion I have ever felt, and I am no longer afraid to say it. When I am with you, I no longer feel like a lost child – I feel like a man. I once swore I would always be alone. But you have stripped me of my armour. I have been travelling a dark and weary road and you have lit up my life with your brilliance, with your beauty, with your love. You have given me so much, but now I ask you for more - not because I deserve it, but because I cannot live without it.

'Marry me, Isabel Audley. Be my own light, always before me, always beside me. Whatever is good in me, whatever is true: it is yours. Will you have me?'

Tears were streaming down my face, the happiest tears I had ever cried. It was not a question. There was no decision. You can give your heart fully but once. I gave John Treador my heart on that hillside, and he placed the star on my finger.

Over his shoulder, the dawn began in all its glory. The new year had begun.

# XXX

I wake and find myself in a green room under the eaves. I hover on the surface of waking and try to find myself. I wonder where I am – am I at school, back in my old dormitory?

The sun gleams through the window and I sit up on the bed. I have been dreaming all night and I try to untangle myself from the fictions and step into reality. Something glitters in the sunlight, catching the morning light and sending sprays of rainbow sparkles across my bedcovers. I look down in surprise - it is my ring. There is a ring on my finger and I am engaged – engaged to the most wonderful man I have ever met. I am loved: finally, finally I belong to someone, like I have never belonged to anyone before.

The morning is full of sunlight and hope. I can see before me only joy. On the floor I can see a tumble of blankets and pillows where John slept last night. They still hold his scent – deep and warm. I step over them to the small, white-painted dressing table. I can hear John and the innkeeper talking downstairs, through the cracks in the wooden floor. I lift my hairbrush; I want to look beautiful for him.

### THE STORY CONTINUED BY THE EDITOR

John was still speaking with innkeeper when Isabel came down the stairs. She was dressed in a fresh muslin gown of the palest yellow. Her hair was gathered in a loose knot at the base of her neck. It was still early morning and the morning light illuminated her youthful beauty perfectly, bringing out each dimple and sparkle with a fresh charm. She wore a radiant expression as she smiled at him, glowing with fervent beauty.

'Here comes a young woman in the very exultation of love,' said the old man, his voice almost lyrical.

John stared at her for a moment longer, his eyes saying all that his voice could not. He said later that it was because he realised that his life could never be more wonderful than it was at this moment. The joy and sadness of it made his eyes shine with tears.

'You look beautiful,' he said, his voice full of emotion. 'I will not forget this moment. It will stay with me for the rest of my life.'

Isabel stepped towards him and took his hand. He kissed her tenderly, adoringly. She could feel joy coursing through him and felt like she had finally come home.

'Well, I think I will leave you two young lovers alone now,' said the innkeeper jovially.

Isabel looked up with radiant eyes and then a blushing face – she had completely forgotten he was there.

'No, you must stay and eat with us,' said John, pulling out a chair for Isabel. 'It is your home, after all.'

The innkeeper laughed and then assented.

Soon they had eaten a hearty breakfast and the innkeeper went outside to hail the Dover coach that would take them to their next destination. Once he was out of earshot, John turned to Isabel, and pulled out a parcel wrapped in brown paper from under the table.

'What is that?' she asked curiously.

'You must put it on – and quickly,' said John in a low voice. 'Then put your cloak over the top so the innkeeper does not see.'

Isabel wrapped it the paper – inside was a black and white maid's outfit.

'Why must I wear this?' she asked, confused.

'Because there will be people looking for us now, and you must not be recognised. If they hear of a lady travelling in this direction, they will be straight after us. As ludicrous as it sounds, if we are stopped, you must pretend to be my maid and I will pretend I am a travelling teacher.'

Isabel smiled half-heartedly. As foolish as it was, she was reluctant to step out of her gown into the drab items in her lap. John understood her expression.

'It is for your safety, Isabel.'

She looked up at him, knowing he was right.

'Very well,' she said, in mock resignation. 'I shall sacrifice my dignity for one day, for you.'

A few minutes later, she was dressed in the uniform, her golden hair tucked under a black cap. She turned up her nose in the mirror at her reflection, putting her pretty muslin dress back inside her suitcase.

'It is not for long,' John whispered in her ear when she joined him outside where the carriage was waiting. 'And besides,' he added, 'you are the prettiest maid I have ever seen.'

They bade farewell to the innkeeper and thanked him for his food and service. Isabel climbed inside the coach – it was in need of repair and smelt of damp, but she did not care. Soon John was beside her and they were off.

The bright winter weather that they had enjoyed when they set off did not last for long. As they travelled south, the rain began and soon it was very cold in the carriage. John pulled Isabel close for warmth.

Outside, the skies grew steadily darker and the coach journey steadily rougher – the road was full of potholes that the wheels continually managed to hit. Yet Isabel did not mind. She and John were going to be together; the terror was over now.

'I love you, John,' she said, with all sincerity, moving deeper into the fold of his arm.

He kissed her lightly on the forehead.

Two hours later, the sky was black and the rain falling in great sheets, while wind ripped through the trees on either side of the road. They heard a roar of thunder and John put his arm out in front of Isabel.

'What is it?' she cried out in alarm.

'The thunder – it means lightning is not far off.'

She did not know why this was the cause for such alarm, but soon realised. When the lightning struck with its blazing white light, the horses reared up in terror, shaking the coach from side to side. Isabel would have fallen from her seat had it not been for John's arm holding her upright. The coach drew to a halt.

'What is wrong?' John called out the window to the coach driver.

'Tess kicked Bessie in the leg in her fright,' the driver called back as he leapt down from his seat. 'She's in a lot of pain.'

'I am going to help,' said John to Isabel. 'Stay here in the dry.'

Isabel sat in the semi-darkness for a few moments. The rain continued to plummet from the sky, the wind continued to bellow. Then, from far off, she heard the second call of thunder.

Concerned, she glanced out of the window. The two men were on their knees in the mud, assessing the damage, shouting to one another over the storm.

'John!' she called out in alarm, but he could not hear her.

She got out of the carriage, her feet sinking into deep mud.

'John!'

He looked round as she ran towards them, just as the lightning struck. The men managed to steady the injured mare but the larger horse reared with a deafening whinny, its eyes wild and terrified, its hooves striking outwards in fear and terror. For a second the great creature was lit up against the black sky, tall and majestic in the light of the white fire.

Then, hoof connected with bone; flesh with mire. A great cry rent the air, as blood scored the ground. Red against brown, a white face against a black sky. The thunder roared again.

# VOLUME THREE

# XXXI

POLICE REPORT
By Constable Barnes of Little Wharton

*2ⁿᵈ January 1867*

I have come to the end of my investigation. There is no trail, nor any witnesses to be found. Whoever took the girl planned it very carefully and time is serving only to remove any final traces of her departure. I can do no more from here.

Harringdon Court is now completely closed up and I am sending an officer once a week to check it is secure, until Mr and Mrs Leicester are able to sell it. I understand that they married a few weeks ago, once the search for Miss Audley was declared over. Mrs Catherine Leicester came to me very upset at this news, but there is simply nothing else I can do. The wider search I have finally sanctioned, albeit unwillingly, but I do not wish to make her aware of this until it yields some results, which I am doubtful it will.

The investigation into the disappearance of Lady Harringdon has also proved fruitless. Since the night when she vanished without explanation – on the day when we discovered the bloody rag at the bottom of the garden - she has not been seen. I regret showing her this now. It seemed only to confirm fears that her niece had been killed. However, I agree with Officer Hardy that this seemed more likely to be a well-planted diversion to lead us off the trail.

I should note that my junior officer Fielding has reported a story that has been going around the villagers. It is said that a tramp who has recently turned up in Ashton been telling the story of how he passed a well-dressed woman on his travels, coming from the Harringdon direction on the night Lady Harringdon disappeared. He said she was dressed in black, her face covered with a veil, tearing down the country road that led to the coast. He said she kept calling out a name: 'Marianne.' She seemed to be following something, but he could see nothing before her: it seemed visible only to her. The tramp followed her for a while until she took the path that led to the sea, and then she disappeared into the darkness and he lost her.

Whether this has any bearing on the case or not, Lady Harringdon has not been seen since and is now also presumed dead.

# THE STORY CONTINUED BY THE EDITOR

A servant girl is on her knees in a stone-flagged entrance hall. Her sleeves are rolled up, a scrubbing brush is in her hand and she has a pailof water by her side. The front doors stand open and a cold wind sweeps in. Although thinly dressed, she does not seem to notice.

A group of male pupils walk past. One of them kicks over the girl's pail with a laugh and cold water soaks through her skirt. The girl does not move, does not even blink, but carries on scrubbing, her fingers raw, her eyes dead.

A door opens on her right. Out walks a teacher, dressed in black school robes. This time, the girl looks up, her eyes on his face – but he does not see her. He walks past, stepping around the spilt water, and exits into a room behind her.

If you looked back at her, you would see the despair etched across her face.


## ISABEL'S NARRATIVE
### (Extract from Isabel's Diary)

*LANCEFIELD, account written 16<sup>th</sup> January 1867*

It helped me once to write down all that had happened. I will do so again, but this time I do not think it will bring me any comfort.

The first thing I saw of this place was the sign. Even then I hardly noticed it, so focused was I on what was going on around me. They carried him past, and out of the corner of my eye I saw the words 'Lancefield School'.

But I am getting ahead of myself. The accident...no, I do not want to remember it. There was so much blood coming from his head...The hoof had caught him on his right temple. Terror such as I have never known gripped my heart like a stone vice. Blindly, I stumbled forwards through the mud towards him, my feet feeling completely unconnected to my legs. I heard the driver shout that he was going for help, and then he disappeared into the rain.

I held John's head in my hands. I remember the way that the raindrops created little rivers through the blood running down the side of his face. His eyes were closed, his breathing slow and ragged. I could not believe that my world had shifted so suddenly in just a few seconds.

Then, the driver returned with a few men. They lifted John – I remember calling out for them to be careful, his head was unsupported and lolled frighteningly – but they did not hear me and carried him down a path to the right. I followed behind – that was when we passed the sign – and then a great building reared up out of the darkness.

They carried him into this house, across a great hallway and into a room on the left. I was about to enter when the door was shut suddenly in my face.

'No servants,' a man said to me. 'The doctor will see to him now.'


## THE STORY CONTINUED BY THE EDITOR

The men stood in the hallway, smoking their pipes. One of them cast a glance at the pale, dirt-splattered girl in the doorway.

'Who is she?' he asked the other.

'She arrived with the injured man, most likely his servant,' replied the second man.

'Well,' said the first, gesturing with his pipe, 'he has no need of her now. Get rid of her, will you?'

The second gentleman glanced back at her with some sympathy in his eyes.

'Oh, let her stay a day, at least. She seems genuinely concerned about her master and I think she may be in shock - she has not spoken a word since she arrived.'

The first man glanced at her again. Her face was paper-white; her eyes, huge with worry, seemed to convey a certain desperation. She barely blinked as she gazed transfixed through the half-open door at the injured man lying motionless inside. Her expression was stricken, full of fear and uncertainty as she listened to the snatches of conversation from inside the room, spoken by a gentleman whom she understood to be the headmaster of the school and the doctor who had just arrived:

'Severe blow to the head... may suffer trauma... memory loss... extremely lucky to have survived.'

'One day, then,' the first man replied, turning back to his companion. 'And then send her home.'

'What is your name?'

'Isabel - Snow,' she replied, thinking fast.

She was now inside the room where John lay, dried blood crusting around his eye. She had finally been allowed in by the doctor, who had listened to her plea with kindness, and allowed her to sit in the corner of the room on a wooden chair while he examined his patient.

'And where were you headed when this accident occurred?' the doctor asked.

'Dover – we were heading to Dover...John has family there,' she lied quickly.

'John?' the doctor said in surprise.

'I mean, Mr Fenn,' said Isabel, realising her mistake too late.

A woman, a little older than Isabel, entered the room. She had a sweet heart-shaped face, wide doe-like eyes and soft brown curly hair. She was dressed in a simple calico gown.

'Ah, Miss Part,' said the doctor with a smile. 'Thank you for coming down. I must away, and I wondered if you would sit with my patient tonight?'

'I will sit with him,' said Isabel quickly.

The doctor and Miss Part looked round at her in surprise.

'I am his servant, it is my position to sit with him,' Isabel continued. Her tone was agitated, but also commanding; the voice of a woman accustomed to getting her own way.

The nurse glanced at the doctor and he glanced back at Isabel, looking rather taken aback.

'I would be happier if Miss Part stayed with him – she is, after all, experienced in these matters.'

'Why, is she a nurse?' said Isabel, aware that she sounded insolent, but not caring.

'No, but she has assisted me before,' replied the doctor, surprised.

'Then she is no more experienced than I, and knows him less,' said Isabel, a hint of desperation now in her voice. 'I must stay with him.'

Her eyes flicked back from one to the other. Miss Part exchanged a look with the doctor, wariness in her eyes.

'Very well,' said the doctor resignedly. 'You may stay. But you must call Miss Part if you notice any change. She is the niece of the headmaster of this school and lived here for many years, often aiding me in the sick room.'

'So you see, I do know a little about these matters,' said Miss Part, though not unkindly. She paused and then said, 'You will find me on the first floor, the last room on your right. Please come at once if his condition alters in the least. I can then get in touch with Doctor McKenzie'

'I will,' said Isabel, visibly relieved.

'Then I wish you a good night,' said the doctor, tipping his hat to Miss Part, and casting Isabel a slightly troubled glance. 'I will be back first thing in the morning.'

'Good night, Doctor McKenzie,' replied Miss Part. She too glanced quizzically at Isabel, before following the doctor out and closing the door.

## ISABEL'S NARRATIVE
*(Extract from Isabel's Diary)*

*LANCEFIELD, account written 16<sup>th</sup> January 1867*

The silence. That was the worst part.

I sat quite still and listened to the heavy, laboured beating of my heart.

At first, I simply stared at him in disbelief. I wondered if he were playing some sort of charade, half-expecting him to sit up now that everyone had left the room - to leap up with all his usual energy, grab my hand and we would run. But something in the colour of his cheeks told me this would not happen.

I felt my chest begin to heave. For the first time I let myself look at him fully. I took in his pale face, his bandaged head, the blueish tinge of his eyelids. For the first time I let the fear that I had held off for so long, flood me with the force of an ocean that had finally burst its gates. The doctor had said the wound was deep, that he had shown no sign of consciousness since they brought him in. He said he was not hopeful…and yet John looked so peaceful, so unaware that his life was hanging like a thread waiting to be cut. Panic, seething and unstoppable, surged up in my throat. I thought I would be sick. 'John – John. Can you hear me?' I said urgently, seizing his cold hand. 'You must not leave me, John. You cannot leave me alone here.' He could not hear me, lost in his swirling world, far away.

I looked around at the unfamiliar room. I realised fully how lost I was, how far I was from anyone I knew... how terrible my situation was. I was alone, in a place I did not know, with ruthless men most likely on my trail. I had no family or friends to turn to, no money at my aid. With John by my side, all of that had not seemed to matter. He was the hero, he would protect me. With John, nothing could go wrong. But John was silent and still now. He was slipping away from me.

And yet, I realised - it was not just his protection that I might lose. I had never considered what it was like to live and breathe without the one you loved. We were two parts of one whole - but part of me was fading now, and I felt it physically. How could I live if he – I could not

265

think it. The thoughts that now crowded my mind were too terrible and incomprehensible to bear. I tried to overcome them, to remember the few positive things that the doctor had said. There was a chance, he had said - a chance that he might come back to me.

I held his clammy hand and listened to the unstoppable tick of the mantle clock. I swept his hair out of his eyes. Time stretched out before me like a dark and endless void. I crouched closer to him, so that I could hear the sound of his heart. That was my lifeline.

Beat, quiet heart, beat.


## THE STORY CONTINUED BY THE EDITOR

Doctor McKenzie arrived about eight o'clock the next morning. He found Isabel with her chair drawn up to his patient, her hand in his, her eyes red-rimmed with weariness.

'You can go now,' he said kindly. Isabel looked round stiffly. She had not moved in many hours.

'No, I will stay,' she said. She sounded exhausted.

'You must get some rest,' he urged.

'I will not leave him,' she said, this time quite firmly. The doctor opened his mouth and then resisted.

'Very well,' he replied. 'Move back and let me examine him.'

There had been no change. The doctor lifted his eyelids, felt John's pulse, moved his hands; all the while Isabel sat on the chair, her fingers knitted together, silently praying for some sign of life.

The door opened and Miss Part entered. She was carrying a small bowl of porridge.

'For you,' she said gently to Isabel, and placed it in her cold hands.

The warmth was pleasant, but Isabel could not eat. Her stomach felt tight and sick.

'Is there any change, Doctor McKenzie?' Miss Part asked gently.

'None,' the doctor replied. 'His pulse is good, but he is in a very deep sleep, completely insensible.'

'Is there anything we could to try and rouse him?'

'No – and to do so would be dangerous. He must come round in his own time, if at all.'

'What can I do for him?' she asked, resignedly.

'Will the headmaster let him stay?' asked the doctor.

'Of course,' she replied.

'Then he must be kept under constant supervision. I suggest that you two young ladies share the watch, and send a message to me as soon as anything changes. Do not give him anything to drink as he cannot swallow and it will choke him.'

'How long can he survive in this condition?' asked Miss Part, with an anxious glance towards John.

'Three days,' replied the doctor gravely. 'At the most.'

## ISABEL'S NARRATIVE
### (Extract from Isabel's Diary)

*LANCEFIELD, account written 16th January 1867*

Day one came and went with no change. I allowed myself to be shown to a small room on the fourth floor with a narrow bed and was told to sleep. I tossed and turned for a few hours, feeling fretful and anxious at being parted from John. When I saw the sky darkening outside, I went back downstairs and relieved Miss Part. Night fell and I resumed my vigil through the watchful hours.

The next morning, she entered once more and sent me upstairs to rest, but I was ill with worry. There had been no alteration in John's condition. No matter how I squeezed his hand, cooled his brow or pleaded with him to wake, he did not respond. It may have been my imagination but his breathing seemed slower, less steady.

Sleep would not come to me and as soon as it was time to take over from her, I rushed back downstairs, desperate for some news, some sign – but her sombre face told me he was no better. She left and I took my post. His face was paler, his hand colder. I did not even notice that she had not closed the door behind her. I was holding his hand with both of mine, and then reached up to brush his hair from his eyes. A noise made me look round – two maids were standing by the door, staring at us.

'Leave us!' I said, displeasure in my voice.

They glanced at each other, their eyebrows raised. It was a moment before I remembered that I too was dressed in their uniform and not the lady of the house.

'He needs rest,' I said, trying to cover up my mistake. 'Please close the door.'

The taller girl looked at me challengingly with (she could not have been much older than me) and obtusely pushed the door a little further open. With a glance at each other, they walked away. Frustrated, I got up from my seat and shut the door firmly.

The night was long and dealt its hours with painstaking slowness.

And still there was no change.

I was woken by a knock on the door. I had not realised I was sleeping, and a wave of guilt washed over me. I stood up as Miss Part entered and watched her as she searched John's face anxiously. His mind was still far away, sleeping in its silent graveyard. She did not need to ask me if there had been a change.

'Let me take over now,' she said gently.

I suddenly realised it was two days since the doctor had been. John's lips were dry and cracked; his skin looked papery and translucent.

'No – I cannot leave. It is the second day…'

'Sleep,' she said firmly. 'By tonight…we will know.'

I did not sleep. And yet, I did not want to go down again that evening. I could not face what I felt was almost inevitable. For the first time I tried to force myself to think of what I would do if…it happened. But I could not even contemplate it – it felt like a brick wall that my brain could not get past. Eventually, I knew it was time to do downstairs.

I felt like a ghost, gliding through those corridors, passing by the pupils as I went. I knew that there had been no change. She would have woken me if there had been.

She opened the door before I had even raised my hand to knock. I heard her three words as though they were bells ringing out across the whole world:

'He is awake.'

# XXXII

## ISABEL'S NARRATIVE
*(Extract from Isabel's Diary)*

*LANCEFIELD, account written 16<sup>th</sup> January 1867*

He is awake. I hold onto this thought like a mother clutching her child.

I have barely seen him since he opened his eyes. Immediately, when Miss Part opened the door, I was sent to call for the doctor who arrived just ten minutes later. We were both kept out of the room while he conducted his examinations. Finally, he opened the door and came out to speak to us.

'He is troubled and suffering some memory loss, but after some food and a good long drink, all his other faculties are in perfect working order. He is a very fortunate man.'

'Oh thank goodness,' breathed Miss Part.

I could say nothing. Waves of relief surged through me and I longed to open to door and see him. Doctor McKenzie turned to Miss Part.

'You must get him settled, Miss Part – that is extremely important in a case such as this. His mind is darting about like a fish trapped in a small bowl. He must feel safe and secure in his environment until he finds himself again. You know this school well, you know its grounds and its people - can I entrust you with that task?'

Her face lit up with a sweet smile.

'Of course Doctor. You can leave that to me.'

She turned and went into the room. I turned to follow her, but the doctor laid a hand upon my arm.

'You must let Miss Part look after him now. He is very confused and needs rest and proper care.'

'But I must - '

'I am afraid I must insist,' said the doctor firmly, taking me by the arm. 'You have done very well but now you must have some proper rest. I can see,' he interrupted her protest, 'that you have not slept in many days now, despite my advice. You must look after yourself. The worst is over now.'

Reluctantly, I let him lead me to the foot of the stairs and he turned to leave.

'Doctor McKenzie?'

He turned.

'Thank you,' I said in a voice that was weary but filled with gratitude, 'for looking after him. I appreciate your services more than you could know.'

'It is my pleasure,' he said, looking touched, and his eyes lingered on me for a moment. There seemed to be a question in them, but I was too tired to try and decipher what it was.

## THE STORY CONTINUED BY THE EDITOR

It was not until the next morning that Isabel was allowed to visit John. He had a cushion propped behind his head and his eyes were open – but something was wrong. Although the room was well lit and several people were bustling around him, it was as though he were looking into darkness. She looked at him closely and realised with a cold shock that while he looked awake, he was still not with them. He took no notice of the people in the room with him; they may as well have not been there. His eyes were wide, his pupils searching - searching for something that he could not find, seeing nothing but whatever prison kept him captive inside.

'Ah, Isabel,' said Doctor McKenzie, when he saw her. 'Come in. I want to see if he will recognise you.'

Tentatively, Isabel approached the bed.

'John?' she said softly.

There was no response. John's eyes were fixed on the emptiness in front of him.

'It is me, Isabel,' she continued with forced calmness. 'You gave me quite a fright.'

Still he did not look at her, or give any sign that he had heard her. He simply stared and stared, as if she were not there at all. She felt her heart sinking inside her.

'Do not worry,' said Doctor McKenzie, noticing the hope fading from her face. 'It is still early days and he is doing remarkably well, considering what he has been through. I am confident that he will recover.'

'May I stay for a while?' Isabel asked.

'Yes, you can stay,' the doctor agreed. 'It is good for him to have familiar faces around him at this time.'

The room in which John was recovering was constantly busy, Doctor McKenzie checked in on his patient twice a day and the headmaster, who Isabel discovered was called Mr Penderton, also paid frequent visits. Miss Part was in constant attendance, fussing around him on a regular basis. At such times, Isabel held her composure and let her attend to him, although there was nothing she did that Isabel felt she could not do – mopping his brow, feeling his pulse, taking his temperature.

John's condition did not change over the next few days. It was like he did not know himself and he looked troubled and constantly bewildered. His right hand was always twitching, as if reaching out for something that used to be there and was now missing. From her position in the corner, Isabel's hand ached for his.

A few days later, Isabel was called to the headmaster's study. Mr Penderton was a tall man, in his late forties, and he spoke to her gently. He explained that he was very happy to keep her master here at Lancefield while he recovered, and to provide Isabel with bed and board in the meantime, as long as she was happy to work for her keep. Unable to think of any other response, Isabel agreed. As she left the room, she noticed that his eye was upon her ring that was sparkling in the late morning sunshine.

'How long have you worked for Mr Fenn, did you say?' he asked, as she was about to shut the door.

'Just over three years,' she replied quickly, snatching a number from the air.

He nodded, and Isabel closed the door behind her.

You will not be surprised, therefore, that rumours soon began at Lancefield, about the injured man and his strange servant girl who wore such a dazzling ring. They conversations were started by the teachers, innocently discussing the situation, and were then taken up by the servants. Lancefield was a large senior boys' school that had many boarders, but also some day pupils who came from well-to-do families in the nearby areas. As a result, it had a sizeable workforce, consisting mostly of female servants, including the kitchen maids who worked downstairs, preparing and serving up three meals a day for the hungry pupils, and a fleet of housemaids who kept the four vast floors of classrooms and dormitories clean and tidy.

Any small piece of gossip was eagerly seized upon and dissected by these women, and Isabel had quickly become the topic of much discussion. As she walked down the stairs to begin work in the dining hall, she caught snatches of their conversation:

'I heard that she will not leave his side, even during the night.'

'Do you think she could be his lover – and that is why he gave her the ring?'

'Do you think it is a real diamond?'

'I have never seen a paste imitation that sparkles like that.'

'No – it is no fake. I think that she has stolen it!'

'But surely her master would have noticed.'

'Maybe he did - and maybe it was she who attacked him!'

'He was kicked by a horse, Sal, not attacked.'

'You do not know that – she could have made it up.'

'But if she did attack him, when he comes round he will tell everyone.'

'Perhaps she will slip up to his room at night and kill him while he sleeps!'

There was a collective gasp. Wearily, Isabel turned past them and took her place at the end of the hall as the boys filed in for dinner. She felt ten pairs of female eyes turn upon her and then the muttering began again. She kept her eyes down and told herself not to mind them, that she would not be here long.

Isabel's tasks at Lancefield were simple – help serve the food at each meal and then tidy up at the end. That was all – the headmaster felt she should not be tasked too much as she did not know the ways of the house – and for that Isabel was grateful.

She had no training in serving food, but it was not difficult and she kept her head down and her hands busy. She did not wish to talk to anyone, nor did she wish to draw any more attention to herself. At the end of her final shift each day, she was allowed to go to John.

Pulling off her apron with anxious hands, she rushed through the hallway to his room. Miss Part was there already, bathing his brow. Isabel felt a sting of irritation when she entered. It was bad enough that the woman was allowed to remain with him most of the day, but now Isabel wanted some brief time alone with him – for perhaps, she thought to herself, perhaps all this confusion was feigned? Perhaps, if they were alone, he would look at her with his clear eyes, tell her it was all an act to conceal their identities, and they could make their plans to leave.

But they were not alone, and Isabel could do no more than sit in the same wooden chair and ask Miss Part how John was doing. He was sleeping now and his wound was freshly bathed and healing: he looked almost peaceful.

'He seems more comfortable – and less bewildered,' she told Isabel. 'I think he is getting accustomed to the faces in the room.'

Your face, thought Isabel bitterly.

'That is good,' she replied.

'Doctor McKenzie is very pleased with his progress,' Miss Part continued with a smile.

She brushed John's fringe out of his eyes as she continued to dab his forehead with the cool cloth. Isabel bristled at the familiar act and Miss Part glanced round at her.

'I am glad,' Isabel replied, with a stiff smile. 'I am sure he will be fully recovered very soon.'

Three days passed, each following the same pattern. Small improvements were made: John was taking a small amount of soup; he was sleeping well; his wound was almost closed. But something troubled Isabel, something was still not right when she saw him each day – either sleeping, or awake. He may have opened his eyes and be partaking in all the usual human functions, but he was still not with them. It made her very uneasy.

On the fourth day, Isabel arrived at his room. The door was ajar, and she pushed it open, surprised.

The bed was empty, the white sheets pulled up. The window that had been closed for so long to prevent John from catching a chill was now open, and birds were singing outside. There was no nurse, doctor, or carer to be seen. Isabel felt panic rising up in her. She opened the door to the adjoining room, where the doctor had kept some medical supplies. It, too, was empty. It was as if John had never been here. Isabel touched the corner of the pillow upon which his head had rested the last time she had been in here. A small drop of blood had imprinted itself upon it. There was only one explanation:

'It is over', said a small voice inside her head.

No, she told herself. She would not believe it.

The door behind her opened. It was Doctor McKenzie. His face was impassive.

'Where is he, Doctor?' Isabel cried, unable to contain herself any longer.

'Mr Fenn?'

'Yes – Mr Fenn!'

'Oh – but he has been moved, did you not know?'

'Why has he been moved?' she said, desperately.

'Why? Well, because he is much better. I thought it would be best to move him to a brighter room, get him out of this stuffy place and give him some fresh surroundings.'

The relief that flooded Isabel was immense. She shut her eyes, letting his words sink in, and the fear leave her. Doctor McKenzie took her by the arm.

'Why, you look quite overcome, Miss Snow. What did you think had happened?'

'I thought…I thought…' The room swam a little. 'It does not matter now.'

'Mr Fenn is on the second floor now,' the doctor continued in a steady, comforting tone. 'He woke up this morning quite restored and completely himself again - it was a near miracle - and after seeing him eat a hearty breakfast, I felt it would do him good to be in a fresh room, with more space and more light.'

'I am sure it will,' Isabel replied, every word he spoke a blessing to her.

'I have advised him to rest for a few days more, but I do believe he will be on his feet very soon. There is no need to worry anymore,' he said kindly to her. 'You obviously care very much for your master.'

'I do,' said Isabel fervently.

To her great frustration, Isabel was not allowed to visit John in his new room as she was told by the headmaster that he had adequate care for the moment. To fill her spare time, she was given some dusting to do in addition to her serving at meals, but she did not mind the extra chores too much. In a few days John would be on his feet and soon after that, they would be away. She hoped he did not miss her too much – it must have been so strange waking up in a whole new place, surrounded by a sea of new people. But she heard that he was talking and walking perfectly once more, and that was all she needed to know. He would know she was near. He would know she was waiting.

It was upon that third day that she was summoned to the headmaster's office.

'Ah, Miss Snow,' he said, motioning for her to enter.

'Mr Penderton,' she replied politely.

'I am pleased to report that your master is much better and able to continue his life again.'

Isabel could not contain the joyful smile that broke forth from her lips.

'I am so very glad,' she replied.

'He is complaining of some memory loss,' continued Mr Penderton, (clever John, what a good way to cover our tracks, thought Isabel), 'so he will need security and stabilisation over the next few months. He is still too weak to travel, but does need to get back into working and a routine. He has told me that he is a teacher, and as luck would have it, we have a position for an English teacher that has just opened up. He has agreed to take the position and we are looking forward to having him here as part of the school.'

This last part of the conversation confused her. Why would John agree to take a job at Lancefield? But perhaps it was only to mislead Mr Penderton into complacency, and then, in the dead of night, they could disappear.

'That is very good news,' she replied sweetly.

'Of course, we would not force you to leave him, after everything you have been through,' he smiled at Isabel. 'I have spoken to our housekeeper, Mrs Clegg, and she has found you a place among our serving staff. You will have bed and board and be paid £1 a month.' Isabel forced back the horror of such a presumptuous idea, focused on the joy of being back with John soon enough, and replied,

'That is most kind of you, Mr Penderton. I gladly accept your kind offer.'

He smiled at her, perhaps wondering at how Mr Fenn had come by such a well-spoken servant.

'Excellent. I am meeting with him in an hour's time so I will let him know your decision.' He smiled once more. 'Well, well, well. Who would have thought that good things could have come out of such a terrible accident?'

'Indeed,' replied Isabel, with a convincing smile.


ISABEL'S NARRATIVE
*(Extract from Isabel's Diary)*

*LANCEFIELD, account written 16<sup>th</sup> January 1867*

I left Mr Penderton's office, thinking hard. I knew what my plan must be.

I rushed to my room, and grabbed my already-packed case. I had already worked out the quickest way to the stables, and silently I stole out round the side of the house. The stable boys must have been at their lunch. I found the deepest pile of hay in the pungent darkness at the back of an empty stall, and buried my case deep within the mound. Necessity has made me resourceful.

Mr Penderton's office was on the ground floor, overlooking a grassy courtyard and so I made my way upstairs to an overlooking classroom that I knew would be empty at this time of the morning. If I tucked myself behind the curtain in the corner of the bay window, I would be able to see anyone coming out of the study, but anyone who entered the classroom could not see me.

After an hour – John appeared below me. Tall, striding, as lithe as ever, he walked up the path towards the office door that opened on to the garden. He seemed full of life; he was no longer wearing his bandage. I could not see his face, but just seeing his sweet brown head was enough to fill me with hope. It was all I could do to stop myself from running down to him now - the stairs I had run up led down to the same garden courtyard – but he was expected by Mr Penderton, and I must be patient...

An hour later, the door opened. John appeared once more. I stood up, breathless. The charade was over. I knew that I should be cautious, that John was pretending to take the job to avoid suspicion, but I could wait no longer. I was prepared: we could take two horses - we could be on our way in moments, heading onwards to our life together.

The steps seemed uneven and too close together as my feet tumbled down them in my haste to reach him. I swung open the heavy door and stepped into the sunlit courtyard. When I turned, he was there – at the end of the path, walking towards me. Forgetting all pretences, I rushed to him and threw my arms around him.

'Oh John, I thought I had lost you.'

I buried my face in his familiar, sweet-smelling jacket, my hands around his soft neck. Finally, I was home. The joy was almost too much to bear. We had been apart only days, but it felt like forever since I had been in his arms.

But someone was pulling me from behind, hands dragging me away from him. I grasped his jacket, but it was pulled from my grip. I opened my eyes, and felt hands digging into my shoulders. I was a foot apart from John. Anger flooded through me - who dared to separate us? Half-expecting to see Branden's brutes upon me, I looked down at the hands that held me – long and smooth, and grasping me forcefully. They were familiar hands. And then I realised – I was not being pulled, I was being pushed.

I blinked: it was John who was holding me back, keeping me at arms length. The realisation hurt, even though I knew I was being foolish for embracing him so publicly; we must keep up pretences. But surely he was as desperate to hold me close as I was to hold him? We had been apart for too long.

I lowered my voice:

'I am sorry John, I cannot help myself! But there is no need to wait any longer – let us be gone now! I know the way to the stables, my bag is packed – we can be together once more.'

The words tumbled from me as I stared beseechingly into his eyes. Such wonderful eyes...such *empty* eyes? A stranger was staring back at me. I searched for myself in them and found no sign of recognition. 'John? What is wrong?' I asked in utter bewilderment.

Suddenly I became aware of the pressure upon my shoulders, of the force holding me from him. He was not gently grasping me - he was roughly, harshly forcing me from him. His fingers dug into my skin and his arms shook with what seemed like some kind of rage.

A cold, unrecognisable voice came forth from his lips:

'What is the meaning of your behaviour?' it said. 'How dare you speak and act towards me in such a way! Take your hands from me this instant.'

He was not jesting. I was not dreaming. The world seemed to tilt and I grasped his arm tightly to keep me steady. He threw me off and I stumbled unsteadily. Everything whirled. He did not try to help me; indeed he seemed to be still rebuking me. His face was stern and shocked. I tried to find my legs but they seemed suddenly made of paper. I felt my lips try to form a coherent sentence while my brain whirled in a frenzy.

'John – John, what do you mean? It is me, Isabel!' I cried, trying desperately to connect the space between us.

I felt terrified at his words, terrified by his actions – but terrified most of all by his eyes. They looked at me as though I was a stranger. It was the way you would look at someone you had just met, but whom you instantly detested. The coldness of his glance turned my insides to ice. He dropped his arms and took a step back. He seemed to tower over me in his rage.

'For a servant to behave in such a way towards a teacher is unacceptable. Now whether you are rebellious or delusional, I do not know. But I know that if you behave in such a way again I will see that you are punished. Do not approach me again, do you understand?' He started to walk past me and I tried to call out his name, but for a moment it seemed as if there was no air in the world.

'Wait – wait!' I gasped, and then managed to call out desperately, 'It is me – your Isabel!'

He glanced back, distaste etched in his face,

'*My* Isabel?' He turned to me, his eyes blazing. 'I have never seen you before.'

I watched him walk away. I heard his footsteps echo along the path and into the school. I felt the ground cave in and the sun went out.

# XXXIII

*LANCEFIELD, 15<sup>th</sup> January 1867*

The world ended today. It ended quietly, and with a few little words: 'I have never seen you before.'

ISABEL'S NARRATIVE
*(Extract from Isabel's Diary)*

*LANCEFIELD, account completed 16<sup>th</sup> January 1867*

So now you know all that has happened since I arrived here.

Writing it all down has brought me no relief, no catharsis. If anything it has made me think more upon those terrible things I would rather forget. But I will carry on in the hope that one day I will read back over these pages and appreciate how my life has changed for the better - for surely this is my darkest hour?

Apparently I was found lying upon the path by one of the other girls. I was brought round and then helped up to my room. When I awoke this morning, I found a small pile of clothes and a coarse cap at the end of my bed, which I presume is my uniform. The dress is plainer than even the outfit that I arrived in, and very worn.

A knock on my door roused me to my feet, though my head spun when I stood up. Before I could answer the door, it opened. It was the housekeeper, Mrs Clegg.

I had not met her properly before, but had seen her around the house and heard the other girls speak of her. Despite having served at Lancefield for most of her fifty years, it seems she is not a favourite. She had a thickset neck, rounded shoulders and small pale eyes that eyed me with dislike.

'So you are up and about then?' she said, her large teeth protruding slightly as she spoke. 'They told me you were unwell?'

'I do feel very faint,' I replied, grasping the bedpost as her sturdy form swayed before my eyes.

'Faint?' She snorted. 'Fainting is for ladies. Well – you managed to swindle yourself a whole day off work so you will make up for it

278

tomorrow. You will be up at five, and make sure this room is cleared.'

'Why?' I asked, glancing round at the small, sparse bedroom I had presumed I was to call home.

'Because this is a guest room, not a room for the likes of you! You'll be given a room in the attic. The other girls share a dormitory, but there's no room for you – so they say,' she added, with a malicious smile.

The she closed the door in my face.

I tried not to think of what awaited me tomorrow. I tried not to think of what had happened yesterday. I told myself to breathe in and breathe out, and by some miracle, I fell asleep.


## THE STORY CONTINUED BY THE EDITOR

'Get up you lazy creature. Up!'

Hands shook Isabel from her sleep. The room was in darkness but two black figures stood in front of her.

'It is a quarter past five and you were supposed to be downstairs fifteen minutes ago. Mrs Clegg is after your blood – so for all our sakes, get dressed now!' one of them commanded angrily before turning on her heel and leaving the room, the second girl behind her.

Unsettled, Isabel reached for her uniform and got dressed. Something smelled of damp and when the scent followed her downstairs, she realised it was the dress. Before she knew it she was on her knees scrubbing the kitchen floor with a rough brush, at the command of the red-faced cook, Mrs Fowler. All around her was a hive of activity as the house sprung into life, but Isabel barely noticed – her mind was somewhere else completely.

Somewhere in this house, perhaps in the very room above, John was walking and talking. All she wanted was to be in his arms. She needed to see him, needed to be with him. But the memories of his words stung her so badly that she did not know if she had the courage. Nor did she have the chance, with the cook's beady eye upon her and an endless stream of commands shouted at her. She only knew that the harder she worked at them, the less she would be reprimanded and the more chance she would have to think.

The doctor had been right – John's memory had been affected, that much was clear. But surely it would recover? Surely, no matter how severe the injury, she could never fully be wiped from his consciousness? Yet (she scrubbed harder and harder as though to blot out the memory), the way he had looked at her - it was as if he hated

279

her! What would make him remember the truth? Thoughts swirled back and forth in her head like great metal balls rolling from one side to the other as she moved in time with the scrubbing brush.

One thing was clear to her – she must speak with the doctor. She must understand more about this condition. When Miss Part appeared downstairs to ask for some hot water, Isabel ran over to her and asked when the doctor would next be back.

'Not for another month, I am afraid,' she replied, a little surprised, as ever, by Isabel's forwardness. 'Doctor McKenzie splits his time between here and Warmstone, a few hours north. He was quite pleased with your master's progress when he left, however – there is no need to worry.'

Isabel thanked her distractedly, her brain working quickly.

When they paused for lunch at midday, she asked one of the other maids from whom she might borrow some writing paper. The girl laughed in her face.

The rest of the day was a blur – loud voices, rough shoves, a sea of new faces. By four o'clock exhaustion had kicked in. As the sky outside the tall windows darkened, Isabel's legs began to feel like lead, her body desperately cold. But the work did not stop – there was no relief until nine o'clock, which to Isabel felt like midnight.

When Mrs Clegg called out that it was time for bed, Isabel forced herself alert. She had been told her room was the last door on the fourth floor. While the other girls filed up the back stairs, she held back until the last voice had disappeared. Then, quickly and silently (she had Gaunt to thank for that training), she made her way round to Mr Penderton's office. The door was unlocked and the room empty. Lighting a candle, and conducting a hurried investigation, Isabel quickly found what she was looking for: his address book. Flicking through the pages, she came to the one she needed,

*'Doctor George McKenzie, 3 Hearn Place, South Warmstone.'*

Copying it down onto a piece of paper that she had found, she pilfered a few more sheets and an envelope (she already had pen and ink in her case). She did not agree with stealing, but she decided that God would forgive her a few sheets of paper in a time of such need. Then, tiptoeing upstairs, she made her way to her room.

Fortunately it was dark enough to conceal the full extent of how foul the room was, but she could see just well enough by the moonlight to get what she needed from her case (which had been left on the bed) and write her letter. In it, she feigned to be John's sister: a Miss

Charlotte Fenn, who was desperately concerned for her brother's mental well-being. Once she had dried the ink and slid the letter into the addressed envelope, she crept back downstairs, and put the letter in the mailing pile for the next morning.

Only when she returned to her room did she appreciate how cold it was, and how uncomfortable her bed was. Several large springs poked out from the sagging mattress and she was sure she heard a scuttling noise from underneath. Too chilled to take her clothes off, she drew the raggedy blanket over her. It was then that she realised how much she hurt. Her hands were dry and scratched, her back was aching and her feet throbbing. She felt as though every inch of her was covered in the dust that she had been sweeping up all afternoon and her head – how it pounded!

It was only for a little while…only a little while, she told herself, as she waited for sleep to take her.

The doctor's reply came quicker than Isabel had expected. Fortunately she noticed it in the delivery pile one morning before anyone could discover that there was no Charlotte Fenn at Lancefield. It read:

*Dear Charlotte,*

*Thank you for your letter. I am glad to hear that your brother is settling in well to his new position and that you are there to help him. The memory loss is to be expected, I am afraid. The human head is a very fragile thing and John sustained an extremely heavy blow. Many parts of his brain will be struggling to reconnect and this will cause several blanks for him. The best medicine for this is time, and frequent exposure to people from his past who can help him put the pieces back together. I understand that this may be painful for you, but do not lose hope. Many patients recover fully over time. Unfortunately I cannot specify how long this may take, but as John is a young, healthy and intelligent man, I have every confidence that with your help he will be able to regain a full and strong hold over his bruised mind.*

*With regards and every good wish,*

*Dr. McKenzie*

Isabel could not define how this made her feel. She was glad, certainly, that this was all fairly normal behaviour for someone who had suffered a head injury. But she was also worried – how long was it going to take for John to remember? And what was she to do in the meantime?

She was trying to process all her thoughts as she walked along with her bucket and pail and nearly collided with Mr Penderton.

'Ah, Miss Snow.'

Isabel turned, her thoughts disrupted.

'Mr Penderton, forgive me, I did not see you.'

'I have been speaking with your master,' he said gravely. 'I understand he does not recognise you?'

A terrible fear rose up with within Isabel.

'Yes, but I am his servant – I swear to it! Do not send me away!'

He held up a hand to calm her fears, sympathy in his eyes.

'Of course, of course I believe you. I know that memory loss is a very common effect in the case of head injuries.'

He looked at the maid with sympathy in his eyes. Already she looked quite different from the girl who had arrived – she seemed to have aged many years in just a few days.

'It must be hard to have a master that you have worked hard for, to forget you,' he said gently.

Isabel tried to fight the tears in her eyes.

'Yes, it is,' she replied simply.

This passing sympathy Isabel received from Mr Penderton was the only kindness that she received at Lancefield during those first few weeks. The other servants were openly hostile – both jealous and wary of the new face thrust so suddenly into their midst. Mutters and grumbles soon gave way to complaints: the new girl did not know how to clean properly, she had too many high and mighty manners about her, she was not to be trusted. At first Isabel, numb and exhausted as she was, brushed off these comments, but soon she realised that the ring upon her finger was at the root of most of the trouble. The other girls' eyes were constantly upon it, like greedy birds watching a crust of bread.

'She has stolen it, that's for sure.'

'She should not be allowed to keep it!'

'She has no more right to it than anyone – that little thief.'

It was when they begin to deliberately push and jostle her in the corridors, tugging at her hair, pulling at her fingers, that Isabel realised what must be done. The trouble was – where to put it?

That night, Isabel put her mind to the task. Her room was as small as a closet, with a sloping roof and one small cracked window high above her. The mattress was thinner than the towels she was accustomed to drying with – no use for hiding anything it at all – and there was no furniture save a rickety table next to her bed upon which her candle (which was to last a month) was set. And so, Isabel turned to the filthy, ill-fitting floorboards beneath her feet. One was particularly loose and with a few pulls, Isabel was able to get it up. Underneath was a dark space, about half a foot deep. It would have to do.

Then came the hard part. Try as she may, she could not seem to bring herself to draw the ring from her finger. She pushed it down towards her knuckle and the stone caught fire in the candlelight. Suddenly she was back on that hillside: the ring was in its box and John was kneeling before her, presenting it to her with such a look of love in his eyes that the world itself seemed to stand still, watching. That wondrous, wondrous night. He had put it on her finger for eternity – why should she have to remove it here, kneeling in the dirt? Tears began to fall from her eyes. It was only for a little while, she told herself, still staring at the stone on her finger. But she had been telling herself that all too often lately.

Reluctantly Isabel dragged her suitcase towards her and retrieved the beautiful little ring box. With fingers of ice she drew the band from her hand and set it inside. Then she placed the precious box into the dark space and drew the board over to hide it from view. It was safe now. That must be her comfort.

A deep cold stole over Isabel. It did not seem to touch her skin, but penetrated deep down into her bones. She shivered and climbed onto her bed.

## ISABEL'S NARRATIVE
### (Extract from Isabel's Diary)

### LANCEFIELD, 26<sup>th</sup> January 1867

I work, and sleep and listen – always listen, for some news that he has come round; that he has remembered.

Every night I rush back to my room. As I close the door, blissful silence surrounds me and finally I am alone. But it not the solitude that I crave. Down on my knees, I scrabble for the loose floorboard. I lift it aside and reach for the small blue box. Opening it, the sparkle that greets me brings comfort to my lonely heart. There it is - my star. I take it from its velvet bed and slide it onto my finger. The feel of the cold metal against my skin, and the weight of the stone cause me to sigh with relief and I lean back against my bed. I am myself again. He is mine again. The putting on of this ring each night is as oxygen to a drowning man. It gives me hope; it gives me strength.


## THE STORY CONTINUED BY THE EDITOR

I can only commend Isabel as she worked away; completely exhausted, completely bewildered. I think her mind was too numb to look too far ahead. Keep working, stay near him, pray he remembers: those were her thoughts – that was her focus.

But her body, raised on years of rest and good food, was not as strong as her mind. Each morning was harder, each day longer, and soon constant aching and continual headaches were her daily companions. The food was plain and her portions meagre. Her stomach hurt from the sudden change in diet and struggled to produce the energy she so badly needed. She longed for meal times – but not because of the food, simply for a chance to sit down, where she was not at the beck and call of the omniscient Mrs Clegg, whom she continued to displease.

The girls ate and left in their usual time slots, for there was not enough room for everyone to eat at once in the servant's hall. Isabel usually waited until the final serving, when the numbers were fewer and the privacy greater. She did not normally look at the unwanted newspapers which were left out on the table from previous days, in case any of the servants wished to read them before they were thrown out, but the conversation of two of the girls who were turning through one of the copies made her look up.

'Killed with a single blow – they say there's a huge reward.'

'My aunt lives near Enderton, I wonder if she knows anything.'

Isabel looked up like a shot. Enderton? The name sent a shiver down her spine. Waiting anxiously for them to finish, she then grabbed the paper and flicked through it breathlessly. It was a copy from some weeks ago – but there was the headline: 'Enderton burns: Master dead.'

Feverishly, she read:

*The ancient estate of Mount Enderton has been devastated by a terrible fire. Discovered amidst the ruins was the body of Sir Aubrey Branden, lying on the floor of a third-floor bedroom. However, the local doctor has claimed that his death was not caused by the fire, but by a severe blow to the back of his head.*

*The cause of the fire has not yet been ascertained, but it seems to have generated from a room on the ground floor. It seems clear that it was a deliberate attack. Not a room stands untouched by the flames. The great and ancient house is now a ruin, lacking most of its roof, and part of the west wing has completely crumbled to the ground.*

*The sudden death of the nobleman has been a matter of great scandal. Police are asking for any witnesses to come forward. The acting owner of the estate, a Mr Rester Gaunt, has put out a reward for any information on the whereabouts of a young man and woman who were seen leaving the estate the night of the fire. The man is tall, with brown hair, estimated to be in his mid-thirties. The woman is around eighteen years old, mid-height, with long fair hair. Please direct any information to the address below...'*

Isabel looked up slowly from the paper. She expected every pair of eyes in the room to be upon her, ready to turn her in, but in fact the room was nearly empty.

'Get on with you,' shouted Mrs Clegg from the back of the room. 'There is plenty more work to do and sitting there on your backside will not get it done.'

Isabel rose, trying to refocus her mind on the task in hand, but there was too much going on inside her head. Sir Branden was dead? She picked up her pail and brush and made her way up to the top floor classrooms where she could have some peace to think.

The news of his death was an utter shock. Frantically she tried to think back to that night. She remembered John coming in, and his rage that had burned so fiercely; she remembered the men backing off as he overcame two of them; she remembered the pain as Sir Branden grabbed her by the hair – and then...did John hit him? Yes, she could remember that. But killed him? Never! Branden had hit his head as he went down - she half-remembered noticing that he had been unconscious when they left, but then she recalled that dead look in his eyes. Had he been killed? Had he hit his head with a deadly force when he went down? It must be so. Her memories of that night had been so overcome with the joyous events that followed that it was like trying to remember a dream from the night before - only fragments were left now.

As she set her pail down, she was overcome by a wave of guilt. She brushed her hands against her skirt: she felt as though she had blood on them. Then a terrible thought shot through her – had John seen that article? Did he know what he had done? Or... had he always known? He had seemed so different when he had entered the room that night, so…wild. Had he meant to kill Branden? And if so - had the murder driven him out of his mind? Surely killing someone, even to protect the one you love, must have a profound effect on you. And John was so sensitive…

Hearing Mrs Clegg outside, Isabel got to her knees and began to scrub back and forth, still thinking. Gaunt had put out a reward for them. A reward for murderers…. but it was not the information Gaunt wanted, it was a chance to see them hung - she was certain of that. She could picture his rage, the complete devastation on his face when he found his master's body; the master to whom he had been so devoted for so many years. He would stop at nothing to find them… but surely they could explain what had really happened to the police if they were found? Surely…

And yet, presuming Branden's five friends men had survived the fire, it would be two statements against five, some of whom had been brutally attacked by the same man they would claim had killed their friend. Suddenly Isabel realised what John had been doing all along.


### ISABEL'S NARRATIVE
*(Extract from Isabel's Diary)*


*LANCEFIELD, 28<sup>th</sup> January 1867*

He is trying to protect me! Oh, how could I have been so stupid? He knows we are being hunted; he must have realised this when he woke up from his accident and read the paper. We found ourselves in a busy place, he had an excellent back-story – of course integration would make us invisible – it was our only hope!

And how could I have been so stupid as to throw my arms around him in public – to expose us so openly! He must have been terrified that we would be found out. Perhaps the headmaster had even been watching from his window. John's only way to cover up my indiscretion was to act so coldly, reacting quickly to try and salvage the situation, I see that now. Every word, every gesture he made may have been being monitored.

Warmth surges through me…how did I not see this before! But no matter now, I understand it all and my mind is at peace. I know we must keep up our roles, and yet surely he will contact me soon… but there are eyes everywhere at the school. No, I must bide my time and wait patiently for his signal.

## ISABEL'S NARRATIVE
*(Extract from Isabel's Diary)*

*LANCEFIELD, 2<sup>nd</sup> February 1867*

I know I must be patient…but the days are passing by so slowly. He is so near, and yet so far. I do not know how he manages to keep apart – he used to struggle with just a few days before!

I must make contact with him again. Even just a glance – just to let him know that I know what he is doing, and why. I could not bear for him to be rebuking himself for his behaviour now that I understand completely.

## THE STORY CONTINUED BY THE EDITOR

The next few days, Isabel did her best to catch John alone. Their paths did not usually cross and she had to risk the fury of Mrs Clegg in using the main stairs when she guessed he might be changing classrooms between lessons. For three days she had no success, but on the fourth day she learned that the teachers were having a meeting that evening in the main hall. Isabel waited nearby, her pail in hand; ready to start cleaning in case any one saw her. The hall door opened and a line of teachers filed out. John was not among them. She waited in the semi darkness: surely he had been there. Then she saw him, the last one to leave the hall, and he was coming towards her. It was so strange to see him in the teacher's robes, the black hat upon his head, but it was him, all the same.

Trying hard not to cry out his name, she made her way slowly up the corridor towards him, still clutching her pail. She must be careful, and very subtle; she understood that now.

'Mr Fenn,' she said, her voice trembling with joy as she drew near and looked up at him.

He was so close to her, but she must play her role, no one must suspect. Yet just to be close to him was wonderful.

'Yes?' he said brusquely, an inscrutable expression on his handsome face.

'I just wanted to say that I found that paper you wanted.'

Isabel held out the paper she had read, folded over at the Enderton article. This was the only way she could think of letting him know that she understood.

'What are you talking about?' he asked.

'The newspaper – I wanted to give it to you and let you know that I had read it.'

She fixed her eyes searchingly on him, but there was no response, no flicker of understanding. He glanced down at the paper with distaste.

'And why would I want an out of date newspaper?'

'I...' Isabel struggled to find any words. He was looking at her with such abhorrence that her mind had frozen. There was no light of recognition, no reassurance. And yet they were alone – there was no risk in just smiling at her, of letting her know he knew what she was trying to say. He stared at her with growing exasperation. Then something seemed to snap.

'This is ridiculous,' he barked. 'Get out of my way. Now!' His voice was almost a snarl.

Isabel stared back. John – her John – did not exist in those eyes, in that dead face. Her John would never speak to her in that manner. She knew then, in that instant, that he had no memory of her. A hurt more intense than any she had ever experienced flooded through her. She felt him push past her, his schoolteacher's cloak sweeping out behind him, and Isabel felt her final hopes shatter on the stone floor beneath her.


## ISABEL'S NARRATIVE
*(Extract from Isabel's Diary)*

*LANCEFIELD, 5$^{th}$ February 1867*

You must have thought me a fool for thinking that it was all an act, that he was only doing it to protect me. But I needed something to hold on to, so desperately. It is gone now.

He has no memory of me, or of the months that led up to us being here. And if I confront him with the truth and he does not make the connection, he will report me, that much is clear. Not only could I lose my job and be separated from him (with nowhere to go, I might add), but he would be sure to tell Mr Penderton who may connect my name with the article in the papers and call the police. We would be arrested, or worse – Gaunt might find us first. I can only imagine what his rage would be like.

The only small thing that keeps me going is that I know John is safe for now. No matter how damaged his mind is, it is ironically providing his best protection. The situation, no matter how horrible, really is perfect, for he cannot give himself away and is acting so naturally in the role that no one would ever suspect him. But I did not think that his safety would come at so high a price.

I should be glad, really. But instead I feel sick and wretched. And so alone.

# XXXIV

ISABEL'S NARRATIVE
*(Extract from Isabel's Diary)*

*LANCEFIELD, 6<sup>th</sup> February 1867*

I woke up today, long after I had physically woken up, and found myself working as a servant, kneeling on a cold, hard floor, my hand scrubbing mechanically. I know it sounds foolish, for I have been doing this job for several weeks now – but today I realised I actually am a servant. It is not a pretence. It is not a charade. It is my life.

But I suppose I have not told you much about my life here...I have tried to tell myself that it would soon be gone, that there was no need to record a place I would sooner forget, but I see now that I will not be leaving any time in the foreseeable future. So let me recount what life as a servant at Lancefield involves.

I am one of forty-three servants here at Lancefield. We rise before dawn breaks... That sounds romantic. I will reword it. We rise when the sky is grey and the sun refuses to wake, at roughly five o'clock. I put on my loose-fitting grey gown and clumpy brown shoes. The dress is thin yet the material chafes my skin and the shoes rub around my ankles. I tuck my hair under my cap and join the line of girls filing downstairs. We form one long grey streak down the stairway, our eyes half-closed, our faces ashen in the darkness.

The back stairs twist steeply down into a long corridor with many doors leading off it to store cupboards, pantries, the laundry room, scullery, the cellars and at the very end, the large kitchen. Once we have snatched a piece of bread to eat (bread, always bread), we begin cleaning the lower halls and work begins. I am a maid-of-all-work, as are most of the younger women, except the laundry maids. My tasks are filling the pails and scrubbing the floors before the day begins (I have such bruises on my knees from this – I have not had bruises on my knees since I was six years old!), cleaning the classrooms after lessons and serving the pupils their meals. Our own meals are meagre, made up from leftovers, and even after eating I am still hungry. Afterwards, the cook puts out the fire beneath the kitchen hotplate and I help the kitchen maids sluice down the kitchen. We then fasten the ground floor windows and the kitchen, laundry and back doors. I am in bed just after ten o'clock, the soles of my feet burning and my back aching. Most of the female servants share a bed for warmth, but I have

290

been told that I am unwelcome in the main dormitory. When I explained to one of them how cold my room was, she eyed me sourly and then told me to stick rags in the gaps. I have done so. It has not helped.

My bed is narrow and clearly I am too tall for it as my feet stick out further than the end. So I curl myself up and wait for the day to begin again.

This is what I do each day, every day, for six and a half days a week.

*LANCEFIELD, 7<sup>th</sup> February 1867*

I realise for the first time how finite everything is in this world. I spend hours washing floors that are dirty again within hours. I wash them again and the water in my pail runs out, so I refill my bucket, over and over. I eat, and am then hungry, so I eat again. I sleep, and then spend that meagre energy gained within a matter of moments in all manner of endless tasks. Over and over, the endless, dreary cycle of it all. The days fade away slowly, one after another, or perhaps several at a time – I can no longer tell.

The other servants continue to resent my appointment with a sullen unison of distrust. Their looks plainly say that they want nothing to do with me. They mock my 'yellow' hair and 'white' skin, and while my lack of experience in the job has been put down to the fact that I have not worked in this kind of establishment before, my inadequacy is commented upon at every turn. Had it not been for the fact that Mr Penderton had appointed me, I do believe I would be out on the street by now. I keep my head down and try to work as hard as I can, but they do their best to rile me.

I turned my back on one girl yesterday as she continued to insult me and she pulled my cap off in spite. My long hair fell down in a disarray of curls, a conspicuous contrast to their dull bobs. The other girls around us stopped to stare. I felt naked, somehow.

'It's just not appropriate,' one of them whispered. 'It's indecent for a servant to have such long hair.'

Other similar comments rippled around the hushed group. Ignoring them, I tucked my hair back up into my cap. I refuse to listen to their jibes.

I have little to do with the many teachers who both work and live at the school. Mind you, there is only one I have any interest in. It is the pupils that are more troublesome – and one group in particular. The Head Boy is a young gentleman called Adam Halthorp who seems to fancy himself something of a ladies man. I have gathered he is involved with several of the other girls, and seems to like to make himself a nuisance around me. I try to ignore him whenever possible but he has a nasty habit of turning up wherever I am. His partners in crime, Walter Yates and Herbert Messing always accompany him, swanning along beside him as if they own the whole school. I treat all three of them with the disdain their immaturity deserves. Somehow this has served to make me even less popular with the girls ... I can do nothing right in this place!

Do not get me wrong; I understand why I am so disliked. I am different, and say not a word to them apart from what is needed. I make them uneasy. I hear their spiteful remarks on my breeding, my manners, but I cannot criticise them. They have been dulled by years of labour, hardened by their harsh lifestyle ... Had I some emotion to spare, I would pity them. And yet they make this almost impossible by their growing animosity. I overheard a plan that they were going to steal something from Mr Penderton's office and hide it in my room to get rid of me. So I have taken to locking my door whenever I am out (fortunately there was a key). It seems I am destined to live my whole life behind a locked door. Only now I do not feel trapped. I feel abandoned.


## THE STORY CONTINUED BY THE EDITOR

The strangely mild January had given way to a bitterly cold February. Outside, there was no movement in the trees, as if the barks themselves had turned to ice. The skies were bright blue, but the colour was deceptive: the sun gave off no warmth and the air hung still in the frozen expanse.

Isabel could feel the cold her very core. Even indoors, her ears hurt and sometimes she found it hard to breathe – as though the air was freezing in her lungs. When she went outside to collect wood or water, the bitter wind was like knives against her face. It cracked her skin and reddened her face. The cold crept into her bones, curling itself up inside her, sitting upon her heart, her hands, her feet. There was no escape. At night she would automatically reach out for a fur or blanket to try and defend herself from its villainy, only to realise her mistake. She was not Isabel Audley any more.

She looked up from her work and glanced outside. There was a light silver frosting over the grounds and the trees cast long wintry shadows, as long as the dark night that was to come. Tiredness overcame her in a wave and her feet burned as though they were on fire. She slumped against the wall to ease the pressure and pain.

'Get up, you!' called Sal, the unspoken leader of the other maids.

Isabel rose back up onto her aching soles. She had not realised she had company.

'You think you can just take a break whenever you feel like it?' spat Sal, her pockmarked face now inches from Isabel's weary one.

'I am just so very tired,' said Isabel faintly.

'Then leave. We all want you to.'

Isabel let the words wash over her and carried on with her work. Sal watched her with an expression of dislike and then turned to leave.

Isabel waited until she was sure that Sal had gone, and then gathered up her mop, bucket and scrubbing brush. Surely the day was nearly over. As she crossed the entrance hall, she glanced up at the coat of arms carved into the stone above the front door. She had heard that Lancefield used to be a grand house, but its owner, Sir Whitcombe, could not afford the upkeep, and so he turned it into a school to ensure a steady flow of money and because it could house children that he had so great a love for, but had never been able to have. The school only took on boys from the upper classes, mostly because of the high fees charged in order to keep the house running, and many more servants had been added to the ranks to cater for the additional numbers. As Isabel sat down in the servant's hall, she wondered at the vast workforce and the number of tasks they carried out for those living at Lancefield. She had always thought of herself as quite independent, but since working at the school, she had realised just how much had always been done for her.

On the way to her room she passed Miss Part. Isabel looked up in surprise; she had never seen the nurse in the servants' quarters before. Indeed, she had not seen her since she had asked about Doctor McKenzie in the kitchen.

'Is anything the matter?' Isabel asked.

'No, not at all,' said Miss Part. 'I just wanted to give you this.'

In her arms was a thick rug. She held it out to Isabel, sympathy blurring the usual wariness in her eyes.

'I heard you were not sleeping with the others and your room must be cold.'

'Thank you, Miss Part,' replied Isabel, taken aback by her kindness.

'John is doing well,' she said with a soft smile. 'You need not worry.'

Isabel's heart lurched at the sound of his name.

'I am so glad,' she replied numbly.

'You may call me Constance,' she said, with a smile.


ISABEL'S NARRATIVE
*(Extract from Isabel's Diary)*


*LANCEFIELD, 8<sup>th</sup> February 1867*

It is my favourite part of the day. It is eleven o'clock and I am in my room. I have taken off my tight-fitting shoes and grubby dress. I have locked my door and lit my tiny candle stub. The house is almost silent and the stars are out; I can see them through the filthy windowpane. I have this paper and my pen, and I am writing - the one thing they cannot take from me. Every so often I will set my pen down, flick back several pages and read extracts from my months with John at Enderton. I let my mind wander back into the memories that rise up before me in the darkness. I cannot enter those memories fully: they are too painful at the moment, too fresh - but I indulge myself by lingering around the edges, an on-looker on a beautiful scene. The minutes creep by. It is almost midnight now. The rooster will crow at five. It is time for me to put my diary back, curl up under my new rug and sink into sleep. I am touched by Miss Part's kindness. Tiredness creeps over me like blackest night. I will be gone in a moment.

Good night.


*'But the windows of the house of memory…are not so easily closed as windows of glass and wood. They fly open unexpectedly; they rattle in the night.'*

'His Boots' from *Somebody's Luggage*, Charles Dickens


*LANCEFIELD, 10<sup>th</sup> February 1867*

Last night the dreams started – oh, terrible dreams. All my worst fears brought alive in vivid wretchedness behind my closed and trembling eyelids. For the first time I realise how much of a beating my mind has taken. It is bruised and broken and I have lost all control. For I have never dreamed like that before – the dreams were more vivid than life - figures and scenes dancing before my eyes in an endless dark nightmare that I could not escape.

The dreams continued last night. I could feel them hovering in the darkness, waiting for my fears to give them shape. I tried to calm myself, comforting my troubled mind so that I would slip into pleasant reveries, but once again I fell into nightmarish fantasies that brought to life all my most terrible memories from the last few months – the church, the blindfolding, the faces on the wall, the knocking, that flash of red hair – and always, always finishing with those eyes, those dead eyes telling me that they knew not who I was. I woke with a terrible cry, drenched with sweat and shaking like a small child.

*LANCEFIELD, 12<sup>th</sup> February 1867*

Again and again he came to me last night.

At first we were together at the folly, the sun was shining. But then evening began to fall and he was insistent that we return to the house. When we entered the ballroom – there she was – a woman more beautiful than anyone I had ever seen before, with scarlet hair and dangerous eyes. John was captivated, striding towards her as though he could see no one else. I watched them, dancing together, their hands touching, their mouths a breath apart. He had forgotten I was there, even when I called his name, over and over. She looked at me over his shoulder, a terrible laughing look in her eyes. I knew I had lost him, I knew she would never let him go...

Then we were in my old room at Enderton, on that terrible night when I thought all was lost. I watched the door break down before my eyes, the men advancing and then – there he was, jumping down from the portrait hole. I cried out to him to save me, my voice full of relief, but when he turned towards me, he could not see me. I was invisible to him. Confused, he left the room, deaf to my cries as the men attacked...

Finally we were at the concert, on that fateful night. The orchestra was playing and I looked over at him. He looked back, but his eyes were cold – there was no warmth in them when he looked at me. It was empty eyes that watched me, full of shadows. I watched the shadows come to life, dark and creeping, terrible and malevolent, and screaming, they devoured him before my very eyes...

...And on and on. Rejection, abuse, blindness, despair... His face appears before me each time I shut my eyes, and he is the first thought on my mind when I awake each morning. I cannot bear it. I cannot bear that his face, which once gave me such hope, should now fill me with such despair.

The dreams are getting worse. Last night when I fell asleep, Sir Branden, Gaunt and John stood before me, each one as terrifying as the next. Laughing, they seemed to blur and merge into an inescapable shadowy figure that advanced upon me as I ran down endless black corridors until I woke with a cry, bathed in sweat. I heard the girls making comment this morning that I was half-mad, talking in my sleep and shrieking in the night. I worry that they will tell Mrs Clegg, who is already finding more fault than usual with my work. I cannot help it, I find myself more exhausted when I wake than when I went to sleep.

I was struggling to clean the main stairway this morning, so heavy were my arms. Tiredness seemed to course through my body instead of blood. I had paused for a moment when I heard Mrs Clegg behind me.

'If you are not fit for your place, Miss Snow, you will be removed from it.'

So the girls had been talking. Normally I could have brushed this off but I was so exhausted I felt the tears welling up in my weary eyes. I could feel her looking at me, judging me. Desperately, I tried to hold myself together as the tears trembled on the rims of my eyes. I reached for my brush and began to work furiously at the rug that covered the stairs. Seemingly satisfied, she turned away. I could hold them back no longer. Down fell the tears, tumbling through my lashes onto my dirty cheeks below. I brushed them away hastily, lest anyone should see. It is my greatest fear that I will be removed from here, away from John. I had no choice but to work even harder for the rest of the morning, though I know not from where I found the strength.

In the afternoon, Sal came up to me with a bowl in her hands. Mrs Clegg had kept me back from lunch claiming that my work on the stairs was insufficient. I was almost faint with hunger. I looked down at the bowl and the foodstuff inside.

'This is for you,' she said.

I wondered dazedly if it was my lunch.

'What is it?' I asked.

'It's for the chickens, you fool. It's your task to feed them now – no one else wants to go in the cold.' She smiled at me with her crooked teeth. 'See, I told them you'd be useful for something.'

Strangely enough, although it was very cold, I enjoyed being outside. The chickens were kept in another small courtyard at the back of the house, by the gate in the stone wall where the trades would come and go. It was oddly calming to stand there, tossing feed to those curious birds that pecked around at my feet, clucking contentedly. It was nice to be needed.

The rooster strutted round the yard as though he owned the place, deigning to eat but making sure the chickens left him the best of the feed. He reminded me of Branden, the Lord of the Manor... but then I felt suddenly guilty. I remembered the unseeing look in his eyes as we left Enderton... I remembered that he was dead. The thought made me shiver.

Afterwards we were all called to the servants' hall and given our wages in a small envelope. I opened it and held the dull tarnished coins in my dirt-smeared hand. I had never seen coins of such little worth. I do not even know what to do with them.

*LANCEFIELD 16th February 1867*

The blood spread towards me in a seeping pool. A red tide of guilt. I tried to run from it, but it enclosed me, running up my body and dripping over my hands.

'You did this,' said Gaunt from behind me. 'And I will do the same to you.'

*LANCEFIELD 18th February 1867*

I can stand it no longer. I have decided that the only way to overcome these night terrors, so full of such terrible memories, is to try and focus on the good memories. Yet I have put such effort into keeping them from me, so fearful of the pain they might cause, that it is hard to let them back in again. Last night I lay in bed and cautiously tiptoed towards the corner of my mind where I had tucked them away. As I approached, it was like unlocking the door of a tightly packed cupboard: the memories tumbled out before me, bursting from their place of concealment, suddenly coming back to life.

It was like a clockwork jewellery box was playing for me – a cascade of colours, gowns, music, firelight and faces danced and twirled before me – memories all mixed into one glorious haze that came alive as I turned the silver handle in my mind. They danced around me, so full of wonder and happiness, they seemed almost real, almost within my grasp; yet I knew if I reached out a hand, they would dissolve.

One face stood out more clearly than any of the others. He stood at the back of the scene, so near and yet so far. Tall, silent and watching, he did not dance to the medley, but when he caught my eye he would smile.

'All will be well,' his eyes would say. 'Soon we will be together again.'

But as time went on I realised that I had no control over the box. All too soon the music began to wind down, the dancers became slower, and he began to fade away into the terrible darkness of my room, leaving the last note to play and send a shiver down my spine.

And the dreams began again...

## THE STORY CONTINUED BY THE EDITOR

Wise men have said that once the outer barriers of the mind break down, there is no stopping that which follows. Isabel was very weak already, and the peaceful sleep that her body so desperately craved was being denied her each night by her unsteady mind.

To make matters worse, the class schedule seemed to have changed and Isabel was now passing John several times a day. At one time, this may have been a blessing, but now it was torture. His reaction to her was worse than just blankness now: he eyed her with dislike, uncertainty. She could see that her presence upset him, and once she saw him go out of his way to try and avoid her. It was torture. She told herself that she would do the same if a servant she had never seen before had behaved so strangely towards her, but it did not stop her feeling wretched. Part of her wondered if somehow his consciousness associated her with the night of the killing – perhaps his injured mind wanted to repress anything to do with that terrible scene, that fateful act he must want to forget...But did he even know what he had done?

Emotions and fears that she had tried for so long to keep at bay slowly began to overwhelm her. Every part of her ached to be with him, but it was worse than impossible. She felt as if there were two locked doors with an empty dark room between them; an impenetrable darkness that she could not, and did not know how to pierce.

For he could see her, but he could not *see* her. It was an unrequited love that was yet not unrequited. Isabel wondered one morning if there had ever been a woman in the same situation, so bizarre it seemed to her. If it had not been happening to her, she may have appreciated the irony if it.

'I cannot be with you, I cannot mourn you, I cannot search for you,' she whispered as she watched him pass by the classroom in which she was cleaning.

Tears of hot, salty, irredeemable grief fell from her eyes to mingle with the soapy water below. She brushed them away. She knew she must not pine like some lovesick heroine. She wanted to continue in a manner that would make him proud - and yet it was so hard. It would be easier if he were trapped on some remote island, or locked up in prison, she thought, half-ashamedly. If she could just know that he was aware of her existence, this would all be bearable, and she looked often for some flicker of recognition when he passed by. But then she would remember in full force the coldness in his eyes that day in the courtyard, and she would silently acknowledge that even the greatest stage actor could not have played a part so well. Those eyes used to fascinate her. Now they frightened her, so alien was their glance.

She thought back to a night where a man lay sleeping beside her. She had run her fingers through his hair and pressed his features into her mind. She used to fear that she would lose him, that one day he would leave, or disappear without a trace, so perfect did he seem – but she had never thought that she would lose him even as he stood before her. That he would be there in presence, but John - her John - would be gone. Sometimes, in her weakest moments, she wished that he really had gone, that he had left her. She thought it might have hurt less.

*'Or Scorne, or pittie on me take,*
*I must the true Relation make,*
*I am undone tonight;*
*Love in a subtile Dreame disguis'd,*
*Hath both my heart and me surpriz'd,*
*Whom never yet he durst attempt t' awake;*
*Nor will he tell me for whose sake*
*He did me the Delight,*
*Or Spight,*
*But leaves me to inquire,*
*In all my wild desire*
*Of sleepe againe; who was his Aid,*
*And sleepe so guiltie and afraid,*
*As since he dares not come within my sight.'*

*The Dream*, Ben Jonson

ISABEL'S NARRATIVE
*(Extract from Isabel's Diary)*

Two nights ago (I know not what brought on the change), I had a different dream. I was back at the folly. It was late afternoon and the sun was shining, the sea blue and glistening far below. I looked round and saw John coming towards me. Upon seeing me, he broke into a run, and with a great cry he gathered me up in his arms and spun me around, joy in his eyes. And then, holding me close, he kissed me. Describing it to you, it seems only a short dream, but to me every second seemed like hours. We were lost in each other once again; I could feel his touch and his breath and his kiss. I could feel his arms holding me close, so close - and I knew he still loved me. Then I woke up.

Anger and frustration flowed through me. No, no, not yet! I cried. I did not want to be back here, I wanted to be where I had just come from, for a little longer. Fragments of the dream hung round me like ghosts and I concentrated, willing them not to disappear. But the rooster crowed outside and they scattered amongst the dust that drifted down from the ceiling boards.

Never mind, I thought, I will go back tonight.

And I did. As soon as I tucked myself under my rug I slipped easily back into sleep and this time we were in the ballroom at Enderton. But there was no other woman there this time – we were dancing together, with many others around us, but I could see only him. Our bodies moved in time with the music and I felt his lips brush my neck as I turned under his arm towards him. A secret smile spread across my face and he held me closer. His fringe was ruffled from the dancing and he looked so handsome in his black suit and green waistcoat, dressed almost as if he were going to a wedding.

'Shall we have dancing at our wedding?' he whispered to me.

And then I woke up, the feel of his lips still on my ear.

The dreams are becoming more and more real.

I find myself rushing through the day, holding on to the hope that I will soon be with him once more. When I close my eyes, I felt reality slowly slipping away from me. Memories, so lucid, so beautiful, begin to take over. I let them grow stronger and stronger, until they are before me, in all their beauty.

You might say it is foolish - dangerous, even, to live in the past like this. But these memories belong to me. They are the only possession I have not relinquished, that has not been taken from me. It is the only resistance I have made in these wretched weeks and months gone by.

*LANCEFIELD, 25<sup>th</sup> February 1867*

Another glorious night! I feel as though I am losing my grip on reality, but oh so happily. My days blur together…I hardly feel the pain of them anymore.

Indeed, it almost seems as though it is my dreams that are real, and not this miserable life. I marvel at how real the details are, how vivid the scenes. Every word is beautiful, every moment precious. In them, John looks at me like he used to, he holds me like he should do. When I am there, I am happy. My waking hours slip past in great chunks, dark and unremembered; I yearn to be asleep that he might come to me. When I get to my room each night I put my ring back on and slip back into a glorious release.

*LANCEFIELD, 26<sup>th</sup> February 1867*

I dreamt of a figure standing in a beautiful garden at night. I felt a deep, piercing, wonderful pain, and alongside it, I heard a woman's voice, high above, singing in a key that I could not quite define. But I understood the melody. The voices – more and more joined in the song - grew louder, drawing me nearer and nearer to that figure in the garden. On and on, nearer and nearer, and then – oh joy – he turned, and it was him. It was John, and we were together, his hands drawing me to him, his sweet voice whispering in my ear, his lips finally on mine. All around us, the snow began to fall, and the voices kept singing – on and on and on, until all was white, and the world was snow and even the voices stopped.

And then it all fades into nothingness and I am alone in the bare room, at the end of the world. I search frantically for my key back into that place; that world between the worlds where the stories come alive, but it tumbles from my fingers and is lost in the darkness.

Morning has come and he is not here, and I feel more alone than ever before.

# XXXV

## THE STORY CONTINUED BY THE EDITOR

Isabel stood at the back of Little Acton village church, surrounded by her fellow servants (well, I say surrounded – they had left an empty chair at either side of her in castigation). She could see John at the front from where she stood, but she scarcely glanced at him. She found it easier now to think of him as two separate people – the man she loved and who was still in there somewhere – and the man who stood there now; the man who would rebuke her had she dared look at him. For the moment, she preferred her dream John to the real one.

The occupants of Lancefield School took up the entire left hand side of the church. At the front of the church sat Sir Whitcombe, the owner of Lancefield, and his wife. Then there were two rows of teachers, resplendent in their black robes. Miss Part stood beside her uncle, Mr Penderton, at the far end of the row, and behind them were row upon row of Lancefield pupils, from which intermittent scuffles and whispers occasionally broke out. John turned round to silence one particularly loud disruption, a stern look on his face. Miss Part smiled at him mildly as he turned back.

Isabel sighed and shuffled in the uncomfortable pew. She could barely even focus on what the vicar was saying; her attention levels seemed to have dropped considerably over the past few weeks. Even to sing seemed to take up energy she did not have. She tried to comfort herself with the thought that at least she was sitting down, even it was on a hard pew, and not kneeling upon a cold stone floor.

Before long, the service was over and the congregation began to file out into the bleak March morning. The servants waited outside for Mrs Clegg, who was busy gossiping with some of her friends from the village. Isabel watched as the teachers came out of the church and began to organise the boys into a straggling procession to walk back towards the school. John appeared then – she could just see his face above the sea of pupils. He looked happier than Isabel had seen him in a long time; his eyes were bright and his fringe slightly ruffled, as it always was when he was feeling slightly exhilarated. The sight of him looking so familiar brought a smile to her lips and hope to her heart: was he becoming himself again?

He seemed to be talking to someone – she presumed it was a pupil as they stood much shorter than him, but then she saw that Miss Part stood beside him. She looked flushed as she glanced shyly up at the tall gentleman before her. Isabel wished Miss Part would leave; already she was contemplating speaking with John again - perhaps this time he would remember? He looked so much better, all those old expressions and habits reasserting themselves on his smiling face. Miss Part turned to leave, but something held her back. Isabel watched impatiently for the crowds that blocked her view to move. The last of the boys standing in front of John were now filing down the road in their pairs and finally she could see clearly. John was holding Miss Part's glove, which she appeared to have dropped. Gently he slipped it back onto her hand. Miss Part looked up at him, adoration in her eyes. John said something to her, quietly, that only she could hear. She nodded, a tiny smile upon her lips.

*'Oh heart! Oh, blood that freezes, blood that burns!'*

*Love Among the Ruins*, Robert Browning

## ISABEL'S NARRATIVE
*(Extract from Isabel's Diary)*

LANCEFIELD, 3rd *March 1867*

It cannot be. I am sure it meant nothing...
But there was something in his eyes...something different.
And as for her...well, she is clearly in love with him. For that I cannot blame her, but it must go no further.

## THE STORY CONTINUED BY THE EDITOR

Isabel had felt the first deep, agonising stab of jealousy. Never had she felt so helpless, so lacking in any measure of control. Her first instinct was to make sure that no more moments like the one she had witnessed could happen again, but this was impossible. She was a maid-of-all-work, forbidden to enter many of the areas in which the teaching staff circulated, and she was forced to accept that she had no control over what may or may not be occurring between John and Constance Part. The tension of it was unbearable.

She tried to keep an eye on them as much as possible, but during school hours they were never together, each occupied with their individual tasks - John in the classroom, and Miss Part helping out in whatever way she could around the school: teaching piano to the younger children, helping her uncle in his study, or aiding the matron in the sick room. Isabel was there now, a silent shadow cleaning the washbasin in the corner, while Constance bound up a cut elbow of a rather flushed-looking young boy. As she tightened the bandage, he began to cry softly and she spoke gently to him in a soothing tone. He looked up at her, sniffing. Her hair curled around her face, framing her small rounded nose and wide brown eyes. She reminded Isabel of a pretty dormouse. Her manner was kind as she dealt with the boy, wiping his eyes with a damp cloth and then slipping him a brightly coloured sweet when Matron was not looking. Isabel watched, and worried, and tried her best to dislike her.

One thing was certain: she could not afford to live in her dreams any longer or she would lose the real John for an imaginary one. He may well have been coming back to himself with time, but she needed to be there beside him - not Constance Part.

The following week, Isabel watched them closely from the back of the church. They may have been in separate rows, but they could not have been any closer if they had tried. Surely it was no coincidence that Constance Part was standing right behind John when she could have sat anywhere in that empty row behind? And there – Isabel watched as Miss Part leaned forward to speak to him again – another exchange when they had only spoken together a moment before! Isabel sat at the back, an indiscernible pale face amidst a sea of grey, feeling her infinite isolation more acutely than ever.

Once outside, she braced herself for the pain she would feel if they exited together. There they were. They spoke for a long time, perhaps making the most of the crowd around them, and then he left with his pupils. Isabel looked over at Constance. She knew that face – it was the same face that had looked back at her from the mirror not so many months ago. It was the face of a woman falling in love.

### ISABEL'S NARRATIVE
*(Extract from Isabel's Diary)*

*LANCEFIELD, 10th March 1867*

My heart is a pit of agony and despair. More and more they speak together; they exchange glances; they take another step down that path... And amidst the panic all I can think is of how much I miss him.

I feel as though I have been physically ripped from him. I ache for his presence like a starving man must ache for food. I feel as though a part of me is missing, as though it has been carved from me and I am constantly searching for that missing piece. I feel like I have forgotten how to breathe without him by my side. The thought of a life without him is impossible. I cannot live without him, I cannot!

I am in a situation where there is no resolution. I was on my way to the most perfect life, and then everything crashed down around me. Everything is perpetually suspended for me, while his new world grows every day.

My mind is about to burst with the pain of it all.

*'Set me as a seal upon thine heart...for love is strong as death; jealousy is cruel as the grave: the coals thereof are coals of fire, which hath a most vehement flame.'*

*Song of Songs* (Chapter 8, verse 6), King James Bible

THE STORY CONTINUED BY THE EDITOR

Isabel's one consolation was that she had seen nothing, bar some glances, to confirm that John's heart had been unfaithful. Yet she still had plenty to torture herself with.

She had noticed that Constance had started to linger around corridors that John often used. Isabel, of course, knew this as she did the same thing. Each time she saw her there, Isabel felt anxiety kindle within her. She knew what Constance was doing - creating opportunities, accidental meetings...the knowledge made her sick.

One night, as she passed the corridor that led to John's office, she heard a sudden, glorious laugh – John's laugh. Isabel had not heard that sound for so many months now and it filled her with joy. Without thinking, she turned and rushed down the corridor – only to see him standing there with Constance, mirth on both their faces. Lost in whatever joke they shared, they did not see her standing there, framed between them; their happiness masking her growing hopelessness.

## ISABEL'S NARRATIVE
*(Extract from Isabel's Diary)*

*LANCEFIELD, 12<sup>th</sup> March 1867*

Each day I feel him slipping away from me. By all accounts he is returning to himself, but someone else is waking him up.

What am I to do?


## THE STORY CONTINUED BY THE EDITOR

Night was falling and Isabel was finishing feeding the chickens outside. They pecked hungrily at the last of their feed. With unseeing eyes, Isabel turned to make her way back into the house.

'Oh there you are.'

Sal stood before her, hands on her hips. Isabel braced herself for another onslaught from her unsought adversary. She knew Sal was the one most eager to report her every misdemeanour to the implacable Mrs Clegg.

'I need to show you something. Now.'

'What is it?' asked Isabel wearily, her mind trying to recall anything that she have missed during her morning's duties.

'Something you will want to see – don't worry, it's not to do with work.'

Sal's face was almost pleasant, and she took Isabel's arm in her stockier one. Confusion reigned in Isabel's mind – was the girl being nice to her for once?

Sal led her up the servants' stairs to the first floor where a window looked out over the courtyard below. It was the same courtyard where Isabel had run down to John for that most horrible of encounters. She recoiled at the memory. Three of the other servant's were gathered there, staring out at something below and giggling.

'What is it?' asked Isabel, perturbed by Sal's friendliness.

'A gift, from me,' she said, smiling. Gently, she pushed Isabel forward.

Isabel walked towards the window and the other girls parted. Below, silhouetted by the large windows behind them, were two figures who stood alone in the quadrangle: a tall man and a petite woman, their breath misting in the cold air. Isabel felt her knees suddenly ache sickeningly: she did not want to see. She tried to turn, but the other girls held her firmly. Down below, the man's hand touched the woman's cheek; she turned her face up to him, and their lips met with the awkwardness and anticipation of a long-awaited first kiss. A queer feeling of unreality stole over Isabel as she watched their nervousness melt, overcome with joy. For a long time they held together, their moment of beauty cruelly savaging the withered hope Isabel had held for so long.

'Let me go,' she said numbly, pulling against the firm grip of the girls who held her.

'No, we want you to see,' said Sal, malice dancing in her eyes. 'We want you to see that you are no better than us. No matter what you did to that man, he does not love you any more. You see? So you drop your high and mighty airs – he's not coming back to you. Not ever.'

A sudden strength flooded through Isabel and she threw them off with ferocity. They stared back at her, a little uncertain.

'You have done your job,' she said quietly. 'Now leave me alone.'

With her last ounce of dignity, she strode from the room.


### ISABEL'S NARRATIVE
*(Extract from Isabel's Diary)*


*LANCEFIELD, 14ᵗʰ March 1867*

Someone left me a yellow rose by my pail at the well yesterday morning. I cannot imagine who it was, but it lifted my spirits, just a little. It somehow gave me the strength to get through the day, and at night its gentle scent helped me drift off into an exhausted, dreamless sleep.


*LANCEFIELD, 15ᵗʰ March 1867*

Each day this week a new flower has appeared there, in the same spot. Sometimes a large gardenia, sometimes just a tiny buttercup, but always yellow. I find my eyes searching eagerly for them each morning, those bright little gifts. I hide them in a gap in the wall during the day and collect them at night to take them up to my room. When their colour begins to fade, I press them in this diary, each one on the day it was given, even if I have nothing to write.

I have not even spent time wondering who puts them there, or how I know they are meant for me. They are there, and that is all I need to know.

## THE STORY CONTINUED BY THE EDITOR

Isabel had kept herself miraculously calm during those first few days when she learned of John and Constance's relationship. Perhaps it was so that she would not give the other girls the satisfaction of seeing her upset. But after coping with the initial shock, she was still not prepared for seeing the couple around the school, and witnessing all the little tendresses that came with the beginnings of a new relationship. Of course they were subtle at first: the brushing of a hand, shy glances across a busy hall – but Isabel saw them all.

While the weather outside continued to improve, the storms in Isabel's heart raged ever darker. Returning to her room after a particularly draining day, she sat down on her bed, aching in every part, and drew her rug to her for comfort.

'John is doing well,' Constance had told her when she gave it to her.

Suddenly it all became so clear to Isabel – she had used his Christian name – was she trying to tell her, even then? She threw the rug off in anger. The kindness was a thorn in her side.

A sudden shiver shook her thin frame.


ISABEL'S NARRATIVE
*(Extract from Isabel's Diary)*

*LANCEFIELD, 16ᵗʰ March 1867*

I cannot, I *cannot* – live like this! I thought I could keep myself calm, but I cannot. To see all he was with me - with her! Everything is reawakened within me. The cold deadness inside turns to terrible heat, the scars reopen as fresh and raw as they ever were, bleeding afresh every time I see him with her. It is a mockery of all we ever were!

They are out walking in the garden just now; I saw them from the classroom window as I came upstairs. She picked him a flower and tucked it into his buttonhole. He watched her hands fumble with the stem, and as she looked up at him he kissed her softly on the lips. Kissed her - as he once kissed me! I cannot endure it. It is too much.

My heart is pounding in my ears as I think of it. There must be some resolution to this. I must be able to make him see. He cannot forget all that we were. Surely, he cannot just forget me.

You are breaking my heart, John.

308

My eyes are puffy and red and my forehead pulses with a steady throb. I have tried not to cry but I indulged myself last night, giving in fully to my emotions. I do not know whether it has helped: I am continually torn between feeling nothing and feeling everything. Sometimes the numbness is too much to bear, but this headache certainly has not helped to make my day any more enjoyable.

Knowing he is with someone else makes me feel his absence all the more. My world suddenly seems emptier than ever before – no one around me seems alive without him there. My link with life has gone.

And yet it is the future that scares me most. To think of those long years stretching out ahead of me. What will I do? Where will I go? Without him, I do not know. All his glorious, wonderful protective strength has gone.

The worst thing is not that he has simply forgotten all memory of me – it is that my presence continues to physically upset him. If I pass him by, he will avert his gaze and walk faster to pass me quickly. Today I watched him consciously retrace his steps when he saw me working in the corridor in which he was about to pass. I feel horrendous, repulsive. It is always horrible to have someone avoid you, but to be avoided by the one you love...

Every little fear that germinates within is fed by these daily tortures. If he truly does not remember who I am, then why is he avoiding me? I have tried to rationally think this through and I can think of only one reason for this. Doctor McKenzie said that his memories would start to return. Perhaps they are – and perhaps his mind is reacting defensively. None of us want to remember the terrible things we have done, and I must undoubtedly be linked in his mind to that terrible killing...

I am resourceful, I always have been. I am the child of the empty house, the brave girl, the adventurer. I have never let anything stop me or force me to give up. I am the girl who survived the lightning-struck church, the knocking and the broken door. I know John loved me then – and I know part of him must love me still. He risked everything to free me at Enderton and gave me everything he had to give when he gave me this ring. My star, he called it.

I will not give up on him, for he never gave up on me. I must show courage. I glance at the yellow flowers by my bedside – those strange, small beacons of hope. They give me strength. I will go to him; I will go to his own room, where we can speak in privacy. I will show him our ring, for it still holds our memories, so fresh from that night when he asked me to be forever by his side. I will remind him why he fell in love with me, the girl who loves him still.


## THE STORY CONTINUED BY THE EDITOR

When you resolve to do something that terrifies you, it is always best to do it as soon as possible. Following this thought, the following morning Isabel went immediately to speak to Dorothy, the girl in charge of cleaning the teacher's rooms and offered her services that evening. Dorothy surveyed her suspiciously.

'Why do you want to take on extra chores?'

'Mrs Clegg is not best pleased with my cleaning skills,' Isabel replied truthfully,' and I wish to gain some extra practice in rooms other than a classroom. I used to work for Mr Fenn, so I am sure he will not mind.'

Dorothy still looked doubtful.

'I know you need the practice – there's no denying that, but I don't want to get into trouble over this. Only the housemaids are supposed to clean upstairs.'

'No one will know – and I will do one of your rooms tomorrow in return,' Isabel added quickly. 'That way, you can finish early.'

That clinched it.

'Very well,' said Dorothy in as begrudging a tone as she could muster, though Isabel could tell she was secretly pleased.

Isabel knew she had a boy that she met after work, a couple of nights a week, and tomorrow was one of them.

'Just make sure you do a good job,' Dorothy added.

'I will,' replied Isabel fervently.

At eight o'clock, having finished her other rooms with somewhat unscrupulous haste, Isabel walked down the corridor towards John's rooms, a duster in one hand and a brush in the other. John would be in the staff room at that moment, but she knew he usually returned to his room not long after this hour. Hands trembling slightly, she gripped the door handle. Her face was pale, but determined; her heart full of misgiving, but also hope. She had not been near to anything that belonged to him in so long, and inside would be so many fragments, so many memories. She feared that stepping into the room might be too much to bear, and yet she needed to enter as much as she needed the air in her lungs. Slowly, she turned the handle.

An odd confusion of pain and comfort swept over her as she stepped into the study. John was everywhere and in everything she saw. All around lay papers written in his familiar hand – there on the sofa was his coat – there his pen. Through the door to her right she could see his bed, upon which lay his open notebook, full of scribblings. Everything moved her with fresh recollection, filling her with unbelievable longing: they were all pieces of John, pieces that had formed their lives together. But hardest of all was the scent of the room. Everything smelled of him, so strongly that she could have sworn he was there in the room with her. She lifted his travelling cloak from the coat stand - the one he had worn that night they fled - and buried her face in it. The smell enveloped her and for a moment she was back at the inn, held fast in his arms, feeling safer and more secure than she had ever done in her life. And he was holding her and telling her what their life would be like together.

For a moment she luxuriated in her pain – a wild, aching, lonely pain. It made her feel so alive. She gloried in the feeling, in having sensation, so dead had she felt for so many weeks. Then, slowly and inevitably, the illusion faded. She glanced up into a mirror that hung in front of her and the pitiless polished surface reflected herself as she was – a servant, alone in a draughty study, an apron tied around her waist, grasping a stranger's woollen coat to her face. The cold March wind swept in at the open window and brought her back to her senses with a shiver, just as the door opened. John stood before her.

Lost in some kind of reverie, he looked up in surprise to find her standing there. Recovering herself quickly, Isabel reached up and flicked some imaginary specks of dust from the top of the coat stand.

'Oh excuse me sir, I am carrying out Dorothy's duties tonight – I hope you do not mind.'

John glanced at her indifferently, signalled his permission with a careless flick of his hand, and picked up a pile of work from the table, easing himself into his chair with a deep sigh. She took this as a good sign: he did not, at least, seem to want to avoid her tonight.

She glanced surreptitiously at him as he marked the papers, taking advantage of their closeness. He looked older than she had ever seen him: dark semi-circles were under his eyes and deep lines carved into his forehead and down the sides of his mouth. Once again she found herself wondering how old he was – at Enderton he had looked in his twenties, now – well, he could have been forty years old. It was as though a mask had slipped on his face.

His exuberance, his energy, were all gone. His eyes looked weary and distant. As he read, he paused every so often, as if some half-forgotten memory had come back to him, troubling him. But as soon as it passed before his eyes, it was gone again. She watched the way he used his pen, the way he checked his watch, rubbed his eyes... his patterns of behaviour, expressions, nuances, once so dear, now seemed distanced and strange. She barely knew the man in front of her with his flat, weary gestures and deadened eyes. Turning away to begin dusting the bookshelves, she asked herself: was this a version of him that could have existed in another life? It seemed so unlike his true self - that man so full of life that she had loved and laughed with not so very long ago.

A book of poetry lay open on the shelf she was cleaning. She did not recognise the author and the pages were old and crumbling. A marked verse caught her eye:

*'I have lost my way, and all is night,*
*But yet I still put up no fight.'*

Gingerly she closed the book and slid it back onto the shelf.
Unexpectedly, John's voice broke the silence:
'I did not mean it, you know.'
Isabel spun round to face him.
'What did you not mean?' she asked breathlessly.
She had recognised that tone – that natural, throwaway tone that had belonged to a man that had not spoken to her in several months.
He looked up, as though startled to see a maid standing in front of him, duster in hand, cheeks suddenly flushed. Surprise crossed his face.
'What are you talking about?' he said, his brow darkening, 'Get back to your work.'
He pulled the papers back to him and set back to work, frowning slightly. Slowly, Isabel turned back to the bookshelves, her heart pounding. What was he referring to? Were the first dull memories starting to creep back into his consciousness? This gave her confidence and she took a deep breath. She tried to imagine she was in one of her fine gowns, looking her very best, rather than dirt-smeared and wearing a drab grey dress. But it would not have mattered to him - to her John - she reminded herself.
She started gently:
'Mr Fenn, I know you do not want to be disturbed, but I must speak with you.'
He glanced up, surprised. Isabel took a deep breath.
'As you know, a few months ago you had an accident. I was with you – indeed, I had been with you for many months. That is why I take the liberty of speaking with you.'
He looked confused, as though trying to piece together a jumbled

jigsaw.

'I do not remember any time before I came here,' he said, and the words seemed to pain him.

'I know that,' she said tenderly. 'And I want to help you, for I remember it all – so clearly.'

A troubled, almost childlike look came into his eyes.

'I do not know why I need to remember. I am quite well now, I am quite happy.'

'But it is important that you know who you were,' she said earnestly, '– and to understand what you wanted. That is why there is something that I to tell you. Something that I know you would not want to forget.'

His hand was gripping the workbook so tightly it crumpled under his grasp; a tension seemed to be creeping through him.

'I do not think…I do not think I want to know.'

'You *must* know,' Isabel said firmly. Anticipation reigned in her: she was getting further with him than she had in many months. She took a deep breath and asked, 'Do you remember staying at a house called Mount Enderton?'

'No, I do not,' he replied staunchly.

'You stayed there for a few months before you came here,' Isabel explained. 'You were invited by Sir Aubrey Branden.'

His eyes were a wilderness. She continued, undaunted.

'Do you remember a girl called Miss Audley?'

'No.'

She tried not to flinch. John seemed quite agitated now, his right hand was twitching and he shifted restlessly in his seat.

'You knew her very well. You saw her, for the first time, on a snowy night. You said she was the most beautiful sight you ever saw.'

'No, I did not see it. I do not remember that,' he said disconcertedly.

'Do you remember rescuing her, riding away with her in the night,' Isabel continued, her voice full of passion, 'taking her somewhere safe, and then going down on one knee on a hillside and asking her to marry you?'

'No – I – no, I did not do any of that!' he said, very agitated. 'I do not remember – why are you making all this up?'

He stood up, seeming taller than ever, but she did not stop.

'I am making none of this up!' said Isabel. Her eyes were on fire now. 'This is your life – this all happened. Every word I speak is true!'

'Then where is this girl, this Miss Audley, you speak of?' he demanded.

'She is standing right here,' said Isabel, with as much confidence as she could muster.

John stared at her back at her, confused and distressed. Not knowing what else to do, she held out her hand, on which sparkled her beautiful ring.

'And this is the ring that you gave me when you asked me to become your wife,' she said, her voice quiet, mingled with love 'and sadness.

The sight seemed to rouse him.

'You?' he said, in disgust. 'You are a servant – you are Annabel, Imogen – Snow, not Audley!'

'I am Isabel Audley, daughter of James and Marianne Audley. I am the girl who you love and who you wanted to spend the rest of your life with, whom you were willing to lay down your life to protect.'

His eyes danced with fear and uncertainty as he stared at her, trying to take in her words. She gazed back at him, willing him to remember with every fibre of her being, but then his eyes flickered like blown candles and she felt the air around them grow cold. With a chill, Isabel realised that whatever advantage she had had, she had just lost.

'You lie! I never gave you that ring,' he exclaimed.

'You did!' She tried to stop her voice from faltering, '...I remember it as clear as day.'

'Then you are the mad one – you are the one who is confused,' he shouted. 'For I would remember such a thing – I would.... I know I would...' he clutched his head.

Isabel put out a hand to calm him. It hurt her to see him so disturbed.

'John, I - '

'Do not lay a finger on me,' he said, pushing her hand away. 'Remember your station!'

'My station?' said Isabel, burning with the indignity of her situation. 'You are the one who gave me this station! I could have been dressed as anyone when you sat me in that carriage – a queen, or a pauper. I am what you made me!'

'You are a liar – everything you say is lies!'

'This ring does not lie, John!'

She held up her hand again. He bristled with anger.

'It does when it is on your finger!'

He grabbed at her hand and pulled at the ring - it slid off like silk on skin, so thin were her fingers now.

'This does not belong to you,' he said, holding it up accusingly. 'If I bought this, as you say, then you must have stolen it for I would not have given such a thing to you. But there is someone who does deserve it, someone that I care about very much.'

'That someone is me!' Isabel said imploringly

John's expression was cold, dispassionate. His voice turned her veins to ice.

'That someone is Miss Constance Part. She is the only woman I have ever cared about. She is real – unlike your…fantasies. Now I do not want to hear from you again. I do not want to even see you. Let there be no more of these unacceptable familiarities. You will keep out of my rooms, out of my way, out of my life, or I will see to it that you are made to leave this place. If you truly are my servant, as they say, then I will get rid of you. Do you understand me?'

There was silence.

'I do, sir.'

### ISABEL'S NARRATIVE
*(Extract from Isabel's Diary)*

*LANCEFIELD, 18<sup>th</sup> March 1867*

Full of sorrow, I left him. That was my final attempt. It failed. And he has taken from me the only real evidence that he had ever loved me.

*'I have lost my way, and all is night*
*But yet I still put up no fight.'*

The ditty played round and round my head as I climbed the stairs, the words dancing in front of my eyes, the rhythm becoming a mantra in my mind. I tried to shake it off as I entered my room, but it continued: '*Yet I still put up no fight, put up no fight, no fight…*'

A queer nebulous idea began to take shape in my mind, a fear that chilled me more than all the rest… I put up no fight… Was this all an act, this memory loss? - even a sub-conscious act? The shadowy dread began to grow within me… How much had John forgotten, and how much had he wanted to forget?

'We are eternally shifting creatures,' he had told me. 'The past is just leaves in the wind.'

How he had seemed to want to forget his past – it had troubled, nay tormented him, all the time we had been together. Well he had got his wish. It was all gone now, truly gone – as was all memory of me… But surely he did not want to be lost? Surely, he had been happy with me? I tried to convince myself that this was the truth, yet that sick little fear continued to burrow itself into my mind, the doubt building like a canker, eating away at my hollow insides. It was so very convenient, this 'forgetfulness'. Some might say it was the perfect way to rid himself of a troublesome girl that he had become entangled with, all too quickly, all too deeply.

At last I laid my weary head on the pillow, and passed a rough hand over my tired eyes that bristled with threatening tears. Try as I might, I could not rid myself of these shapeless fears, that it was all deliberate, that he wanted rid of me, that it had been his plan all along. I tried to buttress myself from these thoughts, but they were like water and crept their way through my defences. I closed my hand around my other one, the way John used to, but my hand was too small, too cold to convince my mind that he was there. The old John existed only inside me now. I must keep him alive.

'I love you,' I tried to remember him saying to me. 'I love you.'

I repeated the words over and over again to myself, trying to make them take shape before me, trying to hold them to me, like a child holding a precious toy.

I fell asleep, fighting the biting conviction that I have lost that which I had loved.

*LANCEFIELD, 19<sup>th</sup> March 1867*

Last night I dreamt of a twirling red ribbon, suspended in utter blackness. It rippled and swayed, and while I watched, the top slowly began to fray, beautiful strands splaying out, and thread by thread, the ribbon began to fall apart.

When I awoke, it was morning. Dawn had broken on a different world lit with the unforgiving light of reality. It was a world of doubt and uncertainty, where nothing was secure anymore, not even the past.

The light was watery, grey and incomparably sad. It was a landscape of despair.

# XXXVI

*'How hard...to have the natural affection of a true and earnest nature turned to agony; and slight, or stern repulse, substituted for the tenderest protection and the dearest care. It had been hard to feel in her deep heart what she had felt, and never know the happiness of one touch of response. But it was much more hard to be compelled to... and to think of her love...by turns, with fear, distrust, and wonder.'*

*Dombey and Son* (Chapter 43), Charles Dickens

## ISABEL'S NARRATIVE
*(Extract from Isabel's Diary)*

*LANCEFIELD, 20ᵗʰ March 1867*

I walked slowly to my assigned classroom; to clean the windows there was my final task of the day. I knew what I might see. I knew they often met in the garden that the classroom overlooked, once dinner was over. And, such was my life, they were there tonight.

I knew I should not have watched them. I should have done my duties and left that place as quickly as possible; but I was drawn to the window like an onlooker to a hanging.

My hand tightened on the filthy cloth that I held to the window, my other palm pressed against the cold glass. Down below they sat together on the cast iron bench, her hand in his, their gazes locked as they talked about their day, about their future...I did not know. I never would.

All I knew was that down there sat my whole world. But now his stars and moon circled around another. I had lost my place in time and space with just a few words. He had left me hanging motionless in the dark, with nothing to anchor me.

My hands were cold, my fingers like ice. And yet my heart was beating so fast within me... Where was the warm blood going, for I felt like one already dead... Had I been frozen in time? Would I be stuck here, watching and waiting until everything ended?

The girl at the window, watching, always watching. I had watched my parents leave as I waved from the front garden at Greenwood, I had watched Cathy leave as I stood at the front steps at Harringdon...

They were gone now, all gone – but none had hurt so much as him.

I stared at them with increasing sorrow through the terrible divide until I could not stand it any more. I finished my tasks and returned to my room.

There is no need to wake or sleep: the nightmares are reality now - only the woman I feared looks more innocent than I could ever have imagined.

*LANCEFIELD, 21ˢᵗ March 1867*

I have always been quite a cheerful person. Perhaps not in an overly happy sort of sense, but always content on the inside. And I would like to think that was not just a result of material things.

Yet now I feel as though my whole existence has been dulled, like a room in which the light had gone out. I look forward only to the dreary wretchedness of my days. My future is all darkness, all uncertainty.

For he is gone, but he is not gone. If he had left me, I could hate him. If he was far away, I could miss him. If he had - God forgive me – died, I could mourn him. But I can do none of these things. I feel like the dream-walker from my school days – the girl who walked the dormitories at night, her eyes open, yet still asleep. She used to terrify me.

I heard Matron and one of the teachers speaking about me as I went past yesterday:

'Dear me, what is the matter with that girl? She looks like she is dead already.'

'I hear she is quite unhinged. The girls say she cries out in her sleep.'

'Do you know where she came from?'

'She came with Mr Fenn, she was his servant. I heard some whispers that she was recently jilted by a lover. Engaged, they saw she was. She had a ring, but she does not wear it any more.'

'Always the way with men – have their fun with the young ones, with no real intentions, and then leave them as damaged goods.'

Damaged goods. I feel damaged.


## THE STORY CONTINUED BY THE EDITOR

Life does not stop, even when we feel that we cannot go on. The rooster continued to crow each morning at the waking hour, the days continued to roll onwards, and John and Constance continued to become more obviously attached day by day.

In the same way, questions and appalling suspicious continued to force themselves on Isabel's mind. Had John truly forgotten her, or had he simply wanted to forget? Was he pretending? Had it all been a lie? Thoughts raced around inside her head like a disorientated swarm of bees. The uncertainty of it all tormented her, but again and again, she was faced with the fact that she could not know. It gnawed at her, oppressed her day and night: she could not rid herself of it.

She went to bed, exhausted, weary, and heartsick to her very core, the same questions beating monotonously in her brain. There was no rest, no oblivion.

## ISABEL'S NARRATIVE
*(Extract from Isabel's Diary)*

*LANCEFIELD, 22nd March 1867*

How can I live with all these uncertainties?

I must believe that he loved me once. Otherwise, I do not know who I am.

And what next? Will I follow him all my life? Distanced and remote, like a lonely shadow always behind him, with him never seeing me, never comprehending who I am, what I once was to him.

Or should I break free - *could* I break free?

Where has all the light and laughter gone? I feel as though I am fading away, fighting to keep a hold of who I am…who I was…

I look down at myself. My hands are dry and cracked. I hold them out before me to survey the damage, turning them this way and that. The skin is breaking around my nails and knuckles. I feel as though the cracks are lengthening and running up my arms, across my chest, deepening and pulling me apart. And then I will crumble, my broken parts crashing down against the ground like fired clay.

## THE STORY CONTINUED BY THE EDITOR

Let me go back to where we opened: A servant girl is on her knees in a stone-flagged entrance hall. Her sleeves are rolled up, a scrubbing brush is in her hand and she has a pail of water by her side. The front doors stand open and a cold wind sweeps in. Although thinly dressed, she does not seem to notice.

A group of male pupils walk past. One of them kicks over the girl's pail with a laugh and cold water soaks through her skirt. The girl does not move, does not even blink, but carries on scrubbing, her fingers raw, her eyes dead.

A door opens on her right. Out walks a teacher, dressed in black school robes. This time, the girl looks up, her eyes on his face – but he does not see her. He walks past, stepping around the spilt water, and exits into a room behind her.

If you looked back at her, you would see the despair etched across her face.

This is Isabel.


### ISABEL'S NARRATIVE
*(Extract from Isabel's Diary)*

*LANCEFIELD, 23$^{rd}$ March 1867*

Tired…so tired. Brain numb, eyes heavy, legs aching. Day after day of the same mindless, exhausting, never-ending routine. There is no changing the awful truth that greets me daily when I awake. Hour, after hour of back-breaking work: I spend my life staring at floor tiles, stone stairs, smeared glass, my red raw hands grasping at sodden, ruined cloths that pull apart even as I clean. I am so tired it hurts - mind, body and heart.

I can tell when it is him approaching, even as I am bent over on the filthy floor, my nose inches from the tiles as I scrub. I know his footsteps, I sense his gaze. But it dwells on me only for a second, as you would acknowledge a fly on a windowpane. It is there, but has no interest for you. He moves past quickly, as though I am emitting a foul stench. He walks over my clean floor with his outdoor shoes. I hardly notice. I am watching him disappear though the far doorway. I have never felt so despised and alone.

The bell rings for dinner. I get wearily to my feet, straightening my aching shoulders. There is a long mirror in the hall in which I am cleaning. I have not looked in one for many weeks. Who is that woman who looks back at me?

Her skin is hardy and red from the cold. Her eyes are bloodshot, with dark circles underneath. Her hands look raw, with dirt pushed far up the unkempt nails. Her fingers twitch strangely in the glass. I gaze at her until my eyes begin to swim. Was it any wonder that he does not love me anymore? That sad, drab girl who hides in the shadows. I was beautiful once.

Constance walks past. I find myself envying the simple embroidery on her muslin gown. I brush this thought away and head to the servant's hall. It is soon time for bed and I walk upstairs to my tiny room. There is a revolting smell in the air coming from the washrooms below and I see the glinting eyes of a rat watching me from the corner. Shooing the rat away, I find myself contrasting this room with my one at Enderton. The four-poster bed, the flowers, the soft cushions – they had meant so little to me then. But, I remind myself, life is not measured in terms of comforts, but in terms of the relationships that we share. Both are gone from my life now.

*'I have sewed sackcloth upon my skin, and defiled my horn in the dust. My face is foul with weeping, and on my eyelids is the shadow of death.'*

*Job* (Chapter 16, verses 15-6), King James Bible

### THE STORY CONTINUED BY THE EDITOR

'Your hair would be very beautiful, you know – if you washed and brushed it. But I suppose, as a servant, you see no need to do such things.'

Isabel kept her mouth shut. Adam Halthorp, the Head Boy, was standing at the entrance to the classroom in which she was cleaning, with Yates and Messing at his side.

'Why do not you wear it down? Surely you do not have to wear that cap all the time?'

'You know full well I do, so why do you not leave me alone and apply yourself to your studies, which after all, are the reason why you are here, are they not?' Isabel snapped, unable to maintain her meek reserve.

'Why d'you speak differently from all the other servants?' asked Messing, with some curiosity.

'Because I am not from around here,' replied Isabel primly, continuing to scrub at the ink-stained desk.

'No, that's not it. You speak like a lady,' said Messing, scrutinizing her.

'I used to serve in a large house,' said Isabel casually, sensing danger. 'I have picked up many of their mannerisms, I expect.'

'Trying to rise above your station?' asked Halthorp impertinently.

'Or just trying to impress the gentlemen of the household?' He circled round her, mischief in his eyes. 'Hoping they might marry you – or just have a bit of fun with you and give you a nice piece of jewellery in return?'

'Leave me be,' she replied, irritated.

'You know, the other girls, they speak to me with respect, not impudence,' he said, a little indignantly.

'Perhaps they have a higher opinion of you than you deserve,' replied Isabel, forgetting to feign mildness.

Halthorp looked stung.

'You know, I do think you would suit your hair down,' he said suddenly, 'Let's see what it looks like.'

And before she had a chance to react, he had whipped off her cap and her hair tumbled down, bright and golden in the evening sunlight.

'How dare you,' she cried angrily. 'Give me that now!'

'Snow!'

Isabel spun round. Mrs Clegg was standing at the doorway.

'Put your cap back on this instant! How dare you display yourself so wantonly!'

'She has been behaving most oddly,' replied Halthorp quickly. 'I think she was trying to entice me.'

'You lie!' shouted Isabel, her eyes blazing.

'Enough!' Mrs Clegg looked incensed. 'Isabel, get downstairs this instant. Halthorp, get back to your lessons. I do not want to see you speaking with the maids again.'

Halthorp shrugged and sauntered out with the other two boys. Isabel picked up her bucket and scrubbing brush.

'I have told you before, Snow, your long hair is not acceptable,' said Mrs Clegg, turning on Isabel, her hands on her hips. 'Keep it short, or keep it out of my sight.'

'Yes, Mrs Clegg,' Isabel replied coolly, gathering up her things.

As she left the classroom, still furious, she saw John in the corridor. She wanted to run to him, to tell him how she had been treated – for him to defend her as he used to. He did not look at her as she passed. She fancied he did not even notice her.


ISABEL'S NARRATIVE
*(Extract from Isabel's Diary)*


LANCEFIELD, 25*th* March 1867

He refuses to recognise me. So I will make myself unrecognisable.

## THE STORY CONTINUED BY THE EDITOR

She found the glass in the outside toilet. One of the girls must have put it there so that they could apply rouge or style their hair when they were going out. She took the scissors from the kitchen – old ones, so that no one would notice that they were gone. She slipped them in her apron pocket after dinner.

She set the glass upon her rickety little table. It was small and chipped around the edges. Before her stood the dripping candle in its rusty holder. It gave off an unpleasant, oily smell as it burned; the smell of cheap wax that stuck in her nose and throat. Beside the candle lay the scissors. They were blackened and blunt with age and overuse. They looked like they had nasty secrets to share, each nick and scratch on the blade brought alive by the flickering candlelight. Isabel lifted them and drew the blades apart. The metal screeched as they opened, as though angered by the awakening.

Isabel looked at herself in the mirror, her reflection greased with the dirt on the surface. She stared into it. There she was: eyes, nose, mouth – she was all still there, in one piece. The mirror lied, she thought bitterly: it did not show what she had lost. She would make it see.

Her hair was brushed out across her shoulders, just as her mother used to lay it after the treasured one hundred strokes. It too, flickered in the candlelight, like gleaming rivulets tumbling downwards from a pool of gold to form a beautiful waterfall. How she had loved that vain crown; how she had delighted in every curl, every compliment.

'But I am not her anymore,' she said in a voice not her own.

And cruelly, determinedly, she sliced the savaged metal through her golden glory.

## ISABEL'S NARRATIVE
### (Extract from Isabel's Diary)

### LANCEFIELD, 26th March 1867

Today I made it rain money. Those coins had been bothering me – those worthless pieces of metal that I had earned with sweat and tears - so I took them, all of them, and dropped them down the well, one by one. I do not know why I did it, but I liked the sound.

When I looked up, I saw the half moon in the early evening sky.

The sky seemed ashamed at its appearance and had tried to cover it with clouds, but the dim semicircle burned through them, the dark blemishes still visible on its scarred face. It hung there, incomplete and unwanted; the world around it trying to pretend it was not there.

I feel a strange empathy with this moon. We are both unnecessary beings in this bitter world. We have no purpose; we have appeared in the wrong place at the wrong time and now have no escape. Like its scarred face, I too am in ruins, inside and out. I feel as though I will never leave this place.

There is thick ivy wrapped around Lancefield School. I want it to constrict and crush us all to oblivion.

*LANCEFIELD, 27th March 1867*

Does love always involve some measure of fear? Fear of losing, fear of being let go... Or is that where it starts, is that when you know it is real? For how can you know how strongly you feel until you bleed from the pain of it...

For me, this fear is becoming a growing sickness in the darkness that eats me from inside... a voice screaming silently and continually inside my head that the pain will never end.

But the worst of it is that he feels nothing I do. I know this just by looking at him. He looks numb, he sees and feels nothing. He turns my burning pain into sickening waves of ice.

Here we are, breathing the same air, sharing the same life – and yet we are further apart than we have ever been. It is tortuous to look at him. Those hands I cannot hold, that voice that will not speak to me, those eyes that destroy me to look at. I want to break into his world – I want him to see me as he used to.

'I am here, I am right here!' I feel like screaming at him every time he passes me.

But he can see that. And he does not remember.

How can the world change so suddenly? My heart is still beating, my chest still rising and falling... but nothing is the same anymore.

I remember when I was a little girl, when I stood before the moon and asked to leave. I knew then that my world had the propensity to change. I wanted it to. But I did not realise how terrible that change might be. How my heart would break and the tears stored up inside me would overflow like acid over an open wound, and my soul would cry out with the anguish of it all. Just give him back to me! Please. Just give him back and all will be well. Just give him back and I can live. For I cannot survive in this world of blackness and despair.

I glance up at the face of the moon. It is screaming.

*LANCEFIELD, 28<sup>th</sup> March 1867*

Last night I had the sweetest vision of John weeping at my deathbed, with all memory returned to him. How sorry he was to see my pale quiet face. How I long for such a release.

For I cannot even seem to cry anymore. I suppose I have used up all my tears.

All I have left are the memories. Memories that burn and burn in my mind until they are nothing more than scars, for the person I shared them with is as good as dead to me. Worse than dead.

*LANCEFIELD, 29<sup>th</sup> March 1867*

What is silence? Is it when you cannot hear anything? When everything stops? But your heart never stops. Is it when there is no one else there but you? You and your thoughts. If so, I hear a lot of silence these days.

Alone with my thoughts. I have been alone with my thoughts for much of my life, but never has it been so terrible a thing. Indeed, I used to enjoy it. Now they come upon me like an invading army – no longer are they the welcome friends that used to visit. I try to keep them from my mind, but still they come, filling me with despair and doubt, hopelessness and pain. They overcome me every time I think of that day… That day when he disowned and rejected me. That day when I ceased to exist.

I feel like a castaway. It is as though I have discovered a footprint on an abandoned beach and then realised it was my own. There is no one here for me.

*LANCEFIELD, 30<sup>th</sup> March 1867*

Me. Alone again. Are you bored of this yet, diary? Would you have traversed the long roads, great stairs, and tempests with me, if you had known it would end here? On a filthy floor in a tiny room where the rats screech from behind the broken walls, and the tiny stub of candle dies down and down until I can hardly write. Would you have chosen this life? I would not have.

But what does it matter. What does anything matter if he does not love me? I think I should hardly notice if the sun did not rise tomorrow, if the sky turned black and the stars fell from the sky. They could shatter around my feet and I would not blink, stepping upon the crystal shards until they cut my feet to shreds and I could walk no longer. Then I would sit amongst the darkness, gathering the folds of my garments around me and burying my head in my knees. The world could stop and I would not see. For already all is darkness to me, and I walk as one dead.


## THE STORY CONTINUED BY THE EDITOR

We all have one moment in our lives when we are at our very lowest; when things seem at their very worst. That one time when life has never looked blacker and you can see no escape. We might not know it at the time, but at the very end, when you look back, you would be able to point and say,

'There! - There was my darkest night.'

Now comes Isabel's. Be patient with her.


*'Yea, though I walk through the valley of the shadow of death, I will fear no evil: for thou art with me; thy rod and thy staff they comfort me.'*

*Psalm 24*, verse 4, King James Bible


## ISABEL'S NARRATIVE
*(Extract from Isabel's Diary)*

*LANCEFIELD, account written 1st April*

It was the midnight hour. Sleep had deserted me. My candle had burned its last. I watched the glow of the wick slowly die as the shadows grew around me.

Then, darkness entered the room, filling out with such force and volume that I could almost feel its weight upon me. Inside the darkness was the silence – that terrible, never-ending sound. I struggled to breathe against the weight of the darkness, against the sound of the silence; I felt them crushing me from outside and within. As I looked into them, in their combined power, I began to think I could see a face. It formed itself out of the blackness and the abyss of noise. It was the saddest face I had ever seen – full of grief, fear and despair, but completely void of pity. It opened its mouth and spoke to me.

'I am the future,' it said to me. 'I am your future, Isabel.'

Desolation surrounded me. It felt like ice and tasted like ash. All at once the room seemed very small and yet somehow very large at the same time, and I could not place myself in the world. I reached out for my comfort:

'Isabel, I will love, protect and comfort you for as much time is given to me. That is my promise to you.'

I heard John's voice all around me, echoing in my ears and inside my heart but his very words, instead of being a comfort, were a mockery to me.

And then the pain stabbed me, like a knife – a silent knife that slid out from the infinite darkness. It cut me right underneath my ribs, bitter and full of hate. I was so alone – no one heard me cry. I did not know what to do with this feeling - it was too much, too much for one person, too much for my head, for my heart. I wanted to curl up and die, for surely oblivion was better than this? And yet I feared that too. Fear in front and fear behind, and sadness all around me. Where did those days go, so full of love and hope? They seemed like shadows now.

A sudden paroxysm of feeling took me.

'I need you, John!' I cried out. 'I need you to come back to me!'

Desperately I tried to hold all his promises against my chest, but they were too heavy for me and slipped from my arms, falling down into the darkness. The pain haemorrhaged within me, spreading and tormenting every part of me. I thought I would die with the unbearable torment of it. My heart was a waste of grief as I stared into the void. All I wanted was his arms around me and his voice in my ear. I wanted to be back with him on that hillside, beneath the stars, but there were no stars now. The blackness had taken them and their light was no more.

I watched the darkest places in my soul came to life before my very eyes. All my foulest fears, my most hopeless thoughts, awoke and dragged themselves up towards my struggling, trembling heart. The house seemed to shake around me – was there a storm outside? I did not know, I did not care – there was a far more terrible storm raging inside me, ravaging every part of me, drowning out all else. In that darkness, I wished for an end. I wished for nothingness. I beckoned death.

I sank down and from the depths of my heart, uttered a cry of utter abandonment. I was more alone than I had ever been in my life and then – suddenly, I was not. Even as I began to give myself up, the very air in the room seemed to shift and a presence stole all around me, indescribable yet utterly wonderful. I found that out of my despair rose a different sort of cry – a call to someone I had not thought of in many months. I felt like a stranger saying his name, full of shame at how far I had travelled, and yet I cried to him from the depths of my heart:

'God, help me!'

The darkness did not disappear. The fear, despair and loneliness did not lessen. But little by little I realised that he was right there beside me, his arms around me - and that they always had been. And somehow that knowledge made everything else bearable.

In the quiet, a small, still voice spoke to me:

'Isabel, my child. Know that you are loved.'

I knew then, that this suffering would not be taken from me. But I knew that he would be there with me, no matter what happened. Slowly, the feeling of suffocation began to fade and I glanced up at the tiny window. Outside, I could see a faint greyness in the east.

The night was over and dawn had come.

That night changed me. It did not make my situation any better. It did not make me a better, nobler person. But it reminded me that underneath was not darkness, but a foundation, that had existed from before the dawn of time. I had come closer to the edge than ever before and fallen back into my Father's open arms.

# XXXVII

## THE STORY CONTINUED BY THE EDITOR

It was Easter Sunday, the first day of spring. In celebration, after the evening church service, cook had made several piles of hot cross buns and in light of the long-awaited holiday the next day, the mood in the servant's hall was jubilant. Several bottles of wine had been procured and soon most pairs of cheeks were flushed and feet unsteady.

Sitting at the back, small and unnoticed, Isabel waited, praying that it would all end soon and they could go to their rooms. She did not want to seem ungrateful by leaving early (it was only seven o'clock), but as the voices rose and more people jostled past her without so much as a glance, she was overcome by a longing to get away from it all. Besides, many of the girls were now disappearing out the back door with various men from the village that had turned up in search of some fun. Surely no one would notice if she left?

She turned to leave through the door that led to the servant's stair, when she realised, with the change of routine that day, she had forgotten to retrieve her yellow flower. Squeezing past several couples that were too absorbed in each other to pay much attention to her, she managed to get to the side door that led to the courtyard. As she glanced back at them, she thought dryly of what Mr Penderton would say if he knew of what was going on downstairs on Easter Sunday.

She glanced over at the well, to the small flat stone where her flower would usually await, half-ashamed of the increased beating of her heart as her eyes searched for the small flash of colour. But it was not there. Trying to overcome the inexplicable rush of despair that rose up inside her at the absence of the flower, she looked away, blinking back tears.

Through her blurry vision she saw a figure standing at the far gate. The outline seemed familiar. She swallowed, and blinking again, brought the figure into focus. That brown overcoat, the sturdy build, the tightly cropped hair –

'Sam?' she called out, forgetting herself amidst a whirl of emotions.

His responding smile brought a surge of joy to her heart. Her dazed steps became steadier and faster as she broke into a run down the path to meet him at the gate. There she paused, unsure as how to greet him, but he put out his hand, and she shook it warmly, glad of the familiar gesture. He smiled at her just as he had done back at Harringdon, during those few happy months, and she smiled back.

'It is good to see you,' he said sincerely, his eyes searching her face. Isabel felt his gaze keenly, and her cheeks burned as she realised how very different she must look to him. Joy turned to wounded pride as her hand dropped against the dirty dress she wore; the wind blew against her bare neck, and she dropped her gaze, putting her chaffed working hands behind her back. He seemed to sense her discomfort.

'I am so pleased that we have met again,' he said, his tone light and friendly.

Isabel glanced up at him, encouraged that she sensed no aversion in his voice.

'I am staying in a small cottage not far from here,' he continued. 'If you are not needed tonight, would you like to come for a visit?'

He spoke warmly, just as he had always done. There was no change, no less respect in his tone. Isabel smiled at him, the invitation brightening the colour in her cheeks.

'I would like that very much,' she said.

She glanced behind. Sal was stumbling out of the doorway, hand in hand with the local butcher boy.

'May we go now?' she asked.

He smiled at her.

'Of course.'

Putting his coat carefully around her shoulders, he led her through the gate. He did not ask why she was here, so very far from home. He did not ask why she was dressed as a maid. They simply walked together, as old friends, out into the deepening twilight.

They had been walking for about fifteen minutes across the fields, when Sam led her through a gap in the hedge and turned into a narrow road named Shambledown Lane. Over the hill to their right Isabel could see a small village that she supposed must be Little Hamble, which she had heard the other girls speak of. However, they were heading in the opposite direction. It was nearly dark when they took a turning down a narrow path lined with bramble bushes and intertwined honeysuckle, the smell strong and sweet in the night air. At the end of the path, set amongst the trees, stood a little white cottage, its windows alight, with a thatched roof and roses around the doorway.

'Welcome to my home,' said Sam, with a welcoming smile.

It was an unpretending little house, modest in every sense, but Isabel thought it looked beautiful. Before she could speak, a series of excited barks broke out and Killie came bounding down the path, her ears up and her tail wagging expectantly. She ran to Isabel, jumping up in excitement and Isabel dropped to her knees to fondle her.

'She remembers me!' Isabel said in surprise. 'But I look so different!'

'Nonsense,' replied Sam. 'And even if you did, Killie remembers people's voices, and the way they smell – appearances matter very little to her.'

Isabel smiled into the dog's big tawny eyes and sank her hands into her soft fur, feeling her lean body gently panting underneath.

'She was always fond of you,' said Sam warmly. 'Now, let us go inside before it gets too chilly out here.'

Opening the front door, he led her into the small hallway. Three doors opened off it – one into a little sitting room, the other to a kitchen and the third, she presumed, to his bedroom. He lifted his coat from her shoulders and hung it on a hook by the front door.

'Have a seat while I make up the fire,' he said kindly, indicating a worn but comfortable looking rocking chair in the sitting room. 'There is a blanket on the side if you are cold.'

His little shows of kindness made Isabel's lip tremble. Such gestures had not been towards her for a long time.

Isabel sat down in the chair, her aching body rejoicing in the soft cushions. She had not sat in any chair other than a hard wooden one for months, and the gentle rocking motion comforted her. It reminded her of her father's chair. As Sam built up the fire with skill and precision, she looked around the room.

It was maintained in perfect order; everything was neat and tidy, but it felt homely, to Isabel at least. The window looked out over a pretty garden and white flowers peeped in around the edges. On the window ledge was a penknife, an old magnifying glass, and a small vase containing some buttercups. There was a small low table next to her on which lay a battered-looking copy of *David Copperfield*. Several of the page corners had been turned down to mark favourite sections. The bookcase set into the wall beside her held a few theologies and several more Dickens novels. The smell of honeysuckle lingered in the air, mixed with a smell that she had come to associate with Sam – a mixture of fresh soap, apples and old books – masculine, but with a certain softness.

'Your cottage is lovely,' she said gently.

He smiled, grateful for the compliment.

'Thank you – it is only temporary, but I like it.'

The fire had taken now, its flames dancing and filling the room with a cosy light. Sam hung the kettle above it and before long it was singing merrily.

'Can I make you a hot drink?' he asked.

'Yes please,' Isabel replied gratefully, holding out her hands to the flames to warm them.

A few moments later he handed her a cup of sweet warm milk. She held it close, the heat comforting against the dry cracked skin on her hands, and breathed in its aroma – it had a hint of chamomile that calmed her and made her relax back into her seat. Sam pulled up another easy chair to the fire and looked over at her as Killie curled up at his feet.

'Would you like me to take your cap for you?' he asked, realising she still had it on.

Isabel hesitated. She had deliberately not taken it off, fearing his response. Not wanting to offend him, she reached up and slid it from her head to reveal her short bob, her eyes cast down, ashamed.

'It is not very...pretty, anymore,' she said in a low voice. She wished she had taken more care when she had cut it, rather than hacking at it like a savage.

'I like it,' he replied. 'Very smart'

Her eyes searched his face, but there was no hint of a lie there, just that old familiar beam of kindness in his eyes. Isabel felt a weight fall from her, and for the first time in a long time she felt a smile touch the corners of her mouth.

'I have missed our conversations,' she said, a little shyly. 'I know it was only months ago that we met, but it seems like many years have passed since then.'

'It does indeed,' he replied softly. 'Many years.'

She looked at him closely in the flame light and realised that it was not just herself that had changed – Sam also looked older; there were faint lines around his eyes and on his forehead that had not been there before. She wondered what the past few months had held for him – and then realised he must be thinking the same thing about her.

'You must be wondered why I am dressed as a maid,' she said, glancing down at her uniform.

'I want only to hear what it will help you to tell me,' he replied gently.

Isabel took a sip of her drink, the sweet taste flooding through her. She looked into the fire, and then up into his eyes. They looked a deep red-brown colour in the firelight, warming her more than the flames.

'I want to tell you everything,' she said simply.

'Then I am ready to listen,' he replied.

Isabel began with the night that she had bade him farewell at the gate. There was a lot to tell, but she did not want to rush it; she surprised herself with her own honesty as she got deeper and deeper into the events that had unfolded. With every word, she felt Sam and Killie's eyes upon her: both patient, both kind. It was a relief to have someone to talk to. Words flowed out without effort, released at last from their pent-up cage. And the longer she spoke, the more she was aware of the generosity of Sam's attention. He listened so patiently, with unflagging interest. She felt as though every word was being taken in, considered and remembered.

As she spoke, Sam was able to look at her fully for the first time. Though he said nothing, he did notice the change in her. Her reserves of youth and strength had been sorely drawn upon, there was no denying that – and not just physically. At points her voice was close to breaking, and he grasped her hand to give her strength – it felt rough and warm and she held it gladly.

She was reaching the end now. She spoke of her despair, of that terrible moment when she wished she were dead rather than having to deal with the burden which was crushing her. She looked up, suddenly afraid, but Sam laid a hand gently on her shoulder and she saw no judgement in his eyes.

'If I could take your pain away, I would,' he said, his voice rough.

She felt the strength of his fingers on her hands as he said,

'I only wish you had not been alone through all of this.'

'I was not alone,' she said. 'Only I did not realise it at the time. It was like when you told me of the time you tried to run away – you had shut God out for so long, only to realise he was all around you. It is amazing what you do not see when you do not want to. He had not left me - I had left him.'

'What was it God said about the floods and the fire?' said Sam softly. 'He will be with you *in* them. He will carry you *through* them. And yet we so often think we can do it all ourselves.'

Isabel smiled.

'I certainly did. Until life showed me otherwise.'

'And yet often it is the things we do not choose – the things in life that are forced upon us – which make us who we are. Make sure you write down what happened to you last night Isabel, and never forget it. Your life is not going to be instantly easy from now on, but you are not alone.'

'I know that now,' said Isabel, setting down her now-cold mug, and stroking Killie who was lying across her feet. 'But I have spoken so much of myself – why are you here, in Little Hamble?'

Sam looked at her for a moment, measuring his words.

'I was needed, and so I am here,' he replied.

After that, they spoke no more of what had happened. Chatting of books and dogs and the weather, they glided back into their old easy habits without an effort. In an unspoken agreement, there was no more 'Mr Hardy' or 'Miss Audley', just Sam and Isabel. Isabel realised how much she had missed friendship and companionship over the past few months. She drank it in like fresh oxygen, and felt it revive her heart.

When the clock struck eleven o'clock, Sam looked up.

'We had best get you back,' he said. 'Although you are not working tomorrow I imagine your Mrs Clegg will want you back in your bed very soon.'

Isabel's heart sank a little. She knew of course that she could not stay here, but the thought of returning to the school was a not a pleasant one.

She wore Sam's coat again on the way home and laughed at Killie trying to find sticks they threw for her into the darkness. But all too soon they were back at Lancefield, and memories of the last night they parted rose up before her.

'The last time I said goodbye to you, I never saw you again,' Isabel said softly, concern in her eyes.

'That will not happen this time,' Sam said pointedly.

A figure moved past one of the windows above them and Isabel glanced up: it was John. She did not need to tell Sam who it was – he saw it in her eyes.

'You will not let me take you away from here, will you?' he asked quietly.

'I cannot leave,' replied Isabel. 'I cannot leave him.' She looked back at Sam, suddenly unsure. 'I can trust you – not to tell anyone of what I have spoken? John's life will be in danger if anyone knows who he is. I must be here to watch over him, even if...even if he does not remember me. Can I trust you?'

Sam looked back at her with his frank gaze.

'I am your friend, Isabel, as I always have been. You can trust me.'

She looked relieved.

'And I will see you again?'

'I shall be at this gate at lunchtime tomorrow. I hope that this time you will be able to make our appointment?'

'I will,' she said, her face brightening.

'Until then,' Sam said, lifting his hat to her with a smile - and then he departed.

## ISABEL'S NARRATIVE
*(Extract from Isabel's Diary)*

*LANCEFIELD, 2ⁿᵈ April*

Last night I dreamt of a candle burning on a beach. It was tall and white, set firmly in the sand. Although the wind blew all around it, its flame burned straight and still, bold and bright, for all the world to see.

# XXXVIII

## THE STORY CONTINUED BY THE EDITOR

Isabel woke feeling strangely refreshed despite her late night. She paused, waiting to hear the cockcrow and then realised the sun was far higher in the sky that she had seen it in many months. With a rush of panic she realised she had overslept, but then hearing no other sounds in the house below she remembered that today was Easter Monday and the day was hers to do with as she would.

She got dressed and sat down upon her bed, her Bible in her hands.

'Today is the day when we remember why we are free,' she said quietly.

She took a deep breath and turned to the Easter story in Matthew's gospel and read it through. It was the first time in months she had turned through the pages of the once-familiar text. Then she turned to the same story in Mark's gospel, then Luke and John. Quietly, she put the book down and ran her fingers over the leather cover. It felt like an old friend that she had not spoken to in many years.

In her mind, she tried to form a prayer, but somehow could not find the words. So she sat in silence for a while, thinking over what she had read until her stomach groaned, and presuming it must be nearly lunchtime, she went downstairs. The servant's hall was quiet as the maids nursed the effects of their over-indulgences last night and Isabel met no one as she passed through the corridors and then outside through the courtyard towards the gate.

There he was; his cap on his head, Killie by his heels.

'I was worried you would not know exactly when lunch time was – by my clock, anyway,' said Sam, smiling broadly.

'I slept in, so I am afraid I have very little idea of the time, but I did not want to miss you,' Isabel replied, a little shyly.

'Well lunch is ready – on the table, I mean...well, it is a cold lunch,' he explained, his words rushed. 'I hope that you will not mind a cold lunch?'

Isabel realised he was a little embarrassed.

'It will seem like a feast to me,' she replied, without a shadow of a lie.

Relief flooded his face and he offered her his arm.

'Then let us go.'

A pair of curious eyes watched them from a window above.

The cottage looked as welcoming in daylight as it had done the previous night. The little chimney smoked merrily as they approached. Killie bounded ahead and waited expectantly by the door as Sam walked up the path with his keys.Opening the door, he motioned her into the kitchen where a small, well-used wooden table was laid with food – cold meats, some cheese, a bowl of apples, and a loaf of bread. Isabel felt her mouth start to water. It was a far cry from the bowl of lukewarm, tasteless stew she usually was given at lunchtime. When she took her seat, she noticed a small bottle by her plate. It was a pretty ceramic bottle with a small paper label on the side that read: 'Hand balm'. Sam noticed her looking at it.

'I thought you might like some – my neighbour makes it for the ladies in the village. Apparently it is very good.'

Isabel undid the tiny stopper. The cream inside was white and thick and smelt of lavender.

'Thank you,' she said, sincerely touched by his kindness. 'My hands are so dry I do not know what do to with them. This will work wonders. You are very thoughtful.'

'You are having to make do without many of the things you are accustomed to,' he said, taking his seat and starting to carve the ham. 'It is the least I can do.'

The lunch was the most delicious meal she had eaten in many months. Finishing up their platefuls, he then invited her through to the sitting room where he put a pot of tea on the fire. Although it was April, there was still a chill in the air. Isabel glanced up above the fire and in the daylight recognised a small line drawing of a row of houses that hung there in a black frame.

'That's Cranwell!' she said in surprise

'Yes,' Sam smiled. 'A little reminder of home.'

Isabel's brow furrowed.

'Why did you leave Cranwell?' she asked. 'I thought you were happy there.'

She watched him pause for a moment, and then answered,

'This is only a temporary posting. I was chasing a lead – a very important lead – and this was the nearest available village that had an opening for a constable.'

'And to think that it was exactly where I was!' said Isabel wonderingly.

'Indeed,' replied Sam, turning away to tend the fire.

The rest of the afternoon passed by in a delightful haze. For Isabel, it was sheer bliss to spend hours sitting with her feet up, gradually working the cool balm into her parched hands. When she closed her eyes for a welcome nap, she was surprised to find she felt almost content.


ISABEL'S NARRATIVE
*(Extract from Isabel's Diary)*

*LANCEFIELD, 2$^{nd}$ April*

He walked me home through the village of Little Hamble. It is very small, consisting of a number of picturesque but dilapidated cottages, two shops and a forge. Indeed, I am surprised they can justify a policeman here. When I asked him about it, he changed the subject so quickly that for a second I was reminded of John. But really, he is nothing like John.

It is surprising how his Northern accent is barely noticeable now, his hands no longer look so rough – indeed, they look just like mine - and his eyes, once so unfamiliar, now seem more recognisable than my own. There are so many details about him I had not noticed before - the light scar by his chin, the faint shadow where his beard begins to show as the evening creeps on, and the hint of curls around the crown of his head. I store up all these observances with gentle pleasure and look forward to the time when I shall next see him again.

*LANCEFIELD, 14$^{th}$ April*

Sam meets me after work on a Wednesday and a Saturday. Saturdays are particularly pleasant as is my half day and I finish work at one o'clock so we can spend most of the day together. We talk about what we have done since we saw each other last, about what has been in the local paper that day (he always has one with him), about the conversations we have had, who we have met. He is interested in every detail of my day which makes the very days themselves seem more bearable, for I enjoy noting things to tell him, no matter how insignificant.

And he always knows when I want to – need to – talk. He waits until we have reached his cottage and has set a hot drink before me, and then he leans back, his face is parallel with mine, and asks a kind question in a light tone – not probing, not anxious – just, caring.

I do not deserve his kindness. But I do not know what I would do without it.

## THE STORY CONTINUED BY THE EDITOR

Killie padded noiselessly into the room, her tail wagging. Isabel was sitting in her favourite chair – the rocking chair. Sam had said it was her seat, and she did not argue. Although it was now April, it was still cold outside and the fire was crackling. Isabel loved the smell, for Sam often burned old pinecones and sprigs of lavender that filled the room with a hazy scent. It warmed her very insides, calming her after a busy day. Sam always seemed to know instinctively what she needed. A mug of hot milk, a footstool for her feet...Isabel found herself accepting all these things as she would have done, had an unseen servant done them for her, but then she would remember herself, and thank him, and he would assure her it was nothing.

She stared into the golden flames of the fire. She had had a busy day and although she finished a little early on Wednesdays as the pupils had recreation time, her feet and back were aching. The flames distracted her and made her think of lions dancing far away in another world – ancient and beautiful and ever changing. Sitting there in her chair, with Sam to her right and Killie at her feet she felt safe and drowsy.

Sam had made her a dinner of roast mutton with cabbage and potatoes that night. It had seemed such a luxury to have both meat and fresh vegetables on one plate. Curious, Isabel asked who his cook was. Sam had laughed.

'I am not on such a very large wage that I can afford my own cook,' he said merrily. 'I did it myself!'

The look of surprise on Isabel's face was evident as she sat down.

'I know most men do not cook, but people do not always have to adhere to the roles allotted to them by society,' Sam had said with a smile, serving her a particularly large portion. 'I thought you, of all people, would understand that.'

She had smiled in agreement.

Now, comfortably full and sitting in her chair, Isabel began to doze off, but her slumbers were cut short when Sam's small wooden clock tolled the time: eleven o'clock. Isabel looked up to find Sam standing there, holding out her cloak.

'I am afraid it is time we should be getting you back,' he said, an apologetic smile on his face.

Isabel rose, brushing sleep from her eyes.

'It is indeed – and I must apologise for I fear I have been very poor company tonight, drowsing in front of your fire.'

'Not at all – it is good for you to rest. You get very little of it at Lancefield, I fear.'

Isabel smiled and let him help her on with her cloak. Putting his own coat on, he opened the door for her and she went out, Killie at her heels, always glad of an extra walk. The night-time smells excited Killie and she sniffed around eagerly.

'I am sorry you must always walk me home,' Isabel said to Sam, suddenly aware of how late it was, and that he too had to work the following morning.

'Nonsense, it does us both good to have some exercise,' replied Sam amiably.

'But you are on your feet all day already!'

'God did not make us to sit still,' he replied, gesturing at Killie who was bounding around in the long grass, chasing some imagined prey, her long ears flapping.

Isabel laughed at her enthusiasm and then stopped suddenly. It felt strange, the sudden noise. Sam looked round at her.

'I have not laughed for a long time,' Isabel admitted.

'Then I am pleased that you are once more.'

'It almost feels too soon,' she said, feeling a little foolish as she said it.

'Nonsense,' he replied, quite firmly. 'Life has not treated you kindly, Isabel, but behind those tired eyes and blistered hands is the same buoyant girl you once were. It will take more than weariness and disappointment to crush you.'

Isabel took a deep breath. He was her friend and she must be honest with him – perhaps he could even help her.

'I am trying to be strong Sam, truly I am,' she said slowly. 'But every morning when I wake, I remember, and I feel as though I have lost him all over again. It is worse than grief, in a way, because he is still there – right in front of me, and yet so far away. He looks right through me…it should not kill me, but it does. The pain rankles and smarts in my breast like a poisoned arrow.'

'Well you know the best thing to do with a poisoned arrow,' he said, as though the answer were obvious.

'What?'

'You must pull it out —sharply, and quickly, before the poison spreads. It will hurt, but it is better in the long run.'

She breathed in sharply at his response.

'No, I cannot. It is too painful.'

'It will get easier,' he said in a gentler tone. 'I lost someone once –

and I felt as you did. One moment they were there and the next they were gone and I had no idea why. But I survived it, and you will too.'

'Who did you lose?' asked Isabel, forgetting herself in her curiosity.

'Someone very important to me.'

Isabel could tell by his tone that he did not wish to speak of it any further and she respected this. She knew by now that if Sam did not want to say something, he had good reason for it. She stared at him a few moments and then said thoughtfully,

'You are much graver than you once were, Sam. I fear much has happened to you since we have been apart.'

'It has been a difficult few months for both of us,' he replied.

'Has your mother been ill – your sisters?' she asked, concern in her voice.

'No, they are all well.' He glanced away and then added, 'It was…a personal matter.'

'I hope it has been resolved?

'No, not yet,' Sam said tentatively. 'But I hope, in time, it might reach a conclusion.'

They walked together in sympathy and silence, both lost in their own thoughts. Isabel thought of the last time they had walked together along Harringdon beach, when the future had seemed as bright as the blue skies above them. She suddenly felt desperately sad. So much had gone wrong, so quickly, and even Sam, strong cheerful Sam, now seemed to be struggling.

'I always thought experience would be a wonderful thing,' she said in a small voice. 'Something that I would learn and enjoy learning. But I have found that it is not something you learn – it is something you have to survive – or not.'

Sam turned to face her. He saw the fear in her eyes.

'We are surviving,' he said, reassuringly.

She managed to smile at him.

'And I hope we might learn to laugh more, together?' he said, gently.

For some reason Isabel felt tears rising up in her eyes.

'I would like that,' she replied, fighting them back to smile at him.

'Then we have a deal,' he said, lightly.

They were nearing the end of the fields and the bright lights of Lancefield were coming into view.

'I will see you on Saturday?' Sam asked.

'Of course,' Isabel replied warmly. 'Thank you for this evening.'

He raised his hand to touch his hat to her, but she reached out and held it tightly for a second, then turned and walked down towards the school.


## ISABEL'S NARRATIVE
*(Extract from Isabel's Diary)*


*LANCEFIELD, 22<sup>nd</sup> April*

Do you know, I had not even noticed that the flowers have stopped coming. The good thing is, it does not upset me, though I cannot explain why.

My weeks are so different now. Each morning I have found comfort in reading a chapter from my Bible. It comforts me and gives me strength for the day. That book, that living word, has begun to fit back into my life. Or have I simply fitted myself back into the way things were meant to be? Sam is an encouragement, always asking what I have read, or talking through any questions I might have.

Sometimes he has to work late in the village and as the nights are so much lighter now, I often make my way to his cottage on my own as this saves him a long walk. The walking seems to alleviate my spirits. I pass through the fields and each time notice more of the world beginning to wake from its slumbers. The sun's strengthening rays warm my cold bones and with each new spring flower I see, I am filled with a little more hope. Then, finally, his cottage comes into view. When I see the wisps of blue smoke drifting up from the chimney, I know that he is home. I also know that there will be a hot drink waiting for me by my favourite seat by the fire. I walk towards the door, down the narrow path, towards my refuge.


## THE STORY CONTINUED BY THE EDITOR

'You know, I think these walks are doing you the world of good,' said Sam, opening the door to her with a smile.

Isabel entered, her cheeks pinched and glowing, a healthy look returning to her face.

'That, or the two good meals I get a week,' Isabel replied happily as she took off her cloak and hung it in the hall.

'Have you had a good day?' Sam asked, leading her into the kitchen where a roast chicken sat on the table.

She breathed in the appetising smell appreciatively.

'Not particularly,' she replied. 'Sal and the girls did their best to make me miserable – but did not succeed.'

'I am glad,' Sam replied, gesturing her to sit down.

'I wish I knew why they hated me so,' Isabel said, with a touch of bitterness.

'It is because they can see you are no servant,' replied Sam.

'Well I have almost convinced myself that I am,' said Isabel dryly. 'So surely they should believe it too.'

Sam placed two glasses of water before them.

'Would you mind if I prayed before dinner?' he asked gently, changing the subject.

Isabel looked up, surprised. He always said grace before they ate – it was usually short and succinct, and he had never asked her permission beforehand.

'Of course,' she replied, a little taken aback.

'Thank you.'

She folded her hands in front of her and waited for him to begin to speak. When he did, his voice was warm and relaxed, full of a strange kind of ease that she had not heard before.

'Father, we thank you for this day. We thank you for all that you have provided for us, for this food, for this house. We thank you for company, for friendship. We thank you for your word, which gives us hope. And most of all, Father, we thank you for Jesus. We thank you for the new life that his death has granted us. We thank you that we are your children. We thank you that we are loved.

'Father, we thank you that you know every detail of our ordinary, everyday lives. Help us to remember that we are never alone. You know when our days are easy, and when they are hard, but we thank you that your strength is always enough.

'And Father, in our lives, help us to honour and lift up your name. May we bring you glory in everything that we do, whether it is speaking your truth to others or carrying out even the most menial of tasks. Help us to love others, as you have loved us.

'In your name, we pray.

Amen.'

Isabel knew then why he had asked her permission. It was not a short, simple grace. It was the most open, personal prayer she had ever heard anyone pray. At first she felt as though she had intruded upon a private scene, somewhere she was not meant to be, for it was so intimate - but then she realised that they were both included in his words. They moved her; they were so refreshing, open and somehow unspeakably true. As they sat there and he continued to pray, she had felt hot tears pricking her eyes. Unable to stop them, they fell down her cheeks. She could not explain them, except that she felt Sam bringing her into God's presence with him, perhaps closer than she had ever been. For so long she had not been able to find the words to pray. Now, with his words, he had taken her hand and brought her to her Father.

He finished speaking. Swallowing, she opened her eyes. She kept them focused on her hands for a moment and when she looked up she found him looking at her, the serving spoon in his hand.

'Would you like some potatoes?' he asked mildly.

'Yes please,' she replied, hastily brushing the tears from her eyes.

He served up a generous portion.

'Are you feeling quite well?' he asked, looking at her a little more closely.

'Yes,' she said, sitting up a little straighter. Then she added, 'I have never heard anyone pray like that before.'

'Have you ever heard anyone pray outside of church?' he asked.

She thought about this for a moment.

'No,' she admitted.

'Personal prayers are very different,' he said. 'Just read David's psalms. That was why I wanted to make sure you were comfortable with it.'

They began to eat. She thought about his words.

'You know, I do believe I found my relationship with God much simpler when I was a child than I ever have since,' she said with a little sadness. She thought of her walks to church, her Bible clutched in hand, and that small girl waiting on the steps for Jesus. 'I seem to have let it all slip away since then.'

'I think many of us find that,' said Sam. 'It is why Jesus told us to come to him as little children, not literally, of course – but with all our worldly 'wisdom', cast off – so that we can present ourselves to him just as we are.'

'I do not think he would like the woman he found standing in front of him then,' said Isabel, half in jest, half serious.

'That is why we need him – he is perfect though we are not,' said Sam simply, mashing a potato with his fork and scooping it up. He glanced at her, the fork halfway to his mouth, 'Excuse me – old habit.'

'No, I do not mind,' said Isabel. She glanced out of the window at the green fields, and then back at Sam. Somehow everything made sense when he spoke.

'You should become a vicar,' she said after a moment. 'You are very good at all this.' She gestured 'all this' with her hand, and then wished she had not – it seemed to generalise something that was too important to be generalised.

'I would be the worst vicar in the world,' he replied, grinning. 'I have neither the patience, nor the temperament. No, I will let better men do that job.'

'I think you are very patient – you put up with me,' said Isabel with a half-laugh.

'And you with me,' said Sam, smiling. 'More potatoes?'

The rest of the meal passed in silence as they ate together.

'That was a wonderful meal,' said Isabel sincerely, as Sam began to gather up the plates, once they had finished. 'Where did you learn to cook?'

'My mother taught me the basics before I left home and I have been very grateful ever since.'

'The basics are more than I know,' said Isabel wonderingly. She glanced up at him, 'You know, you are not exactly what is expected of a man.'

'And you are not exactly what is expected of a woman' he said teasingly, taking her plate from her.

Isabel stood up and took the plate back.

'No – let me. I want to be able to contribute, and you do so much.'

'Very well,' he said, letting go with mock resignation.

'You can sit down and watch me participate in my expected role,' Isabel replied playfully, with a jesting curtsy before turning and beginning to fill up the sink with the bucket of clean water that stood beside it and piling the used dishes into it.

'Have you ever washed dishes before?' he asked with a smile.

She put her hands on her hips.

'I am a maid you know,' she exclaimed, but then admitted, 'but if you had asked me that question four months ago, the answer would have been a resounding 'no'.'

'Then at least you are learning valuable life skills, in an albeit difficult situation.'

'Yes, I am being shaped into the woman I am meant to be,' she said, with a touch of irony. 'It is a shame – I quite liked the way I was before.'

'Well you know what they say,' said Sam, leaning back leisurely. 'Steel is not worth polishing – but much sweat and many hours are spent to shine gold.'

'You say the nicest things,' she said, her arms elbow-deep in water.

'Only because you do not realise them yourself.' He glanced at her, scrubbing at the dishes, a determined look on her face. 'I do not think God is finished with you yet, Isabel.'

'Then I worry about what else he might need to put me through, before I become the woman he wants me to be,' she said, only half-jokingly.

That night Isabel took out her mother's brush and ran it through her cropped hair one hundred times.

'One hundred fold will keep it gold,' she said quietly into the darkness.

## ISABEL'S NARRATIVE
### *(Extract from Isabel's Diary)*

*LANCEFIELD, 26<sup>th</sup> March*

My evening absences are giving rise to questions.

I arrived in the kitchen this morning to find Sal standing there, curiosity burning in her eyes.

'Where do you go every night,' she asked, with more than a hint of jealousy. 'Do you have a beau?'

I felt myself blush a deep red and, angry with myself, replied quickly,

'No, of course not.'

'But Jessie said she seen you in the fields with a man. Who is he?'

I kept my eyes on the floor as I lifted my bucket and brush.

'He is just a friend, a good friend, who I see occasionally.'

She raised her eyebrows.

'More than occasionally – you are out all the time!'

'Excuse me, I have an urgent appointment,' I said, pushing past her with my bucket.

'A good friend,' I heard her say sneeringly as I walked away. 'You watch Mrs Clegg does not find out about your *friend*.'

The morning did not go well. Her question had put me out of temper, though I could not put my finger on why. I found myself justifying my answer to her.... Sam was not my beau. We are friends, nothing more. Anyone who saw us together could see that. Anyone who saw my heart would know that for definite.

But several of the girls had noticed.

'A fine figure of a man, that one,' Bets said to me as I walked past her and Helen in them in the corridor that afternoon.

'Very handsome,' added Helen. 'Does he have a friend for me?'

As the day progressed and I realised that word had got out about my 'romance', I slowly realised that the liaison seemed to have gained me some measure of respect. I was suddenly interesting, rather than just the shadow in the corner. Girls that had never spoken to me before were coming up to me, with no malice in their eyes, to talk about my gentleman friend.

'You're doing well for yourself, there,' said Mary. 'A policeman - he'll take home a fair wage. You will not need to work here when you get married.'

I muttered something about not wanting to get married and decided to miss dinner that evening. I could not bear to be in the servant's hall with them all. There were only so many denials I could make without sounding like I 'protested too much'.

It had never occurred to me to question my relationship with Sam. It was a simple friendship and gave me such blessed relief. That was all I needed to know.


## THE STORY CONTINUED BY THE EDITOR

'Those girls are simply brimming with gossip and idle talk,' Isabel said bitterly as she and Sam passed two of the maids on their way to his house that Saturday. The girls had given Sam an approving glance and then smiled at Isabel.

'Their lives consist of little else,' said Sam gently. 'It is all they know.'

Isabel felt ashamed. Sam always seemed to be able to understand people without judging them, a gift she seemed to have been born entirely without.

'Do you get on with any of the other girls?' he asked her.

She pursed her lips before she replied.

'No. I think they all find me...prickly.'

'Prickly? Hmm, that's not a bad description.'

Isabel laughed, half-offended.

'What do you mean?'

He glanced at her, in mock apology.

'The first time I met you, I think that 'prickly' would be a good description of your attitude towards me.'

'You were a strange man I had never met before, who approached me while I was on my own on an empty lane!' exclaimed Isabel.

'And had I been wearing a top hat and riding a black mare, would you have treated me in the same manner?' he asked, a little curiously.

Isabel was slightly shocked by his insinuation – and even more shocked by the fact that she knew he was right.

'If I did not like the look of him, then, yes, I would have treated such a gentleman in the same manner.'

'So why did you treat me in a similar way?'

'If I recall correctly, it was because of your impudence,' she replied, slightly put out.

'Ah yes, I believe I took the liberty of offering you a yellow rose.'

'Yes, that was quite shocking,' she muttered, unwilling to move from her position.

She glanced at him then and they both burst out laughing.

Recovering herself, she said, 'It is nice to have someone with whom I share memories. Even if they are memories of a past that was less than a year ago.'

'Less than a year ago,' said Sam, wonderingly. 'Yes, it seems a lot longer than that.'

'Things are quite changed,' said Isabel. Then she smiled mischievously and bumped against his shoulder: 'Mind you do not *prick* yourself upon my thorns.'

Flocks of rooks rose up in alarm in a neighbouring field as Isabel approached. It was still light as she walked back alone that evening; Sam had been called down to the village on what she presumed was a police matter and she had left early. The tall hedgerows laced with cow parsley gave way to wide green fields as the countryside rolled out around her. She strode through the mounds of grass, their blades still laced with drops from where it had rained that afternoon. The ground was damp and clingy underfoot and the pleasing smell of wild garlic filled her nostrils. She liked it; it reminded her of her childhood when garlic had grown in the gardens at Greenwood.

The evening spring light had a touch of green to it as it filtered down through the tender new leaves of the trees around her. Spring had been calling forth nature from its slumbers. But there was one tree that stood out. While the others stood rejoicing in their glorious new foliage, one great tree (she did not know what type it was) stood unadorned. There was not a single bloom on its stark branches. It seemed to watch the others silently – whether envious or stubborn, she could not decide.

By the time she got back it was nearly dark but the lamps were not yet lit. Passing from the servants' hall into the main hallway, she almost collided with a tall figure: it was Mr Penderton.

'Oh I am sorry, Mr Penderton!' she exclaimed, stepping back to let him pass.

'No, my fault. I was not looking where I was going,' he said genially.

At that moment one of the other maids came out from the dining hall with her taper and candle to light the lamps. The flame glowed and the wick took and Isabel realised the headmaster was staring at her.

'You are looking much better Miss Snow,' he said, looking pleased. 'You have some colour in your cheeks at last.'

Isabel put her hand to her face, a little self-consciously.

'I hope you are settling in well?' he asked.

'Things are better,' she said, with some honesty. 'Thank you for asking.'


### ISABEL'S NARRATIVE
*(Extract from Isabel's Diary)*


*LANCEFIELD, 27th April*


Why did I feel a flush of guilt when Mr Penderton said that to me? It is good that I am looking better, that I am not pining...and yet perhaps I am letting my focus slip.

It is just the walking that is putting colour in my cheeks. I am still his, heart and soul. And surely he would not mind my going out in the evenings? I find myself laughing as I think on it... He does not even notice I exist, never mind where I spend my evenings.

But that will change - things will never work out with Constance and soon he will remember. I must simply be patient.


*LANCEFIELD, 2nd May*


Her voice broke through my reveries as I cleaned the downstairs windows this morning.

'He has not slept since the concert – I can hear him tossing and turning through the wall. What should I do? I have never seen him so troubled!'

I was standing outside, carefully trying to avoid the border plants as I cleaned the exterior glass. I had thought the room was empty, but Constance and the Matron had obviously just entered. I did not think, before I spoke, too consumed by my concern for John:

'Was it an orchestra – was he listening to the violins?'

They both looked up, surprised, and saw me at the open window, cloth in hand. Matron gave me a look of great disapproval, but Constance stepped forward.

'Yes it was.'

She held her hands tightly in front of her - I could see the concern and desperation in her face.

'You were his servant - do you know why he could be so upset?' Constance asked me.

'Violin music seems to upset him,' I replied slowly. 'I am not sure not know why, but I have seen it before. It raises some deep emotion in him that he finds it hard to dispel.'

'He seems completely distracted and so very sad,' said Constance. 'I do not know how to help him.'

'Just be kind and gentle with him,' I told her. 'After a few days he will forget about it.'

I could not believe I was speaking to Constance in this way, giving her advice - but somehow it was good to be able to help John, even if it was indirectly. I ached to be able to go to him, to comfort him.

'Thank you, Miss Snow,' said Constance fervently. 'I was afraid I had done something wrong.'

'You have done nothing wrong,' I replied as kindly as I could. 'It is something far beyond your control. I doubt anyone will be able to fully understand it.'

Constance looked at her and I was surprised to see sympathy in her mild brown eyes.

'I am sorry he does not remember you, Miss Snow. You obviously knew him very well.'

'I do. And I will be here until he remembers,' I replied.

*LANCEFIELD, 4<sup>th</sup> May*

Today, for the first time since I arrived at Lancefield, I am wearing a new outfit. Ironically, it is still a maid's uniform, but it is the dress I wore when I first arrived here. I laugh to think how dowdy I thought it at the time – but the shapeless sack that I wear everyday has made it look positively fashionable. I have washed it and hung it, and when I put it on, for the first time in a long time, I was not ashamed of my appearance. Even my hair is growing. I have trimmed it, to give it a better shape than when I first cut it. It is no London head-turner, but it will do.

We are going for a picnic today, Sam and I. He is being called away on police business for a week so we planned this as a special trip before he leaves. The sun is shining outside and it is my half-day. Were it not for the man downstairs who does not know my name, I should feel quite jubilant.


## THE STORY CONTINUED BY THE EDITOR

Waiting for Sam, Isabel smoothed her dress and searched the horizon for his figure. There he was – striding over the hill with Killie at his heels. His welcoming eyes greeted her with a smile.

'You look quite lovely,' he said as he approached. 'Is that a new dress?'

'An old one,' she replied with a smile. 'But I have only worn it once.'

'It suits you.'

He carried a basket laden with food. Isabel was reminded for a moment of going off to picnic with Cathy on the beach at Harringdon. She stiffened: such memories were still painful.

'Come on then, we will show you a lovely spot,' said Sam, throwing a stick ahead for Killie.

She bounded on, and together the two of them followed.

They walked for about half an hour, through fields and over hillocks, when they came to what seemed like the entrance to a great wood. Pushing aside some branches that hung over an opening, Sam gestured for Isabel to pass through. She blinked: she seemed to have entered a magical green cave, with tall trees reaching right up to the sky. In the centre was a small lake, surrounded by rushes and smaller trees with low-hanging branches that reached in on all sides as though straining to drink from the cool green pool. All around danced iridescent dragonflies and she could hear the gentle call of tiny birds darting around in the branches overhead.

'Oh, it is beautiful!' said Isabel, stepping inside the tranquil grotto.

'I stumbled across it quite by accident,' said Sam, entering behind her. 'I thought you would like it – it is like a scene from one of your books.'

They picked a spot close to the water and spread out the blanket Sam had brought with him, laying out the food carefully. It was the first warm day of the season and Isabel slowly felt her body re-awakening; the sun's rays, filtering through the branches above, brushed her gently with their long fingers. As they ate, they watched the jewel-coloured dragonflies dancing over the water, sending ripples in all directions - and from time to time the silver flash of a small fish could be seen not far beneath the surface of the water.

'It is a shame we did not have such a lovely location for our last picnic,' said Isabel, the memories of Harringdon still playing in her mind, when they sat and ate at the roadside.

'Ah yes, this is not the first time we have eaten outdoors together!' said Sam, remembering.

'Only this time we do not have an unpleasant gentleman spying on us from the bushes,' said Isabel.

Almost by habit, she glanced over her shoulder.

'No Gaunt is definitely not here,' said Sam firmly. He finished eating his apple. 'I was going to ask you – have you thought of writing to your cousin at all?'

Isabel looked up, surprised.

'Cathy? But what would I say?'

'You could tell her what has happened, where you are?'

'I would not know what to say…she would not understand,' said Isabel falteringly. 'We are worlds apart now, Cathy and I. Besides, I cannot give away where we are. Any small clue may lead Gaunt to us, and I must protect John.'

'You must also protect yourself,' said Sam firmly.

'What do you mean?'

'Do not shut yourself off from those who love you, Isabel. Your life does not have to stop just because of John.'

Isabel shifted a little on the grass. She thought of Cathy seeing her now: dirty, weary, worn.

'I am not the person I was,' she said, shaking her head. 'I could not bear for her to see me like this.'

'What do you mean?'

She turned to face him.

'Tell me I do not look worse than I did when you first met me.'

He considered her gravely, his eyes clear and honest.

'I think you look older, as you naturally would. And your hair is shorter – which I like,' he replied with unshakeable equanimity.

Isabel shook her head a little in embarrassed disagreement. The broken sunlight danced upon her head.

'And your hair is regaining its gold,' said Sam with a smile.

Isabel's eyes brightened.

'Really? The colour is coming back? - It does not look so brown anymore?'

'It does not – look!' Sam reached out and gently held up a strand of her hair to the sunlight. 'Look at that and tell me it is not gold.'

Isabel smiled at the golden gleam, overjoyed.

'There,' said Sam, with some satisfaction. '*That* is a real smile, I can tell!'

'What do you mean?' she asked, with curiosity.

'Your nose wrinkles when you really smile,' he said, grinning.

Isabel stiffened slightly at the unladylike compliment and stared at Sam very hard. He stared back, merriment in his eyes – and then they both began to laugh.

'I am glad to see you are so observant,' she said, regaining some of her dignity.

'I am.' He took a long drink from his bottle and then added jovially, 'And now you have to tell me something you have observed about me.'

She stared at him, trying to think of something clever to say – but all she could think was,

'Your eyes are so different from his.'

Sam stiffened slightly.

'Who – John?'

'Yes.'

'In what way?' he asked, although he looked as though he did not want to know the answer to the question.

Isabel looked deeply at him, and then said,

'In John's eyes there are fires – fires that burn and flare up suddenly, and darkness that swirls and conceals so much – sometimes I cannot read them at all. But your eyes are so very, very…'

'Empty?' he asked, with false brightness.

'No!' Isabel struggled to explain herself. 'Clear – and honest, I can always tell exactly what you are thinking.'

'Can you tell what I am thinking now?' he asked.

She stared at him, hard.

'No…' she admitted.

'And if I think of something else…can you tell me what I am thinking?'

'Your thought has not changed,' she said slowly. 'You are thinking exactly what you were thinking before.'

Sam smiled at her, but it seemed forced.

'Correct. It is one thought that never leaves my mind.'

'What is it?' she asked, with curiosity.

'I will tell you one day,' he said. 'Not now. But hopefully I have proved I am not so easy to read as a book.'

He began to gather up the picnic items and Isabel helped him, tossing Killie the few leftovers. She hoped she had not upset him.

'How long will you be based here, Sam?' Isabel asked, stroking

Killie who was searching for more leftovers in the folds of her skirt.

The question seemed to catch him off-guard.

'I am not exactly sure. Perhaps a few more months. How long will you be at Lancefield?'

His question also caught her off-guard.

'For as long as I am needed,' she replied.

'But what about your dreams – your plans to travel. You cannot expect to stay here all your life.'

She half-laughed, despite the kind turn of his voice.

'Ah yes…I wanted to do so much with my life. I wanted to travel, to see wondrous places, to meet new people, to experience incredible things…I am afraid those dreams are ashes now, Sam.'

'Well why do not you take a poker and dig about in those ashes for a while,' he said, matter-of-factly. 'I think you may find there are still many adventures to have, many new places to see. Nothing is stopping you from doing everything you ever wanted to do.'

Isabel stared into his blue eyes. She did not want to mention John again, the one thing that kept her at Lancefield. He did not seem to have a place there, in their secret grotto; indeed, he seemed almost shadowy at that moment. Above them, the wind stirred the trees, and around them apple blossom fell gently down. The petals settled in her hair and the folds of her skirt like snow.

'We shall see,' she said, a little more hopefully, and for a moment she looked like the girl Sam had met all those months ago: young, beautiful and excited about what lay ahead. 'Perhaps I shall yet get to do all those things I wanted to.'

Sam smiled at her.

'I am glad to see that experience has not entirely cured your propensity to hope.'

She looked at him, feeling his reassuring, steady presence; feeling his willingness for her to have a life beyond everything that had happened. His kind face, his steady eyes: not overly expressive, but always attentive, listening, noticing each shift in her face. She felt suddenly touched, but also saddened that he was leaving her for a while.

'Come back soon, Sam,' she said, gently.

He looked at her, a strange expression in his face that looked something like expectancy.

'I will,' he replied.

# XXXIX

## ISABEL'S NARRATIVE
*(Extract from Isabel's Diary)*

*LANCEFIELD, 11<sup>th</sup> May*

I have a secret to tell you. I turn eighteen tomorrow.

I suppose I shall feel different? If I were a normal girl, my parents would throw a huge ball to celebrate my coming of age and all the young men of the county would come to see if I was worth pursuing. I would be given gifts – of jewellery, clothes and perhaps a horse. A white one, tall and beautiful.

As it is, not one person knows of this happening, not even Sam. But he returns tonight and I will tell him then. I can already see his smile when I tell him.


## THE STORY CONTINUED BY THE EDITOR

It was Saturday, that much-awaited half day for all the staff at Lancefield. Isabel was just completing the last of her tasks when Helen, the scullery maid came towards her.

'Mrs Clegg says I am to give you this.'

She held out a letter addressed to Isabel. It was the first piece of post Isabel had ever received at Lancefield, and with relief she saw that is was addressed to 'Miss Isabel Snow'.

'She says it came yesterday but you were not to have it til you finished work today.'

Isabel took the envelope. Helen stood beside her, looking eager as Isabel opened it.

'Thank you Helen,' said Isabel, pointedly.

Frowning, Helen left the room and Isabel slid out the letter. The address at the top was Little Bridges, Grove End. She did not recognise the area. The letter read:

*Dear Isabel,*

*I am sorry, but I am going to be detained here for a few more days. There is a matter that I must attend to before I return. Killie and I look forward to seeing you soon - no later than Wednesday, I expect.*

*Yours,*
*Sam*

Isabel tried not to let the deep sinking feeling of disappointment envelop her. She had counted on him coming back today. The week had been so long without him and now it would be several more days before he returned. And he would miss her birthday! Sadly, she contemplated the fact that she would be turning eighteen on her own, with no one to know, or even care.

She gathered up her cleaning pieces and walked slowly to the kitchen.

'Seeing your beau tonight?' asked Sal, who was scrubbing the table.

'No,' replied Isabel miserably, too downcast to correct her.

To Sal's credit, she almost looked disappointed on Isabel's behalf.

The afternoon came and went and soon it was evening. There was no food provided for the girls on their half day, as most of them went down to the village inn, so Isabel went without, her stomach growling at the unexpected fast. She could hear the other servants coming and going in the courtyard. There was a dance going on at the local hall, which Mr Penderton and his family were attending. Isabel had made sure not to look out of her window when she heard the carriages arriving. Seeing John help Constance into her carriage would do nothing to improve her mood.

It was around nine o'clock, when dusk was falling, that Isabel suddenly grabbed her pen and a sheet torn from her diary. She would write to Sam and tell him it was her birthday tomorrow, she decided. The letter would most likely not reach him in time but she needed to tell someone - and a dialogue on paper was better than nothing.

*Dear Sam,*

*I hope all is going well where you are. It has been strange not seeing you this week. The days have seemed very long.*

*I did not tell you beforehand – but it is my eighteenth birthday tomorrow. I know it will be past by the time you read this, but I wanted you to know.*

*Give Killie a hug from me and I will see you next Saturday.*

*Your friend,*
*Isabel*

She surveyed it with satisfaction. She could see him reading it, Killie at his heels. He would be pleased to know she had missed him. Getting up, she pulled a box from under her bed. Sam had given her some basic essentials: stamps, envelopes, a fresh supply of ink – should she need it. She had not, so far, but was grateful now.

Addressing the letter to the location he had given, she sealed the envelope and attached a stamp. She could leave the letter out at the back gate to be posted on Monday, but she was wary of prying eyes. Instead, she decided to take it herself to the local post box that was a short walk away at the crossroads that led to the village. Putting on her cap, she set out into the warm evening air.

It took her less than ten minutes to reach the post box and she enjoyed the walk. Dropping her precious piece of mail through the slot, she turned to head back. It was then she saw the two figures, framed against the lilac evening sky, standing amongst the gently swaying grass of the field. She knew who they were instantly: no amount of time could erase that tall figure from her mind. Constance was dressed in a pretty coral gown; the fading light shone through it, the ends of the pink ribbon tied around her waist fluttering slightly in the soft breeze. Her heart-shaped face was turned upwards towards John. He leaned forward towards her and Isabel turned away: seeing that soft kiss bestowed on someone else still rankled more than she could bear.

Isabel took a deep breath. She must walk away. Watching them would do her no good: but instinct turned her eyes towards them for one last glance. At first she thought John had left Constance for she seemed to be standing on her own in the field – but then she saw him, kneeling at her feet. Isabel's heart stopped. She watched Constance breathe in, lost for words, and then with her outward breath gasp, she said, loudly and clearly,

'Yes.'

There was the tiniest twinkle of light coming from the most beautiful star Isabel had ever seen – and then it was gone. Now it was just a ring, on Constance's finger. The past was being erased even as Isabel stood there.

With a great cry of delight, John caught Constance up in his arms. They exchanged words and kisses, warm and excited, and then, pulling her forward, John began to run – presumably heading back to the village to share their joyous news. Isabel stayed standing, watching Constance's pink gauze skirts dance through the long grass as John led her onwards by the hand.

'You are breaking my heart, John,' Isabel murmured softly.

ISABEL'S NARRATIVE
*(Extract from Isabel's Diary)*

LANCEFIELD, 12[h] May

The clock has struck, the hour has come. I am now eighteen. But what does it matter now.

He has found someone else that he wants to spend the rest of his life with him. He looked so – happy. There is no turning back from this. As I walked back from that fateful place, I felt as though everything we had shared together was being cast behind me: sunlight and grass, memories of a folly and breaking waves, a cliff top, a tiny star, bright hopes and an unfulfilled future.

Slowly, I forced myself to think that he will never hold me again. He will never call my voice or look up with pleasure when I enter a room. We will never go back to the folly. The red book will never be filled. We will live lives apart....No! I cannot, it is too much. I will not accept that this is my future.

And then I realised that I had almost forgotten what it was to miss him. For the past few weeks, the warmth of Sam's friendship has kept the misery at bay. But now it has returned, with a roaring vengeance. And part of me is thankful. Because as much as it destroys me, I cannot live without it.

I feel the dark red tide of misery rising up inside me and do not choke it back down. Then, all too late I remember why I was ignoring it: because the pain is too raw, too real... Too late now, I think numbly as I see the wave of agony approach me. It rises up, taller and taller and then it engulfs me.

THE STORY CONTINUED BY THE EDITOR

A young man waited at the gate to the school. Each time a maid came out to fill her bucket at the well, he looked up expectantly, ready to call out to her. But she was not there. She did not come.

Upstairs, a servant entered a teacher's room. Her face was defiant, her eyes unnaturally bright. She should not have been there without permission, but she felt she had a right. She needed to find something – some token, some evidence of a past that she alone knew had taken place. Something that would prove they had existed together.

Another woman entered – her cheeks aglow with happiness, the pink ribbon she had worn the previous evening still tied around her day dress. Finding the servant before her, she almost cried out in alarm. 'What are you doing here?' said Constance, gasping for breath. 'My job,' said Isabel vehemently.

'It is not your job to clean the offices.'

'It is not your job to check my duties,' Isabel retorted.

Constance struggled to stay calm, but then noticed how the girl was staring at the ring upon her finger. Realisation dawned in her eyes and she stared back with pity. The sympathy burned Isabel like acid.

'I know you were his servant,' Constance said quietly, 'and it must be hard for you as there is no need for you in his life anymore. But he has a new life now, and he does not need you any more. I can now do all you used to do for him and more.'

She gestured emphatically with her final words and the ring sparkled darkly on her finger.

'You know nothing of him!' Isabel broke out, fighting the desire to snatch the ring from Constance's hand. 'Nothing!'

'Do not speak to me in that manner,' Constance replied, blood rising in her pink cheeks to match Isabel's, which were hot and flushed.

'He does not love you,' Isabel said heatedly. 'He is confused and ill and reaching out to you because he thinks he has no one else. But he does – indeed, he is already engaged to another!'

She clasped her hand to her mouth, already fearing that she had said too much. Constance was silent: Isabel's words had knocked the breath out of her, but to her credit she did not lose her temper. She took a deep breath.

'You are lying, Miss Snow. You dislike me, and I can understand that. A master holds a very dear place in a servant's heart. But things have changed now, and if you do not keep to your place, I will be forced to have you removed from this school. Do you understand me?'

'Do you understand him?' was all Isabel replied, and while Constance stood in stunned silence, Isabel turned and ran down the stairs to the courtyard.

Once outside, she paused, putting out a hand against the wall to steady herself and taking in deep breaths of fresh, cold air. She felt unsteady and her head was pounding.

'Isabel?'

She glanced round, her cheeks still flushed.

'Sam?'

He strode forward, his cap in hand.

'What are you doing in the school, Sam? – and why are you back so soon?' Isabel asked, confused.

'I managed to leave early and here as soon as I could, but I could not see you. I was worried something had happened to you'.

Isabel took a deep breath.

'I am fine.'

'You do not look it.'

Isabel felt her temper rising once more. She turned away from his probing eyes.

'You had better go – only staff are allowed in here,' she said shortly.

Sam felt the rebuff but it did not stall him.

'I am a policeman – I can go where I want,' he replied. 'Now tell me what is wrong.'

She stared back at him, fighting back a sharp response.

'John and Constance are engaged,' she replied at last.

'I see,' he replied calmly.

She gave him a look of disbelief. He seemed completely unfazed by her news.

'Engaged – to be married,' she said, by way of elaboration.

'Yes, I do know what the word 'engaged' means,' said Sam replied mildly.

Isabel cried out, frustration painting her cheeks:

'It is just impossible – he barely knows her –'

'Did he not only know you a few weeks before he proposed to you?'

She ignored him and continued,

' - I just do not know what does he sees in that simpering fool.'

'I hear in the village that she is kind and goodhearted,' replied Sam gently, but firmly.

Isabel wanted to slap Sam. Why was he not on her side? She stared at him fiercely, feeling both ashamed of her words and furious at his response. He stared back and suddenly she felt very limp, as though all the blood was rushing from her body.

'You are exhausted, Isabel,' said Sam, getting to the heart of the matter as usual. 'Put your arm around my shoulder and come with me.'

Silently, she obeyed.

They sat on the hillside behind Sam's cottage. The day was warm, but somehow Isabel could not feel the sun's comfort.

'Talk to me, Isabel,' said Sam.

They had been sitting in silence for some time.

'What do you want me to say?' she replied dully.

'What are you feeling?'

Isabel stared straight ahead. Hatred, she thought to herself. She felt hatred.

Her sudden rush of feelings towards Constance frightened her. She had never felt this way about anyone – not even Gaunt. Yes, she had feared Gaunt. But she hated Constance.

Sam seemed to read her thoughts.

'I know you will want to place blame – and you will place it on Miss Part. But doing so will not help you.'

'She has stolen him from me!' Isabel burst out bitterly.

'Not intentionally,' replied Sam. 'Remember that she knows nothing of you and John's relationship.'

'She has been trying to trap him since we arrived,' said Isabel fiercely. 'I could see it in her eyes from the moment I first met her.'

'Did you not say she helped you when you arrived there?'

Isabel ignored him and continued in a low voice:

'You should have seen her today – she was triumphant, gloating - there was a cruel gleam in her eye. I could tell she has always hated me!'

Sam sighed, deeply, and then said,

'Isabel, be calm. We both know the truth of the matter. You put that gleam in her eye and you imagined her triumph.' He looked saddened. 'You have such a wonderful imagination Isabel but do not use it for evil. Do not let the bad experiences you have had taint who you are. Remember the hopeful, happy Isabel I first met in the lane – '

'- The Isabel you met in that lane was a child,' she said quickly, defending herself before he could finish. 'She had no idea of what the real world she was about to be thrust into was like. She was lost in dreams and fancy.'

'Wonderful dreams and beautiful fancy,' replied Sam, just as quickly. 'Things you should not lose for they are just as real as the nightmares that you create – and better for you. The world is not made entirely of hard fact and tough experiences – it is also made of beautiful imagination and incredible creation. The God that made this world did not create the mountains, lakes and valleys without a great deal of what you call 'dreams and fancy'.'

Isabel was silent. It was frustratingly difficult to argue with Sam.

She wanted to hate Constance – she *needed* to hate her. For, a quiet voice inside told her, if she did not hate her, she would have to hate John. And that, she could never do.

'I used to think that my destiny would be of my choosing,' said Isabel in a harsh voice, 'that I would be in control of my life. Now, I feel I have been cast afloat in a leaking boat, tossed and turned wherever the winds decide to hurl me, the only certainty being that soon I shall surely end up cast lifeless on the ocean floor.'

Her foot was tapping on the ground rapidly, insistently, shaking her whole body. Sam put his hand on her arm.

'Be still,' he said with firmness.

Isabel could feel all her frustrations, all her disappointments pouring out of her. This final blow seemed to have broken the floodgates. She carried on angrily:

'I never questioned God for taking my parents, or for what Sir Branden did to me – I did not complain that I have had to work as a servant, completely cut off from everyone I love - but this, this is too much! I do not know what I have done to deserve this.'

'So you believe that you deserve a perfect life?' asked Sam bluntly.

Isabel was taken aback. Sam took advantage of the silence.

'I used to blame God for all that he had allowed to happen to me, for allowing my father to abandon us and leave me with such responsibility. But how can anyone know who they really are – and who God is – until they experience the real world, which includes suffering and hardships? God can make good of all that happens in your life, Isabel. But that does not mean the pain is not real. If we did not feel pain, we would not be alive.'

'Sometimes I find God's love hard to understand' said Isabel, still with a trace of bitterness in her voice.

'And how do you describe love?' Sam asked her.

Isabel's forehead creased.

'It is...desperately needing to be with someone - indescribable happiness when you are together, or incredible pain when you are separated...it is what binds two people together, and once you have tasted it, you cannot live without it.'

The look on Sam's face was strange.

'Why?' she asked. 'How would you describe love?'

'How would I describe love...' his voice tailed off.

He looked out across the sky. For a moment Isabel appreciated his rare gift of allowing himself to be silent before speaking so that he always said exactly what he meant. He took a deep breath and then said,

'Love is hard. It is often lonely. Love wants the best for another at the cost of yourself. Love takes the blows, pays the price...It does not ever give up.'

Isabel looked at him.

'I think we see the world very differently,' she replied, her voice softer.

'Well we are looking at it from different places,' he said. 'A mountain looks rather different when you are standing at the top of it.'

'And where do I stand?' she asked.

'You are busy climbing it, Isabel,' he said. 'Wait until you have reached the top and then tell me what you see.'

'That will be many years from now,' she said with a half-smile, 'when I am old and grey'.

'Well I hope I am still around then to ask you' said Sam. 'And I pray to God that you will get there sooner than you think.'

Isabel toyed with some long grass with her fingers, breaking off the heads and scattering the seeds.

'How do you know it is true?' she asked, in a voice suddenly uncertain. 'How do you know there is a God, and that he is in control?'

Sam thought for a moment. A rush of wind carried the seeds from her fingers up into the air.

'I know God exists, just as I know that the wind blows,' he said steadily. 'Because I feel it, and I see its power. It is something I will never fully understand until the end, but until them, I am content.'

They were silent for a few moments, each lost in their own thoughts. Then Sam stood up,

'Come, it mutt be nearly dinnertime. Let us eat.'


## ISABEL'S NARRATIVE
*(Extract from Isabel's Diary)*

*LANCEFIELD, 12th May*

I felt calmer when I walked back from Sam's, and a little ashamed of my outburst, but as I passed through the courtyard, I saw them there – her hand in his. John's fringe hung low over his eyes and my hand twitched, longing to sweep it back, but her hand was there instead.

As I looked at him, I could see how his eyes had begun to take on life again. They were no longer dull and empty, but full of life and love. But not for me. When I saw him look at her, I almost wished the deadness back again, though I hated myself for it. Constance saw me then and looked at me, her eyes as threatening as someone as meek as her could make them. If I was a cat, I would have hissed at her and spread my claws. But I was a girl, a servant girl, and I walked away.

How can it be that his world can go on – as if I never existed? I, who was his everything – his love, his joy, his future. Or was that just talk? But if that was not real – those moments, those days of wonder and of joy, where every word was sacred and every glance an adventure - then what is?

I thought of Constance, so pretty and mild, so loved by all around her. The one person at the school that even Sal could not speak ill of. Perhaps she is more suited to him, a voice in my head said gently. Had I been too much for him? Too intense, too demanding? Constance seemed so simple, so straightforward...

Hot blood flows into my veins and I repel a savage urge to rush back out there and pull Constance from him, to hurt her... I wrestle with this sudden madness. No, it would do no good. I look out of the window – they are still down there, making the most of the last moments of the warm spring evening. Constance glances down at the beautiful ring on her finger and I wonder if any engagement ring has been worn by two such different people in such a short space of time...

How ironic that I now look down on him from a window when I used to look up at him from his arms. We should be miles from here, married and starting our lives together. Instead I am trapped watching him begin life with another.

There is a strange feel in the air tonight. I think I am going slightly mad. I must try and sleep.


## THE STORY CONTINUED BY THE EDITOR

But sleep was far from Isabel. She was right when she said there was a madness in the air – it was the night of the full moon and as the darkness increased, so did the moon's brightness. The rag that attempted to cover her window could not keep the unearthly light from her eyes as she tossed and turned on her narrow bed, trying to grasp onto the last threads of sanity amidst her world of chaos. Unable to bear the light any longer, Isabel rose and with a violent gesture, snatched the covering from the glass. The moon met her with all its power: challenging, bold. In a flash, she remembered all the other times it had met her there, in her excitement, in her fear, and now in her brokenness – and yet it was just the same, as if nothing had changed. Embittered, she held her head high as her words thundered forth:

'Why will you not leave me alone? I do not want you outside my window. You no longer comfort me – you taunt me! You taunt me with what was and what will now never be.' Her voice broke and she beat her hands against the glass. 'You are no friend to me. You are nothing but a mirror that has hung outside my window capturing the best and happiest of times, and now you shine them back upon me when I am broken and alone. I see now that your smiling face is not smiling at all – you are mocking me and I can stand it no more!'

She railed her small frame against the beaming circular face of the great orb. It seemed to shine brighter and brighter; the more she stared at it, the larger it seemed to grow until she fancied in her dreamlike state that it would grow so immense that it would encompass and devour her. Its callousness chilled her.

'Every tear I have cried before your shining face I will gather up in my heart and one day I will drown you in them,' she said bitterly. 'Your light will die and then your smile will finally fade.'

There were no velvet curtains to draw. She returned to her bed and imagined the deepest darkness possible, trying to find some comfort in its obscurity.

Isabel's mood the next morning was less than pleasant. Even Sal avoided her in the servant's hall, noting the dark look in her eye. The girls were glad when she went outside to see to the hens.

The sky was dark overhead and just as Isabel stepped outside into the courtyard, the first drops of rain splattered unevenly over the cobbles. Isabel stood by the hens and scattered the food at their feet without looking at them. The rain fell more heavily. She looked down - the hens were pecking round her feet as her hand was still making scattering movements but had no feed left. She dropped the basket and began to walk towards the gate, her feet unsteady on the soaking cobbles. She heard someone shout to her from the doorway, but she did not turn round, walking through the gate and out into the fields.

She strode through the long wet grass, soon becoming completely drenched. She suddenly felt an incredible need for John to be there and to feel his arms around her. The intensity of the moment stopped her in her tracks. The rain passed by her in a huge magnificent cloud and she was alone and soaked - and wanting him.

'I did not know if you would want to come tonight,' said Sam tacitly.

'I did not know where else to go,' Isabel replied numbly, taking off her soaking cloak and cap.

It had not ceased raining all week, as though the skies somehow knew her dark mood and were determined to mirror it.

It was a Monday, not her usual evening for visiting Sam, but the servants had been allowed to finish early that night as there was a dance being held in the village in honour of John and Constance's engagement, courtesy of Mr Penderton who was delighted by the union. Isabel had slipped away before any of them came downstairs: she could not bear to be part of their celebrations.

Sam noted the redness around her eyes and the weary way in which she held her head as she entered his living room. He hung up her dripping cloak and watched Isabel as she sat down in the rocking chair. Killie was sitting by it, her tail wagging expectantly but Isabel could not even bring herself to give her a pat. Killie's tail slowly dropped at the lack of attention.

'There is some food on the kitchen table,' said Sam gently.

'I am not hungry,' she replied absently.

'Come Isabel, you must eat,' he said reasonably. 'Let me make a plate up for you.'

He went into the kitchen and came back with a plate of cold chicken and some potatoes that he sat on the low table beside her. Then he lit the fire to warm the room; her misery seemed to have chilled the air when she entered. Isabel watched the flames come alive, but did not touch the food.

Sam observed her astutely for a while: her hands that hung limply by her side, red and hardened from months of labour, her stopped shoulders, weary from lifting and carrying endless buckets of water, her face tired and wretched from many sleepless nights.

'Why do you stay here, Isabel?' he asked at last.

She looked up, as though confused by his question.

'Why? For John,' she answered, as if the answer was too obvious to state.

'But, now that he has moved on, would it not be better to leave him?'

The bluntness of the question shocked her – she started away from him as though he had burned her.

'No!' she exclaimed. 'I cannot!'

He stared at her with pity in his eyes and then asked,

'But if he does marry Constance – will you still stay at Lancefield? Will you carry on working there, watching them start their lives together?'

'They are not married,' she muttered. 'There is still hope. This is just…a misunderstanding.'

Sam made a noise of frustration.

'How much pain will you take, Isabel? You need to set yourself free. The time has come to leave, surely you must see that.'

'I will never leave him,' she replied in a strangely dry voice. 'I cannot. If I let him go, I have nothing else. He is my all. I cannot give up all that was – all that could still be. To give him up… it would be to tear off a part of myself.'

'Better one painful tear than the ache of a thousand disappointed hopes, surely?' said Sam, imploringly.

Isabel did not reply. She stared ahead into nothingness, her hands hanging limply by her sides. Sam took one of them.

'Isabel, you are standing on a cliff, over a great ravine. On the other side is another cliff, level with you but several metres away. On your side of the cliff are all the horrors of your past, everything you want to forget. On the other side is a rolling valley – peaceful and quiet. You want to get there, but to do so you have to jump – a very high, very frightening jump. But once you have made it, you will be free.' His voice was urging, pleading.

Isabel turned to him, her face stubborn.

'What side is John on?'

He ran a keen gaze over her face.

'He is on your side.'

'Then I stay where I am,' she said with finality.

Sam sighed. 'You will stay in the land of dead and turn your back on the land of the living,' he said, a clear note of disappointment in his voice.

'John is not dead,' she said in a brittle voice. 'And as long as he has breath in his body, I will remain with him. He is everything to me, Sam. I have been waiting for him, my whole life, and now I have found him. I cannot leave him.'

'Your whole life,' Sam murmured softly, surveying the young girl before him.

She felt his pity. She felt anger rising up in her.

'You think you know better than I – you think I am wrong in what I choose?' she said bitterly. 'You think I should trust God and walk away from all of this? Well I have been speaking to him – I have *begged* him to answer me and restore John to me, and how has he replied? With silence!'

Sam's face was grave. She continued, aggravated by his expression:

'Tell me then, why will not God answer my prayers, why will he not make things right?'

Sam thought a moment before he replied.

'Sometimes you must put your hope in God, and not in the hope that things will change. We do not know what is best for ourselves, only he does. True obedience is when you stop pleading for what you want and lay your future down at his feet and give it to him.'

'You make it sound so easy, sacrificing your dreams,' she said dryly.

'Perhaps that is because you do not know what my dreams are, Isabel,' he said, somewhat sharply. 'It is not easy – far from it. But in doing so, there is peace.'

Isabel fell silent, galled and irritated with herself. But the sullen, stubborn demon that possessed her raised its head again and she said obstinately,

'The difference is that I need not give up my dreams, for John will not fail me.'

'We are all human,' said Sam wearily. 'We will all fail.'

Isabel made an exasperated noise.

'Must you be so pragmatic all the time!'

'I apologise,' he replied shortly. 'From now on I will be nothing but nonsense and vagueness. Would that be more useful?'

'Yes!'

There was silence. Sam took a deep breath and exhaled slowly.

'Isabel, can I say two things to you?'

'If you wish,' she replied curtly.

He watched her carefully, weighing the silence before he spoke.

'Firstly – you need to cast aside your doubts and hold fast to your beliefs. Otherwise you are anybody's fool. The girl I spoke to on that beach knew perfectly well what she believed, and you do too.'

Isabel met his eye briefly, and looked away again.

'Secondly, you think you can see no end to this misery. But you must open your eyes wider. There is hope, and there is a future for you. You have suffered much, but so have many people. We only ever see part of people's suffering – most of it is done in silence and solitude and no one around them ever knows the depth of it, or even that it exists at all. Yet few of those people ever give up – they pick themselves up and carry on. So take heart, Isabel Audley. This is not the end for you.'

Isabel turned her face down again. Sam made everything sound better when he spoke, but it was just words. She wanted to tell him to look at her heart – her starving, bleeding heart – and then tell her that it was not the end.

'You do not understand,' she said in a low voice riddled with misery.

'Then explain it to me,' he said patiently.

'I cannot! You do not see things the way I do – the way John does…'

'Am I that different from him?'

'You are as different from John as day from night,' she said ungraciously.

'Is that a compliment or an insult?'

'It is a fact, nothing more.'

Sam rose suddenly.

'We are going for a walk.'

Isabel looked up.

'Why?'

'To stop you sulking.'

Isabel also rose, her eyes furious.

'If you would like me to leave, you can simply tell me.'

'I do not want you to leave,' Sam said, frustration in his voice. 'I want to make you feel better. But at the moment I am at a loss to know how to do that, so I wonder if some fresh air might do you good instead.'

'Then I will walk myself. I want to be alone now. If you would be so good as to fetch my things, I thank you for your time.'

Her face was set like stone, her voice haughty in the extreme. Sam surveyed her with an expression of utmost gravity. She realised suddenly that she wanted him to argue with her, to give her more reason to vent her frustration, but slowly, quietly, he turned and left the room, returning with her cloak and cap. They were still wet.

'Thank you,' she replied coldly, putting the sodden clothing on with an air of stubbornness and, going out into the hall, she opened the door and marched down the garden path, leaving a trail of drops behind her.

Isabel walked so fast she was almost running. Her damp cloak clung to her infuriatingly and in her rage she cast it off, leaving it lying behind her on the grass like a dead animal. Over to the west it was raining again. She could see long grey tendrils of clouds reaching down like fingers to touch the ground. The world shifted around her as the wind blew the clouds overhead with huge force. Great walls of sunlight rushed towards her and then vanished as the sun appeared and then withdrew again behind its covering. She felt as if she was running below a giant sky battle as the scudding clouds rushed past at a great pace. Behind her was a dark cloud, larger than any of the others. She glanced back at it, shivering in her damp dress and bare arms, threatening it to come closer.

As though taking up her challenge, the great black cloud moved faster and faster until it had caught her up and soon Isabel was completely engulfed in its gloom. As it hung above her she sensed in it a presence, as if God himself was walking above her, casting his long shadow across the earth. There was great power in the darkness, its presence sending the countryside around into an awed silence. She felt suddenly cold, afraid, and terribly guilty.

'Leave me be,' she muttered uncomfortably.

As she moved quicker, so the cloud moved with her. Her steps grew faster still. She thrust her shoulders back in defiance, but inside her heart was pounding. She walked faster and faster, trying to outstrip the presence but unwilling to admit her fear by flight.

Suddenly, just as she reached the great oak tree by the school, the wind stopped and the cloud fell back. Isabel was doused in warm sunlight as the sun came out again. Heart still pounding, she broke into a run and did not look back until she had reached the door.


## ISABEL'S NARRATIVE
### (Extract from Isabel's Diary)

*LANCEFIELD, 13th May*

I know why I ran. I was ashamed. The guilt that I carried inside me seemed to become a presence before my very eyes and I feared what it would say to me.

That I am selfish.

That I am unkind.

That I am cruel and thoughtless.

That I have been cruel to the only person that has been both kind and loyal to me throughout everything that has happened.

Why did I act like that? I felt as though some kind of monster, deep within me had been unleashed. It had pillaged and ripped through all that was good in me. But the thing that scares me is that such a monster exists at all. I do not like what this world is doing to me. I need to be stronger and not let it change me so. Sam is right.

Sam. I can hardly bear to think of him. I do not deserve to speak his name. He has been nothing but kind and I have repaid him with nothing but spite. I am overcome by an urgent need to make things right with him – I want to apologise and show how much he means to me. But what if he will not see me again? I would deserve such treatment... but I do not think I could cope with it.

When I think of how he has acted towards me, I feel nothing but gratitude. He has been there for me, cared for me, listened to me – all my hasty, angry words - he has taken it all in, without judgement, and then replied, his words full of measured understanding and sympathy. Even when I have treated him badly, he has never faltered in his kindness.

I wonder suddenly, who I am becoming? I know one thing. It is not who my parents would have wanted me to become. I have bemoaned my loneliness, wept about my abandonment – but they too knew what it was to be lonely. After their marriage, they were cut off from all their friends and family. They must have wished it was not so, but they made the best of it. I appear to be making the worst of it.

I will go to the village after work on Wednesday. I will buy a bone for Killie from the butcher and some food from to cook Sam dinner (I have kept all my wages since Sam returned). I will arrive at his door with flowers in my arms and an apology on my lips. Surely he will give me another chance? I will be better this time. I know I can be.

I glance out of the window. The sun is setting now, the sky streaked with bold washes of deep orange and pink. It is beautiful. What am I in comparison to this? All my worries and troubles – my life – are nothing in the grand scheme of things. And yet he who made this, made me. He loves me, and will not abandon me, even when I bring him nothing but shame.

The sheer wonder and gladness of this thought fills me with such warmth.

Forgive me, Lord.

# XXXX

## ISABEL'S NARRATIVE
*(Extract from Isabel's Diary)*

*HONEYSUCKLE COTTAGE, account written 17<sup>th</sup> May*

I had heard in passing that servants at Lancefield were sometimes punished:

'Matt, the stable boy was horse-whipped for stealing beer from the cellar,' said Helen one morning.

Or, last week, when Sal remarked with some glee,

'Jack got it for letting his lady friend up to his room last night – will not be able to sit for weeks!'

It was always the boys, and I always thought it was an exaggeration, the girls turning a harsh word into a hard blow with their words. Mr Penderton was a fair man, I told myself, he would not allow such violence to take place in his school.


## THE STORY CONTINUED BY THE EDITOR

It was almost nine o'clock but it felt like late afternoon. The sky was still light, the air warm and the birds revelling in the prolonged singing hours. Isabel was busy cleaning the passageway that ran from the back of the house to the stables. It had windows all the way along the right hand side that looked over the gardens. They were not as immaculate as the gardens at Enderton, but Isabel liked their gentle charm: the overgrown hedgerows, sprawling flowerbeds and slightly unkempt grass. The sweet smells of the flowers filtered into the passageway and pleasured her evening chores.

Sharp footsteps from behind made her look up and she lifted her bucket and pail to let whichever teacher or pupil who was approaching walk past. She was half way through cleaning the floor – behind her were glistening flagstones, before her the dust of several hundred footprints of the day's pupils.

When she saw Adam Halthorp and his comrades approaching, she braced herself. Drawing back against the wall, she cast her eyes down to see if she could possibly avoid any more trouble. Since the hair incident she had not seen much of him, but as they approached and she glanced at him subtly through her lashes, she could already seen in his eyes the mischief that was about to play out.

'Oh look, it is the lady of the house – Isabel Snow,' Halthorp said gaily.

He came close to her – much too close - and she smelt the stink of alcohol on his breath. She was not surprised. As the head boy, with plenty of money at his disposal, Halthorp had the means to procure whatever he wished, but she suspected the intoxication would only serve to make their encounter even more unpleasant. Suddenly she wished she was not so far from the main building.

'Good evening, Master Halthorp, Yates, Messing,' she replied quietly.

Halthorp was carrying a long walking stick with a gold beast's head for the handle. She suspected it was a gift from his wealthy father. He swung it back and forth with a merry air. She could already see him in a few years time, Lord of the Estate, anything he wanted readily available to him.

'Oh, it is not Master any longer,' he said portentously. 'This is my final week at Enderton – my studies are complete and a glorious summer of prospects is commencing.'

'I am very glad for you,' said Isabel, keeping her eyes down. 'I am sure you have an illustrious future ahead of you.'

This seemed to annoy him.

'Yes I certainly do!' He stared at her, his gaze unsteady. 'Who are you anyway, Isabel Snow? I always wanted to find that out before I left. The one remaining mystery at Enderton...I think I conquered all the rest.' He cast a smile back at Yates and Messing and they sniggered.

'You know who I am,' said Isabel warily, noticing the slurring of his words and wondering just how much he had had to drink.

'Well you certainly did not start your career as a serving girl in a boarding school, that's for sure. Your manners are too high and mighty and your attitude too condescending. Were you a governess?'

'No,' she said coolly, though rage danced in her eyes. He could see it there.

'Yes, that's what you were!' he said delightedly. 'A poor governess from a once-respectable family. Then there was...' He twirled his stick, '...some scandal. You were dismissed with a ruined reputation!'

His face glowed with triumph. Hot, furious blood had begun to course through Isabel's veins. She breathed slowly, trying to remain calm.

'What was the scandal?' said Yates from behind, greedy for some gossip.

'She let the wrong man into her bedroom and into her skirts!' said Halthorp, half-shouting now, his voice filled with glee as he turned to the other boys,

There was simply nothing else for it. As he turned away, Isabel picked up her pail and promptly dumped the swillage over his head.

For a moment she thought he had frozen to the spot. She could see the dirty water running down through his hair and down the back of his expensively tailored suit. Then, slowly, he turned. His eyes were black.

'You little slut,' he said, each word spiked with hatred. 'How dare you!'

Isabel stood, her arms folded, her eyes defiant. There was a sudden noise at the end of the corridor: they turned – it was John. His tall figure, ghost-like in the semi darkness turned towards them, his face cast in shadow. It was unclear how long he had been standing there. Before Isabel could say anything, Yates called out:

'Sir, this servant has just assaulted the Head Boy!'

'Yes, did you see that Sir? She should be disciplined!' called Messing, who looked genuinely shocked by Isabel's actions.

There was a sudden gleam in Halthorp's eye. He turned, still dripping wet, to face his teacher. He raised his stick.

'Do I have your permission, Sir?'

A silent nod signalled assent and the figure turned away.


### ISABEL'S NARRATIVE
*(Extract from Isabel's Diary)*

*HONEYSUCKLE COTTAGE, account written 17<sup>th</sup> May*

I did not feel anything at first; it was like branches knocking at a window. But then the pain began. It caught, just below my spine, and spread like fire, with an unimaginable ferocity. Pain, such as I had never felt.

I did not even think about where I would go. My legs simply carried me. I only realised it was raining because my head felt wet. Every nerve in my back was screaming. My legs stumbled on, through deep puddles, through the long grass. Looking back, I do not know how I managed it.

By the time I reached the cottage, the sky was dark. I could see his lamp burning steadily in the window: a beacon in my agony. Knocking weakly on the door, I waited, the lamp's light casting a glow around my vision that was coming in and out of focus. There was no answer.

Still I waited, unable to comprehend what to do if he was not there – I could not think for the pain.

Then I heard a loud crack, and looked up, expecting to see lightning above me, but the sky was filled only with rain. Another crack. My feet carried me towards the noise at the back of the house. I saw an axe lifted high in the air, rain running in rivulets down the straining muscles in the bare arms that held it steady. The rain seemed to run in time with the lines of pain streaking down my back. Then the axe fell: the wood cleaved in half as easily as if it were made of paper. I felt the final vestige of energy slip from my body and I was gone.

## THE STORY CONTINUED BY THE EDITOR

As gently as he could, he lifted her off the ground and carried her into the house. When he laid her down on the bed, he heard the small murmur of pain and only then did he notice the spreading blood coming from the back of dress. Gingerly he turned her to lie on her front, and with the movement she woke.

'Sam?' Her voice was as thin and faint as a child's.

'I am here.'

She turned her head to look at him. Dressed in a white vest, braces and trousers, he was soaked through, but it was his eyes that caught her attention, through her haze of pain. They were burning fiercely with an emotion she had never seen in him before: anger.

'What did he do to you, Isabel? Isabel? Tell me!' His voice was fearsome, shaking with suppressed rage.

She could not find the words to tell him. There was a pair of scissors by the bedside. She motioned to them, bracing herself for the pain. Slowly, gently he used them to cut open the back of her dress. Seven dark weals, deep and long, were etched into her back like blood red snakes slicing their way through her ivory skin. Sam made a low, revolted sound at the back of his throat and Isabel knew it was as she had feared. She turned away to let the tears drip down her face, grateful only for the fact that she could not see what he did.

'I am going to have to clean the wounds,' he said, steadying his voice. He came round to the side of the bed where he could see her face and looked straight into her eyes. 'It will hurt.'

With a small nod of her head, she gave her consent, and Sam returned a few moments later with a small bowl of steaming water and several strips of white cloth.

He dipped a strip into the bowl and laid it along the first cut. It

375

calmed the burning pain, but the initial sting of whatever was in the water almost made her cry out. She bit her lip very hard as he prepared the second strip. Sam was very silent as he worked, almost fiercely silent, but his movements were tender. Isabel glanced up at him as she lay there, catching glances of his expression. His face was severe but his anger did not overpower him - his hands and eyes were steady as he worked. For that she was grateful, for every undue movement seemed to create new sensations of pain. As weariness overcame her, she shut her eyes and still he worked, quietly, sternly.

'I have done all I can do,' he said some time later, his voice sounding muffled through the darkness of her slumbers.

Her wide eyes, ringed with long wet lashes opened to gaze up at him.

'Is it so very bad?' she said softly.

She half-expected him to smile, or make a joke. He did neither.

'It will heal,' he said, his voice dry. 'But now you must sleep.'

Gently he eased another pillow under her head. She felt more stabs of pain shoot down her back.

'Are you comfortable?' he asked.

'Yes,' she lied, knowing there was nothing more he could do.

'Then I will leave you to sleep.'

He turned to go, but she called his name and lifted up her pale hand to him. It seemed like the smallest and most fragile thing in the world. He caught hold of it and kneeled down beside her.

'I am so sorry Sam,' she whispered, her voice spent and weary. 'I am so sorry for how I behaved towards you. I never meant to hurt you.'

It took him a moment to realise what she was speaking of.

'Hush,' he said softly. 'It does not matter now. Be still.'

Her eyelids fluttered shut, her eyelashes lying damp upon her flushed cheeks, but she did not let go of his hand. Sam stayed where he was. The purple tinge on her eyelids was more prominent as she slept and they flickered a little as half-remembered dreams passed beneath them. He hoped they were happy ones. He watched as she breathed deeply in and out through her slightly parted lips, the flush in her cheeks gradually fading away as she slept, her hand tight on his.

*'Rest you then, rest, sad eyes!*
*Melt not in weeping,*
*While she lies sleeping*
*Softly, now softly lies*
*Sleeping.'*

*Weep You No More, Sad Fountains* (lines 14-18), John Dowland

## ISABEL'S NARRATIVE
*(Extract from Isabel's Diary)*

*HONEYSUCKLE COTTAGE, account written 17<sup>th</sup> May*

When I awoke, my first thought was that I was in a room I had not been in before, yet it smelled so familiar. I turned my head and looked around me. I was lying on a single, black cast-iron bed and covered with a patchwork quilt, carefully folded. The walls around me were white, appearing very bright compared to the dark brick walls that I usually awoke to. They were sparse, but comforting. The window also was much bigger than my own, filling the room with morning light that streamed through. Beside me on the bedside table lay a well-worn Bible, a small vase of wild yellow roses and a photo of an older woman with three girls. They all had kind faces.

Then I remembered the night before. I remembered that I was in Sam's room. I remembered what John had done. That was when I realised the pain.

'Try not to move too much,' said Sam's voice.

I turned his head to see him standing in the doorway. He looked a little tired, as though he had not slept well. He came round to my side.

'How are you?' he asked gently.

I swallowed and tried to measure the pain.

'I am...better than last night.'

'I am glad. Your body is exhausted from the shock and today you must rest, but first I need to check your wounds.'

I nodded my assent, but only when he began to remove the first strip did I realise why he had said it so apologetically. To stop myself from screaming as he lifted off the bandages, I bit the pillow between my teeth as I lay there upon my front. He had greased the material as best he could but still it stuck to the already-healing wounds. I tried not to whimper as he pulled the material free and I felt the air rush to meet the open weals. For the first time I thought about how my body might look for the rest of my life.

Sam watched Isabel steady herself, gathering what courage she had left, and then clearing her throat, she asked,

'Is it bad?'

Her soft white flesh was ripped and scored; the blood, no longer weeping, stood in thick clots along the centre of each wound. He did not reply, but she could see the answer in his eyes. Spotting an old mirror in the corner of the room, she began to rise and said quickly,

'Let me see.'

'No,' he replied sharply, putting his hands on her shoulders. He looked at her, his eyes full of pity and said, 'Lie still for now.'

Her eyes glistened with fast-forming tears. She swallowed, and looking down, asked softly,

'Will it scar?'

He gazed fast at her.

'Yes', he replied honestly.

He saw the determination in her eyes not to cry. Searching around, she saw again the picture of the four women.

'She has your eyes,' Isabel said, her voice hoarse, 'your youngest sister.'

Sam smiled; he could not help himself.

'That is Grace. I miss her most of all. She is sixteen now. I suppose I will need to chase boys away from her soon.'

'You should,' said Isabel sincerely.

There was a sharp rap at the door.

'Excuse me a moment,' said Sam, rising.

He shut the door behind him but the window was open and Isabel could hear Mrs Clegg's insolent tones from outside.

'Is Miss Snow here?'

'Indeed she is,' Sam replied, his voice pleasant, but with a warning undertone.

'Can you explain to me why she is not at work today and why she is staying, unaccompanied, in your house?' demanded Mrs Clegg

'I think that is a question best asked of Mr Fenn,' said Sam curtly.

Isabel could almost see Mrs Clegg's raised eyebrows. There was an uncertain pause.

'Will she be back at work tomorrow?'

'No she will not.'

'The day after?'

'Neither the day after, nor the day after that.'

'May I remind you that Isabel is already facing expulsion for being found with you, never mind not attending to her duties,' spluttered the housekeeper.

'Madam, may I remind you that you face much worse for unjustly casting judgement upon this young woman, and also inform you that you will need to speak with Mr Penderton before you make any decisions regarding Miss Snow's employment as I believe the final decision lies with him.' Sam spoke with such authority, Isabel could tell Mrs Clegg was quite lost for words.

'Does Mr Penderton know about this?' she said, all authority now slipping from her voice.

'He will in about thirty minutes time,' said Sam boldly. 'And now, I must ask you to leave. Good day madam.'

The door closed. Isabel heard Mrs Clegg shuffle on the doorstep for a moment and then turn and walk back down the path, her mind clearly abuzz with confusion. Sam opened the door and came back into the room.

'That was the milkman,' he said casually. 'Now, do you mind if I go on a short errand?'


ISABEL'S NARRATIVE
*(Extract from Isabel's Diary)*

*HONEYSUCKLE COTTAGE, account written 17ᵗʰ May*

Sam said nothing of what had occurred when he went to Lancefield that morning (for I knew that was where he went, judging by his conversation with Mrs Clegg), but I heard all about it from the girls when I returned. His first call was to Mr Penderton. Apparently the two men were already on friendly terms having met several times in the village and Mr Penderton having a very great respect for the police force. Upon hearing what had taken place in his establishment the night before, he was much angered, and also very surprised, for he liked Mr Fenn and had not thought him a man to sanction such violence towards a female member of staff. Sam asked for his permission to speak with the teacher in question and the permission was granted. No one seems to know what went on during that interview.

It was also told of how Yates, Messing and Halthorp were all called to Mr Penderton's office. Yates and Messing left not long after and were unable to sit down for a week. Halthorp did not leave for many hours and when he did, he was led to a carriage without a word of farewell to anyone and was not seen at Lancefield again. His gilted cane was found in the refuse a few days later, snapped in half.

When Sam returned, he brought with him some fresh clothes for me (including my poor cloak which he found still lying in the field where I had cast it off in my temper), and also my diary. I was feeling a little better by the afternoon and highly bored of lying on my front, so after very slowly changing into a clean dress, I was able to turn and lie on my back, propped up by several pillows. I stared for a long while at the yellow roses beside me: they seemed like old acquaintances and I breathed in their scent with warm familiarity. I felt a great sense of peace in that small, whitewashed room.

## THE STORY CONTINUED BY THE EDITOR

Three days had passed. Time had done its work and Isabel's wounds were healing well. Despite the initial pain, the days had been spent in a pleasant haze of rest, good food and good company. That was what life was like with Sam, she realised: no highs or lows, just as regular and easy as breathing. When she and Sam sat down to breakfast that morning, he spoke the words she had been dreading:

'I think it is time for you to return to Lancefield, Isabel - if you are willing. I can take you back after we have eaten.'

Isabel tried not to feel disappointed. She knew she could not stay forever at the cottage, and she could not deprive Sam from his bed any longer - but it had been such a happy few days she did not think she could bear to leave.

'Of course, I could not presume upon your kindness any longer,' she replied, trying to mask her emotions.

'I have spoken to Mrs Clegg,' he said, 'and requested that you be given lighter duties for the next few weeks to allow for continued healing.'

'I am grateful, thank you.'

She knew Sam had visited Lancefield a few times in the past few days and there had been a question in her mind that she had not yet dared to ask. She glanced up at him.

'Can I ask you something?'

'Of course.'

'Did you speak to John when you went to the school?' she said, hesitantly.

Sam's face changed, taking on a grim expression.

'I did.'

'What did you say?'

'I said that his behaviour was unacceptable and that I would be keeping a close eye on what goes on at the school to ensure that such an incident does not ever happen again,' he said, purposefully.

A cold fear crept through her.

'Even though you are angry with him...you will not say anything...about what happened to Sir Branden?' she asked nervously.

She could see the struggle in Sam's eyes before he answered her. She wondered if he would ask why she was still protecting him, but all he said was,

'I will not.'

'Thank you,' she replied fervently.

There was silence as they both ate, Killie moving from one pair of feet to the other under the table in the hope of catching some scraps. Isabel ate well, knowing it would be the last good meal she would eat in several days. The thought of returning to Lancefield was beginning to fill her with a cold dread – the work, the lonely room, the cold stares...and facing John. Sam seemed to read her thoughts.

'What is wrong, Isabel?' he asked.

'I thought you wanted me to leave Lancefield,' she said, a little uncertainly, 'but now you think I should return?'

He studied her for a moment and then replied,

'If you leave now, you will be running away. You will be leaving because you do not want to face what is there. You need to leave when you are ready, when you have made the choice yourself.'

She looked back down, ashamed to find that her eyes were filling with tears. As she struggled to control them, she felt Sam's hand upon hers.

'Remember that I will be around; I will be watching you - and if you need me, I will be there,' he said steadily. 'You are not alone.'

'Thank you,' she replied gratefully.

She took a deep breath and stood up. It was time to return to Lancefield.


ISABEL'S NARRATIVE
*(Extract from Isabel's Diary)*


*LANCEFIELD, account written 18$^{th}$ May*


I was quite overcome by the amount of sympathy and well wishes I received from the other girls when I returned today. Even Sal begrudgingly asked how I was. My mistreatment seems, strangely, to have made me one of them, in their eyes. They did not even grumble when they were told I would be doing some of the lighter food preparation tasks for the next few weeks and they would have to continue to shoulder my housework chores.

I was therefore not feeling as low as I might have thought when the day drew to its close. Bidding a couple of the girls a good night, I turned to head up the servant's stairs when there he was: tall, commanding, that same strange look in his eyes. He glanced over me, addressing Helen who stood nearby:

'Miss Part requires some hot water for a patient she and Matron are attending to. Please see to it right away,' he said in a commanding tone.

Helen murmured her assent and John turned and left, without a second glance. I felt all eyes on me.

'Good night,' I said quietly and went upstairs.

As I climbed each worn step the wounds on my back twinged and stung. I remembered the day when he had told me that he would never let anyone hurt me. In my head I named him a liar. I realised then just how far apart we had become and that, despite this, his existence still continues to determine my every thought. It exhausts me.

When I reached my room I saw my little case sitting on my bed. Sam had dropped it off when he returned with me earlier in the day. I unpacked it slowly, taking pleasure in handling the few things that were my own. I had not looked at my copy of *Innocence and Experience* for many months now and I took the time now to turn through the pages. The images of *Innocence* filled me with a childish warmth and once again I felt myself back in that rocking chair with my father. But when I read the words – words that as a child I had instinctively understood - I found that the meanings had shifted and become shadowy, obscure. I no longer felt I understood the world they spoke of; it felt unknown and foreign to me, like a country I had once visited, but when I returned, had changed completely. It saddened me. I recalled a verse from Luke that I had always struggled to understand:

*'Jesus rejoiced in spirit, and said, I thank thee, O Father, Lord of heaven and earth, that thou hast hid these things from the wise and prudent, and hast revealed them unto babes.'*
*Luke* (10 verse 21), King James Bible

The meaning of the passage was perfectly clear to me now. When we are children, we are not afraid of truth. We are not weighed down by all the pain and complexity of this world. There is only what is right and wrong, what is true and false, what is good and evil. I ached for that simplicity. I ached for the Songs to sing to me again. But the Songs of Innocence now seemed as false as a fairytale. Where had it all gone wrong?

I think back to those days when I had spoken so excitedly to anyone who would listen of all my hopes and dreams for this life. Life had been like a maiden then, holding out its promises to me as one would hold a handful of bright ribbons to tempt a child. But her wares had been unfulfilling and I had passed by, moving forwards from the light into dusk. When I look back now, I can see that the ribbons were worn and mud-stained. I turn away from them, disillusioned.

Suddenly I feel old, and the last twelve months seem like a blur. Here I sit, a woman grown. A woman who has loved and lost. It has all happened so fast. I have grown up, and I missed the moment when I changed from a girl into a woman. I have passed from innocence to experience without noticing. Suddenly I long for the hand-drawn borders to spring back up and the bright colours to return. The hand of experience had grabbed me from behind and dropped me into a pit too dark for me to see out of.

I took up the book again and turned to the second half. The pages here were smooth and almost unturned. I read the *Songs of Experience* and for the first time, I understood them perfectly. I lifted my weary head and closed the book. The child Isabel was truly gone now.

# XXXXI

## ISABEL'S NARRATIVE
*(Extract from Isabel's Diary)*

*LANCEFIELD, written 22$^{nd}$ May*

I suppose you might ask if I am ready to leave Lancefield. The answer is yes. But I am too afraid.

It started with the hair. Just a single hair, upon my pillow. Why did that frighten me? It was a red hair.

I also have the strangest feeling I am being watched. You know that feeling when you can see something out of the corner of your eye, but when you look back it is gone. It has happened to me all too often these past few days.

Then there was the book, the red book that John gave me. When I came back to my room yesterday the book was lying on the floor. No one knows where I keep my books, under the floorboard where I had hidden the ring, and yet someone has found it and cut the heart out of it with a knife. When I lifted the cover, all I could see inside was a gaping hole, sliced into the pages with a savage hand. It is ruined.

There is only one person who would do such a thing.

*LANCEFIELD, written 24$^{th}$ May*

Now the thought of him has got back into my head, I cannot get it out. I tell myself again and again it is just my imagination, that the hair could have come from anywhere, blown in from any of the dormitories, or from outside, but my mind thinks otherwise.

My dreams are beginning to pick up on little details of my day and turn them into terrors. One of the teacher's young nephews was visiting today – I found him in one of the top classrooms, playing with his top in the corner of the room and singing away to himself. I had smiled at his carefreeness. Then I dreamt of him - crouching in the corner, singing as he played. I walked towards him, calling his name and he turned round, still singing, but he was Gaunt, his face twisted and strange, those terrible eyes staring at me, burning with hatred and murderous intent...

I woke up with a cry.

Isabel slept late the following morning. It was one of the few times she had done so since she started at Lancefield, for the rooster outside her window always woke her promptly at dawn.

Drip. Drip. Drip.

Isabel stirred in her sleep.

Drip. Drip. Drip.

Her eyelashes fluttered as her dreams began to release her into reality.

Drip. Drip. Drip.

She opened her eyes, blinking against the light. The red words before her seared themselves into her brain.

*'The debt will be repaid.'*

Each smeared letter dripped with an excess of blood, the long trails running down her window and distorting the hideous message almost beyond translation. But Isabel could read it. She sat bolt upright, her pupils wide with terror. The letters were large and crude, streaked across the whole window, through which the bright morning light shone, bringing the violent red hues vividly to life.

From the yard below, Isabel heard cries of horror. Too terrified to approach the bloodstained window, she slipped out of bed into her shoes and grabbing her shawl, ran down the stairs to the yard.

'They are all dead!' Helen cried. 'Every single one of them!'

The serving girls stood around her in their nightgowns, looking down. In front of them, on the cold ground lay ten golden brown hens and one great rooster, their throats crudely slit, their wings broken. Isabel stared at the line of bodies, feeling sick.

'Who would do such a thing?' exclaimed Helen.

'It's sick!' declared another girl.

'But why kill them and leave them? That's a strange thing for a robber to do?' said Sal, her usually brash voice shaking a little.

'And an even stranger way to kill them – why would they not just wring their necks?' asked Bets.

'To arrange them on the ground like this. It's like…a message,' said Helen.

The girls fell silent. A chill ran down Isabel's spine.

'We should let Mrs Clegg know,' said Sal, breaking the silence. She'll be shouting for us in a minute anyway.'

'Yes,' the others agreed, beginning to make their way back inside.

Isabel stayed behind, looking at the bodies of the creatures she had cared for, for so long. She pulled her shawl tighter around her shoulders, glanced all around, and then followed the others back into the house.

LANCEFIELD, written 25<sup>th</sup> May

He is watching me. I can see him even now. A flash of red hair disappearing round a corner in the yard. A pair of hideous eyes watching me through a dusty window. It is unnerving.

I had lived with that constant, lurking presence for so long, at first I wondered if he was a figment of my imagination – a phantom spectre forever haunting my steps, who was no more real than my dreams. But someone had killed those birds. There was only one man I knew who took such pleasure in killing innocent creatures.

Of course, I have told Sam. I could not let John's life be put at risk. It is John I fear for, you see. For how else would Gaunt repay the debt than by hurting the man who took his master from him? Sam has promised to stay near. If anyone can keep John safe, he can.

LANCEFIELD, written 27<sup>th</sup> May

It is the end of the month and summer is only one day away. I realised this with surprise this morning as I glanced at the morning paper. Where has all the time gone?

This year, I feel as though I have spent my life in the past. It has been like taking a long journey, but being given a seat that faces backwards so that you cannot see or anticipate what lies ahead, only focus on what has passed and is racing away from you. Life is awakening all around me – a new season, a new start for so many - but my heart hangs heavy in my chest and refuses to reawaken.

For there is a sense of inconclusion all around me. There is so much yet too be decided; so much yet still to happen. I feel as though I am perpetually suspended in mid air, waiting, waiting...

I saw John and Constance together last night. For all that has happened I cannot hate him; the love that burned in my heart still burns, like a silent watch fire – waiting, always waiting. And yet I can see their love also, it is as real as the love we shared, though I hate to admit it. They are so happy together; those gentle touches, quiet smiles – I can see that this is no imagined bond.

I had a sudden soft and aching thought: should I leave him? He is happy and content, with a woman who has a good heart, who would

386

love him, for all the days of his life. Surely if I truly loved him, I should let him go? I do not know, I cannot say. All I know is that I cannot. I am too selfish. But you know that already.

And danger is near.


## THE STORY CONTINUED BY THE EDITOR

The day had been hot and sticky; a storm was in the air. As Isabel stood by the sink, scrubbing the last of the pans, she was reminded of the day at Enderton when the storms had come and she had almost gone mad from the heat. It was late evening now and the temperature more bearable. She had actually enjoyed her work in the kitchen these past few days. Her feet did not ache so much now and although the cook, Mrs Fowler, was rather harsh of tongue, she had a kind heart underneath her imposing exterior and did not pick fault with Isabel as much as Mrs Clegg.

The hot plate was still smoking from a day's worth of school meals and the only light in the room was that of the candle burning next to Isabel. She heard the far off rumble of thunder and looked up to see that the candle was guttering. Within a few seconds, it had gone out.

The first stroke of lightning turned the familiar room into something strange and disturbing – a foreign landscape full of shadows and an unearthly glare. This was followed by a crack of thunder that shook the flagstone floor beneath her feet. Isabel was not usually afraid of the dark, but in the blackness she remembered why she had first feared it as a child. She hurried to the cupboard to fetch a second candle, stumbling over a broom on her way across the room.

There was a flash of light near the doorway and Isabel looked over in alarm. A match flared into life and illuminated a white face with an eerie glow. It was Constance.

'My, you gave me a fright!' exclaimed Isabel, catching her breath.

Constance held up the candle to see who was there.

'Why are you working in the dark?' she asked Isabel in surprise.

'My candle went out,' explained Isabel.

She noticed that Constance was holding a white shirt stained with what looked like red wine and remembered her duty.

'May I help you with anything, Miss Part?'

'Oh no, carry on. I just need to get this stain out of John's shirt before it sets. I did not want to bother anyone.'

The two women had not spoken since their last heated encounter in John's study, but the look in Constance's eyes was not of anger, but of compassion. Isabel slowly realised that Constance must have heard about what happened to her in the stable passageway. She wondered how it must have made her feel about her fiancé, if indeed, she knew the whole story.

'There is hot water in the pan over there and the sink to your right is clean,' said Isabel.

'Thank you,' replied Constance, setting down her candle and putting on apron that lay on the side.

Lightning scored the room again and Isabel looked around, still slightly uneasy. In the brief moment of illumination, something glinted red in the corner. It is just the copper pans, Isabel told herself, the same ones she saw hanging there every day. Constance was now at the sink, beginning to diligently scrub the shirt, her hair hanging loose down her back. Isabel was struck with an uneasy thought that from behind, dressed in an apron in that world of shadows, she looked strangely similar to herself.

Fumbling, now, for another candle, she found that the box was empty. She knew there was a second box somewhere in the large cupboard, but in the gloom, she could not pick it out.

There was the sound of footsteps across the paved floor. Surely Constance was not finished already? No, there she stood, still scrubbing at the shirt. Another noise, closer now. Isabel looked round again, furious with herself for her foolish imaginings, but unable to bear the tension. Lightning flashed again, and for a moment, in the glare of the light, she thought she had gone mad. It was him: it was Branden. She would know that greatcoat anywhere. But...something was wrong. The coat was too big, over-sized for the shrunken frame on which it hung. It was a hideous re-version of Branden, with long red hair and one eye that flashed black in the light. His shadow writhed up the wall behind him, as tall as a giant.

Isabel cried out, and at that moment, Constance's candle went dark. Whether it was caught in the breeze, or put out by Gaunt himself, she did not know. He was behind Constance now. A third stroke of lightning: Isabel caught a glimpse of his face, twisted with rage and seething hatred, his eyes gleaming wildly. His arm was raised, poised, and there was a gleam of sharp steel in his hand. She heard Constance's cry – a shriek of utter terror.

When the next clap of thunder fell, so did she. And then he was gone.

## ISABEL'S NARRATIVE
*(Extract from Isabel's Diary)*

*LANCEFIELD, written 28th May*

Pure horror turns to numbing shock. I could not move, only watch; my eyes wide with disbelief. People entered the room – paper people. They moved on sticks, lit from behind. I felt like I was watching a stage play – one of those performances they put on for children. I smiled as I watched, it was so dreamlike, almost pretty in the candlelight, but someone was tugging on my hand. I shook them off, annoyed at the interruption. When I looked back at the scene before me, the figures had cleared and I saw her again, her pale blank face lying still against the stone floor where she had fallen. Her eyes were wide, staring at me helplessly. I tried to say something, something that mattered, but all that came out was:

'There is blood – blood all over my ring.'

My star lay in a pool of red velvet. The blood had stained the stone, stained the gold. I felt so very sad as I stared at it disorientatedly. It would not shine so brightly now... who had let this happen? It should not be there, on the floor, on that white hand. I sighed. The paper person who had been tugging on my hand started to shake my shoulders and I realised that they could not be made of paper for I would not feel their movements so sharply, and when I turned I saw that it was Sam.

'Did he see it was not you?' he was asking, over and over again, his voice coming in and out of my consciousness. 'Did he see her face - did he see it was not you? Isabel, look at me!' His voice was demanding, urgent, and it woke me from my reverie.

'I...' I paused, uncertain.

'Isabel, tell me now!' he said, with uncharacteristic sharpness.

'I do not know!' I stuttered, finding my voice again, trying to recall what had happened. 'It was so dark. He left so quickly, I do not know if he saw her...her face.'

I glanced back at Constance, her eyes so open and empty. My stomach turned. Sam made a noise of frustration.

'I was following him, but he managed to lose me. I got here just a moment too late.'

I looked at him, still unable to shake the feeling of unreality. He was breathless, his face very white. He kept his hand on me, as though afraid I was going to slip away again. I blinked and looked around me. The room was filled with candles – their light casting tiny halos around the room. I saw Mr Penderton, his eyes very bright, standing in one corner. Matron was with him holding bandages – obviously brought in the hope that she would not be too late. Now they hung pointlessly in her limp hand. Around them were various teachers, but no one seemed to know what to do.

Then, the door opened and John stood before us. We all looked at him, but his eyes were fixed upon her, still lying on the floor. He walked towards her like a man in a dream, kneeled down beside her and lifted her head slightly. Her eyes stared blankly up at him. He looked back at her – his face so terribly confused. His eyes seemed to flicker, as though thousands of images were passing through them at an incredible speed. His face began to shift, though from what, to what, I could not say.

'Come, it is time to leave,' said Sam quietly.

He had a lit a candle and the beam cast a warm glow on his face. He tried to lead me towards the door, but my legs did not seem to want to move. I realised my heart was pounding in my chest like a battle drum. He scanned my face and then said,

'Breathe. Deeply.'

I exhaled.

'Again.'

I did as he said. Slowly, my heart began to fall back into its normal pace and my breathing slowed.

'Now come with me.'

I felt my feet moving in time with his, but my brain was not telling them to do so. We climbed the stairs to my room and he sat me down on my bed.

'How are you feeling, Isabel?' he asked, his face close to mine. His voice sounded so terribly worried.

'I – I cannot feel... anything,' I replied.

'Can you feel my hands around yours,' he asked, his rough hands warm and trying to rub the life back into mine.

'Yes,' I replied.

'Then you can still feel,' he said gently. 'Now, lie down and try and get some sleep.' He pulled the wooden chair out from the end of the bed. 'I will be right outside your door.'

I tried to shut my eyes and sleep but all I saw was her pale blank face against the stone floor. Those unseeing eyes, that look of confusion etched upon her colourless lips...

The wrong woman. She had taken my place by his side and now she has taken my place in death. Should I feel guilty?

I got up and looked outside my window. I had wiped hard, but there were still smears of blood on the glass. The moon was behind it: motionless, suspended in the sky. It seemed further off than usual, but still there - watching. It had a white face too.

*'The darkness deepens; Lord with me abide.'*

*Abide with Me*, Henry Francis Lyte

# XXXXII

'It is my fault,' said Sam. 'I was the one who led him here.'

Isabel stood beside him in the courtyard. At Mr Penderton's request, he had not left the school since the night before and dark circles were beginning to form under his eyes.

'What do you mean?' asked Isabel, perplexed.

Sam ran a weary hand over his eyes.

'When I was away the other week, I was actually at Harringdon. Barnes had sent me a letter telling me he thought he had spotted the man I had been looking for – thin, red hair, skulking around the place. I went up there as fast as I could but there was no sight of him. Now I realise it was a trap – Gaunt needed to know where I was, so he could follow me back to you. And he did.' He sighed heavily.

'How did he know I was with you?'

'I suspect he had a list of people with whom you might be staying. He knew we were friendly, and that I worked with Barnes. I suspect the whole trick worked quite smoothly for him. I am sorry, Isabel.'

'Do not apologise, how could you have known that was his plan?'

'I should have foreseen it. It is my job to think of these things.'

His face looked desperately grave.

'You should go home, Sam,' said Isabel, tenderly. 'You have been awake for a long time and are exhausted.'

'I cannot leave.' He turned to Isabel. 'Do you not understand? You are in danger, Isabel. Terrible danger. It will not take Gaunt long to read the paper and find that he has killed the wrong woman.'

'Surely he will not dare come back here again?' she said, trying to sound incredulous and knowing full well that Gaunt would dare anything – she had seen it in his eyes.

'I think he would risk a lot more than that. He wants you dead Isabel – that much is clear.' A question rose up in Sam's eyes. 'But why you, and not John?'

'He hated me from the moment I entered his household,' said Isabel plainly. She had thought much about this as she lay awake last night. 'John would not have done what he did if he had not been protecting me. And now I think Gaunt wants me dead for fear that if he turns me in to stand trial for Branden's murder, I might be shown mercy. He adored his master, and thinks I took Branden from him.'

Sam nodded and said,

'You agree then. I stay here. There are many bedrooms, and I know Mr Penderton will agree.'

'Very well,' Isabel agreed, with a half-smile. 'You are my watchman.'

There was a strange hush over the school for the next few days. Some of the boys were called home by their parents - it was nearly the end of term and the murder on school grounds had naturally made several parents nervous. Mr Penderton kept himself busy organising the funeral and other affairs. He had loved Constance dearly and felt her loss very keenly. The maids were sent out to pick flowers to decorate the church while John kept himself locked in his rooms, speaking to no one and leaving his meals untouched.

'It is his way of grieving,' Isabel heard Helen say as she crossed the courtyard with Bets. 'Some people like to talk when someone close to them dies, others like to keep themselves to themselves.'

But when Isabel looked up at him, standing at his window, she saw no tears or sorrow. Instead, he looked confused, like a man awakened rudely from a dream that he was enjoying, only to find he is a place he does not know. She longed to go to him, to comfort him; then, suddenly, he looked down at her. Was it her imagination or was there a faint, gentle smile upon his lips? She looked around to see if there was someone nearby, to see if she was mistaken and he was actually smiling at someone else – but she was the only one there. When she looked back, he was gone. She felt a sudden rush of hope rise in her. She tried to quell it, but it was too late. It was burning within her - that bright, shining, yearning expectation of happiness.

She found Sam by the stables, looking out over the fields, and she handed him some bread and ham.

'I thought you might be hungry,' she said, with a smile, 'and you have fed me so many times these past months it is time for me to return the favour.'

'Thank you,' he said gratefully.

It was a warm day and the sun was beating down on him. He had taken off his coat and rolled up his shirtsleeves. Several of the girls walked past, giving him warm smiles and appreciative glances.

'I fear you have been invited into a den of wolves,' said Isabel lightly.

'I think I will survive,' he said, returning her smile.

Isabel looked out over the fields, basking both in the sun and in the warm glow that had filled her heart.

'You look well today,' said Sam.

Isabel looked up at her friend, unable to keep silent about the hope within her.

'I think…I think John might be coming back to himself,' she said tentatively.

'What do you mean?' he asked, wariness leaping into his eyes, but Isabel was staring out over the fields and did not notice.

'He looked at me a moment ago – and his expression was so different from how it has been the past few months…it looked like he was smiling.'

She glanced up at Sam, her face radiant, and instantly realised he did not share her happiness.

'What is wrong, Sam?' she faltered.

'Isabel – I mean this in the kindest possible sense – do not get your hopes up over one throwaway glance.'

'It was not throwaway!' she exclaimed. 'He was looking right at me.'

Sam looked away, shaking his head.

'He is not in his right mind, Isabel.'

'You do not know what is going on in his mind,' she said passionately, unwilling to give up. 'Perhaps the death of Constance triggered something…some kind of reawakening within him.'

'Well that would be convenient timing,' remarked Sam dryly.

'Do not mock me,' said Isabel, softly.

'I am not mocking you, Isabel,' he said, quite seriously. 'I am concerned for you.'

Isabel looked troubled, confused at his reaction. He tried to make her understand.

'The openness of your heart does you credit, Isabel. But do not let it lead you into yet more pain. You must protect yourself. You have overcome so much in the past few months; I do not want to see you made to suffer anymore.'

'But if he remembers, it would not lead to suffering – it would lead to happiness,' she said in a small voice.

He looked at her; it hurt him to see the hope slipping from her face.

'Perhaps,' he said softly.

Sam returned to his usual duties a few days later. Despite the fact that he still stopped by the school whenever he could, Isabel missed his constant presence and therefore was therefore looking forward to the coming Wednesday when they could spend the evening together. She finished her work promptly that day - with the school half-empty, her chores were minimal. As she washed her hands and hung up her apron, she looked out of the window to the green fields that lay beyond the school walls. The evening was warm and she was looking forward to her walk to Sam's.

She left through the kitchen back door that led to the stable yard. As was her custom, she glanced up at John's window, but that evening, no one was there. She tried to feel glad: perhaps he had finally come downstairs to be with the other teachers, relieving himself of his misery, but she missed seeing him.

A hand grabbed her by the arm and she swung round, her heart pounding, fearing that the murderer had returned, but it was not Gaunt. John stood there, his face anguished and hair unkempt. His eyes were wide and wild, staring at her with desperation. Isabel stepped back in fright, aghast at his expression. His eyes bored into her like knives.

'Who are you?' he said, his voice urgent, pleading.

Isabel struggled to catch her breath.

'Isabel. Isabel Audley,' she replied startled. She did not even bother to lower her voice, such was the intensity of his question.

'To me?' he almost cried, 'Who are you to *me*?'

'Unhand her!' said a commanding voice, and they turned to see a figure striding towards them at great speed.

'Sam!' she gasped.

'Who are you?' John asked urgently again, turning her attention back to her.

'I am – ' Isabel began, but John interrupted,

'No! Do not tell me - I cannot bear it!'

He cast a hand over his face so that he could not see her, and then began to stumble off. Isabel made to hasten towards him in concern, but Sam held her back.

'I must go to him,' she said earnestly, pulling against Sam's grip.

'No – I will go,' said Sam firmly.

There was a stern frown on his face; she read in his eyes an angry warning. Unwillingly, Isabel watched him cross the yard after John, following him into the stables. She wanted to go after them, to hear what was said, to protect John, but she stayed still. She could hear the low rumble of Sam's voice from inside, gathering momentum. Then she heard movement, both men's voices, loud and angry. She rushed forward, fearing an altercation, and saw Sam leaving the stable.

'I will not stay and quarrel with you, sir,' he said curtly to John, who was still inside, 'for I see that your life is a quarrel with itself. May you one day find your true nature.'

He turned to see Isabel. His face was still dark.

'I am afraid I have some business to attend to, Isabel. Can I meet you at my house in an hour?'

'Of course,' she replied, staring past him and trying to make out John's figure in the darkness of the stable.

Sam glanced at her for a moment and then walked away brusquely.

Isabel entered the stable. John stood at the back, half-hidden in shadow. A strange look came over his face as walked came towards him and then his expression suddenly softened. It was like a light over dark ripples of water. Hope tugged inside her chest, but the noise of some other servants crossing the yard made him start. Isabel looked round, hoping that they would not enter, but when she turned back round, John was gone.

Her heart sinking, she left the stable yard and made her way down the lane and into the fields, the dry grass brushing against her legs. It was almost up to her waist now, grown tall under the hot summer sun. She grasped a stalk and pulled her fingers up through it, stripping the dry seeds from the grass and scattering them into the balmy air. Absentmindedly she did this again and again as she walked, casting the seeds out into the air. They floated around her in the almost indistinguishable breeze, hiding themselves amongst the folds of her dress and catching in her short curls.

The feel of the grass, the warm air, the scents of the wildflowers, all reminded her of Harringdon. It was almost a year to the day that she had arrived there; she remembered the sunshine, Cathy rushing down the steps to meet her. How much had happened since then. She looked up and noticed that the one tree that had stubbornly refused to blossom when all the others did, was now in full bud. She supposed it had just needed time.

It did not take her long to reach the cottage. The door was unlocked and she left it ajar to allow a gentle breeze into the house. The living room door was open and she went in, breathing in the familiar scents contentedly. Several letters lay open on the small low table in the centre of the room. It looked like Sam had left in a hurry that morning for he did not usually leave things lying around. She sat down in the rocking chair, and glanced down at the letters. One word caught her eye, written across several of the pages. It was her name.

She tried not to glance back, but it was too late – her interest was piqued. Why were people writing to Sam about her? Drawn as to a magnet, she looked back down. The top letter was long and written in a sweet hand, obviously female. The words flashed past her eyes and entered her mind before she could stop them…

*(page 2)*

*I am glad that Isabel is feeling stronger now. She will appreciate your friendship during this time. You have been there almost five months now, have you not?*

*Mother says not to worry too much about the money. She has been doing some mending for a local family and that is bringing in a little extra income, as does my cleaning job. It is not your responsibility to care for us for the rest of your life. You have always put us first Sam, but the time has come for you to seek a life of your own.*

*Why not find another town where you can work – a lovely town near the countryside where you can walk Killie and at the weekend write more of your wonderful stories? You have not sent some for so long and Grace loves to hear them (She is so tall now – you will not recognise her!). We have managed these past months quite well and you must start to save for the future so you can buy a house of your own.*

*It is cruel that you, who have never asked for anything in your whole life, cannot have the one thing you want, but you should try to move on. It would be better for you, Sam. I know you will not admit it, but you were too late.*

*I hope you know that I could not ask for a better brother. You have kept us looking up when times were hard and you always got us through. I only wish that now you might find some happiness of your own. May God grant you that.*

*Your loving sister,*
*Elizabeth*

Mind whirling, Isabel moved this letter away so she could see the one underneath, wanting to read it before her conscience caught hold of her and shook her by the scruff. The writing was larger and more ragged – a man's hand:

*…I have tried again to get you on full pay, Sam, but they will hear none of it. They say you are lucky to be on half in that tiny village. If you are still struggling for money, let me know. No point in spending all your savings just for her. You have your whole life ahead of you.*

*In answer to your question, Isabel is still classed as 'Missing,*

*Presumed Dead.' Do you appreciate the irony in that you, who never stopped searching for her, now want her to remain classed as this? But I appreciate it is for her safety. I will make sure nothing changes.*

*I am sorry to hear of how Treador treated her the other night. You know you could always have him arrested? From what you told me, the conditions around Branden's death were very suspicious. He would be prosecuted for manslaughter at least. But I know your sense of justice would not allow this. I suppose she would never forgive you either. It was certainly Gaunt who started the fire once he knew Branden was dead, I am sure of that. The other five men, and all the servants, have disappeared like water. Knew how to cover their traces that lot. But then, I suppose that was why they were hired.*

*Anyway, I must get on. Think about what I said last time. There are plenty of others out there. You took the only role open to you and now you are stuck in it. It will not lead to what you want.*

*You know where I am.*
*Guy.*

'What are you doing?'

Isabel jumped, and turned to see Sam standing there. His face was white.

'I – I am sorry, I saw my name and…' she stumbled.

'Did you read them?' he demanded tersely.

'Yes,' she admitted, shamefaced.

There was silence. For a moment she thought Sam was going to be furious with her, but his expression changed from fury to sadness.

'Then as atonement for your reading of my letters I will ask you not to mention them again.'

'But Sam!'

'No! They are my private business and I do not want to discuss them.'

She could make no argument, though she could not halt the questions that filled her mind as she watched him gather up the papers and stuff them into a drawer in the corner. The first letter said that Sam had been here five months and yet she had only known him here three; the second letter said that he was on half pay, though the reason was not given – why was this? And why were they both urging him to leave? Isabel felt a sudden panic.

'Are you going away from here soon, Sam?' she asked.

'I said that I do not want to talk about it,' he replied shortly.

'But I need to know.' Her voice was pleading.

He looked round and saw the terror in her eyes. His stern face relented.

'I am not going anywhere at the moment,' he said, a little more gently. 'And I apologise for leaving my personal affairs out. I should have realised they would cause you interest. I was called out unexpectedly to attend a theft in the village this morning and did not have time to clear them away.'

'I am very, very sorry,' said Isabel, and she looked it. 'I have let you down.'

'Let us speak of it no more.'

There was silence between them. Isabel glanced out of the window where night was falling. She searched for a change of conversation. Her glance fell upon the line drawing of Cranwell above the fireplace.

'I was reminded of Harringdon tonight,' she said. 'The summer walks, the beach, Cathy...I was reminded of how much I have changed.'

'You have not changed at all,' said Sam, sitting down beside her. 'You are the same girl that I met all those months ago. You just have a little more experience of the world.'

She looked up at him, wondering at his ability to always see things in such a positive light.

'I wish I could be who you want me to be,' she said with a small smile. 'I wish I could be as good as you want me to be.'

'Isabel – I want, I have only ever wanted, you to be yourself,' he replied steadily.

'And yet so much of myself is tied up with him,' she said, a little wistfully, thinking of his soft glance in the stables.

'I do not believe that,' said Sam forcefully. 'He has no hold on you now if you do not want him to. You are no longer tied to him, Isabel. You are free to leave whenever you wish.'

Isabel wondered at his sudden change of heart – did he now want her to leave Lancefield?

'But why would I leave now, when he is suddenly free again...' The words died on her lips when she remembered at what cost his freedom came. 'And besides,' she hurried on, 'where would I go? – I have no money.'

'Your inheritance is still waiting for you,' reminded Sam.

'But if I claim it - if I come forth - you know that the police will want to speak with me. They will not be as... understanding as you.'

'But what do you have to fear?' he asked.

'It's not me who must fear – it is John!' she exclaimed. 'They will find where he is and arrest him for murder.'

'Why should you have to forsake your future as a result of his actions?' Sam demanded.

'I have no choice,' she said heavily. 'I will not give him up.' 'Isabel, you will have no life if you stand by that man,' said Sam fervidly. 'You are enslaved to him – trapped. And if you do not break free soon, the doors of your cage will close forever...'

'Sam,' she said in a tired voice, holding up her hand to halt his words. 'I will not give him up.'

She watched him turn away in frustration, biting back further words. She wished she could make him understand. Silently, she searched for the words.

'Do you understand what it is to wait for someone?' she asked, after some time had passed.

'I do,' he replied, his voice low.

'Then you will understand that if there is any small hope, you must stay. I must stay.'

He smiled at her, his eyes full of sorrow.

'Do you know, that you have one of the truest hearts I have ever known, Isabel Audley.'

'What do you mean?' she asked, a little uncomfortable.

Sam paused for a moment and then spoke, his voice gentle and full of emotion,

'You had a childhood that would have crushed many, and yet you came out of it full of optimism and overwhelmingly kind. You were betrayed by your family and forced into an entrapment that would have been unbearable to most people, yet your spirit remained strong. You are fiercely loyal to John. I understand that, truly I do.' His expression grew more serious. 'But do not let this last trial crush you when you have overcome so much. Your story would give encouragement to many, Isabel. The girl who was so full of hope when all else seemed black; who overcame despite so many obstacles. Let that be the story they tell of you; not that you gave up in the end, waiting, alone, for something that would never happen.'

Isabel did not know what to say. She stood up slowly and turned towards the window, her heart very heavy. Outside, the moon shone brightly.

'You know, I think the moon follows me wherever I go,' she said softly.

'It does. If you travelled to the far side of the world it would go with you.' Sam's voice came from behind her, deep and steady.

'I believe I have often equated the moon with God,' she admitted. 'It has the same comforting presence,' he acknowledged.

Isabel knew he did not fully understand her, but she gave a small nod in agreement. She felt his hand upon hers and turned.

'You know I will always be there when you need me, Isabel,' he said, his words heartfelt.

She looked up into his warm brown eyes and smiled a gentle smile, though she felt desperately sad.

'I am only sorry if I have caused you any trouble,' she replied.

'No, it has been my pleasure to spend so much time with you here,' he said sincerely.

'Indeed, what would you have done without me these past months?' she said, trying to inject a smile into her voice.

'I would have had a lot of emptiness to fill,' he replied.


## ISABEL'S NARRATIVE
### *(Extract from Isabel's Diary)*

*LANCEFIELD, written 1ˢᵗ June*

I try to walk away, but my legs do not want to make the steps. Something is drawing me back. I force them to move, onwards through the tall grass. I know he is standing behind me at the gate. Inexplicably, tears are falling from my eyes. I feel as though I am making a monumental decision, though I do not fully understand it.

I glance back at Sam and our eyes meet. I want him to call out to me, but he does not, and I look away, feeling the moment fall away to that dark place where all the lost opportunities go, never again to rise.

On the horizon, there is a girl, her outline hazy. She looks very young and has long blonde hair; a daisy chain flutters in her small hand. She looks at me, so sadly. I gaze at her, and she begins to fade. I have made a terrible mistake, I know I have. The girl follows me like my own shadow, full of reproach.

Before me are two tracks through the fields. I walk along one of them, the other is empty. I realise that these are the paths Sam and I have made as we passed through the fields over the past weeks and months. I have always walked on his left hand side on the way there and on the way home, so between my light feet and his sturdier walk, the paths had evened themselves out into equal width and depth. I wonder how long they will stay that way.

I reach the schoolyard, feeling as though I have traversed miles to get there. My eyes are drawn to the window. John stares back at me from above. He gives me a searching look and I stare back, trying to tell him who I am; tell him all that we had been. I feel very lost – I need him more than ever. He glances away. Did he understand? It is too dark – I cannot see. Despair covers me. Will he ever remember?

Sam is right, I am wasting my life here.

After my kidnap, when John entered my life – that terrible, wonderful period – I believed that I had not thought of Sam for many months. But now, I realise that he had always been there. He had been that same, comforting place in my mind that I fled to when I had nowhere else to go. When John left me, when I had felt so alone, Sam was the stable presence that had never left me, even though I was not fully aware of it.

I lie in bed and try to comfort myself with my dreams of John. But they seem misty – like vapours that slip from my fingers even as I try to catch them. They are no comfort compared to Sam's solid presence, his reassuring words of friendship. I realise with a terrible ache that Sam is going to leave me soon. He had seen tonight that my mind would not change, that I am set on this course - and he will not stay to watch himself proved right.

## THE STORY CONTINUED BY THE EDITOR

Morning dawned. There was no cockcrow. Isabel sat up in bed and shivered. Perhaps she knew that this day would reveal all of us for who we truly were.

She got up and dressed. As she went downstairs she could hear quite a commotion in the kitchen.

'What is going on?' she asked Helen, who was standing nearest the door.

'It is Mr Fenn – he has left in the night!' Helen exclaimed. 'He did not tell anyone – just packed up and went. Mr Penderton is so angry.'

Isabel grasped the table, feeling suddenly faint.

'Does anyone know where he went?' she asked breathlessly.

'No – no one saw him go. It was not until Mary went in to clean his room this morning that anyone realised he had gone.'

Isabel swallowed hard. She tried to tell herself that she had known this would happen – that it was a good thing, but she felt nothing but despair. Perhaps she could try and follow him? Someone must have seen something.

'This is for you.'

Isabel looked up. Sal stood there, holding something out to her.

'Excuse me?'

'Mary found it in his room. It's addressed to you.'

Isabel looked down. Sal was holding out an envelope, with her name written on it. She knew that writing – it was John's hand. She struggled to contain her emotion as she took it; her hands were shaking.

'Well, go and read it then,' said Sal.

Isabel looked up and found to her surprise, that Sal looked as eager as she did.

'There's no one in the scullery if you want some privacy,' Sal added, with an almost friendly glance.

Nodding gratefully, Isabel slipped out of the kitchen and down into the empty scullery. She locked the door behind her and held the envelope in both hands. Suddenly, her pleasure turned to panic. What if it was a farewell note? What it if was a letter telling her he had never loved her, that his actions had been borne out of pity and not affection? That he had finally freed himself in the only way he knew how... Her hands began to shake again.

There was a kitchen knife next to her on the worktop. She lifted it up, took a deep breath, and then sliced open the envelope. The words swam before her eyes, and she blinked, calling them into order.

*My darling Isabel,*

*My own one. Every day the memories have become clearer; every day your face shines out more brightly, until at last I remember who you are to me. It is as though you have been hidden by a dark cloud for so long, but slowly the light has pierced through in bright shafts, until at last I realise with some sadness and much joy, who I am, who you are, and all of our precious story.*

*But do not think that I had forgotten you completely during all of this: you were constantly in my mind, beating on the misted pane of glass that stopped me from seeing you fully, from hearing your voice. And when I dreamt, it was always of you. I dreamt of you in a field - a field of white – twirling, twirling, forever twirling, calling the snowflakes down by name. My snow nymph caught forever in a frozen moment of time. If only I could have seen your face through the snow.*

*But it has taken you so long, I hear you say - so long to remember. I am sorry. During these months of darkness and confusion, I have been lost in a maze with no way out - but you have led me to the centre where you waited so patiently. The veil is lifted. I see only you. Still disguised as I disguised you, but living a life I never meant you to live.*

*I can only imagine what you have been through in these long months. I can only thank you for waiting.*

*I know the danger we are in, but I must see you; I can wait no longer. Meet me at the place where it all began. I will be there when the clock strikes midnight.*

*We will be together again my love,*

*John*

Isabel stood, savouring the sweetness of the moment. The power of the words rushed through every fibre of her being – those words she had longed to hear every day for five long months. She was filled with a fire-like heat, there was a sweet taste on her tongue and she trembled with the pure delight of it all, breathing the words in like fresh air to a drowning soul.

'Now,' she said softly, her eyes alight. 'To Enderton.'

It did not take Isabel long to pack, but she did take the time to leave a short note for Mr Penderton, thanking him for his kindness to her during her time at Lancefield. She stood on the threshold of her room, case in hand, and looked back at the small dark space, dumb to all that had been suffered in it. Then she closed the door behind her.

She went down the stairs and through the kitchen. It was empty – the servants must have been called to the great hall for an end of term service. She went out the door and into the yard. She had one final person to see – and just enough time to see him before she caught the coach north back to Enderton. She started to run, through the gateway and into the fields.

'Isabel!' a voice called after her.

She turned, still half-running, her skirts held up amidst the long grass. It was Sal.

'He loves me!' Isabel called out to her, her voice full of joy.

'Then good luck!' Sal called back, and for the first time, Isabel saw her smile.

And so Isabel ran towards the cottage, full of happiness, full of hope.

What fault can be found in this, you may ask? Only the fault of untempered youth. We cannot judge her.

*'But the time will come – at last it will,*
*When, Evelyn Hope, what meant (I shall say)'*

*Evelyn Hope* (lines 33-34), Robert Browning


He saw her coming through the fields from a long way off: she was holding up her skirts and running - running as he had never seen her before. Her hair was loose; it was growing longer now, and glinted gold in the bright sunshine. But one thing caught his attention more than all the rest. She was smiling – smiling with everything she had. Sam stood up a little straighter, placing the last book in his open case, hope rising within him. Then he saw the suitcase in her hand. Joy filled his heart – she had made her choice.

Isabel wondered at his glad expression as she grew nearer. Did he already know the happy news she had to tell him?

'I have not seen you looking so radiant since I first saw you step out of that carriage at Harringdon,' he called out as she approached.

Her face was aglow as she shouted back,

'He has written to me, Sam – he remembers, he remembers everything!'

She held up the letter with elation as she tumbled up the path towards him. A cascade of expressions passed over Sam's face. He controlled himself, with an effort, but when Isabel reached the doorway, she watched him turn away from her smile, as though unwilling to share in its joy. There was a moment's painful silence as she tried to understand his reaction. Finally, with no pretence at good humour, Sam said gruffly,

'So he remembers, does he? What does he say?'

Attempting to overcome his chilly reception, Isabel walked into the living room, holding the letter out before her and reading every word aloud with lips that trembled with delight. Sam's face was tenebrous; he kept his eyes cast down. When she read the final line, Sam struck out at the wall in front of him with violent anguish, and then sunk down into his chair in surrender.

'What is wrong, Sam?' Isabel asked, in shock.

'So you will go to him, will you?' he asked bluntly.

'Of course I will.'

Sam's gaze was grave and unrelenting. Isabel felt the rebuke in his eyes keenly.

'I do not understand; are you not happy for me?' she asked, confused. 'You, of all people, should understand how wonderful this is! You, who alone know what I have been through.' Her voice was filled with appeal as she tried to make him understand, to make him share in her joy: 'You will be able to live your life in peace now; I will no longer be a burden to you.'

The pain in Sam's eyes was immeasurable.

'A burden? Is that what you think you have been to me?'

Isabel looked troubled.

'But I have taken so much of your time, of your efforts. I have been a worry and a care to you that you should not have to deal with. Now you can be free – is that not what your family want, what your sister was referring to, in her letter?'

Sam stared at her, despair in his eyes. Killie slunk in beside him and nuzzled at his leg. The movement seemed to distract him and he stroked her, gently. Then he began to speak softly to her, as though he was reciting something:

'When you finally find the thing you have been looking for all your life and are not willing to fight for it, then what sort of a man are you?'

Killie stared back at him, her eyes soft and sad. Isabel looked at them both, puzzled and Sam sighed deeply.

'Will you not sit, Isabel?'

She took the chair next to him. He looked deeply at her before speaking, as though trying to measure something within her. She looked back, hoping not to be found wanting, and then he began to speak,

'After you were taken, I searched for you, Isabel. I scoured the whole country but there was no trace of you. I exhausted every source, every lead failed. I was frantic in my powerlessness. They all told me you were dead, but I said that was impossible - you could not die. Not you, not yet.' There was an unfaltering clarity in his gaze as he spoke and Isabel stared back, captivated yet confused. He continued, 'And then I found you, quite by chance, here at Lancefield. I cannot tell you what relief I felt when I saw you by the well: exhausted, broken, but alive. I was ready to take you away from that place. To help you live your dreams and accomplish all that you had hoped to accomplish. And then I realised: you belonged to another, and nothing I could do then would change that fact. So I became what was required: you needed a friend, and so I was there. And there I waited, waiting for the world to change.'

Something was building in Isabel's chest, an emotion she could not explain. Sam looked at her anxiously, to see if she understood, but he could see that she had not grasped what he was saying, not fully. His words were straining to touch her, like waves on a shore trying to brush a white shell that was just beyond their reach. He sighed deeply.

'Do you really mean to go back to him, Isabel - after everything that has happened?'

'I do,' she replied sincerely. 'You know I am grateful to you Sam - so grateful - and I respect your advice, as a friend – as my closest friend. But I will do as John asks.'

'Don't go, Isabel – please.' Sam's voice was soft with entreaty

'Why not?' There was a hint of exasperation in her voice now.

'Because the meeting will only disappoint. Because he will let you down – again. Because you are finally beginning to heal, and this will tear you apart. Seeing you in pain breaks my heart, I cannot bear it any longer.'

It was the first time Isabel had heard Sam speak so quickly, so urgently. There were no measured pauses, just pure passion of speech – but it angered her that he disagreed with her so fervently.

'I am in pain no longer!' she exclaimed.

'But you will be again,' he said quickly. 'Going back to him does not secure you a happy future Isabel – the very opposite!'

'But, but he remembers – he remembers me now!' She felt tears springing to her eyes. Why would he not just let her be happy?

'Yes, he remembers *now*,' said Sam. 'But he forgot you for many months - how can you have forgotten?' His words were coming faster now. 'He has ignored you to your face, treated you like dirt, forced you to work like a degraded slave, watched you have the flesh cut from your back – '

'Stop Sam!' Isabel shouted, tears in her eyes. Panic was surging through her. She wanted to stop his words, to clasp her hand over his mouth and make them unsaid – they were too terrible to exist. 'Just stop it! You do not know him – you do not understand. He had an accident. He injured his mind. That was not his fault.'

'How long will you defend him, Isabel,' said Sam bitterly.

'As often as he is maligned,' she retorted.

There was a pregnant silence. Then Isabel spoke, her voice gentler:

'I know I am disappointing you in going back to him, Sam - and this grieves me. But you knew this day would come. It is what I have hoped and prayed for. I cannot turn my back on him now. I cannot give up on all that we were – all that we can be. My suffering is at an end.'

'Your suffering cannot end, as you set its salvation upon the head of its source,' Sam broke out, his voice full of anger.

Isabel felt the heat rising up between them.

'I know you have never liked John, but there is no need to let your prejudice taint my happiness,' she said, with some vexation.

'I care for you,' replied Sam shortly. 'I have always cared for you and I will continue to protect you for as long as you allow me – and a little after that. But sometimes that means protecting you from yourself.'

Something was rising in his eyes – something that Isabel had often glimpsed, but never understood. She felt suddenly afraid. She did not want the next moment to happen, for after it, everything would be different.

'I must go now Sam,' she said quickly, half-rising. 'I will write to you tomorrow and let you know where I am.'

'No,' he said heavily, putting his arm out to stop her. 'There is something I must say to you before you leave.'

'But I will be late,' she said, desperately.

'Isabel, please stay for a moment longer. I must speak with you.'

She relented at the pleading look in his eyes and the urgency in his voice, despite the foreboding in her heart.

'Of course Sam,' she said, sitting back down. 'Of course I will listen to what you want to say. Forgive me.'

She gazed up him, trying to control the misgiving within her. His face was pale, like a man stepping out to his death. He took a deep breath and then spoke,

'I can remain silent no longer, Isabel. Your actions force me to speak. I would have kept this from you, until you were ready, but I cannot let you leave here without knowing how I feel.'

'What do you mean?' she said falteringly.

'Can you not see?' he said, desperation in his voice. 'Isabel, could you not always see, that I love you?' Isabel moved back as though struck.

'What? You do not love me!' The words left her mouth before she could stop them. 'Why would you say that – it is not true!'

Sam's face was full of anger and frustration, but she found herself continuing, her words tumbling out,

'You must not say such things, Sam. You must not. You do not love me, I know it!' She knew she was babbling, but she must keep talking, or else his words would sink in and become a reality that she could not face.

'Do I not love you?' he demanded.

'No!' she exclaimed, her words almost pleading.

'Then why am I here, Isabel?' he appealed. 'Hundreds of miles from my post, living on almost no pay, serving a village that do not need me? Why – Am – I – Here?' He was almost shouting now, his face taut.

'You are here because you are my friend,' she said in a choked voice. 'I – I thought you were my friend…'

'And I am – ', he said, making a visible effort to calm himself. 'I did not lie to you in that. I am and always will be your friend.' He looked at her sadly. 'I could not burden you with any more than that when we met. But I thought you would come to realise...over time, that I am a friend who loves you as a man, a friend who wants to always be by your side, to love you with the first and fiercest love.' He sighed heavily and for a moment, in the fading light, he looked much older than his years. 'It started as a captivation,' he said heavily. 'I thought it would pass – you were a beautiful girl from a beautiful world who was not meant for me. But then, as I came to know you better, that feeling grew into a hope. I tried to stop it but it grew as strong as ivy and bound itself around my heart.'

His voice was hoarse; Isabel could not bear it. She could not be here, listening to this. It was too much. She had made her decision, she did not need to hear this too. She found herself moving away from him as he spoke.

'Isabel?' he said, sounding hurt.

'I took you at your word,' she replied, anguish in her voice. 'You said you were my friend. I cannot give you any more.'

Pain crossed Sam's face and he looked sad, sadder than she had ever seen him.

'I love John,' she said, her voice very small. 'You know that I love John.'

'Yes, I know,' he said, forbearingly. 'And I know that I ask too much – more than you could ever give. You have come here as my friend, and I have burdened you with a load you should not have to bear.'

'And can we not just be friends?' Isabel asked beseechingly. 'Can we not just carry on as we were before?'

Sam sighed heavily.

'Oh Isabel, I will never be satisfied with half of you. I have tried, believe me. I have tried harder than I have ever tried at anything. But I have failed. I cannot only love half of that which makes me whole.'

Isabel turned to stare out of the window and hide her falling tears. This could not be happening; this was not how it was supposed to end. Sam spoke in a gruff voice beside her:

'I love you Isabel. I have always loved you.'

The words smote her soul. She felt his lips brush her hair for an instant and she pushed him from her.

'No,' she said in a strangely dry voice.

She could not cope with this: it was too real, too possible. She wanted John; she wanted to return to her dreams. She turned to face

Sam, her eyes bright, determined, and he saw in that moment that there was no way to break through. His shoulders sagged and he moved away from her once more.

'Then there is nothing more I can say. You do not love me – I will try and accept that....' He sighed heavily and then looked at her, his eyes fierce. 'But do not go to him.'

Anger rose within her at his words.

'Why, Sam? Because if you cannot have me, you do not want anyone else to?' she said, heatedly.

Sam did not reply. She felt the words come tumbling out and she flung them at him defiantly, her hurt making her cruel:

'Why do you tell me of your feelings now, Sam? You have known me for almost a year – why tell me now? Is it because I am a mere servant you see fit to express your feelings?'

'I would have done so whether you were Queen of England or a peasant girl,' he replied crisply, ' – it was circumstance, not station, that sealed my lips.'

'I do not believe it – you would not have dared speak thus if I were still at Harringdon, a lady.'

'You know that is not true,' he said steadily. 'Isabel, I know that you are angry...'

'Do not presume that you know me at all, Sam Hardy,' she lashed out, her anger prevailing. 'You have never known me.'

The words stung him, but he continued:

'That may be true. But by this decision, I will know you better.'

'Then let me reveal myself to you.'

Isabel rose to her feet; he imitated her.

'You go to an unworthy man, Isabel,' he said, his gaze unrelenting.

'You think you can judge him – judge us?' she said wildly. 'You have no idea...you do not even know what it is to love!'

Sam gave a bitter laugh. It sounded cold and alien on his lips.

'You think I do not know love?' he said dryly. 'Do not think you understand my heart, Isabel. Do you think I have not known pain or joy – do you think that I have not known sorrow in the name of love? To find you and then learn that you had been torn from me? To hope again, and again, that you might come back to me, and always have my affections flung back in my face?'

'Come back to you? Sam – I was never yours!' she exclaimed.

'I see that now. I see that I could never have won you. But something in you always inspired me to hope. How foolish I was.'

Isabel said nothing. It hurt her to see him despair, but she had no words of comfort. They stood, staring at each other, the twilight darkening around them.

'I must leave now,' she said at last. 'I have a coach to catch.'

Sam's face was lined with sorrow.

'Do not go,' he said, his voice breaking. 'If I cannot have you, then give yourself to someone who deserves you. Someone who will honour and protect you.'

'He will protect me!'

'But he has not honoured you. He has not shown his affection for you. I would have you *loved* Isabel, loved before all others.'

'I will be,' she said, though this time there was no certainty in her voice.

'Does he love you?' asked Sam quietly. Noting her hesitancy, he shook his head, saying, 'Why must you continue in your quest for happiness with that man? It is hopeless, Isabel.'

She turned away and his eyes darkened.

'Do you know how it kills me to watch you every day, pinning your ragged hopes upon him again and again, only to have them dashed every time?' He paused - he knew his next words would sting, but he could hold back no longer. 'Men do not *forget* the women they love, Isabel. There must be something in them that wants to let them go. God knows, I have tried to forget you,' he said darkly. He could see the anger in her eyes but there was no going back now; there would never be another time. 'Let me tell you something, Isabel - men only forget what they want to forget. No man can have you in his life and not remember you were once his. Look closely! See what you do not want to see! John Treador has used you, and abused you, and is now using you again. He is a liar and a coward and your future with him will be nothing but wretchedness.'

Isabel stood stock still as though frozen, her eyes fixed wide upon him. Then, with the speed of a whip cracking, she struck him sharply across the face. Her eyes blazed with fire.

Sam did not flinch. He said not a word, his left cheek burning a deep red with the force of her blow. His face was dark and weary, worn out by suppressed emotion. He turned away from her, hiding the red mark she had inflicted.

'I first saw you a year ago today, Isabel,' he said sadly.' You were beautiful. You still are.' There were tears in his eyes as he looked at her. 'Do not force me into a goodbye. Not now, not after everything.'

'Goodbye Sam,' she replied, picking up her suitcase - and without glancing back at him, she went from the room, forced open the door and ran down the rose-strewn path, trampling the pale petals under her feet.

## ISABEL'S NARRATIVE
*(Extract from Isabel's Diary)*

I broke my mother's crystal horse a few days after she died. It had been her favourite ornament. I remember sitting on the floor beside the pieces, tears sliding down my face. I knew I had broken something very precious that could never be repaired – the blow had shattered the pieces too small.

I remembered that moment as I fled down the paths that together our feet had so often trod. It was dusk, the time when we would walk back together, talking of the things of the day; I taking quiet comfort in his steady presence.

Now I was weeping while I went. Weeping more than I ever remembered weeping before. Deep, hot tears, coming from a well I never knew existed within me. Why was I weeping? I did not want to know. I am crying because I am weary, I said to myself, I am crying because it is all nearly over. I am crying because the end has come.

# XXXXIII

The coach took me right to the edge of Enderton. When I told the driver where I wanted to go, he had shaken his head.

'Why would you want to go there?' he said in disbelief. 'It is ashes and ruins.'

But my small purse containing several months' wages overcame his reservations.

'On your own head be it,' he said, taking up his reins. 'But I would take no maid there of my own accord.'

The night seemed preternaturally dark as I stepped out of the coach. Ahead of me was the steep path that rose up, leading to the front gates of Enderton. Behind me I could hear the waves roaring themselves hoarse. The air seemed colder here than it had done at Lancefield; cold and full of memories. I heard the driver say something behind me and I waved him away absently, drawn upwards to that place where it had all began. At his soft mutter, the horse neighed and walked on.

I went up the hill, my heart still full of sorrow, but also trembling anticipation. I had to do this. I was certain of it. I felt as though all the pillars of my life were coming together to form one great walkway, and I had no choice but to proceed down it, cast in their shadows. Onwards now, I must go onwards.

I was halfway up the hill, drawn towards those dark gates like a small boat in a current. My breath came out in clouds in the night air and made images before my eyes. I saw myself arriving, so many months ago, bound and blinded; I saw Gaunt following me through the sunlit grounds like an ever-present shadow; I saw John and I riding for our lives down this very path, thinking never to return. I felt old – so old; the air full of remembrances that haunted my every step.

Then, through the gloom I saw the far-off shadow of the gatehouse. A lantern burned in the window, as it had always done and I could just make out the hooded figure of the blind watchman sitting by it, listening for anyone who would dare to cross the threshold, staring out with his unseeing, ever-searching eyes.

Why do you wait? I thought to myself. Why do you wait when everyone else is gone? My footsteps were quiet, muffled in the damp fog, and he did not stir as I went approached. Perhaps he too, was a ghost.

The pillars at either side of the gates rose up before me, those ivy-covered sentinels – but they guarded nothing now, the gates were twisted and broken; anyone could enter. I walked through, my eyes straining towards the house, but all I could see was mist; it hung in the air like a terrible presence, shielding all of Enderton from my sight. I strode through it, leaving it swirling behind me.

Down the dark path I went. Ivy and rotten branches tore at my face and skin and I pushed them away impatiently. It seemed as though I had not been there for years, so wild were the gardens. Perhaps I had not. Perhaps all this had happened decades ago and I was too late – too late for him. Half-frenzied I broke through the overgrown foliage and then suddenly the mist cleared.

Before me was Mount Enderton in all its magnitude. In the lifting fog it seemed to have doubled in its immensity, so huge was the height and mass of the building before me. I was awed once again by its terrible magnificence. But as the mist continued to rise, I saw it for what it truly was: a palace of ruins.

Its once grand walls were blackened and crumbling, like a great cliff that was slowly collapsing into the sea. The roof stood only in partiality; the tower on the west side had collapsed, taking with it most of the upper floors of that wing. The grand leadlight windows were mostly gone, the carnes twisted and broken, and the charred entrance doors hung broken on their great hinges. The high lanterns that hung at either side of the black doorway no longer glowed with the warm promise of a luxurious welcome. I was shadowless on the lawn for the first time.

Suddenly I felt a strange rush of affection for the place where John and I had met, where our relationship had blossomed, where I had first fallen in love. This was the only place where I could remember being happy with John, despite its equal horrors. I had thought it almost beautiful then. But now the burnt house with its sense of lost grandeur filled me with loneliness and despair.

I knew I was early and that I should wait outside for John, but the silent, elegant wreck called me in. I stepped over the crossed swords that once had hung above the doorway. They had seemed so lofty but now they lay, broken and rusty on the ground. Although it was dark inside, the moon shone so brightly through the broken windows that I needed no candle. The hallway was filled with an unearthly light. I was back at Enderton.

# THE STORY CONTINUED BY THE EDITOR

Ash had coated everything. It rose and fell as she walked through the halls, past the piles of rubble. She had only been away months, but it seemed as though centuries of dust now covered each surface. Her every movement disturbed more of the powder, forming shadowy figures behind her as she walked, disappearing whenever she turned to look at them.

She wandered through the despoiled house like a ghost. The first room she came to was the ballroom and she paused in the doorway to look inside. Destruction was everywhere: the great oak beams that had formed the ceiling had cracked and fallen, like trees after a storm. Floorboards from the rooms above, scorched curtains, and shattered remnants of the decadent chandeliers hung down at strange angles throughout the vast hall: it looked like a jungle forest in the gloom. Isabel closed her eyes. Was it really only months ago that she had danced here, amidst all its beauty? If she was very still she could almost hear the music playing still, the tap-tap of the feet on the polished floor, the swish of the fine silks, the gentle clinking of the champagne glasses. Shadowy figures rose up out of her mind; memories so real that she could almost touch them. She opened her eyes, thinking to find herself back there – but it was all a dream and they melted away into the darkness.

She left the ballroom in all its desperate majesty. On she walked through the moonlit house, pausing at each doorway to witness the ravaging effects of the flames. The morning room, the dining room, the study – all were ruined reflections of what they once were. She did not look in the library. She could not bear to think of all those beautiful books destroyed. There was so much devastation wherever she looked. Why had Gaunt created such carnage, she asked herself. Why did he have to ravage this place so? It had become the very depiction of his ruined soul.

She felt her breath coming ever more slowly as she walked back into the hallway. She glanced upwards into the darkness. Up there was her room. The room where her life had begun. She knew she should not go up there, that she should go back outside and wait for John. She had thought that she would be desperate to see him, impatiently biding her time until he arrived, but instead she was quiet, still; content to wander and remember. Standing amidst the wreckage, she felt a new sense of loss; a new sense of definition. This ruin of a house had become the very measure of herself, reflecting all that she had lost, how much she had changed. And now she needed to see her room.

She was at the foot of the stairs. On her right, the marble woman greeted her, as unchangeable as ever, despite her thin veil of ash. Her eyes were still cast down, her arms wrapped around her body. She looked so terribly sad. On her left was a great mirror, its gilt frame now dulled with smoke. Isabel caught her reflection in it, highlighted by the moonlight. Her high forehead, wide bright eyes, curling hair... it was true, her looks were returning. She still did not look as she had done when she was here before – a golden princess dressed in unimaginable finery - but she would be called beautiful once more. She turned away: she found she no longer cared.

The journey upstairs was long and dangerous, the crumbling staircase threatening to give way at her every step, but Isabel reached the third floor without injury, the disturbed ash falling down the stairwell like snow. She stepped around some fallen debris and then, there before her, was the door to her room. She took a deep breath, and entered.

Unlike most of the first floor, the floor and ceiling of this room had stood fast, and as it was on the right-hand side of the house, it had escaped the fury of the flames. Indeed, despite a thin coating of residue, it looked much as she had left it on that fateful night. The coverings were still on the bed, the curtains open, the portrait ajar – it was as though it had been frozen in time. She walked into the airless room, the dust catching in her throat, memories catching at her heart. There – John had entered her room. There still stood the Christmas tree that he had made for her. There, the chest that he had forced in front of the door to protect her. Such precious memories.

But then, there was the moment when he had said he would never hurt her; there he gave her the book in which they were to write their glorious future; there was the red smear of blood where Branden had died, when that dark fire had burned so wildly in John's eyes.

Isabel moved over to the corner where the painting of the knight still hung on the blackened wall. She stood silently and surveyed it. So often had she seen it in her memory since she left; her silent protector, standing firm, even now. Yet while every stroke was just as she remembered, the painting looked different: slightly antique, slightly less real. The knight still stood tall, his visor drawn, but his expression hidden behind the visor had changed in her mind. It was less trustworthy, less true. She found she no longer believed in him.

'I do believe you were a false hero', she said quietly.

She pushed the frame back until it covered the dark space behind it. John was not going to come through that door to her aid again; there was no need for it to stay open.

'Retain your happier memories', she said, turning away. 'As I will try to retain mine.'

She thought for a moment of all the times at Lancefield when she had wished she was back in this room, when she had tried so hard to make these memories that were now before her come alive. Memories made all the sweeter by the knowledge that they could never happen again. This house brought both their past and their future to life. If it was blackened and ravaged, she thought sadly, then we are too. We cannot go back to the way we were; only learn to live with what we have become.

When she had last stood here, John had been a fantasy, a hero such as she had always dreamed of, ready to whisk her away to a life of wonder and excitement. Now he was a man, made solid by understanding and experience. Despite the layers of dust, she could see clearly now.

Yes, she would go back to him, and yes, she would love him. But it would be a very different kind of love: a love that had been hurt, and dreams that had been mud-stained and torn. A relationship that would exist in an imperfect world, which would need to cope with all that had passed and adapt for all that was to come. They had been pure and untried when they were at Enderton. Now, everything had changed.

A clock somewhere in the house began to chime and Isabel counted the strokes. Midnight. She moved to the doorway and looked out along the desolate hall, still lost in her reflections, but after a time, she realised that there was a solitary figure standing there. It seemed to be aware of her, but did not move towards her, instead standing still and watching. Isabel drew nearer and saw it to be the figure of a man. As she drew nearer yet, he seemed about to turn away, but then he faltered, and uttered her name and she cried out:

'John.'

He looked up at her and there was a wonderful softness in his eyes that she had not seen in many long months. When he spoke, his voice broke slightly:

'I did not think you would come... Part of me did not want you to.'

'There are many reasons why I should not be here,' she said honestly.

'And yet you came.' There was hope in his eyes, shining as brightly as the moonlight around them.

She moved towards him, drawn as ever by his voice, by his very presence.

'You are part of me, John. You are part of my very soul. I had no choice but to return - you burn through me like fire and I cannot put it out.'

She stood before him; finally there were no more restrictions, finally they were together.

'You waited for me longer than anyone ever has in my whole life,' said John tenderly, but there was pain in his eyes. He still did not move towards her, but stood, like someone at the other side of a frozen lake, staring at her with longing.

'What choice did I have?' Isabel asked, trying to keep the bitterness from her voice. 'I loved you. You were everything to me. I had no choice.'

John saw the desperation in her eyes and looked away, haunted. For a moment he did not speak, seemingly unable to find the words. Then he said, in a broken voice,

'They told me of what I did to you... Isabel, I can hardly bear to live with myself.'

Isabel breathed deeply, speaking the words she had told herself so many times.

'You were not yourself. You did not know what you were doing. It was another man, not you.'

'But some part of me must have known,' he said frantically. He ran his hands through his thick hair with the face of a wretched man. 'I am not to be trusted, Isabel. I do not deserve you.'

'And yet I love you,' she said, stepping forwards and taking his hands in hers, 'and we will be together. Somehow, we will make this work John. I do not know who I am if I am not with you.'

'You deserve better,' he said flatly.

'I choose you,' she said firmly.

She watched the joy in his eyes; she saw him step forward, so full of hope at her words, and she tried to share his emotions as he grasped her hands fervently. She had wanted this moment to give her such happiness, such peace. Instead, she felt nothing but weary resolution.

'You do not look very happy, Isabel,' John said softly as she tried to fight the tears from her eyes at this realisation.

'I...I thought this would be such a wonderful moment,' she admitted.

'Perhaps...' he said slowly, 'perhaps if we try to forget all that has happened, Isabel, then we can make things right again. If we hold onto the good moments and let go of the bad.' He looked around. 'We were happy here, Isabel, remember? Let us leave with those memories and not the times at Lancefield.' He nodded, as though trying to convince them both. 'Nothing in the past matters now, we never have to speak of it again.'

Isabel shook her head, frustration rising in her.

'Because that is what you always do, John? You have spent your whole life embracing the good moments in your life and fleeing from the ones that make you unhappy. I cannot forget one second of the past months – they are all scarred into my mind and I will never be free of them!' She felt all of her anger awakening as John held up his hands to try and stop her words – but these were words she had to say, and she had to say them now, or they would burn through her. 'My heart was young and untried John – I gave myself to you unreservedly and you let me down. You do not know what you have cost me. I am not like you – I cannot just put all that aside, and if you can...well, that frightens me.'

He drew her closer.

'Hush, now. I am so sorry that I have hurt you, Isabel, my precious Isabel. But you must believe I have always loved you, no matter what happened.'

'How am I to believe that, John?' she demanded, taking a step back. 'When I have watched you with Constance these last three months?'

John's eyes seemed to glaze as he searched about in his memory at the mention of her name.

'Or have you forgotten her too? It is convenient, is it not?' Isabel felt as though someone was at her side, urging her on, prompting her to say the things that had lain silent in her breast for so long. 'But I remember – because I was standing right there!'

'I did not mean to hurt you,' he said desperately. 'I was not myself.'

Isabel paused, and then a memory flooded back on her, as fresh and biting as the day it happened. 'And then you...' He seemed to sense what she was about to say,

'Do not, Isabel,' he said, pleadingly.

'- You stood there like a stranger while they beat me. You betrayed me. Me! Whom your first duty was to protect.'

She knew she should not say these things, having defended him only moments before. He could not really be blamed. He had lost his mind. Surely that was true. Surely...

She looked back at him and saw, like a dagger to the heart, that he felt – oh, how deeply! – all that he had done. The tears ran down his face – the face of a broken man, and it was all she could to do keep from clasping him to her breast.

'I know. I know, Isabel,' he said brokenly. 'That knowledge still freezes my blood.' He continued, desperately. 'It is no common struggle that I have been battling with. These past few months, since the accident, all has been darkness. I did not know myself, I was so angry at everything and everyone around me, so frustrated that I could not manage my own mind. All I could remember was that night in the snow and the girl that I saw there. But I could not see your face, no matter how I tried! You were as a ghost to me, and I was lost in the blizzard...I am so sorry!' He covered his face with his hands as if he could no longer look at her. 'I know that I could never deserve you, that I have let you down beyond forgiveness. But I am the man I want to be when I am with you...when you are gone the chains rise up and I cannot bear it - I cannot be without you Isabel!'

'John, I am not enough to save you!' she said with conviction.

'Yes you are. You have to be. You alone can bring me hope...' The realisation struck him anew, '...and yet I cast you aside as if you meant nothing to me. What kind of a man am I?' He lifted his streaming eyes and said in a broken voice, 'Oh God, forgive me, for I need it very much.'

Torn in two, Isabel embraced him and felt him collapse into her arms. She held him tightly, breathing in his familiar smell, taking comfort in having him close. She looked around them: at the dust, the ash, and all the brokenness. How could their world have collapsed so quickly? Nothing seemed certain any more.

'If I am not true to you then who am I?' she murmured.

They stood there like that for some time; too exhausted to speak, taking solace in each other's embrace, and trying to grasp at the fragile future that drifted before them.

A noise downstairs made Isabel look up. She could hear movement.

'Wait a moment,' she said to John.

He looked so fragile that she did not want him to move. She went to the top of the stairs, trying to see down into the dark hallway.

'I must see what that noise was,' she said to him.

'No, I will go,' he replied, but she was already off, creeping down the stairs like a mouse, stepping from one side to the other to avoid the debris.

She reached the ground floor. There was no one in the hallway and she breathed a sigh of relief. But then she saw it, hanging on the coat hook like a huge dead bear, exactly where it used to be in all her days at Enderton. It was Sir Branden's greatcoat. She could not breathe - that had most definitely not been there when she had entered. She spun round; Branden was dead, he could not have come back, not even to Enderton. And then she remembered that same coat moving towards Constance in the kitchen – and the skeletal figure underneath.

Suddenly she realised: of course Gaunt had followed her here. He had been watching her for weeks, it would not have taken long for him to realise he had killed the wrong woman. But then he would not have been able to get back into the school afterwards, with so many people on high alert. She thought of the watchman at the gate: she had wondered at him remaining there after everyone else had left the ruined house; but that hooded figure had been Gaunt, watching for her. She felt suddenly, sharply, a change in the very air around her. The stakes had risen in that brief instant. Their futures were shifting.

She turned in urgent haste: she must protect John, she could not lose him again. Her feet seemed less sure as she rushed back up the staircase. When she reached the second floor the moon passed behind a cloud and suddenly all was darkness. She paused, uncertain of her footing, and felt something brush against her, like a rat scurrying past her feet, and then the moon appeared once more. She could see no one – but then, she never had been able to see Gaunt when he did not want her to.

'John!' she called out when she reached the third floor. 'It it him – it is Gaunt, I am sure of it.'

John turned, his face very white.

'I know,' he replied, and motioned upwards with a slow and heavy hand.

Gaunt stood above him, halfway up the staircase that led the fourth floor. His hideous face, half-human, half-brute, leered at them in the moonlight. He looked even more unkempt than usual: his hair was longer, his clothes more ragged; Isabel could almost see his skull under his paper-thin skin. Yet there was a gleam of triumph in his mismatched eyes. She followed his glance and saw the coal-black gun that he was pointing straight at John's chest. He smiled at her, the darkest and most malignant smile she had ever seen.

'And there you are,' he said, in a low and deadly voice. 'The two lovers, together again. What insolence you have to return to this place! The place where he died, all because of your shameful affair. But now you two will die here – it is fitting, is it not?' His eyes gleamed with a hungry fire as he continued, 'Did you think you would escape me, after you ran from here, fleeing like cowards into the night? I knew it would be hard to find you if you did not want to be found – like a needle in a haystack. But I had forever to look.' He smiled, slowly. 'You see, if you have forever, you can carefully check every tiny piece of straw, one by one, until you find the needle. And here you are,' he bowed low to Isabel, still keeping the gun trained on John. 'The needle.'

'Very well,' Isabel said steadily, trying to hide the panic in her voice. 'You have found me, Gaunt. Congratulations. Now let John go – and you can do what you want with me.'

'Let him go?' said Gaunt, ignoring John's noise of protest at her words. He took a step downwards, towards them.

She could hear his ragged breathing; see his eyes gleaming large in his sunken face. There was a vein pulsing in his temple that seemed to increase in speed as he approached.

'None of this would have happened if it was not for him!' he almost screamed. 'I watched you, the two of you. I was always there. I *told* my master, but he would not believe me…not until I told him you were planning to leave. You forced him to act…' There was maddening grief on Gaunt's face as he turned to John, '…and then you killed him! My Master! You killed *my* Master, John Treador!' His voice echoed with a ringing fury, raising clouds of dust around them. She thought he was going to strike out at them, but then he stopped, breathed deeply, and said in a cold, calm voice, 'And now, you will die.'

Isabel reached for John's hand. This was it. This was the end. There was no escaping Gaunt now.

'I am glad I came here,' she said clearly to John.

'I am glad of every moment I have spent with you,' he replied his voice also steady.

Together, they faced Gaunt as he cocked his gun, triumph on his face.

'Oh no,' he breathed, as though they were children who had misbehaved. 'No, no, no. You think I will let you stand there, united? My master died alone and afraid.' There was a terrible madness in his eyes: 'Run,' he said softly, menace in his voice. He raised the gun while they stood there, confused and afraid. 'Run!' he screamed.

'Drop your weapon!'

Isabel looked round in terror. Running up the stairs were Sam, Guy Barnes and two men in police uniforms she recognised only from Sam's descriptions. Gaunt let out a howl of rage.

'If you do not drop your gun, we will fire on you,' said Sam, his voice ringing out from the stairwell. The four men had their barrels trained upon Gaunt. Cornered, he shot them a look of vindictive fury.

'This is your last chance,' said Sam, still moving forward without fear. Gaunt stared around at them all, malevolence in his eyes, and then spat upon the floor and threw his gun down. Isabel felt both herself and John exhale in relief as Sam rushed past them towards Gaunt and picked up the gun. Gaunt cowered back in the corner of the stairwell, like a beaten dog.

'Arrest him,' Sam called to the other two men, whom Isabel assumed were Fred Gelding and Will Whitburn. 'Are you hurt?' he asked Isabel.

She stared at him in surprise,

'You came after me?'

She could see the mild exasperation in his eyes.

'Of course I did.'

John glanced between the two of them.

'How did you find us?' Isabel asked.

'I realised the moment you left that Gaunt would try and follow you,' Sam replied. 'I had sent word to Barnes, Fred and Will that I might need their help. They were half-way to Lancefield already, in an inn not far from here, so I rode there to meet them and then we came straight here.' He glanced over at Gaunt, now with one hand in handcuffs. 'But we were almost too late.'

'We have much to thank you for,' said John, in a strained voice.

The two men looked at each other. Feeling a little ill at ease, Isabel looked over at Gaunt. With a jolt, she realised that his eyes were fixed upon her, a vicious expression on his face. Although the two men were holding him fast, she still felt unsafe.

'Please can we leave?' she said to John, not wanting to be near Gaunt a moment longer. 'I want you to take me away from here.'

'Of course,' he replied, putting his arm around her, moved by the appeal in her eyes.

Sam stepped aside as they made to leave but there was a sudden noise of a disturbance behind. Whilst trying to put the second handcuff on Gaunt's wrist, Gaunt had slid a silent knife from his sleeve and stabbed wildly at Fred's hand. Cursing in pain, Fred had released his grip upon Gaunt and in that moment, Gaunt had reached for Fred's gun.

## ISABEL'S NARRATIVE
### (Extract from Isabel's Diary)

It was such a long second. Everyone seemed to be shouting, but my brain could not process the words - they sounded muffled and faint, as if I were far away and watching the scene from a great distance. I saw the panicked faces of the men and it was only then I saw the gun in Gaunt's hand.

I had never given much thought to how I would die. But I had not imagined that it would be like this – so sudden, so strange. I saw him pull the trigger, and tried to brace myself for the pain. Would I feel the bullet pierce me? They never said, in the books, if it hurt. It looked so very smooth, that tiny metal pellet that was flying through the air towards me.

Then I felt someone pull me down – I hit the floor with such a thud, and looked up at him; suddenly it all seemed much more real. I saw the bullet enter his body instead of mine and he gave a soft cry of pain. Everything seemed to slow before my eyes, like grass swaying in a very soft breeze. He began to fall, like a tall young cedar that had been cut with a great axe. The beautiful branches splayed out in fear, the slender trunk falling towards the cold earth. It was ending. All our choices had now been made.

I looked round in horror just in time to see the second man fall. Gaunt had been shot by Barnes the instant after he had pulled the trigger – just a moment too late. I watched him slump down, a fleeting look of shock and anger on his face, and then he was still.

I turned back to the man lying in front of me. He was so very still, so very pale.

John, my sweet John. How could I have ever doubted you?


## THE STORY CONTINUED BY THE EDITOR

He will live, Isabel told herself, as they carried him downstairs. The thread would hold. It would have to – it was the one that held her whole life together.

She had seen Barnes' face when he had opened John's coat to reveal the dark spreading stain.

'Ride out and get a doctor,' he had said sharply to Will.

She had seen the look in Will's face that had asked, whatever for?

'Will he be...' her half-finished sentence died on her lips as she stared up at the men.

A mixture of panic, fear and beseeching anguish was etched on her face. Barnes looked away, as though he could not bear it.

'Help me carry him downstairs,' he had said to Sam.

Together they lifted the long, limp body and carried him as gently as they could down the first flight of stairs. Isabel followed slowly behind, as though sleepwalking. This would be the last time she went down these stairs, she thought absently. She glanced back up to where Gaunt lay. Sorrow was etched in his lonely eyes, his hand reaching out for the master who would never come. She felt a lurch of pity for him, then turned away.

'Put him in here,' said Sam, gesturing towards the door of the small drawing room on the ground floor. There was a dusty sofa in the far corner. Sam brushed aside the debris and they lay John down. He groaned and shifted slightly. Isabel entered the dark room and knelt down beside him.

'John?' She took his hand in hers, but he seemed unaware of her presence.

Sam parted the curtains slightly so that John's face was illuminated in the darkness. It looked very white.

'John, please open your eyes, please speak to me,' said Isabel, her voice breaking slightly.

She squeezed his hand tightly and slowly his eyes flickered open, coming to rest on her pale and anxious face.

'Isabel,' he breathed.

There was silence for a few minutes while Barnes built a small fire in the grate that glowed and came into life. Sam closed the curtains again.

'Come, we must see to Fred's injury,' he said quietly to Barnes and silently the two men left, leaving the couple alone in the small room, the flames crackling softly in the corner. John's eyes flickered closed again.

'I cannot recall what happened,' he muttered. 'Did I get shot...or did I...?' His voice tailed off, weak and confused.

Isabel had tears in her eyes.

'You got shot, John. Gaunt shot you – but it is not serious. I am sure it is not.'

John reached out his hand and touched his damp shirt which was now soaked with blood. He rubbed the blood between his fingers, a hazy look in his eyes.

'Does it hurt very badly?' he asked, his words stumbling.

'I...I do not know, John,' she faltered, unsure of what he meant.

'Does it hurt?' he asked again. 'Does it hurt you, Isabel?'

A sob caught in her throat.

'Yes, it hurts John, it hurts me very much.'

His voice was very weak:

'I do not want to hurt you. Make it stop, Isabel. Make the pain stop.'

Isabel turned, desperately, as if to see if a doctor had arrived. But she knew that was a long time away yet.

'I do not know how, John. You must just squeeze my hand for the pain and keep your eyes open.'

He tried to look down at his wound, but she held him back.

'No John, you must lie still,' she said, as firmly as she could.

'Is there much blood?' he asked.

She looked at the rapidly spreading stain.

'Just a little,' she lied.

'There must be no blood,' he mumbled. 'No one else must get hurt.'

His eyes came in and out of focus. Isabel felt the cold sickening fear inside her tighten its grasp.

'John!' she almost shouted. 'You must look at me. You must stay with me.'

Tremors ran through him and his breathing became very shallow. He held her hand so tightly it hurt.

'Focus on me John,' she said urgently. 'Focus on me and talk to me.'

He opened his eyes and slowly his grip on her hand relaxed. He took a deep breath.

'I am sorry I got in the way,' he said in a slightly shaky voice. 'I did not want him to hurt you.'

'The doctor will not be long' said Isabel, her voice determinedly calm. 'He will know what to do.'

'You look so very sad' he said, with an attempt at a smile that rent her heart. 'Do not be sad – you are safe now. There is no need for these tears.'

He lifted his hand to try and brush them from her cheeks but the effort was too much.

'I am not sad,' she said. 'There is no reason for me to be sad, because the doctor is coming and he will soon have you bandaged, and healed, and…'

'Isabel,' John's voice was pleading, unsteady. 'I do not know if... I think…I am so glad you are here. At the end of it all.'

Isabel trembled from head to foot.

'The end? Oh my dearest, what end? – We are together again, this is just the beginning.'

She stared at his face, and saw the fast-draining colour; she felt the chill creeping into his still hand. Panicked, she looked round again but no one was there.

'John, you must try – you must live – for me.'

The pleading expression in her eyes seemed almost too much for him to bear; he half-turned towards the couch in grief and his chest heaved with unspeakable anguish.

'John? I –'

Suddenly, he cried out in pain and began to gasp for breath with a horrible ragged sound that seemed to tear through them both. Fear and panic rose in John's eyes, and Isabel grasped his cold hand more tightly, half-rising with terror. He gazed up at her through his pain, with great anguish and tenderness. The past months seemed to rush between them like a gull soaring low over the sea: all of the love, the pain, the hurt and the joy, the waiting, the tears, the endless nights of darkness and fear and loss. He burst out in tones both familiar and unbearable:

'Oh, I should have let you go. I should not have put you through this! Oh what have I done, my dearest one, what pain have I caused you? All I ever wanted was to love you and not feel unworthy… I have never deserved you, Isabel, but I never, ever wanted to hurt you. I was just so scared...' His breathing was becoming more unsteady and pain was etched on his face.

'Hush, my darling, you must be still,' she said, urgently.

But he continued despite her protest:

'I knew I would let you down, that I would hurt you in the end. It was not why I wanted; I only wanted to keep you safe.'

'John, please do not talk so, you are only causing yourself more pain.'

'No –' he half-rose, but she held him down, ' - it is you to whom I have caused pain. Oh Isabel! Oh my darling Isabel, forgive me.'

'You know I do, John,' she said desperately. 'You know I have.'

He stared at her for a moment and then a smile passed across his face.

'You do,' he said, relief in his eyes. 'You do forgive me.' He uttered a sigh that came from the very depths of his being and sank back down.

Isabel placed her warm hand on his cold brow as his eyes began to close.

'You are right, John,' she said, trying to keep her voice light. 'You were right about everything that has happened – it does not matter now. All that darkness, it does not matter. This is what matters – here, now…John, I love you, please look at me. Do not abandon me now, after all we have been through'

His weary eyes opened slowly at the sound of someone entering the room behind them. It was Sam.

'The doctor will be here in an hour,' Sam said to Isabel in a low voice.

The last flicker of hope in her heart faded and died.

'It is no matter,' said John, addressing Sam. 'He can do no more than you have done.'

The two men looked at each other fast for a moment. It seemed as though they were having an entire conversation in a single glance. Isabel looked between them, trying to understand the words. There was a sense of passing on, of a promise made that was never to be broken. Then Sam bowed his head slightly, and left the room.

'Isabel,' John was struggling for breath now, struggling for words.

'Hush, hush my love,' she said, unable to stop the tears from falling. 'Let us be quiet together, there is no need to speak any more.'

But with a great effort, John seemed to summon the last of his strength and quietly, painfully, he smiled at her.

'Isabel, purest and best of natures. You are the vision that dances before my eyes even now, when they grow too dim to see it. Thank you. My dearest one, thank you for loving me...for trying to save me. The darkness is fading now and I can see... My dancing girl in the snow... You made me that night, Isabel. You made me who I wanted to be.'

His eyes closed slowly, like a child falling asleep; the smile never leaving his lips. He was watching her still, but from inside his dreams.

'Speak to me John,' Isabel urged, kissing him. His fringe fell over his eyes with her movement and she put it back gently, where it sat quite still, perfectly in place where her fingers had laid it.

It was that strange half-light when dawn was just approaching. The fire in the corner was slowly burning out. John's hand no longer gripped hers, but grew limp and still. She held on to it. She did not want to let it go, just as she had never wanted to let it go. In the quiet, she gazed at his face and tried to look forward into the days that would never come.

She knew when he passed even though there was no outward sign. Time seemed to stop; the pain was wiped clean from his face, and for a moment she thought she sensed his presence by her side. Then it was gone.

She wept. For a long time the tears did not cease and she sobbed beside the silent body. Then she was quiet.

Suddenly there shone into the room a stream of light - a single ray of sun that had escaped through the heavy folds of the wasted curtains. It was quite unmindful of the scene before it, quite unheeding in its brightness. Golden specks of dust twirled and danced in its radiance. Morning had come.

She realised then that Sam was there. She did not hear him come in, but suddenly he was there by her side and she was not alone. He raised her up and when she was ready, led her from the empty room. He took her weight as she leant on him and together they walked through the ruined house towards the light.

The sun was rising before them as they stepped over the crumbling doorway, and dawn spread out across the horizon in all its glory. Sam turned to look at Isabel. The tears were still on her cheeks, grief etched on every feature of her fair, young face.

'Come Isabel, let us leave this place,' he said gently.

She took his hand and together they walked out into the morning.

*'Sleep sweetly, tender heart, in peace;*
*Sleep, holy spirit, blessed soul,*
*While the stars burn, the moons increase,*
*And the great ages onward roll.'*

*'To J.S.'* (lines 69-72), Lord Alfred Tennyson

# XXXXIV

*Isabel's Narrative*

I did not love him immediately. But he was there for me while the wounds healed, and when they began to close over, I realised I could not let him go. He changed my despair to expectancy; he calmed and comforted me day after day, and as I looked forward to what the rest of my life would hold, I could see only him. They say that you should not marry the man you can live with, but the man that you cannot live without. I found this to be good advice.

I have been given three rings in my lifetime. The first was forced upon me, the second was given to me by my fiancé, and the third was given to me by my husband. Sam asked me to marry him exactly a year after John the day I lost John. It was the easiest decision I had ever made. I felt as though I was placing my feet in the footprints already laid before me and they fitted as perfectly as his hand fitted in mine.

We walked to the church one Friday morning and were married. I wore a simple white gown made of crinoline and carried a bouquet of yellow summer roses picked from the hedgerow. Surrounded by Sam's mother and sisters and a few well-wishers, we took our vows and on my finger he placed my mother's simple wedding band. It fitted perfectly.

We bought a cottage just south of Manchester, in a small village called Bidcombe, to be close to his family. Sam got a good post in the local town of Yatton and I helped in the school there, teaching literature to the local girls. It was a quiet life and I liked it very much, but I found that there was still one thing left for me to do before I could settle.

*'Nothing in this world is hidden forever. Sand turns traitor and betrays the footsteps that have passed over it… Look where we will – the law of revelation is one of the laws of nature and the preservation of a secret is a miracle which the world has yet to see.'*

*No Name*, Wilkie Collins

A few weeks after John died, we went to register his passing. When they asked for his details I realised how little I knew of him. I could tell them neither his age, nor where he was from. I did not know his next of kin, or even if any of his family were still alive.

At first, this saddened me beyond belief. I felt I had not done my duty and that somehow, in death, I had let him down. Who was this man who had left so many mysteries behind him? He had meant so much to me and yet I knew so little about him. I needed to know more – there were too many words unspoken, too many questions left unanswered for me to be at peace. I did not even know if his name was real. As the first year of my marriage passed, I found I could not settle: I was filled with an unshakable resolve to discover his story.

The only clue I had was from Mr Penderton, who had mentioned, at his quiet funeral, that John had told him he was originally from Devon. I did not know if this was another fiction, mentioned during his disorientation, but it was a start. The fact played upon my mind until one summer's day, I decided to set off to London to begin my search. Sam gave me his blessing, but he did not accompany me. This was something I had to do on my own.

My first stop was the census office. When the clerk asked me what year I wanted for the district, I said I did not know. I think he thought me mad. Nevertheless, I took all the Devon records between 1824 and 1844 and set to work. I sat up for many nights in that small room, trawling through the tiny handwriting, my eyes hurting and my back aching. I found no record of any John Treador.

I then travelled down to Devon. I spoke to the enumerator who said he could not recall a family of that name. He suggested I look through the parish registers, which I did. Days and days of reading and wondering commenced – what was the lie: his name, or the place – or both? There was no record of him ever being born. The name John Treador did not exist, as I had perhaps expected. Towards the end I was beginning to wonder if the man I knew had ever really existed, or if he was just a fragment of a dream.

I was ready to turn for home when the kindly vicar in the final church I had visited, noting my despondency, directed me to the county's largest library, only ten miles away. I travelled there directly and found it to be a musty old building, stacked high with every kind of book imaginable. At the back of the building there was a small room devoted entirely to a collection of every local newspaper since the turn of the century. It was to these that I turned my last vestiges of energy.

For several days I did not find anything. One fruitless search led to another. Page after page led to nothing but frustration and hopelessness.

I read through scores of articles and more births and deaths. I sat at the desk, weary, despondent, my head pounding with a fierce ache. Finally I decided that today must be the last of my searches. It was not fair on my husband to be away for so long and the chance of me ever finding out the truth about John had been slim, at the very most.

The final article in the *Blackthorn Chronicle* caught my eye. The page had been well read, and the headline stood out in large black letters. I pulled it closer to the light of the candle and, amidst the gathering gloom, began to read.

*January 5$^{th}$, 1845*

### FAMILY TRAGEDY IN BLACKTHORN

*Sir William Westera, the well-known composer and violinist, has been found dead in his house along with his wife and two young sons. The shocking incident look place last Sunday night. Police say the bodies had been dead for several hours when they found them, after being alerted to the crime by locals. Sir Westera's eldest son is missing and has not been seen since. There is one witness who claims to have seen the shocking events unfold.*

*Mr Rook, who lives in the village, alleges to have heard Sir Westera engaged in a furious row with his wife on the night the murders took place. Drawn to the scene by the sound of the loud shouting, Mr Rook watched the events unfold through the front window in horror. Mr Rook reports that he saw Mr Westera take a pistol from the wall and shoot his wife in the head, before turning the gun upon his two youngest sons, Harry and James, killing them outright. At this point, Mr Rook said that the eldest Westera boy, John, entered the room. Sir Westera then aimed the gun straight at John who apparently said not a word, but looked around in horror. Following John's gaze towards the bodies of his dead wife and sons, Rook claims that Sir Westera apparently smiled at the boy, and then turned the gun on himself, killing himself with a single shot to the head.*

*It must be noted that Mr Rook himself was reported as being in an intoxicated state on the night of the event, having previously been dismissed from his position as a labourer for his tendency to drink. As a result, his report is being treated with some caution. John Westera himself is being treated as a suspect and police are on the lookout for him after he fled the scene on the night of the crime. Locals say he was a quiet boy who had often had to protect his mother and brothers against his father who was prone to violent outbursts. Yet they also claim that there is a history of madness in the Westera family, going back several generations, which many feared had been passed down to the boy himself. Mr Thomas of Dean Street reports that John was well known in the village for his 'wild eyes'.*

*Lady Louisa Westera and her two sons are to be buried in the family cemetery in St Peter's Church on Thursday. Sir Westera's body will be taken to a local graveyard. It is felt to be a sad end for the illustrious composer, known for his much-loved concerto 'Ego Somnium Beatitudinis.' Their surviving son is still nowhere to be found.*

*Sir Lounte, who had known the family from childhood, said this of William Westera:*

*'He was a tragic, troubled man. Many people thought he should never have married. The vein of madness ran deep in his family tree and it has finally had its vengeance.'*

*Certainly, reports from the two servants who were cowering outside the sitting room door at the time of the attack, ally with the notion that William Westera had indeed lost his wits. When John entered the room to find the bodies of his family and the gun now trained on him, Misses Joan Howell and Rosie Thomas claim to have heard his father say:*

*'It is because I loved her, John...because I loved her. I loved you all. You are like me, you know. We are the same...I cannot...I cannot...Watch.'*

*They then heard the final shot, presumably marking the death of Sir Westera himself.*

*When the two women finally had the courage to enter the room, they found John standing there 'with huge eyes'. They tried to speak with him, but he said not a word. Shortly afterwards, he left the house and this has led to the widespread view that it was the boy himself who took the lives of his family and then vanished without a trace.*

Just one story - one tragic story, amongst many - yet this one stood out to me. Was it the name of the child? Or was it the ghosts in his eyes that haunted me every day that I knew him, and every day after that?

I shall never be able to prove that this is his past. I shall never know if he was the boy in the story. But I do know that John had been running from something, and running all his life: of that I was certain. Was this what he was running from? Guilt, terror, persecution; fear of an inheritance buried deep within his mind – unable to escape a horrific scene imprinted on his memory forever. Perhaps this is not his story. Perhaps.

And yet, whether I believed that story was his, or not, I found myself often asking the question: why did the father not shoot the boy also? That question troubled me for many years. And as I grew older, I came to believe that it was because he saw himself in that child. He saw all of his hopes embodied in that one small boy – everything that he could have been – and so he destroyed himself instead. But the child bore the scar of his father's actions for the rest of his life.

For me, finding the article felt like finding the central missing piece of a jigsaw. It may have been a piece from another picture; the image was unclear, but the fit was right, and for me, it gave a sense of closure and release and finally I felt I could let him go.

And so it was that I went back to the folly. I had felt for some time that his burial at Lancefield had been less than he deserved: small, hurriedly organised - in a place that he perhaps would not have chosen, though I knew no home to take him to. As time passed I realised a place that he would have preferred: our beautiful folly, where the birds cried out above and the sea glittered below. The one place where we were truly happy.

I could not take him with me, but I took our book, our red book. It had been meant to hold all our hopes and dreams and instead had had a hole cut through it by a bitter servant grieving for his master. So I filled that hole with things I knew John would like: shells from the beach below, some ivy from the folly walls, a bird feather I found on the grass, a lock of my hair.

I buried our red book at the foot of the folly where the sea could roar and the memories live on. It was a glorious day, truly the best. I looked out at the innumerable shades of the sea – shimmering turquoise, deep purple, dazzling azure. The clouds above, of purest white, were suspended in a mirroring canvas of bright blue. The sharp tang of the sea air hit me with a physical force as the memories that flooded back to me. I had not thought I had forgotten anything, but it was those tiny details, those minute sounds, smells and colours that brought the whole scene back to me more vividly than I could ever have imagined. I was there, with the box buried at my feet, a small spade coated with freshly dug soil in my hand – but I was also just over there, on the grassy bank, in my green dress, sitting beside him, holding his hand, talking quietly and fervently of our plans together. How can all that life be buried, I asked myself? But it was not – so much of it lived on with me, and lives on in these pages. And, I pray, lives on with our Father, from whom John ran from for so long.

Peace begins where secrets end. I found, as the years passed and I got older, that I knew John better. Finally I realised what had lurked in those dark shadows. It was not anger or hatred; it was not madness or cruelty. It was fear. Fear of living, fear of loving - fear of being loved and fear of being truly known. John was a lost boy, wandering through the shadows of life. I like to think that during our time, he wandered into a brief period of light and peace. I like to think that.

What I do know is that he was the darkest, most joyous, irresistible, unpredictable man that I have ever, or will ever meet. His entire life he had walked along the outskirts of the world, never fully part of it. He had taken a road in his youth, but the road did not lead where he supposed. He had run so far and so fast that he had got lost along the way. He said that I was his anchor, and he gave his life to stay tied to it. The world would say that he was not entirely successful. But he was the best sort of failure – unusual, brave and fascinating.

If you had told me, at the age of seventeen, that I would spend the rest of my life in a small cottage in a tiny village I would have despaired. How strange then, that I loved it. Life in Bidcombe was gentle, friendly and always enjoyably busy. Sam's mother and sisters were frequent visitors and I became fast friends with them all, especially Grace, the youngest, who reminded me of myself at her age: wide-eyed and eager to experience the world.

Barnes, Will and Fred also visited from time to time, the younger men in the summer and Barnes in the winter months. Sam always enjoyed their visits and hearing the news from Little Wharton and Cranwell, and he in turn introduced them to his new favourite haunts and walks here in Bidcombe. I loved seeing him so happy when his friends were around, and always encouraged them to return whenever they could.

A few years after the furore around the death of Sir Branden had died down, I went to London and claimed my inheritance. It was indeed considerable and the first thing we did was to use some of it to settle Sam's mother and sisters comfortably in a lovely house near ourselves. His eldest sisters, Elizabeth and Rachel, soon married very happily and before long we were uncles and aunts to several beautiful children.

As we settled into our new home, I realised there was one thing missing from its pretty rooms: my books. It was Sam who reminded me that I had an entire library at my disposal and it did not take me long to have a selection sent down from Greenwood.

Thinking of my childhood home, boarded and empty, still filled me with regret and so, with the help of a lawyer, I managed to get in touch with dear Mr Ronald and Mrs Tabitha (forgive me for continuing to use their childhood names - they have stuck!). Seeing them again was such a joy and after several meetings, it transpired that my old head teacher, Mr William Arthur, had recently found himself quite without a school and so I gave him the keys to Greenwood, with the request that he open it up to teach the local children and be as 'progressive' as he wanted. And so, it was opened up, cleaned up, and before long was filled with many children who I believe were given most excellent and happy educations. I think my parents would have been very pleased.

And as all the strands of my life drew together I suppose you must wonder, what about Cathy? I must admit, I did not contact her myself during those first few years. The thought of explaining everything that had happened to me was just too much and so I waited, often thinking of her, and then one day a letter arrived.

*My dearest Isabel,*

*Where do I begin? With an apology, I think. I should have written to you much sooner, but I did not have the words. I asked Sam to send me your address when you first married; I hope you do not mind. I was in touch with him ever since he began to search for you after the kidnapping and he has kept me apprised of your safety ever since.*

*I have something to tell you Isabel, and yet I do not know quite how to tell you, for it breaks my heart and I cannot even begin to imagine how it will break yours. It was my mother, your own aunt, who felicitated your kidnapping. I do not know what possessed her. I can only hope she had lost her mind.*

*She wrote to me after my marriage. She asked me to forgive her and said that everything that had happened to you was her fault. Along with her letter was a bundle of letters – your letters - that you wrote to me during your last fateful weeks at Harringdon. Somehow Mother had managed to intercept them and they never reached me. It all makes sense now – she kept your letters from me and mine from you. I suppose it was a final attempt to make sure that we did not run away together.*

*That letter, along with yours, was her last act – whether of remorse of repentance. I have not heard from her since.*

*I think my mother is dead, Isabel. In fact, I am sure of it.*

*I did not enjoy my wedding day. I wept because you were not beside me and your fate was so uncertain. But married life is neither what you*

436

*feared, nor what I hoped. It is a different kind of life. Matthew is kind and distant. I am busy and yet often bored. I have a beautiful house and no true friends. My one joy is our son – a beautiful, healthy boy called George. Oh, how I long for him to meet his Aunt Isabel and see you bounce him on your knee.*

*Will you come and stay with us Isabel? I dearly wish to see you again. I know it has been such a long time and we will be both much changed, but I hope that we can still be friends as well as cousins.*

*I have sold Harringdon (with tears, for the many summers we spent there) but Sam has my address. If you want to see me, please write by return of post. If you do not, I understand.*

*Your cousin,*
*Cathy*

Of course I went to see her, and her adorable baby boy. She was right: things had changed. There were things I could not tell her and others I would not. I did not want her to feel any worse towards her mother than she already did: some things are best left unsaid.

What matter is that she is happy, and the best wife and mother that she can be, in a marriage that was never designed for love. I realise now that she is much braver than I.

And so to Sam. My life with Sam.

It is amazing how well you can think you know someone until you marry them. I already knew he was kind, and as selfless as any man could be (and I do not mean that disparagingly!). What I did not know was that he was so creative, skilful with his hands and with his pen. He has a mind furnished by reading good books and thinking on the best things in life. He writes well and is always coming up with engaging stories for the younger children in my classes. He is also deeply intelligent and, as you may have gathered, has a very deep understanding of the Bible and all its mysteries. For the first time, with a man, I am able to discuss sermons equally and at length. I can go to him with any question, no matter how deep, or how menial, and he will talk with me about it with such patience and interest that I never feel foolish in any way.

Indeed, I love how open all our conversations are. No area is out of bounds, no comment too trivial. We take delight in speaking our minds and there has been no question I have asked that Sam has ever refused to answer. I find that the world is a far better place when nothing is too hard to say to one another.

I always knew that marriage for a woman involved duty and submission, but I did not realise that when you are married to a good man, a godly man, it is also filled with joy. I realise also, through his acts of duty and surrender, that it is the man who often has the harder job – making the sacrifices and carrying the burdens for us both. I do not pity the wives of this world nearly so much if they are married to a man such as mine.

I started to apologise once, for how I had spoken to him and treated him on that dreadful eve when I left for Enderton. But before the words had left my mouth, before he finished telling me I did not have to, I realised I had already been forgiven long ago. We had both spoken out of turn on that day, but my words had not been borne out of many months of worry, fear and silent suffering. For that I made sure he knew I was sorry.

When I think of how I took his kindness and sacrifice so wordlessly, so unthinkingly during those many months, I cringe at my selfishness. He gave himself so fully and selflessly and I took - nay, expected it. I know I am unworthy of him and I try each day to be deserving of his love as each day he shows me how to love, a little better. Each day he leads me further up that hill.

But the days are growing dim now and my body grows weary. In this worn notebook, there is not room for much more. I must choose my words with care, for they say your final words define you.

It is warm now, but I feel cold. When I open my diary there is the smell of the past – of thoughts, dreams, joys and sorrows. Pressed between the pages are the flowers, each on the day they were given, always beautiful, always yellow. They are little fragment of hope, each with their own memories.

I read once that lost memories grow into trees. This is true, for you can cut down the ones that you do not want to remember, but they always grow back, their roots deeper than before. Sometimes I like to climb the memory trees, but only when I am very strong.

When I read back over those pages, I seem like such a young girl, only a child, really. Can I use that as an excuse for some of my behaviour? You only have to read a few pages to see that I have been far from perfect. I have not been as kind as I should have been – nor as understanding, patient or giving. For that I am very sorry.

I am still not a saint, yet neither am I as untethered and rebellious as I was in my younger years, when I thought I could do it all alone. I have much to learn – but then, I always will, no matter how many more days I am given. I am still somewhere in the middle I suppose, but fortunately my future does not depend on my best efforts. It is my God that matters, not my faith. I know that now.

I learned once, and I learn again every day, the truth of this verse:

*'Thou hast beset me behind and before, and laid thine hand upon me.'*
*Psalm 139*, verse 5, King James Bible

I think I have finally realised what this means. As a child, I used to think of it as a great comfort – that I was completely surrounded by God's protection and that he would never let anything terrible or upsetting happen to me. As I grew up, I realised this was not true. For while we are surrounded by God's protection, He does not protect us from life, and all its horrors, terrors and, worst of all, its pains. He does not lock us in a padded crib, kept far away from the trials of this world. No - he lets us experience these terrors and pains in all their desperate agony. He lets us wander the world, delving into its dark places and darker nights. I know, for I have been there.

So how does God beset us, you may ask? He surrounds us with his spirit; he hems us in with his love. We may experience the terrors of this world – we must, to be able to grow and to need him – but as we do, we realise that we do not go through them alone. In the darkest night, there will be a light shining in our hearts; in the agony of despair, there will be a voice calling out words of peace. This I know. This I have experienced. And it is a greater comfort than I could ever comprehend, for while his protective arms are less restrictive than I would once have wished, his love is more wondrously powerful than I could ever have imagined. You do not abandon the works of your hands, Lord. Thank you.

As you will have gathered, several of the most special things in my life have been books. But there is only one that that has changed my past, my present and my future. It is the book of hope - but not the one that lies buried at the foot of the folly. This one can never be buried, no matter how hard mankind tries. Its words run through my blood. I have hated it and I have loved it. But I could never forget it, no more than I could forget how to breathe. It was written by the author who also wrote my life. Every time I read it, his prose pierces my soul and fills me with joy. The structure is exquisite: the prelude tells of my creation, the finale points to my future.

I think much about my future now. I am old you see, dear reader, and I feel that my days here are drawing to an end. Is it strange, then, that I find myself looking back almost daily, to that most eventful period of my life when everything changed. I realise more and more that I have been blessed with the love of two wonderful men. I have been loved more than I could ever deserve to be loved. I have had my dreams fulfilled according to God's plan. And it has been far greater than any of mine could have been.

Dickens said that a woman's heart can be yielded only once. With the greatest of respect, I believe he is wrong. I think it can be yielded twice. Once, with innocence. Once, with experience. I have done both. John was my fairytale and Sam was my truth. I would not change it for all the world.

Looking back, would I tell a younger woman not to fall for such a man as John? There is no point in answering. If the woman had already met him then no words, nor any advice in all the wide world would stop her from loving him. I would tell her only that I lost such a man, and it did not kill me.

John's face is hazy in my memory now. Sam's face is before me. Outside my window the stars throng the sky with their patient, eternal light and in the centre is the moon. I think of you, Sam. I know you will read this when my time has come and I am gone. The world is a maze and you have been my one constant.

When I look back, I see that you were the first person to really know me, that day, in the lane. All my foolishness and all my folly was laid bare before you for you to see, but you did not despise me. When I was taken, your love was relentless, pursuing me farther than anyone else was willing to. In my need, you were there. During my lowest moments, even when I was bound to another, you alone remained true and stable: a rock I could cling to, a light pointing the way. You never wavered, and you never left me. Your love has been as faithful as the morning. When I married you, it felt like coming home.

I asked you once, after we were married, if there was anything you were afraid of. You always seemed so brave, so strong, you see. You did not answer me for a long time and then you said you feared that you would never be enough for me; that you would never be all that he was to me. Yes, Sam, John was my first love. But you were my first friend, and you waited while he forgot. You had faith. You gave me hope.

You have seen me from start to finish, Sam. I have never been able to hide anything from you – much as I would often have liked to.

Thank you for the memories we have made together – and for those that we have yet to make, though I fear there are not many more. You have been my husband, my lover, and my friend.

I sit in your rocking chair, wrapped in my shawl, looking out over the garden. I ache so much now, deep within my bones. Nothing the doctor gives me seems to help. But I enjoy sitting here, looking out over our little garden. The yellow roses are in bloom.

I wait for you to climb the stairs to me. I am ready and my suitcase is packed. Just as I had once packed my clothes and my books in readiness for my Father's return, I have now gathered up my dearest memories and faces and placed them carefully inside my mind, ready to take with me. I know, somehow that I will not need them – that the beauty and rightness of where I am going will so supercede everything that has come before so that this life and all its joys and sorrows will seem nothing but a daydream. But I want to take them anyway. They are what have made me myself and it seems only fitting to take them as far as they can go before everything melts away and I become the person I have always wanted, but never deserved to be.

That time is not so far off now.

Then you are here and we say very little for we do not need to. That radiant peace that comes only at the very end is approaching and this world is cast in soft shadow by the light of the approaching tomorrow. I seem to hear faint voices singing – such a strange and wonderful sound – outside the window. My hand aches and I fear I must put my pen down soon, for the final time. I only wish you did not look so sad.

I ask myself for the last time: to whom am I writing? At first I thought I was writing to my parents, and then, when they faded from my memory, I believed I was writing to Cathy. But now I know – it was you. It has always been you, Sam. I wrote this book for my husband, my one and only husband who would know me better than any other. I wanted him to know all of me; the parts of my life he had missed, even the parts I am ashamed of. You never hid anything from me and now I have hidden nothing from you. I know you will pick this diary up once I am gone and, with my permission, read it for the first time. This is my life, my darling. This is me. Remember me with love, with much love.

Your own
Isabel.

I close these pages with a tear, a quiet smile, and a great hope.

# XXXXV

*'I have lived, I shall say, so much since then,*
*Given myself up so many times…*
*Yet one thing, one, in my soul's full scope,*
*Either I missed or itself missed me –*
*And I want and find you, Evelyn Hope!'*

*Evelyn Hope* (lines 41-2, 45-7*)*, Robert Browning

*Account written by Sam Hardy, The Editor*

The year is 1899. Many are saying it is the dawn of a great new era. I have found it hard to share their excitement. I am alone, you see. Alone with my pen and with my memories.

I never thought of myself as a writer. It is just as well I have had so much of her to put into this story. I have tried to narrate as fair and accurate a portrayal of events as possible, according to my memories and her diaries. I have tried to insert her own voice through selecting certain excerpts, but much of it I have paraphrased into a third person narrative to make events more straightforward, for a diary writer often assumes you know exactly what happened on a certain day. But please excuse my crude hand. I am no master of prose.

I have even taken the liberty of working through the text a poem that is very dear to me. There is real beauty in the words and felt somehow absolutely relevant. I have always felt the same certainty of my relationship with Isabel as the unnamed man did of Evelyn. I knew she was the most beautiful woman I had ever seen. I knew I would always love her, no matter what our futures held.

I do not believe I have been false to the facts. If in any place I have, then I must hope that my good intentions will absolve me. Isabel did not know of my plan to write this text – indeed, even I did not know that the half-formed thought to commit her life to paper would one day become a reality. I only know that I needed to write this. I hope that the memories are as vivid on paper as they were when I listened to her recalling them over the days and months and years that we spent together.

It was strange, going back through her life in such detail, from her childhood to her adulthood, and all that happened in between. I did not find it as hard to write about her time with John at Enderton as I thought I would. But I am an old man now, and jealousy seems to belong to the very young. I see now that he was meant to be a part of her life as much as I was. And both of us were very blessed, in that respect.

I did not hate him, in the end. He saved her for me, and for that I am eternally grateful. He gave me the greatest blessing I had ever hoped for. And how I had hoped.

From the moment I saw those beautifully shaped eyes, fixed upon me, her face was fixed upon my heart. What did I do to deserve having her look at me, I thought, as she stood on that forecourt outside Enderton? What did I do to deserve having seen such a sight?

She was all the more charming in her allure because she was innocent of it. There was no artifice in her. She was captivating and gracious, and beautiful – so beautiful. Some men wanted to capture her, to keep her in a cage simply so that they could look upon her and take in every inch of her perfect form. Others, like me, wanted to set her free – to see what she would become and to witness what her future held, in the hope that we might be a part of it.

In the end, she did what she wanted. For she was no ordinary girl. In fact, she was the most extraordinary girl I have ever known. She loved with a raging fire, that, once kindled, nothing could put it out. She learned hard lessons and came through them, stronger and better than she was before. I was so proud of her, even before she was mine.

There are things that I regret, of course. I should have guarded her more closely. I should have read the signs when that dark gentleman arrived at Harringdon. That first month when she was taken was unbearable. My heart had never loved in that way before and it ached with the fury of it. To think that she was hurt, or in pain was unbearable - and she was both. She needed me and another took my place.

And I should not have let her walk away from me, that fateful night when she went to meet John, alone and unguarded in the gathering gloom. I should not have let my feelings affect my conduct towards her. Perhaps if I had stayed by her side as her protector and her friend, the horrors of that night would never have unfolded. But there is no 'perhaps' in God's plans.

I find myself continually drawn back to that time. To the three of us – the oddest trio there ever was. I think often of John. I believe I was too hard on him then. I am still undecided on whether he wilfully hurt her through his actions at Lancefield, but I prefer to think that he did not. I remember him on that couch, quiet and pale, with death so very near. That moment when the boy stopped running and came home at last.

By the time Isabel loved me she was a woman and her love had changed. I do not say this with regret. It is my one great pride that she did love me – and so fully – so faithfully. I met her as a girl. I married her as a woman. My heart had never been so joyful as on that day when she walked down that short aisle, put her arm in mine, and agreed to be my wife.

Most novels would end here: a jubilant ending with a joyous wedding and confetti thrown high into a summer sky. That is the fitting conclusion, is it not? But a wedding is only a beginning and I am glad that we lived long after that. I can remember every evening we spent together in our little cottage, reading and talking; all the walks we went on together in sunshine and rain; and every kiss we ever shared.

We did hope to have children. But it was not God's will. I think I was more mournful of it than she was. She was content with what we had, yet always keen to learn and explore. Our library was filled with more books than we had room for, her appointment book always packed with visits and visitors, her diary filled with notes and thoughts and stories. She loved life, and wanted to experience every part of it - that never changed. She was my rose, with the curious eyes.

She was a beauty when I met her, still beautiful when we married, and grew still more beautiful every day after that. Her mother's trick served her well, and even at the age of fifty, strands of pure gold still ran through her beautiful grey hair. She often bemoaned the soft lines around her eyes and mouth, but I loved them. It is a privilege to grow old with someone and witness the tiny changes in their countenance over the years. Wisdom and experience only enhanced her looks to me and truly I thought her every day as enchanting as the day we first met.

But slowly she started to fade. It became more difficult for her to write, to climb the stairs, to do many things. First I had to take her hand more often, and then her arm. Her body grew weak, and her eyes and mind tired. And finally I carried her upstairs, both of us wondering if she would ever come down again.

I think we both knew when the last days dawned. She said she was glad it was her time and not mine, for she could not have borne to have lived without me. It seemed strangely out of sequence – she was ten years younger than I – yet she joked that fifty-two was quite a good age for an Audley. I smiled back at her as my heart ripped in two. It was the first time we had acknowledged the fact that I would be entering this new century alone.

She passed late one afternoon as dusk fell. I held her soft hand as the sweet final breath passed from her lips, her eyes slowly closed and her body was at last at peace.

I know I will see her again. Be still my soul.

It was my great sorrow and great honour to bury her. Many people asked me why I put the name Isabel Hope on her grave. I had that name inscribed because that was the meaning of her name and also because as much as I loved her, and she loved me, she was not fully mine. I never fooled myself into thinking that. She belonged firstly to her mother and father, then she belonged to John for a time, and finally she was mine. No one of us has a greater claim than the other. She was given to us by God and taken by him. When we all meet with her in heaven, she will belong to all of us and none of us, the earthly bonds will fall away. I named her after what she brought into this world, and what she left behind. I gave her that name because death will not contain her. Let that be her title, and her legacy.

Every day I place a fresh flower on her grave. Yellow, as always. Every day my heart swells with joy – that painful, aching, wonderful knowledge that this is not the end, but how I wish for that end to come. My mother once told me that power and wealth do not define a man. Rather, he is defined by the God he serves, and the woman who accepts him. That has been true for me.

It was a weary walk home from the churchyard today; it seems to take me longer every day. I enter our cottage and place my cap on the coat stand, glancing in the mirror where I see the white hairs upon my head. You said they were like a sprinkling of snow - this makes me smile. I walk to the window to look out over our garden. It looks quite lovely with the late afternoon sun casting long shadows across the grass, and the sweet scent of the honeysuckle, planted so many years ago, creeping in through the window. There is a lark singing in the blossom tree.

I lift your diary and hold it close. This is all that I have left of you, Isabel. It is almost cruel: I flick through the pages, and your beautiful hand is before me – with those swirling curlicues on the ascenders and descenders - but the soft hand that wrote it is gone. How I want to hold that hand just now. You know I would have followed you if I could, but God has willed that I should stay here a little longer. The house is so empty without you, my darling. I miss your touch. I miss seeing your face when I lie down to sleep at night. I miss you.

I turn back the pages, now yellowed with age, and I must be careful not to disturb the sleeping petals, paper-thin now and so fragile, but still slightly scented and full of memories. You might say that you never got to write your great masterpiece. But you did – only it was written with actions as well as words – for only part of it is recorded in this diary. It has been my joy and my privilege to put the whole story together. I only hope I have done you justice.

I have only a few more days to visit your grave and place the flowers – today a buttercup, tomorrow a rose. I am old now and feel all of my many years, as though I am carrying them upon my back. My time of twilight is drawing to a close and I look to my God, who holds me in his Almighty hands, and look forward to meeting him soon, along with all the others who have walked this long road. To God be the glory, great things he has done.

Can love last a lifetime? Ours has. And I will believe that it will continue into a glorious future – that is my firm hope. Our God, who has created so many wonderful things on this earth, will not let them fade. No, he will make them grow, until they become all they were ever meant to be, united forever in his glorious presence. To those who say love will end, I say love is only the dawn. Watch and wait. And Isabel – wait for me. Keep a place beside you, for I am on my way to you.

I love you Isabel. I have always loved you. This was your story, and now it is at an end. But ours is only beginning.

I sign this document,
Sam Hardy, September 1899

'May these words hold true'

> 'I loved you, Evelyn, all the while;
> My heart seemed as full as it could hold –
> There was place and to spare for the frank young smile
> And the red young mouth and the hair's young gold.
> So hush, - I will give you this leaf to keep –
> So shut it inside the sweet cold hand.
> There, that is our secret! Go to sleep;
> You will wake, and remember, and understand.'

*Evelyn Hope* (lines 49-56), Robert Browning

# Author's Note

Thank you for taking the time to read this novel. It has been a labour of love and I know I may have preyed upon your good humour with its structure and length. It has been my aim, from the beginning, to stay as true to the form of the Victorian three-volume novel (from which 'Isabel Hope' takes its inspiration) as possible.

I began writing this particular story over five years ago, during the time when I was also writing my fourth year university dissertation (not the best time to begin a novel!). It was without a doubt a creative escape and influenced heavily by the topic of the dissertation: Victorian melodrama - although hopefully my re-imagining contains less than the usual amount of 'revolting sentimentality' that Wilde so reviled! It is not a historical novel, it is not a, in truth, a romance; in fact, I am not really sure what it is. But it is everything I ever wanted to write.

It all started with a piece of music from one of my favourite sci-fi series. Sci-fi, I hear you say? Not exactly the perfect fit, but that's the way with so much of this novel – it has taken inspiration from the strangest places... And so, one dark rainy night as I sat in my little red Micra in the Asda car park waiting for my brother, the music put in my head the strange image of two men, standing as far apart as you can be, and a girl, running. That was the first image of this story, and where it all began.

I carried on writing when I moved to Bristol in 2008, although the story took a while to take shape. When I began my first role at the BBC, a writer there told me, 'If you want to write a good book, stick your hero up a tree and throw rocks at them.' So I did, and somehow it all began to flow much more smoothly from there.

And so, five years later this strange little story has finally found its way into your hands. It wouldn't have done so without the help of several very special people. Thanks to Jen and Julie, for being my very first test subjects and for reading through copious spelling mistakes and outrageous lapses in logic. Their encouragement and insight was invaluable. Thanks also to them for being willing to write my first reviews (non-bribed, I might add!).

A big thanks to James for risking grass stains all over his white T-shirt whilst taking the cover photos – I love them. And thanks to Mary for the beautiful cover design – her talent never ceases to amaze me!

Thanks to my husband Nathan for supporting me in every sense during the writing of this book and for always believing it would be a success (here's hoping I won't let him down...).

And finally, a special thanks goes to two very special family members. Firstly to my great Uncle Ronald, one of the most creative men I have ever met. From a young age he immersed me in poetry and great literature and sparked an interest that has continued to grow. I never got to thank him and so I am doing it now. Secondly, a special thanks goes to my Mum. If you met her, she'd recount the story of how, for many years, she had looked forward to reading me her beloved Famous Five series. Finally deemed old enough at the age of seven, upon hearing her read the first few lines, I took the book off her, telling her she was reading too slowly and that I would read the rest myself. Sorry Mum – I may have deprived you the joy of reading to me, but reading such great stories quickly read to my beginning to write stories of my own, and so, after many, many years of your unfailing support and belief, this is for you.

www.ingramcontent.com/pod-product-compliance
Lightning Source LLC
Chambersburg PA
CBHW031950060726
47497CB00016B/1043